THE HOWLERS RISE

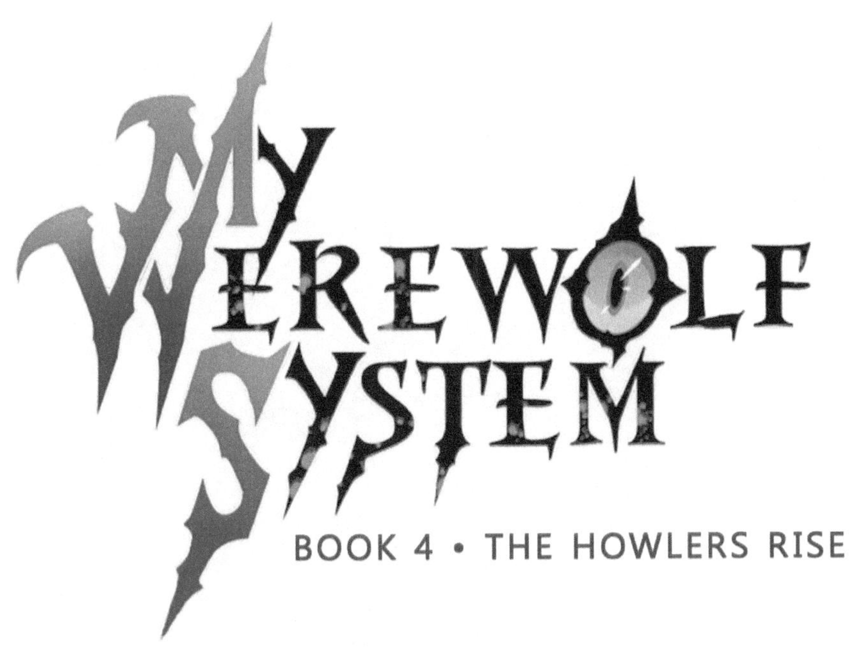

BOOK 4 • THE HOWLERS RISE

JKSMANGA

Podium

Published in 2025 by Podium Publishing
www.podiumaudio.com

THE HOWLERS RISE

CHAPTER 1

NO LONGER A KNIGHT

After his meal, Gary didn't feel like he had been the one in control of his own body, yet somehow he had ended up at home. No longer in his gang clothes, not having met up with any of the others after the great attack, and no longer having the bag of strangers' bedsheets.

There were a few people that Gary went to for help in times like these, but not a single one of them seemed available. He couldn't tell Tom the truth, and Kai hadn't picked up his phone, leaving him to once again deal with matters himself.

As he entered his apartment, he saw that Amy was safe; in fact, the areas of Chavley that he had traversed had shown no signs of damage. How that was possible when such a large attack had occurred, Gary didn't know, nor did he ask questions. It was as if he didn't even care about that right now. In fact, he didn't utter a single word as he proceeded into their room.

Amy had greeted him, but he didn't seem to have registered it. Seeing him in his current state, she knew that she would be unable to get through to him and decided to let him rest on his own in their shared room.

Maybe it's best if I sleep in Mom's room for today? Amy thought. *Gary, were you really involved in what happened on the news today? You told me to stay in, so maybe you were just concerned for me, or it was all a coincidence, but . . . those "coincidences" are starting to pile up.*

The next day, Amy was sure that Gary must have somehow been involved in what had occurred yesterday. Although her brother hadn't openly appeared in the broadcast, Amy had recognized the other members of the Howlers; after all, she had seen them briefly at the Wolf's Pool Club.

Part of her suspected that the green-haired leader was her brother, but a bigger part of her was unable to accept this possibility. Being in a gang was one thing; being an Altered was a completely different one. Ultimately, she came to the same conclusion as Tyler, that Gary must have simply dyed his hair to resemble that person.

As curious as Amy was, she had promised her brother she wasn't going to ask again, and she intended to keep her word. Fortunately, she had never said anything about trying to find things out herself . . .

It was a normal school day, yet she had woken up before him and there was no food out on the kitchen table, as she had grown used to. The door to their room was still closed, and she hadn't heard it open at all during the night.

He hasn't done this before, but I'm not sure if I can make things better, Amy mused. In the end, pulling up her sleeves, she did what she could to help Gary out. She made a simple meal for herself and left a good portion for her big brother out on the table, with a small note underneath, before heading out to school.

It was the middle of the day when Gary realized that he had just been staring at his ceiling. It was hard to say whether he got even a wink of sleep.

Shit, I'm going to be late for . . . ah screw it, after yesterday I doubt anyone will care about me having missed one school day, Gary decided. He stretched his body and looked around. *Hang on, what did I do with the bedsheet? . . . I can't remember. How come I can't remember?*

The green-haired teenager had been completely on autopilot to the point that he couldn't recall where he had put the loose bag filled with bones. He was mildly sure that he must have brought it home, but that might just be wishful thinking on his part. However, he wasn't in the mood to worry about it for the time being.

Since Amy hadn't cried out, she must not have found it, and judging by the time of day, his sister should be at school, leaving him with ample time to find it. He checked his phone to see if there were any messages from the others.

Unsurprisingly, none of them had written anything in the chat. However, there was one personal message from Kai.

Continue today as normal, will let you know more later.

Gary thought that maybe they would continue their attack on the Gray Elephants or the Underdogs, or whatever was left of them, anyway. With their leader gone, someone had to take over, and it was clear they would be scattered.

However, he would leave this stuff to Kai, since he would know best in the first place. There had to be a reason why they wouldn't move out yet, so Gary opted to wait until evening to get an update.

He walked into the kitchen and saw some cooked food on the table. It had already gone cold, but there was a small note underneath.

Big bro, take the day off. Once I'm back, I'll give you a massage to work your sore muscles out. You always look after me, so let me look after you for once.

Next to the message was a little doodle of what he could only guess to be his sister pumping her fist.

That note put a smile on his face, his first expression of emotion that day, but not only that, it reminded him why he had ended up in this crappy situation. He had done some crazy things, but he was doing all of it to make sure his family would stay safe.

Since he wasn't going to go to school in the middle of the day anyway and didn't really feel like doing anything else, he decided to check out his system.

Name: Gary Dem
Class: Warrior
State: Human (Alpha)
Grade: Knight
Level 18
Exp 502/3445
Health 100/100
Energy 300/300
Strength 23 (+1)
Dexterity 24 (+1)
Endurance 20 (+1)

His stats had gained a large boost compared to last time. Currently he had one extra stat point at his disposal, but rather than using it as a way to improve his body, he thought of something else.

1 stat point has been allocated to Health
Your base Health has increased to 110

During the fight with Kirk, he had realized the drawback of overly relying on Claw Drain to refill his Health. It was only useful if he could actually connect his attack, but otherwise it was just a drain on his Energy. His Energy was able to heal his injuries, yet the lost Health would only be replenished once he was outside a fight.

He had the skill Last Stand, but that was exactly what it was, something that should only be used at the last moment. Gary was pretty sure that if he hadn't chosen that skill, he would have died twice already. He had chosen to increase his Health in the hopes of never ending up in those types of situations in the future.

One of his rewards for defeating the Altered was the option to learn one more skill. However, Gary was aware that he wasn't in the right mind for that right now, so he decided to leave that till later, to select a good one.

Instead, he did something that he had been sure about doing from the beginning.

I have three Pawn points and a Knight point. I should be able to use the Knight point to directly upgrade my body to the next grade, so here goes.

> *1 Knight point has been assigned to increase your grade*
> *6/5 Pawn points have been collected*
> *You now have enough points to reach the next grade*
> *Upgrade is now proceeding*
>
> *. . .*

CHAPTER 2

A SPECIAL UPGRADE

This was the first time Gary had consciously done something to increase his grade. Last time, he had simply selected his class, and it had surprisingly upgraded him to a Knight-grade werewolf as well. Since the change in appearance was mostly due to choosing the Warrior Class, Gary hoped that he would be able to gain the system benefits without any pain.

He wasn't completely wrong. His body didn't change much; he only experienced a weird feeling, yet he had gotten somewhat used to it given his frequent transformations. However, he was unprepared for the experience of what could only be described as his brain melting, like being constantly poked from the inside with a hot rod.

It was far more painful than when he had learned new skills; even worse, it lasted longer. He immediately collapsed onto the floor, grabbed his head, and instinctively clawed at it, but stopped himself as he realized that his hands had already transformed.

"Why does everything have to hurt with this damn system?" Gary screamed as he gritted his now-sharp canines in order to try to halt the transformation. He couldn't help but scream at the top of his lungs to try to alleviate even a little of the pain.

"Arghhhh!"

How much time had passed, he was unsure, but as soon as the pain started to recede he knew it was over. As if to stress the fact, the Werewolf System sent him a new notification.

Your grade has been upgraded from Knight to Bishop
1/15 Pawn points to upgrade to the next grade

The first good thing Gary saw was that it had worked; on top of that, it appeared that the extra point had been carried over. However, he was still clueless as to just what going up a grade did for him. After all, Pawn points could be exchanged for skill and stat points, and a Knight point was worth five of them . . .

Gary knew that according to the description of the Alpha Bite skill, he should now be able to create werewolves at the Knight grade. Similarly, he should also be able to invite omega werewolves at this grade to join his pack, since he now outranked them. Of course, he would have to find one . . .

Regardless, these features didn't seem overly useful, at least not yet, so he hoped the system would share some insight that made his investment worth it. He didn't plan on turning any of the others, not until he knew what would happen to Olivia on the night of the full moon. He wasn't going to subject the others to what he had been through.

Checking out his current rank, Gary saw that this information was already present, but there was now additional information below.

An alpha at the Bishop grade can select a class for all his Knight-grade werewolves.
Extra class choices may become available based on the werewolves or their current grade. Meeting certain conditions will allow werewolves to access Special Classes.

Gary thought this was quite the upgrade indeed. He knew that he had improved the most after selecting the Warrior Class. Essentially, it was a way to increase his pack's strength. He also noted that Olivia's grade had changed.

Howlers Pack
Alpha Werewolf: Gary Dem
Grade: Bishop (1/15)
Beta Werewolf: Olivia Pearl
Grade: Pawn (0/1)

"System, are you saying that I need to pay one Pawn point to upgrade Olivia to the Knight grade? Well, I do have the points, and I'm curious if she will have an extra option."

Although Gary was excited about this at first, he paused to think things over. He still was unsure about what to do with Olivia. Sure, she had helped him out; in fact, he was certain that without her whip pulling Kirk's leg in that final attack, he would have been the one who lost his life.

The Lady Boss had also helped the group and saved his sister. Whether she did that because she was simply following his established pack rules or not was another matter, but at least he knew she was somewhat loyal.

If I upgrade Olivia to Knight grade, she will surely get stronger. Even if her increase is as big as mine, I should still be leaps above her. After all, I got a big upgrade myself after yesterday, Gary reasoned. *And if I do have to end up killing her, she will then be a Knight-grade werewolf, which will probably end up giving me another Knight point. That would be exchanging one point for five; it's a win-win situation.*

In the end, Gary convinced himself to do the upgrade, though much of the decision might have been to satisfy his own curiosity. Pressing her name, he granted his point toward her.

Congratulations, one of your beta werewolves (Olivia Pearl) has been upgraded to Knight grade
You may now select her class

Hunter Class (Recommended)
A Werewolf Hunter is fast, agile, and sneaky. It focuses on killing

its prey quickly, out of sight and from the shadows. It is able to track its targets from a great distance and has great focus.
Class perks include: More and better marks, improved tracking.

Protector Class
A Werewolf Protector boasts one of the sturdiest bodies of its race. It uses its own body to shield his pack members from any harm, making sure that they will survive.
Class perks include: 1 extra point in Endurance upon each level-up, faster healing.

Warrior Class
A Werewolf Warrior could be considered the vanguard of its pack. It leads its pack into battle with its strength. It has exceptional fighting ability and courage, but it is because of this trait, and his role, that this class boasts the highest fatality rate.

Class perks include: Wide range of skills to select from, large Energy pool

Gary was a bit disappointed to see that her choices were the same as his. He had hoped for some variety, if only to learn more about werewolf classes. After all, the system had intrigued him with the possibility of those Special Classes.

Under Olivia's name, the system now showed *Grade: Knight (0/5)*. He was tempted to upgrade her further, but that wouldn't be wise. Not to mention, he lacked the necessary Pawn points.

The system recommends the Hunter Class, and I can't really picture her as a Protector or Warrior Class, Gary thought as he selected it. He realized that perhaps he should have texted Olivia beforehand, but it was too late, as her body was already starting to change. Where she was or what she was doing, Gary could only hope she would be safe.

Your Beta Werewolf (Olivia Pearl) has successfully become a Hunter Class Werewolf

Since Kai seems to be busy, I should meet Olivia and find out for myself how her Hunter Class works. Maybe now she will have something like a system, or maybe becoming a Bishop grade has some other benefits I was unaware of, Gary thought.

Then he received one more notification after becoming a Bishop-grade werewolf.

New Quest received
Going up in the world
Reach Level 25
Quest reward: 1st Class Promotion

CHAPTER 3

THE NEXT LEVEL

Once again, it looked like the system had given Gary ample incentive to concentrate on leveling up. Seeing how much he had benefited from becoming a Warrior-Class Werewolf, a class promotion, which should allow him to choose a higher-tier version of that class, would surely make him even more powerful.

I wonder how strong I can get? Gary thought. *So far, each of the grades has corresponded with chess pieces, so queen or king should probably be the highest I can reach. If each new grade allows me to go up a class, just how many class promotions will I need to reach or even surpass someone like Jayden?*

As Gary thought about this, his excitement quickly faded. From what he had seen from the White Tiger Altered, he had a hard time imagining himself beating Xin's brother, even if he became twice as strong as he currently was. Gary had already had a hard time against Kirk, and he was sure that Jayden had yet to show everything he was capable of.

The real question is, how do I even level up to that point? The 50 Exp per day from the Bond Marks is nice and all, but it would simply take a lifetime, especially since the Exp requirement increases with each level. The only other way I have gained Exp so far is from starting fights or running into tough situations.

Gary didn't think he would be doing any of those things soon. After the Underdogs and Gray Elephants were dealt with, Slough would be a pretty safe place for his family. He had already solved the money issue, and would solve it even more after successfully taking over both of the big gangs. Of course, there was still the issue of how exactly he would explain the whole thing to his sister, as well as to his mother once she woke up.

Wait, there is still the matter of who this Werewolf System actually belongs to. If we take over the Underdogs, then whoever the owner should have been might come to us . . . I'll just have to be strong enough to protect everyone when the time comes, and some smaller gangs might make their move. Like those that were at the meeting with Ben Clove.

Gary decided that it was best to use his extra Pawn points. At the moment, he only had two more left. This wasn't enough to allow Olivia to reach Bishop grade, much less for himself to reach his next grade. Since it was so far away, and he believed that more fighting would be coming his way soon, he decided to use them on himself.

Would you like to convert 1 Pawn point into stat point(s)?
Yes
3 stat points have been granted

Gary was happy to see that the conversion granted him more than one stat point. However, now that he seemed to have figured out the importance of his grade, he understood how precious those Pawn points were, making him question why he got relatively few of them. What's more, the last time he had converted a Pawn point, he had received three skill points, which he would have assumed to be more than stat points.

Alas, as the saying went, beggars can't be choosers, so he converted his last remaining Pawn point as well.

Would you like to convert 1 Pawn point into stat point(s)?

Yes

2 stat points have been granted

He was slightly surprised that he ended up receiving fewer stat points this time. Either each Pawn point wasn't worth the same amount, or more likely, the conversion might not be fixed but have a random element to it. He would have to further test it to find out, yet Pawn points weren't exactly a resource he could freely acquire.

Nevertheless, he had a plan for what he wished to do with his five stat points.

5 stat points have been allocated to Health
Your base Health has increased to 160

Just like the one stat point he had received for reaching Level 18, he had put all the others into Health. So far he had yet to find a reliable way to increase his Energy or Health, whereas the other stats could be obtained organically or through eating beasts, and apparently Altered as well.

Now with everything done with his system—apart from selecting a new skill, which he was postponing to another time—Gary was the strongest he had ever been.

He stood up and jumped up and down on his toes, just like Kirk before he started his Altered matches. Once Gary had warmed up enough for his body to feel loose, he threw a couple of punches as fast as possible.

He continued throwing punches, one after another, and eventually stopped with his fist out. He could hear his fists cutting cleanly through the air, and he hadn't even used Controlled Transformation on himself.

This body is amazing . . . If I were to use my full strength at school, everyone would definitely assume me to be an Altered. I better start holding back during rugby practice and PE lessons.

Continuing his little exercise, Gary started to do more, swinging his legs and doing a routine drill that he often practiced when training with Innu. Once again he was surprised at what his body could do now.

His speed had drastically improved, but the speed also gave more power to his punches. The fight against Kirk had opened his eyes to the importance of speed and how frustrating it could be to be unable to touch your opponent.

However, he realized why he was able to do such things in the first place. His Dexterity had improved by leaps and bounds, and it was all because he had eaten his idol—and then the reality hit him once again.

That's right, the bones!

CHAPTER 4

NO LONGER THERE

Quickly, Gary began searching through his room; the last thing he wanted was for Amy to come across an assortment of bones, especially since Kirk's head was also in there. The former would already be hard to explain, but the latter would make it impossible.

Gary spent an entire hour looking through every nook and cranny of the apartment, yet the improvised sack containing the bones was nowhere to be found. He even used his nose to look for signs of blood, yet he was unable to pick up anything.

Why can't I remember where I put it . . . it's like on the night of the full moon. I can't remember anything for some reason. Did I just black out?

Gary was trying hard to replay the events of last night in his head, but there was no such luck. Since the sack definitely wasn't in their apartment, the only thing he could do was go outside. He reached for his hoodie, but then put it back, realizing that he probably didn't need it anymore, not after yesterday.

As he roamed the streets, Gary followed any scent of blood he picked up, searching for any clues to what he could have done with the bones. But he only managed to find some roadkill, as well as a man who seemed to have cut himself shaving.

He increased his search radius along the route between his home and the fighting that had taken place yesterday. Unfortunately, several policemen seemed to be conducting an investigation; they had blocked off the areas that had been attacked.

The biggest change he noticed was the absence of the Underdogs. There were no members in the area. Not needing to hide his face, check behind his back, or put his hood up was something he had never treasured before.

Now it was a freedom he had regained. Gary could finally walk around his own neighborhood without worry. This also meant that he could continue his search, albeit outside the closed-off areas.

Alas, the next few hours were uneventful, with not even a hint, even after retracing the last steps that he could remember.

Well, I guess if even I can't find it with my nose and knowing where I should have passed by yesterday, then hopefully no one else will find him, Gary reasoned.

Since it was getting late, he decided to head home. Just in time too, as Amy entered their apartment a few minutes after he did. Gary welcomed her back and tried his best to act normal, saying that he'd had a falling-out with one of his friends the other day, which was why he wasn't in the best of moods. Of course, Amy saw right through his lie but decided to let it go, just as she had done with all the others. She was just happy that her brother was somewhat back to his usual self.

Gary did a few things before he went to sleep. For one, he messaged Olivia. He had initially wanted to check up on his beta wolf after assigning her the Hunter Class to test a few things out, but thanks to his impromptu scavenger hunt it had gotten too late. The Lady Boss had received the message, but she left it on read without further reply. Gary figured that she must be pissed at him for not giving him any prior warning.

Unfortunately, Olivia wasn't the only one who seemed to be ignoring him. He had constantly checked his phone waiting for Kai's message, but neither he nor any of the others had sent anything.

Still, Gary took it as a good sign, believing that everyone had used today to recuperate. He would just ask Kai personally what had happened. For the first time in a long time, he was able to get a good night's sleep.

Your bloodlust grows
10 days until the next full moon
50 Exp has been gained from current Bond Marks (5)
Exp 552/3445

In a way, Gary was hoping that the matters with the Underdogs and the Gray Elephants could be resolved before the full moon. That way, he would be able to fully focus on himself and Olivia during that period. Unlike last time, when it had annoyed him greatly, he decided to use the notifications as a type of calendar.

The next morning, Gary was the first to leave the apartment, excited to meet up with the rest of the Howlers. He wanted to learn what had happened to them after he had left and what the news was like in their areas, and, most importantly, he wanted to talk to Kai about their next move. Gary wanted to talk to the Howlers in person rather than over the phone, and that was why he hadn't given the others an update.

Tom was still away on his special internship course, so the Howlers were really the only ones Gary would be able to talk to. When he entered his classroom, Tom's seat was empty, of course. However, Innu's seat was empty as well. At first he thought he was just early, but even when the lessons were about to begin, Innu still hadn't arrived.

Did he take the day off? I guess it would make sense for him to take a few days off. After all, he knew those orphans personally. Damn, I've been thinking about my own situation all this time, without even stopping to think about him, Gary thought. Pulling out his phone, he sent Innu a message to try to cheer him up. However, before he could do so, the teacher entered the room.

"Okay, listen up, everyone. I have some news to share with all of you," Mr. Grey announced. "Our recent transfer student, Innu, has decided to transfer out. I'm afraid he will no longer be with us anymore. Let's all wish him the best at his next school . . . or whatever he wishes to do in the future."

Gary stopped in the middle of his message. He couldn't believe it. Why would Innu leave school because of what happened? Everyone started talking.

"Hey, do you think he really transferred to another school?"

"I doubt it. He was definitely the one on the news the other day! Even Mr. Grey seems to think that."

"Yeah, he was with that gang, the black and gold one. What were they called again, the Howlers?"

"I can't believe we had a gangster in our classroom all this time. We should have known; he had those weird bandages all the time."

Crap, this is a big deal, isn't it? Neither Innu, Marie, nor Austin had masks covering their faces! Everyone knows that they would have been involved in that fight. Crap, did the camera manage to capture my face when the mask fell off?

Gary realized that there was at least one person who certainly had seen his face that he would need to deal with. However, the fact that none of the students were talking about him meant it was unlikely that his identity had been revealed.

When the bell went off signaling that it was time for lunch, Gary sent a message to the group asking what was going on and why Innu had dropped out of school. Then he headed upstairs to Kai's classroom.

But Kai was not in his usual place, staring out the window.

"Sorry, but have you seen Kai or Marie anywhere?" Gary asked one of the upperclassmen leaving the room.

"Kai . . . oh, we just got told today. Those two will no longer be attending Westbridge, apparently."

Now Gary was sure that something was seriously up.

CHAPTER 5

HOWLERS NO MORE

The fact that every Howlers member except him had left West-bridge was no joke. Gary was now worried that something very bad must have happened to his friends. After all, he received a personal message from Kai just yesterday, but he had not been able to reach him.

If it had just been Innu who had decided to leave the school, he might have understood. After all, Innu had apparently been captured on film. But if all three had disappeared without any notice, something was definitely up.

Gary pulled out his phone and started writing in the group chat.

I just found out that everyone but me has decided to drop out or transfer. Why didn't anyone tell me? Are you guys okay? Did any of you get hurt from the fight?

He was undergoing a mix of emotions: worry, mixed with anger, as well as the sting of abandonment. Lately, he had gone through so much with the Howlers, and he was prepared to go through thick and thin with them. Seemingly getting ghosted by all of them was making him fear the worst.

I don't understand, aren't I part of the Howlers as well? Aren't I meant to be your friend?

Just as he was about to message each one of them individually, his phone vibrated, and he saw that he had finally gotten a reply from Kai in the group chat.

My bad, Gary, I was so busy yesterday that I didn't get the chance to write to you. This is something that we all agreed on without you. Don't worry, everyone is fine and well. Just enjoy your day at school and come to the Wolf's Pool Club afterward.

Gary didn't know how to feel about this. The pumped-up adrenaline in his body had faded, yet one of his worst thoughts had turned out to be true. The group that he had always felt like he had belonged to since he had founded it together with Kai had done something without him.

Why would they do that? Gary wondered.

Eventually the school day was over, yet Gary had barely paid attention to any of his lessons. His mind was too busy deciding how to react to his situation. Should he accuse them all of abandoning him? Should he pretend everything was normal?

Ultimately, he knew that worrying about it was just making matters worse, especially since he couldn't fix something that had already happened. He just hoped that there was some reasonable explanation for their behavior.

If only Tom were here, then I would at least have someone to talk to about this stuff . . . stupid no-phones rule. At least he said he would be back before the full moon, Gary thought as he pushed open the door to the pool club.

It seemed to be as busy as usual. Plenty of customers had become regulars, and Austin's friends were doing a great job waiting on everyone.

However, all the attention was on the latest addition to the team. White had quickly become the store's idol, which most likely also translated to extra sales. Even now, nobody was paying him any heed, but a group of boys was staring at the waitress.

Other than Miss Degrace, Gary didn't see any of the others, so he could only assume they were downstairs. He went into the storage room that doubled as Kai's office. Walking down the stairs, he could already hear the voices of the other gang members.

He was a bit surprised when his nose picked up another presence: his beta werewolf, Olivia Pearl. Kai, Marie, Austin, Innu, and Olivia turned around, and they all gave him a smile. Marie had the awkwardest look on her face, though, seemingly feeling guilty.

"Guys . . . so do you mind explaining to me what's going on? Please don't lie to me. I thought everything was going our way for once, but should I take it that the Howlers are no longer a thing anymore?" Gary decided to be frank. Throughout the day, that was the worst possible outcome that he could think of.

Although it had never been his idea to create this gang, it had become something like a second family to him, so he didn't want this to be the end of it.

"What? No, of course not!" Marie answered vehemently. "I'm sorry we kept you out of the loop. Let me explain, so these guys don't mess it up, all right?

"I don't know if you know or not, but it turns out that the gang fight was filmed. While they mainly focused on you against Kirk, all of us were shown. I was even recorded using knives. Admittedly it was in self-defense, so according to our lawyer, Mr. Vula, I shouldn't get in trouble with the police, but there were consequences we had to deal with yesterday.

"Although our faces weren't shown too clearly, those who know us should be able to recognize us. It was kinda impossible to go back to school, you know."

Gary understood where Marie was coming from. After all, he had heard all his classmates talking about Innu, and none of it had been flattering.

"On top of that, with the Underdogs and Gray Elephants in shambles, we are the only big-time gang in Slough, which no one can deny anymore. This means that even if we wanted to, we wouldn't actually be safe at school. In fact, we would probably endanger everyone near us just by attending."

"That's not the only reason," Innu chimed in, stepping forward. "All of us have already decided, Gary. There's no real point in us going to school anymore; it would just be a waste of everyone's time. This is the life that we intend to live from now on.

"I have people who rely on me now, so I need to bring in the money so I can look after them. Not in the future when I grow older and get a degree, but now. Surely you understand, right?"

Indeed, as someone who had been in Innu's situation not too long ago, how could he not sympathize. In fact, it was something he had been considering himself as well.

"Then I will—"

"No." Kai immediately interrupted him. "Gary, there is a reason why we decided to do all of this without informing you, and that's because, if anything, you have done far too much for us already. The others may not know the entire story about why you helped me create the Howlers, but I do . . . you agreed to my plans because you didn't really have another choice if you wanted to continue your normal life.

"Part of the reason I gifted you that mask was so you had a chance to live that ordinary life, even if it's just a lie. Gary, I asked everyone to keep quiet about it because I knew you would stop going out of solidarity, that's just the type of person you are, but right now, the thing that is keeping you going is the fact that you could end up with a normal life at the end of this."

Gary opened his mouth to reply, but in the end no words came out, because Kai's words were true. He still wasn't able to fully commit himself to this lifestyle. On top of that, if he did, it would mean dragging his family and close friends like Tom into this, and maybe he would even have to cut ties with them.

Marie's mother was already involved, and then there was Austin, whom they knew little about but who seemed to have already considered this lifestyle. Innu had already said why he needed to do this. And then there was Kai, whose motivations weren't quite clear to Gary. . Either way, they had more reason to do this than he did.

"I understand . . . I'm just glad that I will still see all of you." Gary let out a sigh, and the others all smiled.

After that little talk, it was time the group got down to business. Kai gave everyone an update about the current situation. It turned out that the Gray Elephants were practically no more, and that included the territories they used to run. The few remaining members had disbanded, and without a leader, there wasn't much they could do. On top of that, those who had tried to rally up had been attacked by an unknown force.

However, no one had taken over their territory, and no one dared to. Kai had assumed that was because of the Howlers. So it looked like their plan was working so far.

"Which means that the Underdogs are the only ones that we have to focus on, right?" Gary said, summing it up. "So when do we take them out?"

"There are a few things that I need to sort out before then. We need to get everything perfect, so we can get to Damion. If we don't get him, the Underdogs will always be able to re-form. Right now, our best approach is to let some time pass and wait for the other gangs to choose a side," Kai answered. "Don't worry, it won't be long. At most two weeks. That timeframe should allow Damion to call in every favor he might have, so that we can completely crush him."

The others nodded, but Gary was a little worried. Two weeks' time meant after the full moon. If Olivia turned out to become uncontrollable on the full moon, there was a good chance that he would have to kill her to protect the others.

Without the beta werewolf, he doubted the members of the Pincers would be as courteous as they had been so far. Right now, while the Howlers had Olivia, especially after her upgrade, they needed to attack now.

"Attacking the Underdogs will be dangerous, but there shouldn't be too many members left. I've also placed a Mark on Damion, as well as Gil, so we can simply ambush them if the opportunity arises. With my upgrade in strength, maybe there is no need to put them in harm's way. If we do it close to the full moon, Olivia and I should be strong enough to handle them on our own.

"You guys decided this all on your own without me, so I guess it's time I start acting on my own as well."

CHAPTER 6

THE HUNTER CLASS

"Is it your hobby to take adult women to the woods in the middle of the night?" Olivia asked.

She had met Gary in the woods, where he had told her that she was now a werewolf. The moon was shining brightly in the night sky, allowing the two of them to see, not that they needed it anyway.

She was currently in a new set of clothes that sported the Howlers' color scheme. Because of their position in the gang, she wasn't afraid to be recognized. Heck, if anyone dared to attack her, she looked forward to showing off her strength.

Still, Gary couldn't help but notice that the clothing didn't exactly look warm, not that Olivia seemed cold at all—yet the same could be said about Gary. One of the hidden benefits of becoming a werewolf was that their bodies were able to adapt to the weather conditions.

"No, not really, but I somehow feel quite comfortable here." Gary shrugged. "Also, I've called you over to talk to you about some werewolf stuff, and this seems to be the perfect place for that."

She couldn't help but grin.

"Because it's your big secret?" Olivia asked mockingly. "You should be aware that after what you did, all of them know, right? After all, they know who was hiding under that wolf mask. They all saw you fight that Cheetah Altered.

"The only reason your little buddies didn't mention anything to you was because they're waiting for you to be the one who brings it up first. Although, considering your fallout, earlier didn't seem like the perfect time to ask you any questions anyway."

This saddened Gary a little. Truth be told, he had avoided thinking about it, having been glad that nobody had recognized him at school. However, Olivia was completely right; of course the Howlers knew now.

Most of them had already put two and two together, but now that they had seen it live, there was no denying it. Ironically, Gary wasn't an Altered. No, he was something a lot more menacing, and if the others found that they had almost died because he had been the one to create Billy, he wasn't sure how they would feel.

Sure, Kai had seemingly forgiven him, but would Innu do the same?

Shaking this thought off, Gary decided to concentrate on the reason he had messaged Olivia after the meeting.

"Tell me, have you felt an urge that has been growing? A craving for blood or killing in the last couple of days?" Gary asked. "I need you to be honest."

For a second, Olivia didn't answer; she was thinking about whether to lie, but because it was such a specific question she thought Gary already knew the answer.

"Yes, but I haven't really acted on it, unless you count the fact that I've been eating my steaks a lot bloodier than usual. In fact, it's almost as if my mind is in two states. Every time I consider acting on it, I start to get a headache, forcing me to stop."

Gary could only surmise that this was Olivia's natural instincts as a werewolf colliding with the pack rules he had set up. It was good to know they were still in effect, but on the full moon he doubted that they would be strong enough.

He had a theory, and he was sure it was right. When the system stated that his bloodlust was increasing, it wasn't his lust for blood itself. It wasn't as if drinking blood or eating a human would calm him down.

No, what it meant was the act of killing itself. On the night of a full moon, all a werewolf wanted to do was hunt and kill anything it saw.

"All right, another question about yesterday: Did anything weird happen to you? Anything strange during the day at all?" As he asked this question, Gary put a little more hush in his voice.

This did not go unnoticed.

"You son of a bitch! I should have known that it was *you* who did that shit to me! *You made me collapse in the middle of the department store! Do you have any idea how humiliated I felt from all those eyes staring at me as if I was a damsel in distress?*"

She shouted so loud that Gary was sure even those on the street outside the woods could hear her.

"Look, I'm sorry, I didn't consider your circumstances, but I promise it was in your best interest!" Gary was unable to look her in the eyes for a moment. Instead, he swept his gaze over the Lady Boss's body. Not because he was interested in her or anything, but because he had expected some change in her appearance.

When he had selected the Warrior Class for himself, his body had changed drastically. He had expected something similar to happen to the beta werewolf, but at least outwardly there was nothing different about her.

Could it be that she didn't change because I went with the recommended class? Did my body change because I chose something that I wasn't suited for before that?

"Tell me, have you noticed anything peculiar about yourself? Any messages in front of your eyes, perhaps?" he asked.

"Now that you mention it, I did encounter some strange red smoke that day. It was very faint, though, and it smelled like raw food. I can still see it now, and it hasn't disappeared since that day. Not sure if anything else is new," Olivia replied, before giving the teenager another angry stare. "I didn't exactly have the mind to find out after collapsing out of nowhere, you know?"

So she still doesn't seem to have a system but can see its effects? Did she somehow set targets without realizing it or . . . Then a thought came into Gary's head.

"Can you still see it? If so, can you point me in the direction of where it's coming from?"

Olivia was still unsure what was up, but she humored the alpha werewolf and showed him.

It must be because she is a beta werewolf in the same pack. Now that she is a Hunter she can see my marks as well. However, it seems to be only my Forced Bonds and not the Bond Marks I have made. Not sure if I should be happy about it or not.

"Okay, let's see how much stronger you've gotten, then," Gary suggested with a smile.

There were two reasons he wanted to do this: to test out his own capabilities as well as Olivia's. It was important to know the gap in strength between them; that way he could continue being the alpha werewolf.

Olivia wasn't shy, getting into a fighting stance and holding her whip in her hand. She, too, wanted to know what these changes were. At that moment, her eyes lit up blue.

The beta werewolf (Hunter Class) is within range of the pack leader and has entered into battle
0/15 Marks available
The alpha is able to designate Hunting Marks for the Hunter Class.
The Hunter will prioritize those with marks
Extra Exp will be gained for marked targets hunted by the Hunter
The Hunter's strength will increase when fighting against those who are marked

It was unexpected for Gary to suddenly get multiple notifications, but it looked like he had gotten some of his answers about what a Hunter could do exactly. It was just a shame that he couldn't see Olivia's stats, or whether she benefited from hunting these targets.

Either way, he could find out through a fight.

While Gary was distracted, Olivia lashed out with her whip and Gary grabbed it, catching it with his transformed arm.

"You're faster than before," Gary noted.

"And it looks like you've gotten faster as well!" Olivia shouted as she charged forward.

The two of them were huffing and panting as their training session came to an end. Gary had learned a lot through their small spars. For one, although his speed had increased greatly, this also meant that he used more stamina during a fight.

Which meant that if he wanted to focus on speed, it wasn't wise to just increase his dexterity, because without increasing his stamina, he could only last a few seconds at full capacity.

However, one thing was clear during the fight: although Olivia had improved after gaining Hunter Class, Gary was leaps and bounds stronger than her. He was growing at a much faster rate.

Nevertheless, the Lady Boss had improved in more ways than one. Gary had pushed her significantly in the fight, and in the end, a rage had overcome her, causing her arm to transform slightly. Her nails grew and fur appeared on the top of her forearm. It looked similar to his Controlled Transformation, yet she seemed unable to control it, at least for now.

Without a doubt, though, the two of them were a force to be reckoned with, which strengthened Gary's resolve about his next course of action.

"I've decided, Olivia, that tomorrow you and I will pay the Underdogs a visit and wipe them out."

CHAPTER 7

GETTING A CRYSTAL

It hadn't even been that long since Tom had begun his internship, yet all the things he was discovering at NIRV were unbelievable. He was tempted to share his new findings with the whole world, but he understood that it would lead to enormous trouble.

Still, he couldn't help but search the web about how much of what he had found might be out there. Unsurprisingly, there were only a few rumors here and there that had a hint of truth about what Tom had witnessed. A lot of it was off the mark, and he even imagined himself believing some of these things before he had come here. It appeared that there were no whistleblowers telling the truth, not even on the dark web.

Either everyone was taking their NDA very seriously, or, and Tom was leaning more toward the second possibility, those who had tried to reveal information had been suppressed, never to be given a voice again. You can't stay the market leader without dirtying your own hands; at least Tom wouldn't be surprised to learn of any such news, not that he had found any.

Right now, he was looking into what appeared to be an empty room. The glass windows went all around the room, above the arena floor. The room was occupied by several people who were waiting for something. However, upon closer inspection, there was something very peculiar about this normal-looking room. There were numerous scratch marks on the metal walls, most of them quite deep.

Lucky me; from what Dad told me, I was sure it would be impossible to get permission to watch this, Tom thought with his eyes wide open, not even wanting to blink, as the doors on one side of the large room slowly opened. One could imagine how thick and reinforced they were, based on their slow movement.

Five people entered, yet there was nothing uniform about them; they looked like random people off the street. The only thing they had in common was a strange air of confidence.

These are the Recoverers . . . and . . . and I'm going to see a real beast. Not just a fossil, but a real beast in front of my very eyes!

Tom had often encountered them as he walked around the lab. Many of them looked like gangsters, though he had also encountered some whom he might simply overlook if he met them out on the street. According to his father, they had their own separate lives that NIRV didn't really get involved with.

They could be gangsters, they could even be homeless. Regardless, when they were here, they were known as Recoverers. His father had said that they were Altered who had received NIRV's services, on the condition that they would help out with retrieving the beast crystals.

His father had seen many Altered that were beyond the strength of those at the AFC, which surprised Tom, yet at the same time it also didn't, not after everything else he had come to learn.

The door on the other side of the room opened as well, and a team of people in hazmat suits came in pushing a large fossil on a vehicle, which they then shoved into the center of the room. The group quickly left the room, and then it was time for the final part of the process.

The ceiling partially opened, revealing a specially made and designed clawlike object. Now descending was what Tom had only seen on video so far.

That . . . that should be the Nest Crystal!

Seeing it in person was completely different from the video it-self. There was a certain mystical pattern inside the crystal that was hard to describe. It was as if part of space had been captured and placed there.

"The information that we extract from the fossil gets inputted into the Nest Crystal," his father had explained. "I know it's hard to believe, but the crystal is actually able to read the data. Sometimes it makes me feel that it has learned our language. So after we input the data they extract from the fossil, the crystal can do what it's about to do next. As I said before, though, that's not my department, so I don't know the exact details."

The claw that was holding the crystal started to turn red at its tips, and then it started to glow. At the same time, the Recoverers were getting ready. They had already begun to transform.

One grew to nearly four times the size of his regular self, with thick gray skin and a large horn on his head. Another had grown wings like an insect, flapping at a great speed, and hands that looked like stingers. The rest had turned into even more dangerous-looking creatures, though none of them resembled any earthly creature that Tom had ever seen, but rather something out of a nightmare.

A beam of energy from the Nest Crystal hit the fossil, and flesh and matter began appearing out of thin air, as if someone were 3D printing it, forming on top of the fossilized bones. Some of the bone structure that had been missing was starting to form as well, and soon enough the fossil was no more.

In its place stood what one could only describe as a primordial beast. Honestly, seeing the beast in its full form made Tom instinc-tively want to run away. He didn't know if it was just this beast in particular or if the others were like this, but it looked beyond hor-rifying.

It was as big as a three-story building. It had the body of a centi-pede and the legs to go with it, but its upper half was lifted in the air like the body of a cobra, while on each side it had what looked like the wings of a bat. Its head was mostly a golden triangle shape, and it opened its maw to reveal rows of razor-sharp teeth.

The Hunters got to quick work, with the large horned Altered charging in front. Considering his size, he was quicker than Tom had given him credit for, and he bashed into the beast before it could react. Its horn pierced through the beast's body, and black blood came gushing out.

The beast let out a strange shriek, which stopped the other Hunters from charging in. It used its large maw to bite down on the large Altered, then started to flap its wings, preparing to fly upward.

However, before it could rise, the buglike Altered flew right through its wings, piercing the beast with its stingers. It then quickly flew to the back of the beast's head and hit it a few times. The others joined the attack, overwhelming the monstrous beast. These Altered were strong, and they took out the beast fairly quickly. They extracted the crystal from the beast and presented it to all the onlookers.

With that, the fight was over.

Tom thought it was a good result, but his father looked disappointed.

"Did something go wrong?" Tom asked.

"Nothing went wrong per se," his father answered. "In fact, I would see this as a good day. No Recoverers died today, but others might think this is a bad outcome. After all, this team wasn't very proficient, meaning that the beast was too weak and likely didn't have a strong crystal."

Hearing his father explain this type of logic scared Tom a little. Though he might not have said so outright, it showed how little NIRV seemed to value the lives of the Altered. Of course, they could always create more, but to treat them as an expandable resource . . .

It was then that Tom had felt his phone vibrating, and he pulled it out to see some news about Slough.

"Dad, you have to see this!" Tom cried, shoving the phone in his father's face.

At first, his father didn't seem too bothered. He had a bit of sympathy for his hometown, but the news might have as well been about any other location. However, he started to pay more attention when he saw the images, and he snatched the phone from his son.

"How come there are so many crazed Altered there . . . no, this can't be," his father mumbled.

CHAPTER 8

INFECTED ALTERED

After James Green had read the news about what had occurred in Slough, he mumbled some seemingly incoherent things to himself before heading straight toward his lab, completely ignoring his son.

"What the . . . I know it's shocking news, but aren't you overreacting, Dad?" Tom called after him.

He had only read the headline, so now he was curious about what the article was about. He quickly learned about everything he had missed, about the crazed Altered that were seemingly orphans, the new gang named the Howlers, and on top of that, the fact that there was a "Wolf Altered" in Slough.

I knew it! Tom inwardly shouted. *I knew that Gary was hiding something! So he really did decide to join a gang! That's who all those other people were. Then they must have also been the ones responsible for what happened to the gray color gang, and that means it was really him . . . but why?*

Was it because he got werewolf powers? Did he think that with great power comes great responsibility? But, Gary . . . you don't seem like that type of person. I know you aren't. Otherwise, why would you choose to hide this secret from me?

Tom was trying to put himself in Gary's shoes, to understand why his friend had not shared everything with him. After all, he had already figured out Gary's werewolf identity, so surely he should have been someone Gary could trust.

Wait—what about his story about how he became a werewolf? His part-time job, was he already involved in all of that?

Ultimately, the only reason Tom could come up with was that Gary must have stayed silent to protect him. As he came to this conclusion, a wide grin appeared on his face, and he almost got a tear in his eye.

Ah, man, why am I welling up because he hid a secret from me? And joined a gang? I'm really strange. Tom chuckled.

Of course, after reading the news, Tom was curious to see if he could find out more information. He quickly stumbled on more devastating news, namely that Gary had not only faced Kirk but had delivered a deadly blow.

The articles had headlines such as *AFC Rookie Champion Still Missing!*, *Did the Wolf Altered Kill Kirk Summerfield?*, and *Kirk Summerfield's Double Life as a Gang Member?*

There were too many news articles and headlines about the whole event.

Damn, I need to text Gary . . . Argh, but I can't . . . the NDA mentioned that they check our messages and phone conversations from all calls made here to prevent us from leaking information. They probably have some sort of device that picks up all our communications outside as well. Now that I think about it, I don't think our apartment here is safe either. I should stop going on the dark web in case they keep track of all employees; it could get my dad in trouble. I'll have to wait until I'm back at Slough to talk with him. I just have to hope that he is all right until then, Tom thought.

A short while later, his father returned. He looked winded, like he had run back, and he certainly wasn't the athletic type, just like his son.

"Wanna share what got you so panicked that you left your only son behind, Dad?"

His father needed a moment to catch his breath, but Tom noticed that he didn't seem to be as nervous anymore. Whatever the emergency matter had been, it had apparently been dealt with.

"I apologize, your news just came out of nowhere, and given the things it pertained to, I just had to make a report to the higher-ups about it. I needed to find out if they were already aware of it, since I was worried that it might have come from our lab," James answered, still panting, but then he immediately covered his mouth, earning him a strange look from his son.

"Shoot, that wasn't meant for your ears . . . well, I guess since you're our intern, you might as well learn a bit. Besides, you're family, so surely you would not want your old man in trouble, right? As in, don't tell anyone what I'm about to tell you." He chuckled nervously, hitting Tom on the shoulder as if the two of them were the closest of friends.

In fact, they got along very well, yet the unfortunate reality was that ever since his parents had started working for NIRV, Tom hardly got to spend time with them.

"You see, we are unaware of what state the fossils will come back in once they are hit with the Nest Crystals that you saw earlier, and at times, there have been a few . . . strange results.

"The beasts came out looking a bit sick, covered in strange purple fur and sometimes with a bit of a dark shadow surrounding them. The shadow itself looked almost as if it was alive. Any crystals obtained from them are classified as infected. We don't use those batches of crystal for making Altered, because in nine out of ten cases they end up as crazed Altered."

His father didn't have to say more; Tom had already figured it out. His father was saying that somehow this special batch must have gotten out—either stolen, sold, or maybe even released by the company itself. Either way, he had to inform his friends about what he knew so far.

At the same time, a NIRV employee stood in front of the police station, explaining the exact same thing to Slough's chief of police, as well as the presiding White Rose agents.

"This is the information you are to tell the press. A gang has managed to get their hands on a corrupted batch of Altered DNA that was scheduled to be disposed of. NIRV has started an investigation to find out how it happened, and will share details once the situation is resolved."

Similarly, an employee of NIRV had arrived at the mayor's office, though it wasn't the same employee who had brought the syringes over.

"Are you kidding me? The public won't be content with that! They will ask questions and blame *me* for failing to protect the people of Slough! Do you have any idea how it makes me look, that some gangs were the ones to take care of that problem? *Utterly incompetent!* The fact that you've come all the way here pretty much proves that your company is connected to *all of this*!" Ben Clove shouted.

"Mayor Clove, how are your finances looking after you purchased that second syringe of Altered DNA? Isn't it true that the acquisition has put your family under a financial burden? Sure, you might be able to keep up appearances, but how long will you be able to continue with your current lifestyle? Wouldn't it help you immensely if we were to refund you the payment for that second dosage, and even scratch it off the records?" the man said, and the corpulent mayor quickly calmed down. "Please just read the statement our PR team has prepared, and make sure that the matter doesn't get brought up by anyone other than us in the future."

Although Ben Clove didn't say anything else, he was furious internally. Sure, the freebie was nice, but he hated having to dance to someone else's tune. Fortunately, it was only a matter of time until he was finally free to do as he wished . . .

After his training session with the beta werewolf, Gary had decided to walk home. He had a lot to think about, and with his head now clearer, this was a good time to at least look at the new skills he could learn.

The Last Stand skill had saved him more than once already, and since he planned to attack the Underdogs tomorrow, he needed every advantage he could get. Holding back now would be stupid, if not suicidal.

As he walked along the road, Gary heard an approaching car, but he ignored it, as many cars had already passed him by. However, this car slowed down and came to a halt only a few yards from him.

As he turned around, the car's bright headlights blinded him, making it hard for him to see who had just gotten out.

"Honestly, what are the chances?" The voice sounded surprised. "Here I just decided to give it a shot, and yet I actually found you, streaker boy. This must be some red string of fate between us, and not just as a brother-in-law. You seem to have a tendency to appear near the woods, but perhaps I shouldn't be surprised about that. This makes things easier. Come with me for a ride; there are some things we need to talk about, wolfie."

CHAPTER 9

THE FUTURE OF SLOUGH

As he walked along the road at the edge of the forest, Gary was making mental preparations for what he would do tomorrow. The Underdogs had practically gone into hiding, but since their leader had survived, it was clear that they would gather their strength and try to come back from this. That was just the type of person Damion Hawk was.

Kai seemed to be overly cautious about the Underdogs' resurgence. Gary was sure that with Kirk gone, as long as they could get rid of Damion, it would naturally spell the end of the Underdogs.

And to that end, there was one thing Kai didn't know. Gary knew *exactly* where Damion was!

What's more, due to the Forced Bond he had placed on him, he would be able to find him, most likely until the end of his life.

There's nowhere you can hide from me, Damion. I don't want to be afraid of you any longer. From now on, I'm the one who will become your hunter, Gary thought in satisfaction.

Although the White Tiger Altered wasn't his enemy, Gary couldn't exactly call him an ally either. Nevertheless, he was one of the people that Gary respected wholeheartedly, and not only because of his career as an Altered fighter.

He had seen Jayden get his way when demanding things from the Gray Elephants. A single person had made an entire gang cower in front of him. If that wasn't badass, Gary didn't know what was.

Now that I have improved stats, just how far behind do I lag compared to him? Gary wondered. Ultimately, he decided to enter the car. For one, Gary didn't want to cause trouble, and he also wanted to maintain a good relationship with Xin's brother.

The two of them rode along for a while. Gary had taken the passenger seat as requested; as for where they were going, he wasn't quite sure.

"Let me be frank, it wasn't completely a coincidence that I found you here today. Xin didn't want to hand over your number, and I didn't want to drag her into this mess, so I've been driving around since yesterday evening," Jayden revealed. "With that out of the way, I wanted to talk to you since I saw you on that news channel. You really gave it your all against the cat dude."

Gary's eyes widened. He had been sure that the wolf mask would keep his real identity safe, because no one but the Howlers would know who was underneath. Unfortunately, he had forgotten that that wasn't true. Jayden had seen him use that same mask when he had come to rescue Xin.

"I have to tell you something, Gary," Jayden said as he parked the car in a supermarket lot. They were at the very back toward a hill. "I hate gangs."

As he said these words, there was a fierce change in his voice. Gary immediately opened the door on his side, afraid he was going to be attacked, and rolled out of the car. He stood up in a fighting stance and turned to face the car, but Jayden was no longer in it.

"What exactly do you think you're doing? You're aware that we're not in an action movie, right?" Jayden asked from behind Gary as he walked over toward the hill and sat down on the grass. "I told you that there are things we need to talk about, and I meant using our words, not fists. Gary, I know that you must feel powerful given what you are, but you're just a teenager, practically still a kid. I know that Slough isn't the safest, but did you really have to join a gang? I decided to at least hear you out, since I owe you at least that much for trying to save Xin."

Gary realized that Jayden had chosen his words carefully. After all, he had merely promised to give him a chance to explain himself, but what if he didn't like the answer? Would he attack him? Unfortunately, now seemed like a bad time to ask Jayden his reason for hating gangs.

It should be okay . . . I have an ace up my sleeve. If it comes down to it, I'm sure Jayden doesn't know about his father's involvement with those small-time gangs, Gary thought, calming himself down. He cautiously came over and sat down, though he did so a good two yards away, just in case anything happened.

Jayden couldn't help but let out a laugh at Gary's antics, but he understood why he was behaving like this.

"Well, I'm all ears. How exactly did you get caught up in this mess? How did someone like you become an Altered, and just what was that attack on Slough?" Jayden asked.

Gary let out a big sigh, wondering how much he should tell the Altered. Just enough to make sense, or the whole truth involving Kai and the others?

In the end, he opted to concentrate mostly on his own situation. However, rather than covering up a bunch of lies as he had done in the past, he confessed almost everything. Perhaps it was easier with Jayden, since he still felt a bit like a stranger.

Gary began by sharing his family's financial situation, which had led to him joining the Underdogs in the first place. Then he explained how he had become an Altered and his journey to protect his family from the gang, leaving him no choice but to create his own.

"I see, so I guess what happened the other day was just between the Gray Elephants and the Underdogs. You just saw it as an opportunity to get rid of the Underdogs?" Jayden repeated, making sure he got everything correct.

Gary nodded, though he didn't share the part about how they had gotten involved through Innu's request to save the orphans.

Finally, Jayden let out a big sigh of relief.

"You know, I was worried about Slough, seeing as my old man has no intentions of moving out. Then again, he is the mayor of this town, so I do understand how it would be the end of his career if he did something like that," Jayden revealed. "I went to Chavley and got rid of the crazed Altered there, and it just made me worry whether everyone will be okay. You see, I'm leaving this town soon. I need to get back to the AFC, and without me, I was worried what this place might become.

"However, wolfie, there's someone who has managed to change so much already. I believe what you've told me, but I do have to warn you. If you do change your ways, or become just as bad as the guys who were running the place before your Howlers, I might have to get involved and teach you another lesson." Jayden smiled and made a fist.

Although it sounded like he was joking, Gary was sure that he meant exactly what he said. Thankfully, though, it looked like Jayden wouldn't become an enemy.

Since things had turned out well, Gary decided to keep his little meeting with the mayor a secret for now. In the end, they had never made a move during the fight like they had planned anyway. So there was no need to stir the pot.

"I've told you everything, so I hope you can answer a question of mine now," Gary finally said. "Unlike me, you've had your powers for far longer, and I'm sure what you showed me that day was just a glimpse of it.

"Your presence alone was enough to stop the Gray Elephants from attacking us, so with all your strength, how come you don't stop those gangs? Why not just get rid of the Underdogs altogether?"

It was a question that had been on Gary's mind for a long time. Since Jayden talked about getting rid of his gang if they were to become bullies, why not the current group? He was stronger than Kirk and Damion.

"I . . . am not a leader," Jayden answered. "I'm a single individual. I can't rally people around me, or ask people to fight for me. Simply put, I'm more of a loner. On top of that, there are a few other reasons.

"Even if I take down the leaders, there will just be someone else to replace them. Unless I decide to stay in charge or run the place, things just won't work out. I'm kinda . . . what do they call it, a free bird."

There was a smile on his face as he spoke, but it soon faded.

"Actually, I'm probably not as free a bird as I would like to think. In fact, just like you, Gary, my hands are also tied, but by a far bigger force than just the Underdogs. Remember, I wasn't born into this world with a silver spoon, or as an Altered.

"Even then, I got lucky in the end and have accidentally become a significant someone. Unfortunately, there is a limit to what I can do. I just took an interest in this town because of my family."

Gary understood, because even the AFC was under a large, powerful organization, and possibly behind them was another. He could only guess at the setup and structure in the higher-tier cities, which felt like different worlds from the one he knew.

Finally, Jayden stood up and wiped the back of his trousers. Instead of walking back to his car, he headed toward the woods.

"Why don't we have one final fight before I leave?" Jayden asked. "If you win, you'll still get my autograph, or if you prefer, you can raid my fridge once more? Only this time I would like both of us to go all out, fully use our Altered forms."

CHAPTER 10

TIGER VS. WOLF (PART 1)

From a young age, Gary had always been interested in fighting, though up until recently he had to be content with just watching others fight. However, nowadays, the thought alone was enough to make him feel a rush. He wasn't sure if it was his own personal desire that had manifested—now that he had the capabilities—or another side effect of becoming a werewolf. Especially since it was getting close to the full moon.

Whatever the case, Gary was naturally curious about how much he had improved since his last fight against Jayden, yet this wouldn't be the same type of sparring match that they had before. No, this time it would be the two of them duking it out in their full Altered forms.

Gary looked around to make sure that the area was safe. Jayden's car was the only one in the parking lot. The supermarket itself was actually boarded up, seemingly abandoned. Checking the street-lights next, he found cameras mounted on them. All of them had been destroyed, crushed. They were placed quite high up, so the act was clearly intentional.

"Don't tell me . . . did you drive us here just so we could fight?" Gary asked.

"I told you that I was looking for you since yesterday." Jayden shrugged. "This location also seemed perfect in case things had turned out differently."

Gary gulped hard. It was terrifying to think that if his answer hadn't satisfied Xin's brother, the Altered had been ready to kill him in the middle of nowhere. Even scarier was the possibility that he might not have been able to do anything about it. Hopefully, that would turn out to be a meaningless worry.

Either way, perhaps Gary deserved a death like that, after what he had done to others.

"All right, let's do this," Gary agreed. *I have the system to check up on my Health. If I get too injured, I can stop the fight at any time. The only thing I have to be careful about is not inflicting a dangerous wound on Jayden like I did to Kirk.* He tried to hype himself up as he watched the Altered's face and body structure change in front of him.

There were two techniques Gary could use while fighting against Jayden.

One option was to use Controlled Transformation to the max on all parts of his body. It would increase his stats by a large margin, while also allowing him to conserve his Energy. This would enable him to drag the fight out and try to outlast his opponent.

The other option was to outright use Full Transformation. This would take up more Energy, though, and it would also result in a bigger boost as every single part of him would be fully werewolf. However, it would also mean that their fight would have a time limit.

I ate just after my training with Olivia, so my body is in top shape and I have no excuses.

Skill activated: Full Transformation
−20 Energy
Transformation has begun

Jayden had said that they should both go full out in this fight. So Gary chose his second option, even though the Altered's body didn't seem to have changed as drastically, as when Kirk had gone all out.

Jayden's arms had become like large paws with claws, and his face was now covered in white fur, but other than that, his body had hardly changed apart from his shoulders becoming a little wider.

Still, as soon as his body had finished transforming, Gary felt a slight wind, causing his fur to ruffle slightly.

As for Gary, his whole body had completely changed. However, because of the adjustments that had pretty much been perfected on his clothes, they hadn't ripped for the first time. However, he still had to slip his shoes off. The teenager was the first one to run in, trying to get the jump on his opponent.

With his increased speed, courtesy of Kirk, and his Full Transformation, as well as the nearness of the full moon, he was faster than Jayden had expected him to be. Against the swipe of the werewolf's hand, the White Tiger Altered was forced to bend over backward.

His body was flexible, yet Gary had somewhat expected this as he swung his other arm downward. Still, Jayden swiftly moved out of the way, almost touching the ground with his entire body, somehow managing to support it on a single leg. He pushed off and threw himself directly at Gary. It was a dangerous position to be in, because the werewolf had another weapon that he didn't use much, and that was his maw.

I want to win, so I'm going to use everything I've got! Gary thought as he opened wide. Before his teeth could latch on, though, Jayden's paw had already struck him.

He thought that he could take whatever was coming his way and do more damage to his opponent, but that was when something strange happened. The blow itself wasn't strong. In fact, it seemed as if Jayden's paw had only lightly tapped Gary's chest, but a second later the "light tap" might as well have been a cannonball shot from point-blank distance.

It lifted Gary off his feet and sent him flying through the air.

–50 HP
110/160 HP

Blood poured from Gary's mouth, and it took him a few seconds to embed his clawed feet into the ground, his hands scraping along until he was able to stop himself.

Why was that blow so strong? Is he using that strange power he used before? Gary asked himself, thinking back to Jayden's fight against the red color gang members who had captured Xin. He had attacked all of them from the position he was in.

"You're faster than before, Gary. I'm impressed how much you seem to have improved in such a short amount of time . . . seriously, how are you even still standing right now? I used enough power to have knocked you out for a good while, but here you are still standing," Jayden admitted, not hiding his surprise.

Honestly, this was the strongest blow Gary had ever taken to his HP. It would have taken down half his Health before his upgrade, and probably even more if he had used Controlled Transformation.

Still, thanks to him being at his strongest, Gary knew that he could still take one or two more hits. He didn't want to give up now. If Jayden really was leaving soon, he wanted to find out his own limits beforehand.

"This fight has only just started!" Gary shouted.

CHAPTER 11

TIGER VS. WOLF (PART 2)

Learning how an Altered fighter moves and attacks, and what special traits they possess are all important factors in an Altered fight. Gary had seen Jayden Tiger multiple times on TV, not to mention the countless times he had seen the highlights of the White Tiger Altered's fights on PouTube.

Alas, just as in his fight against Kirk, this supposed advantage turned out to exist only in theory. An Altered fight in the ring on-screen versus in real life proved to be completely different. So much that he had seen on TV seemed to be far from the actual limit of the White Tiger Altered.

The simple punch alone had packed enough power that it would at least severely cripple a normal human for the rest of their life. Gary didn't know if this was the full extent of his power, but he was far deadlier than in his normal human form.

"I see you have the spirit, but are you sure you can continue to fight in your condition?" Jayden asked, not moving from his position.

Gary let the blood dribble out of his mouth, shaking his head a little.

"Yes," he answered, although it wasn't exactly clear what he was saying through his large snout and teeth. The sound was muffled, but his actions were understandable enough. Gary wasn't sure if he was imagining it, but with a single step, Jayden had managed to cross a large distance. It looked like he was almost gliding across the ground, but not only that, he was incredibly fast, even faster than Kirk.

How the hell is a White Tiger faster than a cheetah? That should be impossible. Gary was flabbergasted as he covered his face with his arms in a boxing stance, bracing himself for the attack. However, he only felt a gust of wind; Jayden was able to slow down and stop as quickly as he could move forward. Gary was unable to react as the Altered moved to his side and kicked him in the ribs.

–8 HP

That kick wasn't as heavy as the punch. Is he taking it easy on me because he thinks I'm still hurt? Or is he unable to continuously hit me so hard?

Enduring the pain, Gary swung his own leg out, doing his best not to flinch, and delivered everything he could into the attack. But Jayden had dug his claws into the concrete, his muscles were tense, and the next second he had ripped up a large piece of concrete and thrown it at him. Gary's kick smashed the piece of concrete, destroying it, but he hurt himself in the process as well.

–2 HP

The pain wasn't great, but the impact had slowed him down and thrown several pieces of debris into his line of sight. Although Gary couldn't see anything, his ears picked something up.

Aware that something was coming his way, he lifted his large forearms to block it. But suddenly he felt something deep cutting through his strong hide, and his warm blood started trickling onto the ground.

–8 HP
–8 HP

The attack was strange, and just as Gary sensed something silencing the wind, he noticed that Jayden had moved a good five yards away.

That was strange. He was nowhere near me, so how did he hurt me? Gary pictured the ranged attack he had used against the red color gang members. Jayden must have used it on him now.

I need to stop thinking of him as just a White Tiger. Altered are based on beasts that are different from the animals we have today. On top of that, he seems to be a different type of Altered altogether, Gary told himself. *I shouldn't be surprised that he is faster than Kirk, or about all the strange things he can do.*

Jayden continued his barrage of attacks; he was somehow able to mount an attack from a distance. His slashes broke through the wind and sliced right through Gary's injured forearm, sharper than any knife. The werewolf's hide was strong, but the attack was vicious enough to hurt immensely. *No wonder it had been enough to bisect those gang members.*

−8 HP

The worst thing about the windstrikes was the fact that they were nearly impossible to see. They distorted the airspace a little as they went through. But Gary managed to avoid the attacks and bravely decided to charge toward Jayden once again.

Oh, I have to ask him how he's able to avoid my slashes if he can't see them, Jayden thought. *Xin, your little boyfriend just continues to be full of surprises.*

If Gary had been the same as before the gang war, his speed would not have allowed him to keep up with the Altered's attacks. Once again, he was inwardly thanking Kirk.

The other reason that he was able to evade the attacks was his enhanced hearing. He was able to perceive the noise a wind strike made as it sliced through the air, telling him where not to go if he wanted to avoid it.

Faster, I have to move faster . . . I have yet to use this speed to its full potential! Gary thought as he pushed against the ground with his legs the second they touched it. He focused on drawing strength from every inch of his body, including his toes.

Rolling away, dodging the strange attacks, and moving from side to side, Gary had an image of Kirk in his head. Now, at the perfect place, the werewolf leapt from one side with a claw out, aiming for Jayden.

At that moment, though, just as Gary's claws were about to reach Jayden's face, his arm suddenly moved on its own. Another strong gust of wind lifted it upward, and before Gary knew it, another powerful blow, this time a kick, connected with his stomach and sent him flying across the supermarket parking lot.

–60 HP
16/160 Health

As he lay on the ground, Gary canceled his transformation. As stubborn as he was, he understood that if he continued, he would risk losing all of his Health. Using Last Stand seemed like a waste, since he didn't feel confident in being able to hit Jayden in that one minute.

Seeing that Gary had reverted to his normal self, Jayden did the same. He picked up Gary's shoes and brought them over.

"You did way better than I thought. I know you might be sad or disappointed, but trust me, don't be . . . but I do have one message for you. As long as you are still in this gang business, I can't entrust Xin to you. I want my little sister to be safe and protected.

"*But*, seeing as you're a dumb young teenager, and believe it or not, I used to be one myself, I can't really expect you to just listen to me acting as the voice of reason. I'm sure that you want to have both, right? Here's the deal: the day you can actually beat me, you'll have my blessing." Jayden smiled as he offered Gary his hand.

CHAPTER 12

A COMMON ALTERED

It was rare for people to live outside the cities and towns, since those were the only places one could get work. The higher-tier the city or town, the higher the average pay would be. If they could afford it, people lived in the cities, but most of the workforce commuted to work from a nearby town because of the high cost of rent in the city.

Of course, the Tier 5 "towns" barely deserved the name. They were essentially just giant dumps that housed people who had nothing and lived off the scraps of the other cities. Their "houses" consisted of whatever materials the other cities had discarded that they could slap together.

These cities were why the AFC Academy, more commonly known as the AFA, was a unique place.

It was a school that was the most prominent gathering place for Altered all over the country, and it was the only facility of its kind in the region. Of course, there were academies abroad that trained special Altered, but this academy was unique because, as the name suggested, it was an official part of the AFC.

It was generally considered the best place for any Altered's future, be it as an Altered fighter or in another profession. There were many events for the students to show off to sponsors of the most-watched televised sport worldwide!

The academy was located in a Tier 2 city but wasn't a part of the city itself; rather, it was out in the countryside. The large building was home to around two thousand Altered, which might seem like a large amount, but it was minuscule compared to the world population.

Despite its location, the academy boasted great wealth thanks to the students that attended it. This place was meant to be an independently run facility, away from the Tier 1 cities, although whether people believed that was another thing.

Five new potential students stood inside what looked like an empty white room. Each one wore a plain white uniform, and in front of them stood three older gentlemen. They, too, were wearing white uniforms similar to those of the students, although their styling was a little different.

"Every year, facilities around the world succeed in making breakthrough after breakthrough." The man in the center, with giant round glasses and a tall frame, began to speak while pacing back and forth in front of the five teenagers.

"This has led to an increase in the appearance of Altered in general . . . making them more common."

Although what the professor of the academy was saying was true, *common* seemed to be a horrible word to use in this context. After all, the statement was merely true among the upper class, and even then, less than one percent of people could afford to get their hands on Altered DNA.

"Should this trend continue, there may come a day that everyone in the world will have become an Altered. Be that as it may, our academy *has* always prided and *will* always pride ourselves on one thing! We are *the* place to cultivate the most elite generation of Altered!

"Naturally, that means that we don't accept just anyone. Money can't buy everything, and it won't buy you the right to stay here. You still have to earn that!"

The five students all stood straight and tall, strong and confident; among them was Xin Clove, though she was attending under a fake name. Today was supposed to be her first day at the AFA, yet from the professor's words, she understood that if she didn't show potential, it might also be her last.

I'm not going back! Jayden went through all the trouble to allow me to get a chance to be free, so I need to at least be able to go through all of this!

The bespectacled man stepped back, allowing a bulky professor to step forward. His colleague looked a little strange; he had a large, round belly, but his arms were those of a body builder, with next to no fat visible on them at all.

"The five of you shall now undergo a trial that will determine your positions in the next room," the second professor stated. "There are only two rules: don't get hit, and remain in your human form."

"What?" a boy with blonde spiky hair shouted angrily. "Some of us might have a really rare Altered form or be better at using it than others! If you test us without letting us go all out, how is that fair?"

"Simple," the professor with the glasses replied. "We have done extensive research on Altered. If your Altered form is based on a genuinely strong beast, your body will have changed in accordance to house it, meaning that even in your human form you will be able to display inhuman feats.

"Should that not be the case, then the beast inside you is weak. If you dislike it, you are free to leave and apply to another academy. I can guarantee you that there won't be a shortage of students who wish to apply, and these harsh criteria have allowed us to ensure that only the best of the best get through."

Hearing this, Xin felt confident because she trusted in her own skills even before she became an Altered. However, there was a problem. This supposed change of her body was not something she had experienced for herself.

Maybe we shouldn't have trusted that NIRV guy. After that in-jection, he assured me that everything had gone perfectly fine, but I still struggle to keep up my Altered form, Xin thought. Fortunately, she had passed the Altered test required to get to this stage, which proved that she was no longer human.

"Well, what do we do now?" a tired-looking kid asked once the three professors had left the room. He had large black eyes that made him resemble a panda.

Just then they heard a clicking sound, and a large black ball came hurling out from the side wall and struck one of the students. The ball wasn't heavy, so it didn't hurt, but it stuck to his body, and as the student tried to pull it off, the sticky substance covering the ball just went onto his hand instead.

He then tried to use his foot, but the ball remained stuck to him.

"Rick Toenail, you have been eliminated! Please stand to the side and do not interfere with the test!" A mechanical voice sounded in the room.

"That's your name?" The spiky-haired kid couldn't help but laugh.

The boy with the panda eyes jumped nearly two yards to the side as a large black ball went straight past him, forcing the other three students to evade it. Xin dodged left, while Ryan, the loudmouth blonde, moved in the opposite direction. More and more black balls started coming from the walls, and then from above and below as well, until the students were being blasted from all over the room.

The professors were watching everything through the screen. It had been a minute since the test had begun, and they were getting a clear grasp of the students' abilities.

"Looks like we have a couple of good ones with us," one of the professors noted with a smile.

"Indeed, the panda boy has the best reflexes out of the lot. He's using next to no effort to dodge everything that is coming his way. As for Ryan, although his attitude is quite bad, he appears to have the best physical capabilities of this batch. He can outrun anything coming toward him."

"What about the other two?" another professor asked.

"The other two are nothing special. They're struggling, so I doubt they'll last until the end."

Xin was trying her best to avoid all the black balls, visualizing them as punches and kicks hurling toward her. But as the test continued, the number of balls and their speed increased. Xin was getting tired, mentally as well as physically.

Panda Eyes and Spiky Hair are still doing fine. It's like the first few minutes were just a warm-up for them, Xin thought, glancing at the tall, lanky boy close to her. *If this goes on, he and I aren't going to pass this test.*

Just then, three black balls came flying toward her. Xin knew that she wasn't fast enough to avoid them, but she came up with a plan. She launched a kick toward the struggling boy at her side and landed a blow to his temple, knocking him out cold.

Before he fell to the floor, she grabbed his body and placed it in front of her. Using her fellow candidate as a literal human shield, Xin ran forward, blocking the black balls in front of her. She eventually let go of him, ready to dodge more, but the balls suddenly stopped.

The test was over. However, her actions didn't go unnoticed, by her fellow students as well as by the professors, who had watched everything over the cameras and were now discussing her strategy.

"The rules just stated that we had to avoid touching the balls while staying in human form. I didn't break any rules, right?" Xin asked.

No matter what, she was going to get accepted!

CHAPTER 13

THE NEXT STAGE

On average, there would only be one person for every fifteen batches who would pass this first trial. The three professors had already been happy to see that the current batch had two promising youths . . . and yet, despite having watched dozens of would-be students try to pass, they were nevertheless surprised at Xin's ruthlessness and determination to pass.

The teenage girl had already let go of the student she had used as a meat shield. He was only waking up now, still dazed and confused. It took him a few moments to understand what had happened, and he was staring at the person responsible for his elimination.

"Diego Nascimento, you have been eliminated. Please leave the room together with Rick Toenail!" The mechanical voice sounded as a door opened up. "The rest of you, please be patient for a moment, as we still need to discuss the results."

"Ha ha, are you worried that they're not going to let you pass?" the kid with the spiky blonde hair asked, looking at Xin.

"Why should I be? I never broke any of their rules. Besides, if they don't let me pass . . ." Xin stopped there. She had been about to say who her brother was, but she had entered the academy under a fake name. It wouldn't exactly look good if she were to reveal herself by making use of Jayden's name.

"... I'll just have to argue my own case," she finished.

Indeed, the three professors were discussing whether to let Xin pass. Technically speaking, she had adhered to the rules, yet the purpose of this trial had been to weed out those who wouldn't be worth their time, and from what they had seen so far she would have certainly failed.

"Why are we still discussing this? It should be clear that if she were to take this trial again, there's no way she would pass!" Professor Hai, the man with the large belly and muscular arms, was the most vocal about not letting Xin proceed any further.

"I suppose we could make her retake the test," Professor Wood suggested. "However, the element of surprise would be gone, so it wouldn't be fair to the others. Coming up with a new trial just for her alone seems too troublesome, though."

Professor Humfree adjusted his glasses and let out a huge sigh. "I agree, the trouble does not seem worth it. Perhaps we should adjust the rules in the future if we wish to prevent such a scenario. Either way, this was only a trial to see if they are worthy to get into the next room.

"Let's just allow her to move on to the assessment stage. It will become obvious enough if she's worth our time."

"Are you sure?" Hai said with a worried look on his face. "Those who make it inside can stay for as long as they wish. They only leave when they have to leave, which also means that if we admit someone weak like her ... there's a good chance she won't come out alive."

"A risk that I'm sure she will become aware of quite quickly," Professor Humfree replied, and with that he pressed a button.

"Congratulations, all three of you have passed this trial." The mechanical voice resounded once more. "However, as you might imagine, this was merely a pre-assessment to see if you have earned the right to stay with us a while longer. I look forward to greeting you at the academy itself.

"For now, please head through the door. My colleague, Professor Hai, will lead you to the next trial stage and explain the details."

"Next trial stage?" The panda boy's voice was energetic, yet his expression remained tired-looking. However, he was the first one to head through the door that had opened up, where the man with the large belly was already waiting for them.

"Follow me," the professor said as soon as they all were standing before him.

I did it, Jayden! I passed the first hurdle. It wasn't exactly the way I planned, but I still did it, Xin thought as she followed the other two. The professor turned around from time to time as they walked, yet she was the only one he was staring at, making her feel as if she had done something wrong.

He doesn't seem happy that I passed . . . It doesn't matter; I will show everyone that this is where I'm meant to be. Xin solemnly swore to do everything by the book at the next trial stage.

Eventually, the three of them entered another large building that looked like a stadium. They entered a gigantic room that had several floors, different areas, libraries, and more.

"As you may have already guessed, this isn't the main academy. There are no teachers here, nor are there any lessons," The Professor explained. Immediately, the students who were already inside turned to look at those who had entered. Some smirked before going back to what they had been doing; others didn't even look up, while the rest stared long and hard at the newcomers.

"In fact, this is just a large trial stage set up for all the candidates who have shown promise," the professor continued. "Nevertheless, you'll be provided with everything you need to train yourself. No matter your number, you'll have access to the training rooms, weight lifting equipment, cardio, a gym, the library, and more.

"Each one of you will be assigned to a personal room. How long you stay here is up to you. You are free to leave at any time, though be aware that if you choose to do so, you won't get a second chance to join the AFA again.

"You may be wondering, 'How do I join the real academy?' Well, here." Professor Hai then handed out numbered badges that he instructed them to pin on their white shirts. The new students noticed that the others wore badges as well.

The boy with spiky blonde hair boy had been assigned number 112, the panda boy number 113, and finally Xin had been given number 114.

"Your number indicates what room you sleep in. You will quickly notice that there are some differences in your rooms, and the same will be true for your provided meals. If you don't like it, then I suggest you do your best to try to get a lower number as soon as possible.

"Only the students numbered 1 to 10 are eligible to join the AFA. To do that, you have to keep your badge for a week. After a week has passed, you're permitted to get out of here. Do take note that the higher your ranking is when you leave, the more benefits you will enjoy at the academy, so you might think twice about leaving as number 10."

The new students understood that this was an environment created to force them to improve. They wished to see how much they wanted to become better and stronger. Without teachers to guide them, they needed to motivate themselves.

At the same time, the students who were higher up would be treated better.

"How do we go about getting a lower-numbered badge?" Xin asked, getting straight to the point.

"There are two ways," the professor explained. "One of them is through assessments. Every week, there will be assessments and trials like the one you just went through. The better your result, the higher you place.

"The second option is through a match. Students may challenge anyone they wish once a day. If that person has already been challenged, you are unable to challenge them again."

He explained a few more things to the group as he showed them around the building. Finally he took them to their rooms, and just as he had said, the rooms were horrible. They were cold, and Xin's didn't even have a bed. It was just, a small room.

On the other hand, opposite her room on the second floor was room number 1. She couldn't see inside, but if the extravagant door and pillars were anything to judge by, it might look like the inside of a palace.

"All right, with that you should be aware of everything. Good luck, and remember what I said." Professor Hai looked toward Xin. "You may leave whenever you wish. No one is forcing you to stay here."

After he left, the three of them looked at each other, unsure what to do. They weren't friends, they were practically strangers who had only just met, but they felt the need to stick together, being the new people at this place.

But Xin broke away and headed for the first floor.

"What is she doing?" the boy with spiky blonde hair asked the panda boy.

Xin walked over to a group of boys who were chatting and sitting in a large circular marbled area next to a few plants. No one seemed to dare to come too close to them.

"Hey, you, number 1!" Xin called out. "Fight me!"

CHAPTER 14

CATCH THE RAT!

Since most of the Howlers were no longer going to school, they had decided to regularly meet at the Wolf's Pool Club. Technically, the Howlers owned multiple establishments on Burnham Street. They were larger and perhaps better used, especially since the members were coordinating more with the former members of the Pincers gang.

However, this place seemed more like home for them; it was the place they started, so it was the main base for the Howlers. At the same time, they felt that other gang members would never suspect that the leaders of the Howlers would currently be here.

Austin and Innu were walking down the street. They were a little sweaty, because they had continued their morning training sessions. But now, instead of training early in the morning at school, they did so in the basement of the Wolf's Pool Club.

"Am I the only one who feels put off by this? Do we really have to do this?" Innu asked, as they approached the door of a shoe shop. Innu peeked through the window and saw an old man inside.

"This was a job given to us by Kai. We have to expand the businesses that the Howlers own, and that includes what's near the Wolf's Pool Club. We need to increase our presence now that the other big gangs are gone," Austin reminded him.

Although he didn't go to the same school as the others, Austin too had finally decided to drop out. He had chosen his path, and with everything that was happening, he knew that this was his future.

"But that's the thing, why send *us* out? Just the two of us. I mean, Kai decided to quit school too, right? Isn't he suited better for this stuff? And what even is he doing?" Innu stopped his complaining there, even though there was more on his mind.

Because the truth was, Kai was actually helping them out quite a bit. The fancy new lawyer was trying to find some way to get Innu away from his current foster parents. He and Kevin could live together and look after Suzan. Kai was confident that if they couldn't find out how to do it the legal way, then they would do it the illegal way, only that would cost money and take some time.

Eventually, having no choice and needing to accept what was going to happen to both of them, Innu pushed the door open.

"Oh, it's rare to see two young students at this time of day, and in a shoe shop no less, how can I help?" The old man greeted them with a smile, which made Innu feel a little guilty about what he was about to do.

Just think, you are doing him a favor. These shops are okay now, but sooner or later they'll need someone like us. With this resolve, he clenched his fist, and replied, "We're from the Howlers gang, and we're looking into expanding. We thought that maybe you could collaborate with us on doing some business together."

The smile on the man's face vanished instantly.

Meanwhile, Kai had other important matters to attend to. He was walking toward an extremely run-down apartment building. It appeared to have been abandoned, but that wasn't the case. Kai entered the building and climbed to the top floor, where the hallway was lined with several doors, just like normal apartments. Kai approached the first door and turned a key in the lock. And inside was not what one would expect, because it wasn't a normal apartment at all.

The door led into a large room that took up the entire floor. The other doors were just for appearances. The people in the room gave a silent nod toward Kai.

They were other members of the Underdogs gang. The whole building was actually owned by the Underdogs, and it was one of their many secret hideouts, just in case things like this happened.

Many of the members were working out: lifting weights, hitting bags, training with weapons, and more. At the back of the room, a large table had been set up. Standing there with a few other Underdogs was the one and only Damion Hawk.

"Will you look at that? Now that you're no longer going to school, you're actually starting to resemble an adult," Damion said with a smile. Kai noticed several unopened crates scattered around the room.

"What's with the crates and what's the meeting about today?" Kai asked, getting straight down to business. One of the men started to go over to the crates, but Damion quickly shook his head.

"Now, just because you're starting to get more involved in the gang business doesn't mean you're the head of it just yet. If you want to act like the leader of the Underdogs, you would have to become the leader, and to do that, you would have to take me out . . ."

This was how Damion always talked; there was no special treatment for his son, that was for sure. He pulled a small blade from his back pocket and slammed it onto the table.

"Let's get this meeting started, shall we? After all, we need to figure out who's the rat in the group!"

CHAPTER 15

THE UNDERDOGS BITE!

Kai's heart thudded loudly. Damion was carefully staring at the remaining members of the Underdogs, and finally his eyes landed upon Kai, his very own son.

He doesn't suspect me, does he? Kai started to worry. *He has no way to prove I've done anything against him unless someone can link me to the Howlers, and I did everything necessary to guarantee that there are no connections!* He clenched his fists, forcing himself to not gulp down the saliva that was gathering in his mouth. That would be just the type of weakness Damion was looking for. If Damion figured out that he had betrayed the Underdogs . . . Kai saw his life flashing before his eyes.

Although it had been only a few days between the Underdogs' battle with the Gray Elephants, Kai had been working diligently with the Pincers gang.

At first, the Pincers had naturally been upset when Olivia informed them that they would be working for the Howlers. That might not have been too bad, but once the Lady Boss had told them about the changes the new leadership wanted to implement for Burnham Street, many had left the small-time gang, not least because of the pay cuts all around.

It was pretty much a given considering the loss of their extra source of revenue. Nevertheless, enough of them had chosen to stay, mostly due to their unwavering loyalty for Olivia. Seeing her trust the Howlers reassured them.

Since the Howlers had proven to be a considerable force, they could see a future in which the Howlers would take over the entire town. Once that happened, they would no longer have to rely on those extra streams of revenue, as their wallets would practically fatten themselves!

Now, believing in the Howlers more, the Pincers followed not just Olivia's orders but also Kai's, and she seemed fine with this slight change.

The day under the bridge, after Kai had been given one of the red axes that Damion had used, the gang leader shared his plans for a future counterattack and how they would expand their business back to what it once was. He had done it once, so Damion knew he could do it again. Armed with that knowledge, Kai had ordered the Pincers to stop all those plans in their infancy.

I knew that hitting all of those spots would make him suspicious that someone had joined the Howlers, but I'm the last person he would suspect, Kai reasoned.

He could have chosen to be cautious, ordering the members of the Pincers to slowly attack the Underdog forces and stop only a few of their plans to rebuild, yet there was a reason why he had them take down all possibilities of the Underdogs expanding again even from day one.

He wanted Damion to feel hopeless, defenseless, until he was backed into a corner and he felt like there was nothing else he could do.

I want you to feel the same pain . . . no, I want you to feel the true despair of losing everything you worked so hard for!

"Boss, according to what we found out, the people who have been disrupting our plans are all members of the original Pincers!" One of the men in suits spoke up; he was bruised all over and was one of the members of the Cheetah Squad. Kai recognized him since they had gone toe to toe with each other for a bit, but thanks to his mask, the same didn't apply vice versa.

"From what we have found out, they are now under the new gang that appeared that day, the Howlers. However, the Pincers are the only ones on their side; the other small-time gangs haven't stepped in or claimed to be part of them. We could try to bring them over and ask them to help us, offer them more territory in return for helping us."

What territory are you going to offer them? Kai thought, making sure to hide the schadenfreude he was feeling. *As long as everything goes well, in a few days all of what was once yours will belong to the Howlers. The two big gangs who had been fighting for Slough for over a decade fell that day.*

I've already told Olivia to leave the Gray Elephants area. We have no interest in it other than stopping the Underdogs from claiming it so the small-time gangs can move in and claim that territory for themselves.

With us focusing on what the Underdogs used to own, you have nothing to bargain with, and once the small-time gangs are under the Howlers' territory, why would they go back to the Underdogs? We won't be as harsh with requests for protection money, and with Kirk gone and our very own Altered, only suicidal idiots would offer their help!

The gangs you treated poorly, the people you stumped for every penny, and even your own people you treated like trash . . . all of them will turn against you . . . time is on our side.

Ultimately, Damion stopped scrutinizing Kai and the others and decided to continue on with the meeting. His attempt to flush out the rat had seemingly failed.

"Continue onward with the expansion. If we can't get our old territories, then look for new ones. Step on the toes of the Lock gang, the Blood Triangle gang, whoever. We can't afford to appear weak in front of them! We will hold out our hand for a collaboration; if they refuse to hold out theirs, then chop it off."

Damion smiled as he kicked one of the large crates; the large wooden side panel fell to the floor, revealing what was inside. Kai couldn't stop looking at what he was seeing.

How can this be . . . did he spend every single penny of the Underdogs' money to get these?

"Find out every little thing you can about the Howlers gang! As for that giant mutt Altered who did Kirk in, do whatever it takes to bring him in front of me!" Damion ordered coldly, murder in his eyes.

CHAPTER 16

TWO MINDS

Your bloodlust grows
8 days until the next full moon
50 Exp has been gained from current Bond Marks (5)
Exp 602/3445

Gary had already decided that tonight would be the time for him and Olivia to act. He would meet up with Olivia around nightfall, and they would ambush the Underdogs to finish the gang once and for all.

If I wait any longer, there is a good chance that the moon will influence Olivia to the point where she is no longer following the pack rules or listening to me. At the same time, we now have the boost that the moon gives us to increase our strength further in an attack.

In preparation, Gary had used his quest reward to select a new skill, and he was hoping that it would give them the edge they might need tonight.

I understand that you don't want me to act, Kai, but things are getting too dangerous for you guys. We are not the same, and I can't let the Underdogs come back again.

Before meeting the beta werewolf, Gary headed to the Wolf's Pool Club to make sure everything was running smoothly and there were no other troubles that he would need to deal with first. There, the others filled him in about how they had been signing up the Underdogs' former businesses, as well as those around the Wolf's Pool Club.

Gary was a little worried when he heard this, thinking that perhaps they would cause a stir between other gangs or the public, but at least for now, no such thing had happened. At the mere mention of the name Howlers, the business owners were instantly ready to sign over.

There was still a small standard flat fee, yet the percentage of profits taken was far lower compared to the Underdogs. According to Austin, all the owners instantly became elated once they heard these new rates. It was all thanks to Kai, who knew exactly how much the gang had extorted from those businesses.

In fact, Kai had explained that their new contract was even nice enough to only take money from net profit. In other words, if the businesses were making a loss, there would be no pressure for them to pay the Howlers. Of course, that might lead to people trying to swindle them down the line, but those could be addressed should they occur.

We're still asking them for protection money, which isn't right in itself, but with the other gangs out there and the police doing nothing, we're a necessary evil, Gary thought, aware that he had no right to complain seeing that the money the Pincers were earning, which ended up with him, was being earned the same way.

Eventually Olivia arrived at their usual training spot in the woods; she was wearing the Howlers gang uniform and had her whip ready.

"You sure you have eaten enough to do everything that's needed?" Gary asked.

She paused for a second before answering. "I have, but seeing how you seem to worry so much about my meals, I should probably let you know that I've been eating a lot more lately . . . especially raw meat, and although it is sating my hunger, it still feels like I have an itch that has yet to be scratched, no matter how much I eat."

That must be the bloodlust. It's a good thing we're doing this now; I'll sort this out first and then her next. Gary took out his mask to place it on his face.

"Are you absolutely sure about this?" Olivia said, clearly having more on her mind than just food. "I'm not backing out of what you want to do. In fact, I've found myself quite enjoying your hothead-edness and your determination to charge in first. I can see why you do it when you have this power in you." She stared at her own hands, transforming her fingernails on the spot.

Has she been practicing Controlled Transformation on her own time? Gary wondered.

Not only that, but her transformation looked slightly different from his. She was somehow able to use it on her fingers alone, yet her nails were far longer than Gary's. He estimated that they were twice his maximum length.

Is it perhaps some skill similar to my Claw Drain that she might have gained after becoming a Hunter?

"I haven't known you kids for long, but from what I've seen Kai appears to be a capable right-hand man. He's been using the Pincers to stomp the Underdogs, stopping their growth."

Gary was amazed; he'd thought Kai was doing nothing, just waiting for some opportunity, and it made him think. If he had given them a reason to wait, then it was probably a good one.

"However, he recently asked the Pincers to fall back. I received an urgent response today to clear out all our members from the Un-derdog areas.

"I asked him what he had found, but he wouldn't tell me any-thing. What's more, he seemed to be afraid of something. Now don't get me wrong, at the end of the day, I still follow you . . . not like I had much of a choice in that matter, but I thought it would be best to let you know."

Gary was of two minds about what to do. Originally he'd been so determined to finish things off today. Of course, he had thought about not going; it took a lot to finally decide to go, and now this . . .

"About what you said earlier." Gary finally spoke up. "About following me because you have to. If you weren't part of the pack, and I asked you to do this . . . would you still have come along? Do you think I'm doing the right thing? If you had the choice, would you listen to me or Kai?"

"I would not attack, and I would listen to Kai," Olivia answered, not even hesitating to think about it.

Gary didn't know why, but something came over him at that moment, and his blood was boiling a little as well.

"Fine, then you stay here, and I'll go on my own!" Gary growled, and he was already off, running through the woods.

CHAPTER 17

A CHANGE OF MIND

Although Gary had already experienced his first turning, he wasn't immune to the effect of the full moon approaching. The feelings that he had tried to keep in came out more drastically than he had expected, which had led to his earlier emotional outburst.

His blood was still slightly boiling, and the problem was . . . he didn't really know why.

I've fought so hard, I've trained, and I haven't even had time to relax for a second. Always worried about others. I might have not made the best decisions, they might have not even been the best outcomes, but every time I've gotten us through it all!

While he was thinking of these things, Gary hadn't even activated the system, but his right arm was already turning into that of a werewolf. Fur covered his hand and his muscles bulged as he made a fist.

"This time, I can do the same!" Gary shouted, seemingly to convince himself, as he slammed his fist into the trunk of a tree. The tree got indented, but it still stood strong, not toppling as Gary had expected it to. Swinging his other arm out, he swiped with his claws and took out a good chunk.

"What the hell is this tree made out of?" Gary cursed when there was still no result. He swung his right arm once again, taking out most of the trunk, and finally there was a loud cracking noise as the poor tree started to topple.

For a second Gary was proud of himself, and he let out a smile, but the next moment a shadow cast over his head, making him realize what he had done.

Crap! That's going to make a lot of noise! Gary thought. He activated Controlled Transformation, focusing on his legs to be able to stop the incoming tree.

He grabbed it and bent his knees, as the weight ended up being far more than what he had expected. Then he rolled out of the way, allowing the tree to hit the ground.

Shit . . . I can't just leave it there like this. I need to clean this up somehow.

Gary spent some time making sure the scene did not look like some type of wild beast or Altered had destroyed the tree. This was one of his training spots, and he didn't want to draw attention to the area.

Fortunately, cleaning up his self-created mess had allowed the alpha werewolf to calm down somewhat. Taking in the scene, Gary let out a big sigh.

Olivia is right . . . Kai got us this far already, he really knows what he's doing, so I should trust him . . . Maybe my problem is that I just don't know what he's thinking . . . but at the same time he doesn't know about my situation either.

If I were to tell him about the full moon coming out, and my worries—if he had all the information—perhaps he'd make a different decision. And maybe if I knew everything about him and his reasons for doing things, I wouldn't have to worry so much either.

With these thoughts in his head, Gary decided to just ask Kai why he wanted to take down the Underdogs. At the same time, Gary would talk about his concerns as well. The answer was so obvious: they just needed to talk to each other, but something was holding them back.

After sorting out his thoughts, Gary decided to drop his plans for attacking Damion, especially without Olivia's help.

I'll just spend the night with Amy instead. It's been a while since the two of us had a normal relaxing night.

He headed home, but when he reached his apartment building, many of the residents were gathered in front of the bulletin board. This wouldn't usually concern Gary, but this late at night, something had to be up, and worse, he could smell something . . . blood.

With his interest piqued, Gary walked over, wondering what it was about, and that was when he saw an injured old man lying on the ground. His hand had been severed and the bleeding stump had been crudely stitched up. On top of that, he had wounds all over his body. It wasn't just any old man, though; it was Adam Morten, the landlord of the building.

"Why are you idiots gawking at him? Did anyone call an ambulance?" Gary shouted as he knelt down, checking to see if the old man was okay. He was hurt, but Gary could still hear him breathing, albeit faintly. However, given his age, who knew how long he could last without medical help . . .

Although many of the residents were concerned, there was a reason none of them had called an ambulance. In the state the old man was in, it looked like he couldn't speak, and someone would have to cover the bills for him if he couldn't.

"Just call an ambulance, I'll cover it!" Gary shouted, once he understood why everyone was avoiding his gaze. The residents were wondering how he could afford it, but one of his neighbors took out their phone to call.

"Does anyone know what happened?" Gary asked, since Morten was obviously in no condition to speak.

"I'm not sure." One of the younger residents, who had been kneeling by the landlord's side, spoke up. "I asked him who did this, but he couldn't speak coherently. He mumbled something about the

Underdogs, and some fee . . . From the looks of it, they must have done this to him."

Gary could guess what had happened. Technically, this apartment block was still owned by the landlord. Given Kai's movements, the Underdogs must feel cornered and were trying to apply their pressure to get some money fast to expand and make a move, but the old man must have refused.

No, that's it . . . the Underdogs have to go . . . today!

CHAPTER 18

A JUNK HEAP

In the past, Gary had often been called hotheaded by his family, friends, and classmates, who all thought that he did many things on impulse rather than thinking them through, most prominently his choice to dye his hair green. Once the blood rushed to one part of his body, perhaps another part as of late, he acted based on the first thing that came to mind.

It was the same now.

Gary could have easily gone to Olivia first, or at least called her, or he could have talked about his next course of action with Kai. Any of the other Howlers would also have surely offered him their help, but instead Gary decided to follow the one mark that would lead him to Damion.

None of those monsters deserve to live! How could they be so cruel to someone like Adam Morten? He's one of the kindest people in this shitty world! I can't let them get away with this, otherwise they won't hesitate to do even worse things to others.

Pushing the Underdogs into a corner no longer seemed like it had been the correct move, seeing the consequences of their desperate actions. Gary didn't know if this was also part of Kai's plan, but he was worried that they might come back and try to get the money from the residents soon.

Then more innocent people would get hurt. He couldn't just wait around and watch that happen . . . not when he could do something about it!

I don't want the others to see me like this; I don't want them to see the bloodbath that I'm going to create.

On the way to his target, Gary texted Marie. Initially, he had planned to contact Kai, but things were still weird between them. What's more, he was afraid that Kai might somehow figure out what he was about to do.

Marie seemed like the more reasonable person to contact. He told her to head to the hospital to make sure Morten was treated, and all the bills would be paid.

The reply came within a few seconds. She told him that she would take care of the old man but also asked why he couldn't do it. He didn't reply.

As he followed the mark, Gary found himself going to a part of Slough that wasn't part of the Underdogs' establishments or an area he had been to before.

When he finally saw his target up ahead, he realized that it was simply a junkyard.

What on earth is Damion doing here? Gary wondered. *Never mind . . . the most important question is whether he is on his own. If so, this would be a lot easier. There shouldn't be people around him all the time, right?*

Rather than going through the front entrance, Gary used his powerful legs to leap halfway up the large surrounding gate, then once more straight over the barbed wire that was placed around it. Not that the workers would be concerned if someone was going into a junkyard, but who knew who was and wasn't working for the Underdogs.

Gary could hear many heartbeats in the area. In fact, he could even see the scavengers picking through the trash.

Perhaps they had paid the security guards and asked if they could take whatever they wanted. It was hard to tell if any of the

Underdogs were there, since quite a lot of people were searching through the heaps of junk.

There was one thing the werewolf had not accounted for . . . smell.

The place was filled with expired food, carcasses of dead animals, and other types of waste that he didn't even want to recognize. He never realized how much smell could disorient him. It was to the point that he could no longer detect the nearby mark.

Are my senses being overloaded? Well, Damion is definitely here. Gary was wearing his gang uniform and his mask, because of course if something went wrong he still needed to be careful.

If I remember correctly, the Mark pointed in this direction.

Gary wondered if he was heading toward the right place, but he came up with an idea.

Wait, I can use Controlled Transformation so it only works on my throat, so I should be able to do the same with my ears, right?

Fur started to grow from his ears as he activated the skill, and it worked just the way he had hoped. His already sharp hearing improved another notch. Instead of relying on his sense of smell, which was still being bombarded, he could hear numerous heartbeats close together, as well as the sound of laughter.

It has to be in this direction.

Gary ran forward, expecting to get the jump on Damion. He knew the gang leader was strong, but if he could ambush him when he least expected him, it might all be over with one attack.

As he ran through the piles of garbage, Gary spotted a cleared area containing barrels with hot fires burning inside them, along with several wrecked cars that had been dragged over.

The gang members were sitting around drinking, and the sight reminded him more of a color gang than a regular gang. It really seemed like the Underdogs had fallen compared to where they were before.

Still, Gary didn't care as he ran straight into the center.

"Hey!" a man shouted as he stood up, instantly recognizing the mask in the glow of the orange flames. "It's the Howlers' Altered!"

Gary had planned to do this stealthily, taking out every Underdogs member he found, but he changed his mind once he spotted Damion. The gang leader was on his own, far away from the rest, sitting on an old sofa, drinking away with his shirt off.

Hearing the man's shout, Damion threw his bottle on the ground and lifted the red axe that was by his side.

"I had a feeling that you would come to us. You've come at the perfect time!" Damion laughed.

Gary knew something was up but he still chose to run toward Damion, but then something strange happened as his whole body lit up blue. The werewolf started to shake uncontrollably as he was jolted by thousands of volts.

What is this . . . is this . . . the Altered Hunters' equipment?

CHAPTER 19

SHUTDOWN

It was an all-too-familiar sensation for Gary, who had been on the receiving end of those electrified batons. However, the pain wasn't quite as bad as he remembered, which he took as a good sign of improvement. Nevertheless, the electricity running through his body caused his movement to be sluggish.

Gritting his teeth, he prepared to lash out at whoever had attacked him, but before he got the chance, he felt multiple sharp objects attempt to pierce his back. Fortunately, he had been smart enough to use Controlled Transformation on his back the moment he had been attacked, though he still suffered the aftereffects of the shock.

–1 HP
–1 HP
–1 HP

The amount of damage this attack did was negligible, especially since he had increased his Health pool recently. However, there was one thing worrying him. Though he did not receive a system notification, he noticed that his Energy was dropping which was a first for him.

Gary swung his arm to hit the gang member with the baton . . . yet there was nobody behind him.

Huh?

That was when he noticed that the attack didn't come from his immediate vicinity; instead there were numerous gang members atop the piles of garbage, holding crossbows. Gary had no idea where they had procured those weapons from, but it didn't matter. The problem was that the bolts had a slightly blue glow to them.

Why are these guys better-armed than the Altered Hunters?

While Gary was deciding whether to take those guys out first or continue going for Damion, he saw that more gang members were pulling out weapons. Some were holding the strange batons, but others had swords, spears, and axes, none of which had sharp edges but all of which were producing sparks.

Worst of all, he was in the middle of an area that had been cleared. He felt like a gladiator in the middle of an arena, with no way out other than fighting.

All of them are using Altered hunting weapons, Gary realized, aware that he had ended up trapped, rather than Damion. He reached behind him and pulled out a round object with four sharp prodding ends that had a little blood on them. The blue light was starting to fade.

"I'm not sure whether to call you brave . . . or simply stupid! I knew that you Howlers would try to take me out, so naturally I would prepare something for you, yet you still chose to come by yourself?" Damion shouted, shaking his head in disappointment. "Seriously, has that Alterification process fried your brain?"

A man wielding two large poles ran in, thrusting them like spears at Gary. He hadn't removed all the strange bolts in his back, but their usefulness seemed to have faded already.

Immediately, people with the crossbows started to fire them, and using Controlled Transformation on his legs, Gary ran around the place avoiding all the bolts.

However, he soon noticed the problem with fighting in the junkyard: there was little to no room for him to run or hide, as he had already been surrounded by the attackers with the poles. They all thrust toward him, and the only thing he could do was whack the poles away. Unfortunately, the moment he touched them, the shock coursed through his body again.

Those things are worse than the batons! They're so long that I can't reach the attackers either!

Trying to change tactics, Gary tried to charge forward and ignore the pain, taking at least one of them out, but suddenly his back was hit by three more electrical jolts, zapping his body even more.

Since they weren't sharp objects, Gary wasn't losing a lot of Health, but the worrisome part was the Energy. He was down to less than half.

122/300 Energy

This is the first fight where I'm losing more Energy than actual Health! I don't have any meat on me . . . should I try to bite down on one of them? No, what if I create another Billy . . .

Now that his movements had been slowed as well, finally the crossbow users were able to shoot even more bolts into him. Gary wasn't sure if he was imagining it, but the shocks he was receiving from the crossbows seemed to be more powerful than the Altered Hunters' batons.

They must have spent so much money on these things . . . and to not get weapons that actually do damage . . . what is he . . .

"You bastards took away one of my most prized possessions! Don't you think you should give me something in return? There is no bringing back Kirk, but you might prove to be a useful replacement. There are rumors that there is a way to extract the Altered DNA from an Altered and place it into someone else. Of course, it kills them in the process, but that would just be a win-win for me," Damion explained with a sinister smile.

Now it made sense. So that was why he had decided to purchase such weapons. His plan had always been to capture Gary alive.

Too bad for you that I'm not really an Altered, Gary thought as he activated the one thing he believed might get him out of this situation.

Skill activated: Full Transformation
–20 Energy
Transformation has begun

The werewolf's Energy had fallen to below 100, so he had to use the skill now while he still could. With his body at its strongest he held on to the poles. He was sure that they couldn't stay electrified the whole time; there would have to be a resting period for them to charge up again. It seemed like his attackers were acting in groups to cover up that weakness.

It was in that brief second when the groups were changing that Gary held on to two of the poles. He was still being electrocuted, but bearing through the pain, he gripped to the poles tightly and used all his strength until they snapped in half.

I'll kill you! Gary thought, looking at Damion, and he charged forward, chucking the two pole users off to the side. The others couldn't keep up with the transformed teenager's speed.

However, Damion looked unafraid, still not moving away from the couch behind him. Then ten more gang members appeared from behind the heaps of trash, each of them holding one of those special crossbows.

They fired straight ahead and hit Gary. With each strike his movements slowed, but he continued to charge. By now the others had reloaded their weapons, and they continued to fire.

Slowly, Gary's steps lessened; something dangerous had happened. His mask had fallen off during his transformation and he was looking at a terrible system notification.

Your Energy is now extremely low
Full Transformation canceled
Please replenish your Energy by consuming meat

Gary was turning back to a human, and he didn't have the mask on his face. His body was still receiving shock after shock, until eventually:

Your Energy has been depleted!
Body entering conservation mode

His vision started to fade as he reached out his hand toward Damion, who wore a surprised look that turned into a large grin.

"It looks like today is a great day, after all . . . who would have thought you would come to me on your own, Greeny?"

CHAPTER 20

A LONG TIME AGO

Although Kai was now part of the main operations of the Underdogs, he had managed to convince his father that his position in the gang would be better used elsewhere.

Which was why he was placed in the unit that was in charge of finding out information about the Howlers, the new gang that was there that day. The gang that had gotten rid of Kirk.

However, Although Kai was the leader's son, the other members didn't really pay any attention to him, and they just did their own thing as they roamed the streets and spoke to the other gang members and the public.

Because the Underdogs didn't care for Kai, they weren't really keeping track of him either, and he was currently downstairs in his office space trying to gather all the information he could.

Damion has so many hideouts, not just for the Underdogs members but for himself as well. I doubt I even know them all, but the crucial information will be kept at one of these places. I still don't know why Kirk was so loyal to him, other than being a gift from someone else, and for someone to be able to give away an Altered as good as Kirk, they have to belong to a Tier 1 city.

If the relationship is a really close one, then we could be in trouble; we need to make this look natural. The fall of the Underdogs, or it would be even better to pin it on the other gangs if possible. Then we might also be able to figure out just what Gary was meant to deliver that turned him into that.

Kai circled several points on the large map of Slough. He knew there were more members of the Underdogs who acted as bodyguards for the safe houses, and the more he thought about it, even with all the Underdogs' finances from their years of running Slough, they would have never been able to purchase so many Anti-Altered weapons.

Someone was clearly sponsoring them or working alongside them.

Who should I get to act? I could use the Pincers, or Olivia herself . . . actually it might be the best idea to get Gary in on this. He seems to still hold a grudge about us not informing him about quitting school, and I'm afraid he might do something stupid soon.

His face said it all; he clearly was unhappy about my decision to leave the Underdogs alone. Still, I need time to make sure that we'll be able to handle the aftermath once that bastard is six feet under, Kai thought.

Just then, Kai heard footsteps coming down to the basement. He looked up and was surprised to see Olivia. It was the first time she had come here of her own volition, and usually she would call or text him.

A witty comment was on the tip of Kai's tongue, but when he saw the concerned look on the Lady Boss's face, he swallowed it down.

"What's wrong?" he asked, not wasting any time on small talk.

"I . . . We are . . . He went . . ." Olivia stuttered, unable to continue her sentence. Getting frustrated, she touched her own head. Unsure what else to do, Kai offered her a glass of water, which she gulped down in one shot.

"How much do you know about Gary?"

This was an unexpected question, but he understood what she wanted to know.

"He told me what he really is," Kai replied somewhat cryptically. He had his suspicions that Gary had done something to Olivia that made her this loyal, but since he had no idea what it was, he didn't want to compromise his secret.

The tension in Olivia's face lightened a bit. "So if I tell you that I can 'feel' that he is in big trouble, will you believe me? And no, I'm not talking about some woman's instinct, I physically feel that something is very wrong with him. A big part of me wants to go to his side this instant, but I'm afraid I need help."

Kai stayed quiet, digesting this information. It was hard to believe, but how much did he really know about werewolves? After Gary had revealed his secret, Kai had naturally read up on them, but he had no idea how much truth there was in those fairy tales. Having seen what the green-haired teenager could do, and the fact that he had subdued Olivia, a strange connection between the two might not be the most impossible thing in the world.

"Does that mean you actually know where he is? Is he hurt, injured?" Kai asked. From the look on her face, it seemed like she knew more but either wouldn't or couldn't share.

He wasn't wrong. Olivia was having her own internal struggle. In a way, the Howlers had taken away everything she had built up—but most of all Gary. At the same time, though, he had blessed her with this great power, and what would happen next?

Somehow, the one who had bested her had now been bested himself. Could the Pincers really do anything against the Underdogs in their current situation? At the end of the day, the Howlers were not just one person, they were a group, which was why she had decided to come down here.

"Roughly two hours ago, I met him in the woods, because he wanted the two of us to attack the Underdogs together," Olivia finally revealed. "However, he seemed to be unsure of his own decision and when he asked me for my input, I tried to convince him to stick to your plan. Unfortunately, I seem to have said something wrong, because he ran away from me in anger.

"I was hoping that he wouldn't attack them without me. Honestly, part of me thought that he would be fine even if I wasn't with him. After all, the Underdogs should be on their last legs . . . however, about twenty minutes ago I felt something change. I *know* something has happened to him, and only one thing comes to m—"

Kai slammed both fists on the table as he got up. "That colossal idiot!" he cursed, sweeping everything off his table out of frustration. "ARGH!"

Olivia stared at Kai, not stopping his tantrum, just making sure not to get in his way. It didn't last long, but it was quite a sight to see someone who was usually so collected let his emotions get the better of him.

"No, I'm also to blame," Kai mumbled when he eventually picked up his chair and slumped into it. "I should have explained to him why we had to wait . . . especially after keeping him out of the loop. Damn it, I just never thought that he would act on his own."

"He . . . didn't want any of you guys to get hurt; he wanted to bear the weight of this task on himself. That's what I think anyway," Olivia explained. "So what are you going to do? I've already told the Pincers to gather nearby. Shall we have the Howlers join us and raid the Underdogs together?"

In her mind, it was the only viable option, and ever since her change, she could see the Forced Bonds that Gary had created. She was sure that finding Damion would also lead them to Gary.

After he thought about it for a moment while biting down on his thumb, Kai finally had an answer for her.

"No, I will solve this on my own. I might be away for a few days. In the meantime, tell Miss Degrace and Marie that they're in charge."

With a scorned look on his face, the teenager walked out.

"I should have done this a long time ago."

CHAPTER 21

LOCKED UP

Ever since he had gotten the Werewolf System, Gary had wondered what would happen if his HP reached 0. After all, it represented his Health, so in a way it was the most important stat that he needed to keep track of. Given that his system had a lot of gamelike features, such as his need to gather Exp to level up to allocate stat points, he theorized that if he lost them all it would be *Game Over*, and he very much doubted he would get a chance to have a *Continue*.

Some time ago, he had considered the possibility of merely fainting, but ever since he had seen the description of the Last Stand skill, he was sure that it was the worst-case scenario, something he had to avoid at all costs.

One thing that he hadn't thought about too much, though, was his Energy. His werewolf body somehow used it to passively heal him after a fight, emergency heal his broken bones during a fight, and provide the fuel for a variety of his skills.

Of course, he was aware that it was of great importance to him, and when his Energy went down to extremely low levels, he would experience one of two things: sluggishness and extreme hunger. He had never questioned this, since eating meat would restore his Energy, which in turn allowed him to heal. Now he felt like he had somewhat figured it out.

When the Underdogs had used their Anti-Altered weapons against him, they drained his Energy to the point of depleting it, and when they used the electric batons again, although the weapons hadn't killed him, they had made him pass out.

When Gary woke up, he felt a cold chill on his face, and his body was sore all over. For a moment, he was reminded of the time he woke up in the forest after that fateful night at the construction site. Slowly opening his eyes, he managed to make out a dark surface in front of him. When he tried moving his hands to touch his head, he heard chains rattling against the floor, and worst of all his arms felt incredibly heavy.

Warning, warning
Energy has been depleted
Please replenish your Energy by consuming meat
1/300 Energy
Health reserves will now be used to keep the user awake
–1 HP every thirty minutes
56/160HP

Those aren't the best messages to wake up to, Gary thought. *How long does that even mean I have? . . . My mind is all cloudy, I can't even think properly to work that out . . . Either way . . . where am I?*

Finally opening his eyes fully, Gary saw a single light in the ceiling, but more importantly, he saw metal bars in front of him. The room he was in was small and empty, and as he suspected, his arms and legs had been cuffed.

On top of that, they had been chained to the floor as well. Gary could only see through the bars into the sky as well as into the hallway in front of him; no one was there, nor was anyone in the cell with him. It reminded Gary of when he had attempted to tie himself up. Only back then it hadn't really worked.

Gary tried to tug on the chains, but they were thick, and with his depleted strength, he was weaker than he was in human form.

The Underdogs . . . Damion . . . Now that I'm no longer transformed it means they saw my face. They must now know who I am . . . is that why they've kept me alive?

Well, at least that's good news, I think. Are they going to ask me about the package? What do I do? Should I keep quiet, so they keep me alive as long as possible? . . . but then what? Shit, what the fuck kind of situation did you get yourself into, Gary?

He felt extremely guilty because right now he was hoping that Olivia or maybe someone from the Underdogs would come and save him, yet at the same time he felt like he didn't deserve their help. It was solely because of his stupid pride that he'd ended up in this mess. If he had only asked for help, or listened to Kai, all of this could have surely been avoided . . .

"Hey!" Gary shouted, hoping to get the attention of whoever might be nearby. He had gotten himself into this situation, so he needed to find a way out, and time wasn't exactly on his side.

His call seemed to do its job, as a man smoking a cigarette walked past. Seeing the gang member in front of him made Gary realize how much his senses had dulled compared to his usual state. He could not detect the man's heartbeat or his scent. Even the waft of the cigarette had only entered his nose once he was directly outside.

"Please bring me some food, I'm starving!" Gary pleaded. "You don't want me to die down here, do you? You kept me alive for a reason, you want information, right?"

In this type of situation, the captors would normally at least give food to the prisoner to show that they weren't completely evil. This wasn't something that Gary had picked up from movies, but what he had seen Damion do. The gang leader always treated his captives nicely before either ripping their hearts out or extending a hand to them.

Although the werewolf doubted Damion would work with him, as long as he got a meal, it might allow him to regain enough Energy to break out of his chains and escape. Unfortunately for him, the man ignored his pleas and continued on his way.

Some time had passed, although it was hard to tell how much exactly, because Gary could hardly think on his empty stomach. Going hungry was nothing new to him. He still recalled how bad things had been after his father had disappeared. It had taken his mother some time to find a stable job to provide for her family on her own, especially since it had happened without prior warning.

Those days, they had barely had enough food for two meals a day. As the man of the house, he had often only taken a few bites and insisted that his mother should take the rest.

However, this hunger felt far worse. It was if a hand were reaching into his stomach and pulling his insides out bit by bit. The worst part was that there was nothing he could do about it.

Eventually, though, the man returned carrying a tray with food, nothing too fancy, but Gary nearly started salivating when he saw a small piece of meat. His warden placed it on the floor, and Gary was ready to lunge toward it. Unfortunately, it was slightly outside his reach.

Gary thought that this was on purpose, some sick way to torture him, yet he was willing to endure it, as long as he got to eat eventually. Unfortunately, his hopes were crushed as the sound of another person echoed through the room. A few seconds later, the one person he wanted to avoid seeing at all costs appeared, a wide grin on his face.

"Well, Greeny, I heard you were hungry, but too bad for you this is a prison and not a resort," Damion said, stomping on the meat with his foot, then kicking it away. "You know, I used to believe that you were one of the more promising transporters. I could have even pictured you joining the Cheetah Squad. However . . . you single-handedly caused me more trouble in the span of a month than the Gray Elephants managed to do since their inception.

"You don't get the privilege of an easy death, and I'll make sure that you suffer until the extraction!"

CHAPTER 22

WEAK

Whenever Damion showed off that he was in control of a situation and that your life was in his hands, he did so with a happy face . . . yet his initial grin quickly disappeared, replaced with a deep frown. It was clear that the gang leader was beyond annoyed at his prisoner, and that his threat was anything but empty.

This was bad for Gary, very bad. There was no doubt in his mind that Damion would give the Underdogs the order to starve him out, and while a normal human might last for more than a week without food, and an Altered probably even longer than that, Gary's time was far more limited because of his system.

"I didn't take anything from the package!" he cried, although it wasn't very loud because of the lack of power in his voice. "There was another gang, someone who knew about the package. They attacked me, and they took whatever was inside! Someone else betrayed you!"

As usual, Gary tried to hide his lie by mixing it with part of the truth. At least the first part was all true. He didn't know what group they belonged to, but it didn't exactly matter now anyway.

"You really don't want to live any longer, do you?" Damion asked as he placed one hand on a metal bar and gripped it tightly. "Do you seriously want me to believe that a lowly transporter like you just happened to turn into an Altered out of nowhere? There's nobody in the world who would have sponsored a scrawny high schooler like you. They're a dime a dozen! Do you think I was born under a rock?" Damion screamed as he pulled at the bars.

"It doesn't take a genius to figure out that you opened the package, which must have contained that new type of Altered DNA, which turned you into this! You had your chance, Greeny. If you had come forward and admitted your mistake, I might have even made you my second Kirk, but what did you do instead?

"You created your own gang, made trouble throughout Slough, subdued the Pincers to gather them in an attempt to take me out when the Gray Elephants attacked us! If anything, I have to hand it to you, Greeny, I never believed you would have had the balls, much less the power, to kill Kirk!

"But that wasn't enough for you; no, you still needed to take me down to get rid of the Underdogs! Unfortunately for you, we were prepared! Your actions have caused far worse consequences than you can imagine, and you will pay the price for it!"

Clenching his teeth, Gary thought about how to come back from that one. He knew that he wasn't an Altered, but anything he said right now would just be treated as a lie he made up to save his butt. It looked like even the Underdogs didn't really know about what was in that package.

"Kirk should never have worked for the likes of you," Gary mumbled under his breath, but it was too quiet for Damion to hear. "It should have been you who died that night, not him."

He raised his voice loud enough for Damion to hear him. "Why are you keeping me alive, then? Since you clearly believe that I took your precious package?" If Damion wasn't there to find out information about what had happened that day, was he there just to gloat?

Damion's shoulders started to move up and down as he chuckled to himself.

"You got rid of Kirk, an Altered who happened to be one of my most trusted men. What would I gain from simply killing you? No, you'll have to replace him. Of course, after everything you did there is no way to trust you, and since the Altered DNA is already in your body we have to get it out first.

"I've called in a favor, so once those guys are here, the fun can begin. I don't care what we have to do to make it happen, whether it be to take out your brain and replace it with another, stitch two bodies together, drain you of your blood, or place your organs into another body!

"Don't worry, they've assured me that even in the case of a failure, they'll reimburse me with another Altered. Those guys seem to be overly happy to experiment with your body and get the rights to your corpse! No matter the outcome, I'll have the last laugh."

"Wait . . . there was more in that package, there is another item that I hid!" Gary shouted, as he watched Damion leave with his warden in tow. "I'm not an Altered, I swear! You saw it yourself, I'm a werewolf! Whatever you're planning on doing won't work!" he insisted, trying to buy himself some more time to find a way out. Unfortunately, his words fell on deaf ears.

For some reason, talking to Gary had gotten Damion really riled up. So much so that his hands were shaking with anger; few of the gang members had ever seen him in such a state.

The group was gathered in what looked like an abandoned police station. Damion sat at a desk, lit up a cigar, and started to smoke it, which calmed him down a little, even if only by a tiny fraction.

Alas, it wasn't long until someone knocked at the door. "If you come in, I swear on my life, you better have a good reason, otherwise I'll let you keep that traitor company!"

The man on the other side of the door didn't dare come in, so instead he talked from the other side. "Sir, I'm terribly sorry, but it's your son. He has arrived and is asking to talk to you, claiming that it's very urgent."

"Tell that damn brat to screw off!" Damion instructed.

Surprisingly, the doorknob turned and the speaker entered the room. Damion sprang up from his seat, ready to pound the intruder before throwing him into a cell, but held back when he saw that it was Kai.

"What is it with this blasted night? Does *everyone* want to get a rise out of me? How is it not clear that I'm not in the mood for any of your damn issues?" Damion screeched, Kai immediately closed the door.

"I heard . . . I heard that you managed to capture the wolf Altered, the one that was working with the Howlers."

Damion just puffed air out of his nose. He went back to his seat, opened the desk drawer, and pulled out a bottle of liquor, hoping it would allow him to avoid another outburst.

"What you heard is correct, but I don't see how this concerns you in any way. Unless you want to help me find the rat who ambushed him in the first place! It didn't seem like he was lying about that," Damion said, pouring himself a shot and downing it at once.

As Kai stood in front of his father, his heart was thumping wildly. He put his hand in his pocket, grabbing his trusty knife. In his head, he had gone through the worst possible scenarios, and Gary getting captured was at the top of the list. The problem was that he could see only a few ways to get himself out of this situation, and in the end he chose the best one.

"I am the one who created the Howlers, to get rid of the Underdogs, and get rid of you!"

CHAPTER 23

ROT

Damion grasped his whiskey glass tightly. He didn't move an inch or blink. For most of his life, Kai had been looking forward to this moment of revelation, to admit that he was the one who had ruined everything his father had worked for.

Of course, in his ideal scenario it would have been under far different circumstances, but seeing the cold fury in those eyes nearly made it worth it to have lived in his father's shadow for all these years.

"Didn't you hear me?" Kai said as he strode forward. The man whom he had been afraid of for years suddenly seemed to have gotten a little smaller. "I was the one who created the Howlers.

"Me and that transporter of yours, we've been working together to crush everything you've built up." Kai spoke slowly, making sure to emphasize every single word. "And we're not done yet. It will only be over once I manage to take every single little thing you own."

Damion gripped the glass so hard that it imploded. His eyes had gone bloodshot from not blinking. Getting up from his seat, he leaned across the table and stared his son right in the eyes. He expected the teenager to flinch, perhaps try to talk his way out by claiming that all of this was some sick joke. Instead, the two of them stood there silently.

"*You* . . . You! . . . *You!*" Unable to articulate his frustration, Damion acted upon his feelings. The gang leader threw out his bloodied fist straight toward Kai. It made contact and pushed the teenager back a few feet. However, it didn't connect with his son's face, because Kai had managed to block the attack by lifting his crossed forearms. Still, his arms were throbbing from the powerful blow.

Even though Damion wasn't a large man, he was solidly built, had well-developed muscles, and was just a natural heavy hitter. A wisdom among boxers was that even at the same weight, each fighter's punch strength could vary wildly, and Kai certainly felt the power behind his father's attack.

"I knew you would try to punch me in the face," he admitted with a grin on his face. "Over the years, I've paid close enough attention to your behavior that I know you better than you know yourself! All for this moment!"

Damion began climbing over the desk as he removed his suit jacket, revealing his tight white shirt underneath. "You ungrateful brat! I raised you to take over the Underdogs when I was gone, not burn it to the ground!" He punched the desk in frustration, breaking off a piece of it.

His knuckles were a little red, but his hand was just fine. Damion had large knuckles because he had repeatedly broken them in the past, and they were now solid weapons. Kai got into a fighting stance, which made Damion chuckle.

"What is this? Have you been practicing how to fight? And here I thought you were just a useless brat. No, don't tell me, you've been practicing how to fight, all so you could beat me?" Damion ridiculed his son as he charged in and threw a fist.

Knowing that he probably couldn't take another hit, Kai decided to avoid this one by going low and kicking Damion in the side. It was a solid hit, but it felt as if he had kicked a large tree. Damion pinned Kai's leg under his arm with his elbow, holding on tightly, and turned around.

Kai had thrown another fist toward his face, which he grabbed. Now with two points of Kai's body to hold on to, Damion lifted him and ran straight for the door, then slammed him right into it. The door came flying off its hinge and landed on the floor, with the teenager on top.

The heavy blow knocked the wind completely out of Kai. Furthermore, it was safe to say he wasn't going to get up any time soon, and even if he had tried, several gang members had him surrounded.

"I was wondering what the hell would have made you do this, but now I'm sure of it; it was that bitch, wasn't it? Have you been plotting this ever since then? I guess I always saw you as just a brat, and that was my mistake," Damion admitted. "I can see that you're a man now . . . so it's only fair for you to suffer the consequences like one!"

Inside the cell, Gary was still waiting for someone to come in. Judging by his Health, he could tell that it had been two hours. He had thought about what to say to convince them to let him out, or at least feed him. Finally, two members of the Underdogs approached. They weren't alone either; they were dragging someone by the feet.

"The two of you can rot together!" one of the Underdogs said as they opened the cell door and threw the person inside. Gary was surprised to see a bruised, badly beaten, and unconscious Kai.

CHAPTER 24

BUTTING HEADS

Gary thought his eyes were playing tricks on him. Had the hunger made him start hallucinating? Was he just imprinting the image of the one person that he believed could bail him out of this situation onto his fellow prisoner?

However, even after a few minutes, the person continued to look exactly like Kai. It took some time, but he eventually started to wake up.

"Gary . . ." Kai mumbled, seeing his friend in the cell. As he tried to stand up, he flinched because his entire body was still hurting, especially his chest.

"How long have I been out for?" he asked weakly, slowly looking around the cell. The two gang members who had dragged him in had already left, so only the two teenagers remained.

"Not too long, less than half an hour," Gary answered. On one hand, he was happy to no longer be alone in his cell; on the other hand, he was now worried about Kai. Unlike him, Kai was a normal human, meaning it would take him some time to heal from a beating that had left him unconscious.

Nevertheless, even in his injured state, Kai started checking out the room, looking for a way out: pulling on the bars, inspecting the lock, checking his pockets for something useful, searching for loose bricks.

"Please don't come too close to me!" Gary immediately backed off when Kai approached him. "I . . . I haven't eaten in a while."

Fortunately, despite his hunger pains, he could still think rationally. If it had been another member of the Underdogs, he might have lunged at him and taken a bite, but at least for now, Gary was managing to keep himself in check. Still, he had no idea how long that would be the case, and it would be safer if Kai didn't tempt him, especially in his current state.

Gary hoped that given Kai's intellect, he would understand why he needed to keep a certain distance, without having to go too much into detail. Kai nodded and took one step back, and with a big sigh, he sat down on the floor . . . where he fell into deep contemplation.

"What the fuck, Kai? Do you have nerves of steel?" Gary was astonished. "Shouldn't you at least explain why you were beaten up? Why did they throw you in here? Did they find out that you're in the Howlers? Is all of this part of some plan to get me out?"

The werewolf stared at his new inmate, but all he could see was Kai biting his nails, looking around occasionally, all while continuing to stay silent. Unable to take it any longer, Gary straight up asked him the obvious: "What happened to you, Kai? How did you know that I was here? What about the others?"

Kai stopped what he was doing and turned to Gary. For the first time, he saw a deep frown on Kai's face, and even more surprising was the animosity in his response. "I came here because *someone* seems to be dead set on proving that he's incapable of sitting still and apparently gets a kick out of ignoring the most basic orders!"

"I . . . I'm sorry," Gary stuttered, clearly not prepared to be the target of this kind of aggression. "I know it was stupid of me, b-but I didn't want any of you to get hurt."

"That's great and all, but I had a plan! We were so close to getting rid of the Underdogs once and for all, while reducing the risk to ourselves to a minimum! All I asked for was some time to make sure everything would be perfect! Honestly, I'm not sure whether becoming what you are has made you think of yourself as invincible, or you just had a death wish coming after him on your own."

Kai's words hurt, because Gary had already blamed himself every which way ever since he had woken up, cursing himself for his impulsiveness. Getting chided further by his friend, especially when both of them were in this cell, didn't sit well with him, especially since he felt that he wasn't the only one to blame.

"I'm not a freaking mind reader, okay?" Gary snapped back. "How was I supposed to know what your 'brilliant' plan was if you never told me anything concrete? I thought that we were supposed to be in this whole thing together, but lately I feel like I'm just your discarded pawn!

"I'm not some dog who waits for you to order me to jump and just do it! That may be how our relationship started, but I thought we had become friends . . . that's why I didn't want you guys to do dangerous things anymore."

Now Kai was silent for another reason. He knew that there was some truth to Gary's accusation. He had been afraid that the Howlers' leader might do something irrational because he'd been left out after the night of the gang war, yet he had vastly underestimated just how crazy Gary was willing to act in regard to fighting the Underdogs.

Furthermore, Kai also couldn't deny that at times he did treat others like pawns, yet unlike what Gary seemed to believe, he wasn't willing to sacrifice any of his pieces . . . which was also the reason he had come here on his own.

"Look, you know my reason for wanting to get rid of the Underdogs. You know I'm committed to this entire thing, but what about the other way around?" Gary continued. "I know practically nothing about you. I was worried that you might hesitate too long or think that we had achieved enough already. What if Damion had escaped while you were still planning things and waiting for the 'perfect' moment?

"As I said, I'm sorry for ruining your plans. You should know that I'm not exactly the best when it comes to using my head . . .

which is why I usually do what I feel is right. I've seen how much harm the Underdogs do, especially now that they feel threatened, so I wanted to stop them before it got even worse. I knew it was risky, which is why I didn't want to get you guys involved."

"I've never regarded you as a dog or a pawn," Kai said, after letting out a deep sigh. "I don't want anyone helping me to feel like that. I don't want to be anything like Damion, so if I ever give you that feeling in the future, I want you to tell me immediately, okay? Can you promise me to do that, instead of running headfirst into a death trap?"

Gary remained silent and continued to listen to Kai, who, judging by his change in tone, was being sincere. He didn't know how serious he was when asking Gary to make this kind of promise, but the werewolf had a feeling that it wouldn't be something he could abide by.

"I hope I haven't given the others the same impression. Speaking of them, they have no idea about this place. I only knew of it because I am . . . well, I guess *was* an Underdogs member. Knowing those fools, once they find out what happened to us, they'll risk their lives to bail us out . . . and probably end up in the same state as me, if not worse.

"Now that I think about it, our entire group seems to consist of suicidal teenagers," Kai said with a chuckle, and Gary joined in, since he couldn't really deny it.

"Olivia is the only one who's aware of it all, since she was the one to inform me, but I told her to let me deal with things on my own. That's right, sometimes I can be just as much of a fool as my dear leader.

"However, I want you to know that I haven't come here to fetch you as if you were my dog, Gary. Our relationship might have started off a little strange, but I truly see you as someone who has my back, and in turn I will always have your back as well.

"I wanted to tell all of you once this was over, but you're right, I should have probably informed all of you earlier. You deserve to know the entire truth of why I hate the Underdogs so much, and why I've spent years making plans to do everything in my power to take down Damion Hawk, the bastard who calls himself my father."

CHAPTER 25

FOUR YEARS AGO

Four years ago, in a luxury hotel that had a nice view over the town of Slough, a blonde-haired teenage boy was holding a game controller in his hands. He was sitting on the floor, staring at a seventy-inch TV, courtesy of the hotel, and playing a fighting game.

Next to him sat a teenage girl with black hair who was around the same age. Just like him, she was holding a game controller in her hands, yet her face was filled with visible frustration.

"Kyle, stop it!" Marie complained, looking at him. "You can't just keep using the same move over and over again! That's cheating!"

"If it was cheating, then why would they put it in the game?" Kyle argued cheekily. "Besides, since you know what I'm doing next, you should be able to stop it!"

Out of sheer frustration, Marie began to mash all the buttons she could, hoping it would do something, but in the end, the low kick that Kyle's character repeatedly used continued to decrease her fighter's health until a large *KO* appeared on the screen.

"Hahaha, I win again!" Kyle jumped up and cheered. When the match came to an end, Marie scoffed at his cheap tactics, but she was ready for a rematch. She had always been competitive. But the two teenagers stopped what they were doing when they suddenly heard the door opening.

Someone had entered the hotel room, and without saying a word they went to the main bedroom and locked themselves in.

Using the remote, Kyle quickly turned up the sound of the game while sneakily moving over to the door, trying to make as little noise as possible. Marie shook her head, but she was just as curious, so she joined Kyle at the door, eavesdropping on the ensuing conversation.

In the other room, a black-haired woman in her early thirties was pacing up and down. She looked quite panicked, and she was holding a cold pack to the side of her face.

"Kiki, will you calm down? He won't be able to find you here. I've made the reservation under a fake name, so nobody should know that you're here apart from me." The voice of a second woman tried to calm down the first.

This woman had blonde hair and, despite being a few years older than her friend, still appeared to be in her twenties. She had been blessed with good genes, which made her quite a head turner, even though her years as a model were long since over.

She exuded a presence of kindness, like a real-life angel. People often said she could instantly lighten up a room just by being there. Her voice alone was usually enough to calm anyone down, and in this instance, once again, it managed to work its magic.

Eventually Kiki stopped pacing and put down the ice pack, revealing a large black eye. Unfortunately, that wasn't the only bruise on her body, merely the most recent one.

"It will be okay. I promised I'd look after you . . . you know that. I'm so sorry for bringing you into all of this; this is all my fault." The blonde woman apologized as she stood up and gave her friend a giant hug, which just caused a waterfall of tears to run down her face.

The sobbing continued for a while, and Kyle started to feel bad for listening in. He turned around and saw that Marie had teared up as well. She was clenching her fists, trying to stay strong.

Kyle gently took Marie by the hand and guided her back to the TV. Both of them sat down, neither one in the mood to continue their game. Marie wiped away her tears with some paper towels Kyle had grabbed, for lack of a better alternative.

"This isn't the first time this has happened, is it?" he asked in a low voice, as he turned up the volume so that their mothers wouldn't suspect them of having eavesdropped. "Is it getting worse . . . the hitting, I mean?"

Kyle understood what had been happening, and why Marie and her mother had moved to this hotel. Even though he was young, he wasn't completely oblivious to these things.

"Yeah . . . and I'm afraid that it's only getting worse with each passing day. The hitting has become harder. I hate that I can't do anything about it . . ." Marie curled up into a ball and covered herself. She placed her head on her knees, as there was more that she wanted to say.

"It's not just that, Kyle . . . I'm scared, I'm really scared. Recently, he's been staring at me in a really disturbing way . . . Whenever he grabs me, my mom drags his arms away. However, that only makes him furious, so she ends up getting hurt even more . . . I'm scared what happens if Mom dies, and not just that . . . if that does happen . . . then what happens to me?"

A recurring pattern.

Meanwhile, Kiki Degrace was being comforted by Kyle's mother. Her childhood friend Eleanor was the only person she could rely on during these hard times. She had paid for the hotel room and, without asking for anything in return, had simply handed over the keys, allowing the Degraces to stay in a safe environment. She had promised Kiki that she would do everything she could to help her, but it wasn't that easy.

As a result, Marie and Kyle had become close friends. They had known each other before that and had often played together, but not to this degree. After spending so much time together, they felt like siblings and looked out for each other.

Their relationship outside of school then grew to one in school as well, this was the first time Marie had told Kyle how scared she was.

"Marie, I promise I will do everything in my power to make sure that never happens," Kyle said as he gave her a big hug, making her cry for real.

Gary gulped hard, because it didn't take a genius to figure out that this story wouldn't have a happy ending . . .

CHAPTER 26

A CYCLE

That night, neither Marie, Kyle, nor their mothers left the hotel. In the following days, the four of them continued living together; the two women took turns accompanying the kids to school. This was how the relationship between all of them grew.

But Kyle was no fool; he understood that their happy family life was bound to come to an end eventually. After all, this wasn't the first time something like this had happened. Nevertheless, he was happy while it lasted, and he knew that he could always find Marie at school, even if things returned to normal.

One day, when Kyle and Marie came back from school together, they found Marie's mother with a huge smile on her face, talking with Kyle's mom.

"Are you sure about this?" Eleanor asked, a concerned look on her face. She had been dreading this day, afraid that her childhood friend might get fooled by that bastard once more.

"You saw his message, Ellie! He told me how he's been going to anger management therapy. According to his therapist he's already doing much better, and he promised me the second he raises his voice, I will be free to leave him.

"I didn't believe him at first either, but he showed me the appointments and everything. This time really will be different. He was even crying on the phone. Thank you for always helping out, seriously. I promise we'll pay you back for your help. Let's have brunch over the weekend, and then, once you see I'm okay, you'll have some peace of mind."

Eleanor's face was still filled with doubt, but in the end she gave her friend a smile. She had tried convincing Kiki in the past not to fall for his lies, yet it had proven to be an impossible task.

"Make sure to keep your phone on you at all times, and promise to contact me at the first sign that he's up to no good. I don't care what time of day it might be, if he so much as flinches at you, call me, text me, or simply come to me, okay?" She grabbed Kiki's hand and looked her straight in the eyes. Marie's mother nodded and grabbed the few bags filled with her and her daughter's belongings.

Before leaving, she looked at Kyle.

"Thank you for being such a good friend to my Marie. It's good to know that someone else is looking out for her just as much as I am." Miss Degrace's praise made him blush.

As Marie walked out the door, Kyle caught a glimpse of her face. Unlike her mother, who was all smiles, Marie's eyes were wide, and she looked a little shaken. Clearly she didn't want to leave this place to return to her father's side, not believing in his ability to change.

"Mom, we have lots of money, don't we? Then why can't we help them? You've already been paying for a place for them to live, so why can't we just continue living like this?" Kyle asked dejectedly.

"Oh, Kai, if only it were that easy." Eleanor sighed as she ruffled her son's hair using the name she had wanted to give him, rather than the one his father had insisted on. "Even if Kiki finally decided to break up with that bastard, he wouldn't just let her go. He would make her life here in Slough even more of a living hell.

"Her best option might be to completely leave town and run to the other side of the world to escape him, and that requires a lot of money. Even then, I'm afraid he'd just hunt her down. His reputation and ego wouldn't allow him to be left by a woman.

"Believe me, I've thought long and hard about how to help them, but this simply is a problem that money can't solve. Besides, the money I used to house them . . . it's not really ours to use."

Kyle understood. Although he might not know all the details, his mother had told him about how his father was involved with the underworld. Part of him used to believe that this might be the reason Damion had barely ever interacted with him. Then again, that might just be wishful thinking on his part; he'd always wanted a father figure in his life . . .

The last few times he remembered seeing his father had been on his birthdays, and even that had been for only about an hour, before his father left to take care of "business." Eventually, he had grown used to being treated like a chore rather than a priority in Damion's life.

Kyle also remembered seeing Marie's father on his last birthday, a burly fellow who might as well have been the picture of the word *brute*. Unfortunately, he wasn't just an ordinary Underdogs member but someone in the inner circle.

As for the reason his mother felt guilty, that was because she was the one who had accidentally introduced Kiki into the Underdog world and to Marie's father. She had never expected that the two would fall in love and have a child together, and although they weren't married, the man truly seemed to be obsessed with her childhood friend.

Regardless of his mother's stance, Kyle still thought there must be a way for them to get out of the whole mess, and he believed he might have come up with a couple of possible solutions.

"Don't even think about getting involved, young man!" Eleanor chided her son, recognizing his slight smirk as a sign that he had just come up with an idea. "This is adult business, and you shouldn't meddle with it. It's far more dangerous than you think!"

Heeding his mother's stern warning, especially since it was a rarity for her to raise her voice at him, Kyle decided to disregard his ideas. He trusted that she knew best. After all, while he might think himself clever, he knew exactly who he got his intelligence from.

Nothing unusual happened during the next week. He naturally spent time with Marie at school, and she recounted what was happening at her home. She still had trouble believing it, but there was at least less anger in her father's voice.

Marie had even been dragged into one of those anger management therapy sessions, where her father had apologized to his daughter as well as to her mother. From what Marie had been told, her mother had accompanied him to therapy a few more times.

Then, on the tenth day, something strange happened.

When Kyle took his seat in class, Marie wasn't there. He didn't think much of it until class started and she was still nowhere to be seen. He texted her to see if she had fallen ill, but he got no reply. After first period, he asked a teacher if they knew anything, only to be told that they were just as clueless as he was. There had been no sick note, no call from her parents, or anything.

Immediately, Kyle called his mother, who told him that she was looking after them, that they had booked the hotel once again. He was slightly elated, but also a bit worried. It appeared that the cycle had just started over again, far sooner than before. Last time, Marie and her mother had returned home for a couple of months, yet this time barely any time had passed.

Kyle wrote Marie another text to say that he would bring over their homework later. After school, he reached the hotel room . . . where he immediately dropped his bag the moment he saw Marie.

The teenage girl had a bloody nose and a swollen eye.

CHAPTER 27

THE ABUSIVE MAN

This . . . how could he do this? Anger management therapy, my ass! How dare that scum lay a hand on his own daughter? These wild thoughts went through Kyle's head when he looked at the state Marie was in, and those were just some of the more tame ones.

He knew that Miss Degrace's relationship with Marie's father could only be described as a one-sided relationship filled with domestic violence. Kyle had already grown used to the cycle of the Degraces falling out with the guy, his own mother securing them housing in a hotel like this, and the two of them moving in as well, only for Marie's mother to eventually forgive the bastard and get back together with him.

The only thing that had ever changed in this cycle was the time between rotations . . . yet this time he had done something even more outrageous than the previous times.

As Kyle watched his mother bandaging Marie's damaged face, something was boiling inside him. He had never been a violent child. Despite his being Damion's son, Eleanor had done her best to raise him to be a sensible child who wouldn't resort to violence, even in the world they lived in.

Not wanting to disappoint his mother, Kyle had never gotten into fights, never wished pain on other people, but after seeing the state of the girl he thought of as a sister, for the first time ever the teenager didn't just wish her father bodily harm. No, he wanted him to die in the most brutal way possible.

He was so angry that he didn't even know what to say to Marie as he helplessly looked at her. His heart only hurt all the more when she looked back at him and forced herself to give him a battered smile, wheezing slightly from the pain.

"Ellie, you were right . . . I should have listened to you a long time ago . . . maybe if I had left him after the first time this happened, all of this could have been avoided" Kiki Degrace was sobbing on the couch, a bottle of wine in her shaky hands. Kyle had never seen her so broken before. No matter what had been done to her, she had always managed to keep up a strong façade, though Kyle believed she had done that more for her daughter's sake than her own, but not this time.

This time, Marie's father had crossed the last line. Her mother seemed completely broken, even ignoring her own injuries, which were worse than ever before. So far it had been "just" a black eye or a bruise, yet judging by the swelling on her arm, this time he had broken a bone.

"Kiki, let's talk about this later. First, let's get both of you treated at the hospital. Don't worry, I'll pay for everything, and you can stay here for as long as you like," Eleanor replied, seemingly in her usual voice, but Kyle didn't miss the higher pitch. Even she seemed taken aback at the level of violence on display.

"And then what?" Kiki shouted as she smashed the wine bottle on the floor. "I'll have to go back to him eventually anyway! It's impossible for us to escape that bastard! If we stay here too long, he'll just come looking for us. Even if we run away, the Underdogs will come after us. We'll be on the run for the rest of our lives! Tell me, Ellie, how am I supposed to protect my daughter from that monster?"

Kiki Degrace was neither stupid nor naive. She might have fallen for Marie's father's sugary overtures the first time, but certainly not the ones after. No, her choice to get back with him was born of desperation. She knew perfectly well that she was trapped in that relationship, and the consequences if she truly dared to break it off. Her only hope so far had been that something might happen for him to truly change, her sole solace that he had at least never harmed his own daughter . . . at least until today.

"I have to get out of this. I have to protect Marie. Please help me . . . please . . ." Kiki was begging her oldest friend for help. Unfortunately, Eleanor couldn't bring herself to lie. If she had a way, she would have long since suggested it, so saying anything at this moment would just give the two false hope.

After she finished Marie's treatment, his mother gestured with her eyes for Kyle to take the girl elsewhere while she tried to calm down her friend. Not saying anything, he carefully helped Marie to another room, where she broke out in tears, just like her mother.

If only that man were no longer here, Kyle thought as he did his best to console his friend.

A few days passed.

Miss Degrace had been kept at the hospital overnight before being discharged. By now, the swelling had gone down on both of their faces, and neither Marie nor Kyle had talked about the event. Things were pretty self-explanatory, so he just kept her company, doing what he could to distract her from having to remember that day.

Alas, their somewhat idyllic life suddenly got interrupted.

One day Miss Degrace received a message that made her break out in tears again. Eleanor checked her own phone, and to her dismay, she found that she had received the same text. As she comforted her friend once again, Kyle read the message.

It was from the Underdogs, informing them that there would be a funeral soon. Such a formal event meant that either multiple members of the family had died at once or someone quite important had died. In those cases, attendance was mandatory. This included the entire family.

Kyle would be attending with Eleanor, and Kiki and Marie would have to come as well. If they didn't, the other members would be sure to ask questions, putting him on the spot. There was no telling how he would react. Right now, Marie's father was likely thinking that Marie and Kiki would come back to him in due time; but if they didn't turn up at the funeral, it would only make matters worse.

"What am I supposed to do? Should I go back to him? . . . Maybe you could take Marie, and I could make up some kind of excuse," Kiki suggested.

Eleanor didn't like the sound of that; although she didn't want Marie to get hurt and felt that she should never step foot in that house or near that man again, she was also worried that Kiki's daughter was the only thing keeping Kiki alive. Who knew how far things might go if the two of them were left on their own?

In the end, they had no choice, and the day of the funeral arrived. The venue was a large rented hall. Everyone was wearing black suits, including Kyle, who was scanning the room.

Part of him was hoping to speak to his father and perhaps say a few words, but he was constantly surrounded by other people. Right now, he was next to several caskets with pictures of the deceased. Something had gone very wrong and quite a few people had died, leaving his father in a horrible mood. Kyle understood that today wouldn't be a good time to talk to him.

Eleanor and Kiki were also there, with the latter wearing a veil and heavy makeup to cover her bruises. They stayed in the corner to avoid attention, occasionally exchanging words with a few women nearby, though only briefly.

Meanwhile, the children had been left on their own in a different room. That was until Marie informed Kyle that she really needed to go to the restroom. Naturally, he accompanied her there, and waited outside until she was done.

At that moment, Kyle locked eyes with the man he had been thinking about all too much these past few days. His hatred was written all over his face. Eventually, noticing the stare, the man walked over.

He was in his late twenties and had light brown hair and an average build. Still, he was strong enough to overpower a woman and a young teenage girl. Clenching his fist, Kyle relaxed his expression.

"You got anything to say to me, bastard?" the man said, taunting him. Of course Kyle said nothing, but as the man turned around and left, he had a few last words. "I can't believe I have a brother like you."

CHAPTER 28

A BAD PLAN

"Did you just say 'brother'?" For a second, Gary forgot about his own fatigue. Until today, he hadn't known that Damion had any children at all, yet suddenly he'd learned that he had at least two sons.

Were it not for their current situation, the green-haired teenager would have never believed Kai to have any relation to the Underdogs' leader whatsoever. He appeared to have gotten most of his looks from his mother. Perhaps there was a streak of madness from his old man, but if so, he hid it surprisingly well.

"Hang on, so if Marie's father is actually your brother, then doesn't that make the two of you . . . uncle and niece? Isn't that super weird?"

"The first time we met, I just thought of her as the daughter of my mom's best friend, and to her, I must have just been the son of *her* mom's best friend. Since we were kids, we simply started playing together without a care in the world.

"Over the years, we grew closer together, and I naturally started treating Marie like she was family before eventually finding out that she actually was. Sure, it was weird, but ultimately, nothing changed about our relationship after we discovered the truth.

"However, as for your other question, Simon isn't exactly my biological brother, at least not fully. We only share the same father. He was born when Damion was young, and I believe Simon's mother died giving birth to him. As Damion's firstborn son, he was brought up to take up his mantle in the future.

"Because of her work as a model, my mother caught Damion's eye. Since she was friends with Miss Degrace, it was inevitable that her two lives intertwined, and my half brother apparently fell in love at first sight. I don't know how, but the two of them ended up together, and she was dragged into this whole life."

Gary felt a little sad for Marie. Just because of her father, she had been dragged into the underworld. He suddenly realized that it was the same for Kai. Neither one of them really had a say in the matter.

Still, since he knew that Marie and Miss Degrace were doing okay, the story's resolution couldn't be too bad . . .

"Simon . . . I don't recall ever having heard that name during my time at the Underdogs," Gary muttered to himself. However, it wasn't impossible for him to have never encountered the guy. After all, he had merely been a transporter.

"As I was saying . . ." With a pained look, Kai continued his story.

Watching his half brother walk off, Kyle cursed under his breath. The two of them didn't have the best relationship to start with. Given the large age gap, they had nothing to talk about, and he also suspected that Simon hated him.

He wasn't sure if that was because Damion had remarried his mother, or if he perhaps felt threatened that Kyle might have ambitions regarding the leadership of the Underdogs.

"Hey, Kyle, are you okay? You look a bit flustered," Marie asked as she came out of the restroom.

"Hmm? My bad, I was lost in thought," Kyle replied. He was happy to see her. He felt far closer to her than to the scum who had dared to hurt her.

The funeral continued without any incidents. After the high-ranking people gave their condolences to the friends and family members of the deceased,, the rest of the evening pretty much turned into a meeting of the Underdogs gang members.

Damion and the rest of the leaders were talking about plans for expansion and how to avoid the troubles they were facing. They couldn't afford losses like this to occur more than once. Kyle spotted Simon talking with Kiki; after a short exchange, his half brother walked away toward the other leaders.

I wonder what's going on, Kyle thought.

He sneaked closer to the others. He didn't quite understand what they were talking about since a lot of it was business related, but he got the gist of it. Simon seemed to have been given an important task, and it was one of his first. Damion was all smiles as he patted his favorite son on the back.

"Don't fuck this up for us, all right?" Damion warned him.

Later that night, Kyle thought that Kiki and Marie would be going back to his half brother, so he was positively surprised when the four of them returned to the hotel room together. In the taxi ride over, it seemed that Kiki couldn't believe it either.

"So what happened, Mommy?" Marie eventually asked.

"I'm not quite sure," Kiki replied. "He said that for now it would be best if we stayed wherever we were hiding. He even warned me not to come back to the apartment for a while. It looks like we're okay."

Although that seemed to be true, Kyle knew that it would just be temporary. Perhaps he didn't want them to return so he could concentrate on the big task that had been given to him. Once it was over, Simon would surely be obsessing over Kiki again.

I can't . . . I can't let Marie go back to that damn demon . . . I can't see her like that again, Kyle thought.

Since the next day was a weekend day, Kyle and Marie spent their morning playing games. Her eye was doing a lot better, which meant she was playing better, and for the first time in a while she ended up winning.

"Hey . . . what's up with you?" Marie asked, putting the controller down. "I never win this easily, so something's clearly on your mind. Just look at your fingers, they're moving in slow motion."

Of course it was because Kyle had been thinking every day about what he could do to help Marie and her mother. He had been doing a bit of research on his father's gang. He had found out that the Underdogs didn't take to betrayal or failure nicely.

In some cases, members had been kicked out of the gang, never to be seen again. There were also some shocking stories about what happened to them. Some of this he had learned through his mother, and other things he had picked up just by being around his father and his men.

After yesterday's news, he had come up with an idea.

"Marie . . . I think I know of a way to get that demon off your back."

"Demon?" Marie asked, not sure who Kyle was referring to.

"Simon," Kyle answered, not wanting to acknowledge being related to him. "I've overheard that he's responsible for a massive task at the moment. If he messes it up, there's a good chance that my father would kick him out of the gang entirely.

"It might not work the first time, but if he keeps messing up, or maybe even if I can set it up to look like he stole money from the gang, he might lose all of his backing!"

Hearing Kyle talk this way was somewhat frightening for Marie. He had a dangerous glint in his eyes; he was seemingly obsessed with the idea. And she wasn't wrong. Kyle had spent more time than he would like to admit thinking about how to sabotage Simon.

"Don't you think that's too dangerous? Kyle, this isn't like in the movies! What if you get caught? Listen to yourself, you're trying to sabotage your own brother! What do you think he will do if he finds out?" Marie cautioned him.

"Do we have a choice? Do you have a choice?" Kyle countered. "What if he had gone further that day? I . . . I . . . might have never seen you again! You or your mother! Your mother told me to look after you, Marie, and this is my chance!"

Marie wasn't convinced. In the end they were only young teenagers; what could they even do?

"I won't involve you directly. I'm not asking you to do anything for me, I just need you to tell me one thing. Can you tell me the address . . . the address of where you were staying with him?"

Marie thought about it; the fact that Simon didn't want them to return to the house most likely meant there was something he didn't want them to see or be involved in. If Kyle could sneak in and find something to use against him, mess up his work or frame him for something, all of this could be over.

Unsure of what to say, and seeing the intensity in Kyle's eyes, not quite knowing what he was going to do, Marie decided to give him the address.

CHAPTER 29

A MISTAKE

Throughout his school life Kyle had been called many things by his schoolmates and teachers, ranging from harmless descriptions such as "a smart child" to more outrageous labels such as "a genius in the making." Eleanor Hamper herself had never belittled her son's intelligence; after all, she had personally taught him outside of school, though she had also never called him something as ludicrous as a "talent that only appears once every hundred years."

The only thing she cared about was that her son would grow up and use his gift to do something that would make him happy, not caring about the opinion of others. This was just one of the reasons why Kyle had loved his mother wholeheartedly.

Because of all the praise he received, he had strived to be the best at everything, to live up to the expectations that everyone had for him from the beginning. So knowing that his mother, the one person that Kyle cared about the most, was already pleased with him had done a lot to alleviate that underlying pressure.

At one point, around the time he met Marie, Kyle had started following his mother's advice and concentrated more on finding balance in his life, playing games and doing sports now and then. Nevertheless, thanks to his sharp mind, he had managed to stay at the top of the class, although when teachers volunteered him to participate in special programs, he declined, treasuring his free time more.

In a manner of speaking, despite having been born as the son of a gang leader, young Kyle had lived the life of a goody-two-shoes so far. He had never imagined that he would skip school and do something that was extremely dangerous, if not suicidal.

Marie and Aunt Kiki are happy staying with us, yet you're the one who's ruining it all! Kyle thought as he strode past his school.

Marie watched him with a worried look, wondering what to do. In the end, she still had to go to school.

He won't do anything, right? . . . I mean what can he do? Marie wondered, as part of her hoped that Kyle would back out of doing whatever he planned to do at the last second.

Of course Kyle was heading to his half brother's address. It was the middle of the day, so he was pretty sure that Simon wouldn't be home, but even if he was he had a plan for that as well. Either way, he needed to avoid running into him.

The address wasn't too far from the school; Slough was only a Tier 3 town, far smaller than a city. A person could walk the entire length in about two hours and see most of the main part of the town, so it only took Kyle thirty minutes to get there. He stopped in front of an apartment block; it wasn't in the worst area, nor the best.

Damion could have easily paid for Simon and the Degraces to live in the best area, but he didn't. Since Simon was supposed to take over the gang one day, his father wanted to train him from the bottom up. To do that, he had to live the same life as his old man had, with no extra privileges, so that he could earn the position as leader of the Underdogs.

Of course, Kyle had experienced a completely different life with his mother. They had luxury apartments, an unlimited spending budget, and other benefits. Eleanor hadn't asked much of her husband, yet she had been adamant about one thing. Kyle was not to get involved in the gang business, and since Damion already had a successor, he had agreed to that.

As Kyle thought about it, he realized that this could be another reason his brother seemed to dislike him so much, because the two of them were completely different. Of course, that in no way excused his behavior toward his family. Even his father didn't lay hands on his mother, and he was the leader of the gang.

Marie said that he leaves for work every day at ten a.m. and then doesn't get back till late. Usually around ten p.m. and more often than not drunk as well. That's when she hears her mother and him arguing, Kyle recalled.

He looked at his phone and saw that it was fifteen minutes until ten a.m. It made sense, since gang members had their usual daily runs they needed to do, unless it was a special day. Either way, Kyle was going to wait patiently.

Not long after that, the door opened and he saw that his half brother was leaving right on the dot. Kyle was hiding around the corner of the hallway, at the far end of the staircase. He was certain that Simon would use the upper exit, because his car was parked on that side.

He waited a few minutes to make sure Simon didn't return to pick up anything he might have forgotten, then called the apartment's home phone. He didn't expect anyone to pick up; it was just to check whether anyone else was inside, but after a few rings nobody picked up.

Quickly heading to the door, Kyle pressed his hand against the handle. It was one of the newer types that worked via a fingerprint or a PIN. Marie had given him the code, so after entering the sequence of numbers he went inside.

The door closed behind him, and for the first time he saw the apartment where Marie and her mother occasionally lived with his piece-of-shit half brother.

The first thing Kyle did was head to the kitchen and look for a spoon in the drawer, which he then placed on the door handle. This way he would get an early warning if anyone came home. Of course, the spoon would be a giveaway that someone was inside, but it was better than getting caught red-handed, and with a bit of luck his half brother would choose to ignore it.

"That apartment." Kai spoke weakly, sitting on the hard ground, with Gary not too far away. "If only I had listened to my mother and not stuck my nose where it didn't belong, perhaps I could have continued to live a normal life."

CHAPTER 30

DECISION MADE

The main room of the apartment was a large open-plan kitchen/ living room. Kyle decided to give the area a quick skim, but he didn't look for long as he didn't expect to find anything there anyway.

I have to give him some credit, he's not so stupid to just leave things out in the open, Kyle thought as he closed one of the drawers just under the TV cabinet.

To the right was a hallway that branched off into several rooms, such as the bathroom, the bedrooms, and most importantly the office. Since the last was the most likely place to find information, Kyle checked there first.

I have to be careful, but also hurry in case he plans to work from home and comes back early.

The office was a complete mess. There were things scattered everywhere, and even the papers, pens, and other objects on the desk weren't put away properly. It was nothing like how he would have kept things, showing how different the two half brothers really were.

Crap, this is going to make it harder, Kyle thought. *If it was all neat and tidy I could have put everything back perfectly in its place, but he seems to be the type of person who even though it looks messy, he has his own system. If I move something, he's going to know someone was here.*

He would have to just make do with whatever he could find on the surface. After looking around for a little while and reading over some of the documents, Kyle found more information than he had initially imagined.

For one, several sticky notes were posted all over the front of Simon's laptop, with dates, gang member names, and times. When he matched them up with what he had found in the documents, Kyle was sure that he had hit a gold mine.

Does he not know that he can keep track of his notes on the laptop? . . . Hmmm, maybe he's worried someone might hack it. Oh well, this way made things easy for me. Kyle smiled as he used his phone to compile his own notes after taking photos of the important things he had found in the office.

As Simon was already in a somewhat high position, he had detailed information on planned attacks: dates, safe house areas for the Underdogs, and establishments the gang was planning on taking over or attacking if they didn't cooperate.

The easiest way is probably to sabotage his missions. I just have to find a way to inform the other gangs of what they're planning to do. There even looks to be a whole list of drops that those types of transporters are supposed to do."

On a particular note Kyle saw the word *NIRV* at the top, though he had no idea whether the scribbled *parcel* was meant as something to be delivered or received.

There were also a lot of other things Kyle lacked the context to completely grasp. Nevertheless, with just the few things that were clear enough, he was sure he could sabotage Simon enough to cause a few missions to fail. Then the Underdogs would undoubtedly start wondering about having a rat among them, at which point he would just have to frame Simon . . . though they might even figure out on their own. After all, who would suspect a thirteen-year-old boy?

The only thing I don't understand is what was the big deal? Why would he not want Kiki and Marie back? Kyle wondered. *This just seems like normal everyday business for the Underdogs. It doesn't look like something that would be a shock to anyone.*

Perhaps the big news was hiding on Simon's laptop or under the piles of paper, but in order not to risk himself, he decided to leave everything in place.

Kyle left the room carefully and closed the door behind him, using the pair of gloves he had worn. He was smart enough not to leave any fingerprints, though he doubted the police would get involved. Sure, calling the police wasn't something the Underdogs would do, but it was best to stay cautious.

As soon as he left the room with the information, Kyle started to question whether this was the right thing to do.

Can I really do this? If I give the information to the other gangs, Simon won't be the only one I'm putting at risk. I have no idea how bad things can go. What if they kill him? What if other members die trying to protect him?

His mind was going back and forth. The people he was caring about were gangsters, who might have killed gang members from the other side already, but he didn't know that for a fact. Not everyone had already dirtied their hands . . .

While he was deep in thought, Kyle found himself standing in front of a door with a little sign indicating that it was Marie's room. Without him even thinking about it, his body was moving on its own and he opened the door to what looked like a bright pink paradise.

Whoa, what is all this? Kyle was greeted by countless pink plushies, pink bedsheets, and pink curtains. It took him a bit of time to process this. He couldn't remember a single time having seen Marie wear anything close to pink. The way she behaved around him, playing games and sports with him, gave him a more tomboyish impression of her.

Is she only that way around me or something? Kyle wondered.

With his curiosity getting the better of him, he looked around the room. The bed hadn't been made; it was rumpled a bit, and that was when he noticed something else. Behind the door was a large hole where the wall was indented, as if someone had punched it.

It made Kyle remember why he had come here in the first place. Looking back at the bed, he noticed something by the pillow. A corner of what looked like a notebook stuck out. He pulled it out.

Opening the pages, not caring whether Marie wanted him to read it or not, Kyle found that it was a diary. Marie had written banal things about how her days had gone, and it looked like she had used it a lot in the beginning, but less and less as time went on.

Seems like Marie is also one of those people who try to do this diary stuff, only to give up after a month or so. Kyle had a slight smirk on his face.

However, it didn't remain for long, as he soon discovered a large shift in tone. After a large gap of blank pages, the next page had countless scribbles all over it, as if someone had written in anger. The words didn't fit in the lines, but Kyle could see why.

I don't understand . . . I don't understand . . . why does he get so angry, why does he keep hitting her?

A few pages later:

I wish he was dead! I wish he was out of our lives . . . why do we keep coming back to this god-forsaken place?

The pages looked a little water damaged, and Kyle could imagine that Marie had been crying. The next entry, if one could even call it that, was just the word *die* filling up the entire page, seemingly traced over enough times to damage the paper. There was pure anger, and he knew who it was directed toward.

Alas, the next page was the worst one by far.

I can't take it anymore . . . I don't know what to do. This pain in my heart hurts so much . . . I don't want him to hurt Mommy, and I'm scared. I'm so scared. I feel like I can't breathe when he gets like that . . .

I don't know what to do . . . maybe it would be easier . . . if I weren't there. Without me, Mommy could finally leave him.

After reading the page, Kyle instinctively scrunched it up as he made up his mind.

He has to go.

Before he left the room, Kyle did his best to put it back the way it was, and then he closed the door. As he walked down the hallway, he noticed a faint muffled sound. Stopping for a second, Kyle wondered if it was the sound of his feet on the floorboards, but as he stood still, he heard it again.

It was faint, but it was also constant, and it seemed to go in and out. Continuing forward, Kyle heard it even more clearly. He stopped in front of where the noise seemed to originate . . . the bathroom.

CHAPTER 31

IN THE BATH

With the line of work his family and especially his half brother was in, Kyle could guess what was on the other side of the bathroom door. He already imagined that the muffled screams meant that someone was trapped inside. Now it made perfect sense why Simon had told the Degraces to stay away until he called for them.

I should just leave, I have enough to get Simon into trouble, Kyle told himself, heading to the door, but rather than exiting when he got to the kitchen, he grabbed a knife instead.

No, Dad really cares for Simon, he really does, and maybe just a few failed tasks won't be enough to get him kicked out of the Underdogs. They said that there was something big, and this could be it.

Kyle tiptoed back to the bathroom door and stood outside it, but he could no longer hear the muffled noises. Whoever was inside must have thought that he had left.

If the person was just locked in there, then they would be banging on the door. I'm ninety percent sure that Simon must have tied them up, but just in case . . . I also have this, Kyle thought, looking at the knife.

He had never used a knife as a weapon; although he was quite athletic, he didn't willingly participate in sports or any form of combat. If he tried to be a gang member, he imagined that he would be one of the worst.

Kyle looked down the hallway at Marie's door again and re-membered the diary; this motivated him to push forward, twisting the door handle and pushing it in to find a person in the bathtub.

At first he saw only the person's knees, close together. Kyle couldn't see any rope, but he could tell that they were tied up.

Now, a little braver, he pushed the door further and could fi-nally see the whole bathroom. Stunned by the sight in front of him, Kyle almost dropped the knife, but he managed to control himself just in time, gripping it a little tighter.

A badly injured man lay in the bathtub. He had heavy bruises and his eyes were swollen. On top of that, the bathroom walls were splattered with blood. He couldn't imagine what had happened here, or how much pain the man was in.

The room smelled slightly metallic, and a little like rotten eggs. It was overwhelming, and he felt his insides trying to come up from within.

Calm down . . . I can't afford to throw up . . . It's just a game . . . You've seen plenty of bloody scenes in games and movies! It's just one of those. You're just an actor, Kyle thought, trying to convince himself.

But the man had noticed that someone he had never seen before had entered, and it wasn't Simon. His eyes opened wide, having seen a ray of hope. The muffled noises resumed as the man tried to speak, but of course none of it was audible.

Several pieces of tape were wrapped around his mouth, allow-ing him to breathe through his nose. The fact that the man wasn't using his hands meant they were tied up as well.

Kyle remained frozen in the doorway.

What exactly did I think I was going to do? I knew someone was in here, but then what? If I free the man, Simon will immediately know that I was here . . . Shit, I can't just turn back now either; the guy has already seen me . . . What if he tells Simon about it? What exactly was I expecting to find here? I can't cut the tape from his mouth either.

But Kyle could also see that a lot of the tools that were used to injure and tie up the man were still in the bathroom, including the tape. Perhaps he could just untape his mouth in order to find out why he was here.

At the same time, Kyle realized that this man might die if he left him here.

Simon won't be back for a long time . . . this man doesn't know me . . . I can just undo his mouth for now, Kyle thought.

"Hey, I just wandered in here by accident," Kyle said as he slowly approached the man. "I'm going to remove the tape and let you speak. I'm the only one here, so please don't do anything stupid like scream for help, okay? I'm not supposed to be in here in the first place."

The man quickly nodded. Using the knife, Kyle carefully cut off the tape, then started to pull. It was far more difficult than he thought, and seeing the man up close was making everything he was doing a little harder as reality started to hit him.

Eventually, though, Kyle got the tape off, but not without getting a little bit of blood on his hands.

"Thank you . . ." The man spoke with a weak voice. "If you could free my arms and legs, we can get out of here."

"Um . . . I don't exactly know who you are, mister," Kyle replied, half acting, half serious. "Like I said, I'm not supposed to be here in the first place. Maybe I should call the police, and they can come and get you before he comes back."

"No . . . no . . . please." The man started to beg, with tears falling from his eyes. Just in case the man might try to scream, Kyle picked up the tape, so he could use it if the man made any noise.

But that was when the man realized something. "Wait, I know you! I've seen you before! Your Damion's other son, aren't you?! Your name's Ken . . . no, was it Kevin . . . Ah! It was Kai, right? I'm a member of the Underdogs! Please, just call your dad and tell him that Tim Curdy is still alive and that I'm here, all right?"

Kyle was confused, but then something hit him. Given Tim's current appearance, it was hard to tell, but he remembered seeing someone who resembled him with Damion in the past. But he had seen him even more recently at the funeral. However . . . it had been in one of the photos of the deceased.

What is going on? Kyle wondered, needing some time to sort through the information.

Alas, before he could make heads or tails of it, a metallic clanking sound came from the main room.

CHAPTER 32

FROM THE SAME TREE

At the moment, Eleanor was in a place where she would rather not be. She had come to the Basement, a nightclub that was owned by the Underdogs. Ever since she had gotten pregnant with her son, Eleanor had refrained from getting involved with any gang business, a choice Damion had fully supported.

Nevertheless, everyone in the Underdogs knew about Damion's second family, since he couldn't help but show them off at certain events. It was to ensure unity and strength among the Underdog gang, to demonstrate that he was unafraid of those that might come after their family; that was how confident he was.

Because she was a familiar face, nobody had stopped Eleanor from heading into the main office of the Underdogs, even though Damion only allowed others in under his strict supervision. With nobody bothering her, she went through countless files, business accounts, and more in the hopes of finding something to help out her childhood friend.

Of course she didn't want to hurt Simon. She knew perfectly well how much his firstborn son meant to Damion, yet she cared about her friend more.

This . . . all of this is important information . . . but what exactly am I supposed to do with all of it? Eleanor wondered, sitting down and staring at the files as if they would offer some sort of guidance.

Should I perhaps do what Kyle planned on doing? I have information on some of the shell companies the Underdogs use to launder their money. There are even bank cards here, and I know their PINs. I could just withdraw most of the money and hand it over to Kiki.

She and Marie can run away to another country for a while. If Simon catches his big break, maybe he will become too busy to do anything about them.

Eleanor took a long while to consider her next course of action. If she was caught, it would definitely cause problems. No matter his personal feelings, once everything came to light, Damion would be forced to act, even if she was his lover. It was impossible for him to simply overlook such a treasonous act; he would lose too much face.

I should just do it and come clean to him afterward. So far, He's never done anything bad to me or Kai . . . and if I explain the situation, I'm sure he will understand.

Eleanor knew that she had no guarantee that things would turn out that way, and that this was mostly her hoping it would be okay. Still, she had already spent too much time here, and people might start to get suspicious. So she decided to get to work, transferring the money into her account, so there would be no way to link it to Kiki. After that she could give her friend her own card.

Eleanor regretted that it had come to this. In the past, she had tried to talk to Damion about the situation. Unfortunately, Simon had a way with words toward his father. He knew exactly what to say to convince him. Ultimately, the only thing that came out of it was a sort of unspoken compromise that Kiki was allowed to leave for a period of time whenever Simon "misbehaved."

Everyone involved must have hoped that it would be a onetime thing, yet it had turned into a vicious cycle . . .

There, that's all done, Eleanor thought, mentally exhausted. Everything she was doing was nerve-racking, and she knew that she would eventually be caught. There was no coming back from this.

Her only hope was that it would give Kiki enough time to leave the country. Ideally, Damion would even help her keep it a secret . . .

or at least go easy on her once she confessed.

Interrupting her idle thoughts, her phone started to vibrate on the table. She didn't recognize the number but decided to answer it.

"Hello, is this Mrs. Eleanor Hamper?" the voice on the other end asked.

"Indeed. Who am I speaking to?"

"Ah yes, this is Miss Buckle at Westbridge. I'm just calling to check if everything is okay with Kai at home. He hasn't come in today, and it is school policy that parents should notify the school beforehand. We know you are usually on top of things, and since this is the first time something like this has ever happened, we decided to give you a call."

Eleanor was confused. She had seen her son leave for school that morning, and he wasn't the type to just skip. She didn't know why, but her stomach felt even worse than before.

"I'll be right there." Eleanor hung up the phone and rushed out of the office.

A short while later, Eleanor arrived at the school. She had attempted to call Kyle multiple times to no avail. Normally, this wouldn't be surprising; after all, students were supposed to concentrate on their lessons. However, she knew he wasn't at school. What's more, her calls had gone straight to voice mail, meaning his phone was turned off, which was just worrying her even more.

Eleanor headed straight to the teachers' office, where she got the same story as on the phone.

"Please, would you call Marie Degrace? She should be in the same class. They walk to school every day, and they even left together this morning. I just want to ask her some questions to see what is going on."

The teacher was a bit weary, but Eleanor had been polite, and something in her voice made it hard for them to refuse. A few minutes later Marie was brought in, and straightaway it felt like she knew what was going on, as she avoided eye contact with Eleanor.

"Marie . . . please tell me where Kyle is." Eleanor got down to eye level with her and held her hand. "You know how much I care about you and your mother. You're both like family to me . . . but Kyle is my son. If anything were to happen to him . . ."

Eleanor gulped, as she didn't dare to finish that thought. Of course, Marie found it hard to deny the request of the woman who treated her like her own daughter. Shyly she leaned in and whispered a confession about Kyle's plan to Eleanor, making the mother nearly suffer a heart attack.

CHAPTER 33

STRANGER DANGER

Hmm, that's a little strange, Simon noted as he looked down at the spoon that had fallen on the floor. However, he had more important things to worry about, so he didn't think too much of it, playfully kicking the spoon across the floor before putting his bag on the kitchen counter.

Now . . . let's see how much longer he'll manage to stay obstinate. Simon grinned, looking forward to what he was about to do. He emptied the bag, revealing a large set of pliers, stainless steel skewers, a drill, and other tools.

He hovered over each item, pondering over which one he should use first. Eventually his hands stopped on the pliers. As he walked down the hallway, he passed the spoon, making him halt for a moment.

Don't tell me . . . *Shit!*" Cursing, Simon rushed toward the bathroom door, opening it as fast as he could. Once he had confirmed that his prisoner hadn't gone missing, he let out a sigh of relief.

"Phew, for a moment I was worried you might have escaped," Simon admitted with a smile as he held up the pliers. His prisoner was in the same position he'd left him in, tape still covering his mouth, still alive and stuck in the bathtub.

"Now, Tim . . . our last talk didn't prove too fruitful, and since I have a job to do, we're going to make you speak," Simon revealed as he walked up to the bathtub.

"First, I'm just going to pull off one of your nails, after which I'm going to take the tape off your mouth. Now, if the first thing out of your mouth isn't what I need to know, we'll continue the process all over again. Don't worry, if you should run out of nails, I have plenty of other tools left in the kitchen." Simon was explaining things so casually that one wouldn't believe he was talking about torturing a fellow human being.

Usually, even a gangster would find it hard to resort to these types of things, especially with someone who was in the same gang, but Simon didn't seem to mind. In fact, the smile on his face was testimony to the fact that he was planning on enjoying it. The captive knew this, and he instinctively began to panic.

His body shook like crazy as he did his best to scream. Alas, barely any sound escaped, as the tape muffled his voice. It was then that Tim Curdy looked at Simon . . . but not exactly at him.

Noticing this odd behavior, his captor pulled on the man's hair to lift his head up and shouted at him. "What the fuck do you keep looking at?"

At first, the man couldn't help staring at Simon, but he looked directly behind him once again, and Simon eventually turned his head.

"There's nothing there . . ." Simon muttered, still grasping the man's hair. All he could see was the wide-open door and the rest of the bathroom. He was about to turn back around when he had an epiphany.

The spoon! If he's still here, and I didn't leave it out . . . Simon let go of his captive and went to the bathroom door. He grabbed the doorknob and pulled it closed quickly, revealing a shaking teenage boy . . . one he despised for multiple reasons.

"Well, well, well, if it isn't my dearest brother? To what do I owe the pleasure of your visit?" Simon didn't even try to hide the pure unbridled sarcasm in his question.

Kyle opened and closed his mouth, trying to come up with an excuse. Never before had he come over, and to do so now, in the middle of his half brother being busy with a job . . . There was nothing he could say, so his only choice was to hope that Simon wouldn't hurt him too badly. Surely being half brothers meant something . . . right?

"I've always known you to be a bastard, but to think you would be a goddamn rat on top of that. Thanks for making this easy for me. After sneaking in here, even Dad won't be able to complain that I finally got rid of you," Simon sneered with a sadistic smile as he reached out to grab the teenager by his throat.

Hearing this unveiled threat, Kyle reacted out of instinct, his grip on the knife strengthened, and he immediately slashed it through the air, cutting Simon's hand. His half brother had clearly not expected any resistance from the boy, and the striking pain from the attack was the price he was paying for that.

"You'll pay for this!" Simon shouted in fury as he looked at the gash. "I was gonna make it quick, but you're more than dead now! I'm going to make sure to drain every last drop of your tainted blood!"

Kyle knew he stood no chance against his half brother. He wasn't strong, nor did he have any experience as a fighter. Heck, his body hadn't even fully developed yet, so it was impossible for him to deal with this bona fide gangster.

As Simon charged in, Kyle did the only thing he could think of that might get him out of this situation. Simon was so enraged that even an amateur could predict his next move, and using his smaller body frame to his advantage, Kyle slid onto the floor, right through his half brother's open legs.

Without any hesitation, the teenager slammed the door the other way, attempting to make Simon stumble. He didn't waste any time looking back to see if it had worked, but headed straight for the man in the bathtub.

"Please do something about him!" Kyle pleaded aloud as he used the knife to free the man's arms. Before he could do the same for his legs, though, a grunt came from behind him. He turned around and saw a giant fist coming straight toward his head. The impact connected on the side of his jaw, and the taste of metal filled his mouth.

"Fuck!" Kyle lay collapsed on the floor, with tears in his eyes. Simon was preparing his next strike, this time with the pliers in his hand. This one was going to hurt a lot more and do a lot more damage than a mere fist.

In the middle of his swing, another fist came from behind Kyle and hit Simon's jaw, sending him flying back.

"I'm sorry for outing you," Tim apologized. One of his eyes was still heavily bruised, but the other one could see just fine. "I'll make sure to get us out of here alive and tell Damion everything his rotten son has been doing!"

CHAPTER 34

THE FINAL STRUGGLE

Before entering the apartment, Kyle had considered many ways things could go south, ranging from Simon coming home early to him leaving some sort of incriminating evidence behind. The moment he heard the spoon fall, his heart dropped to his feet. Without hesitation, he used the tape in his hands to cover the gangster's mouth to re-create the scene exactly as he had found it.

He knew that it was too late to leave the bathroom. Simon would either hear or see him long before he could make it into another room, so Kyle quickly hid in the one place most people would normally ignore: behind the door.

As he listened to his half brother's steps coming closer, he racked his brain for a way to make it out alive. He had always known his half brother to be a brute, but the state that Tim was in only proved that he had vastly underestimated him. He was a lot more menacing than Kyle had ever imagined, a true monster that Marie and his aunt Kiki had been forced to live with for far too long.

Kyle's only saving grace was that he wasn't the only one in the room who needed to fight to survive, and unlike him, Tim quickly demonstrated that he wasn't someone who would shy away from using violence. After he delivered his punch, he tried to get out of the bathtub, but his legs were still taped together and he slipped on a bit of his own blood. He barely had the strength to put his hand out to cushion his falling body.

Meanwhile, Simon had already recovered and there wasn't much that Tim could do as Simon kicked at his face. Just before it hit him, though, a flying shampoo bottle struck his assailant right on the nose.

Alas, though Kyle had used all of his strength, the damage was negligible, but it was enough to throw Simon's aim slightly off. Without this intervention, the kick might have fractured Tim's skull. It still hurt, but he could tolerate the pain. Not losing any time, he tackled his torturer. Grabbing Simon around the waist, he pushed with both of his legs to lift him slightly and slam him onto the floor, with his own body on top.

I guess this guy has a lot more strength than I thought. Gangsters are used to fighting for their lives, but . . . what do I do now? Kyle wondered, his inexperience clearly showing.

He still had the knife in his hand, but he hesitated to use it. Slashing and stabbing someone were two different things, especially since he had only done the former in pure self-preservation. The idea that he could end someone's life, even a monster like his half brother . . .

Kyle was ready to make a break for it. Although Simon would know what he had done, he would just have to take the punishment head on.

What if he tells Damion about this, though . . . or what if Simon dies . . . will Mom get punished instead of me? Will Dad get revenge on Marie and Aunt Kiki?

"Hey!" Tim shouted, seeing that Kyle was making a run for it. "If you don't want to get involved, call Damion. Tell him to come here to deal with a traitor!" The gangster continued to punch Simon, who kept both hands up, covering his head.

That's right! He's a traitor! He captured and tortured another member of the Underdogs! Dad won't punish me, and he might even reward me! That will solve all my problems! Simon won't be able to defend himself, and all of us will be able to live in peace without him!

Kyle pulled his phone out of his pocket. He had several messages and missed calls, but he didn't have time to look at them. He pressed the one speed-dial button he had never used before.

Of course he won't answer a call from me during working time. I'll just have to send him a message.

Come to Simon's apartment now! I need help!

With the message sent, Kyle could only hope his father would rush over. But something had happened. Tim had stopped punching. His body was as still as a statue, and as Simon tried to get up, the gangster's body slammed against the floor.

Now that he had a better view, Kyle saw that his would-be savior was dead. Sticking out from his temple was the set of pliers his half brother had brought into the bathroom. During the struggle, he had slammed them into the side of Tim's head.

As he stood up, Simon looked a bit sore himself. His body hurt, but that didn't stop him as he turned to the corpse in anger, slamming his foot right into the pliers, sending them deeper into the man's skull.

"Shit, I didn't want to kill him," Simon grumbled as he approached Kyle. "I still needed the intel he had! This is all your fault! You should have never been born in the first place!"

The teenager rushed toward the door, attempting to get out, but his half brother's steps were bigger than his. Just as Kyle opened the door, Simon kicked him in his side, and he fell to the floor on his back.

Instinctively he put up his arms, though it had little effect. His half brother kicked him once more, destroying his feeble resistance, and he lost consciousness; the last thing he saw was the sadistic smile on Simon's face.

When he woke up, he had no idea how long he had been out, but it felt like all the pain in his body was engulfing him at once. His whole body throbbed with each beat of his heart, and when he opened his eyes, he was surprised to see someone standing there.

"M-Mom . . . i-is that y-you?" Kyle mumbled, unable to comprehend what he was seeing.

As he tried to stand up, he felt his hand touch liquid, and he saw that he was still in the bathroom. This made it even more bizarre that his mother was there. Was it all a dream? Looking more closely, he saw that his mother held a pocketknife . . . and at her feet was Simon, lying motionless in a pool of blood.

Before he could comprehend the situation, someone knocked on the door.

"Simon, are you in there?" a deep and familiar voice resounded.

CHAPTER 35

THE BITE

"... And then ... he ... my mother ..." Kai's voice was shaking, and it was obvious that he was struggling with finding the right words about how to continue with the last part. Eventually, he let out a frustrated sigh.

Gary could tell that the conclusion of the story was difficult for Kai to talk about. The next part was surely the last piece of the puzzle that would explain how the goody-two-shoes Kyle became Kai. Still, he felt that he mustn't rush his friend, and he waited for him to continue once he was ready.

"You know, it's funny, I was kinda mad at you earlier because you ended up in this situation because you can often be hotheaded and rush into situations. However, after telling you about my past, I realize that I pretty much did the exact same thing." Kai let out a dry laugh as he pulled out a small blade with a red handle. "This little blade is the only thing I have left of my mother. It's the one she had used to kill Simon, saving my life but dooming her own ..."

Once more, there was a silence between the two.

"I ... I never found out how long I was out for ... just as I never found out what Simon had attempted to do to me," Kai continued. "All I know is that shortly after I woke up, I saw that my mother had rescued me, by doing what I failed to do. Everything after that happened too fast for any of us to do anything about it. Since none of us answered him, Damion broke the door and rushed in.

"Well . . . things couldn't have looked any worse. He came in, saw his beloved son on the floor, and knelt down. Unable to find a pulse, he turned to my mother, who still held the blade in her hand. He asked only a single question about who had done this to his son.

"I don't know why he even bothered, given the situation, but at that moment I couldn't understand why my mother told him the truth . . . that she had killed Simon to save me . . . it was the first time I had ever seen him hit her, and . . . he just didn't stop . . .

"I don't know how long I watched him let out all the anger and frustration on her defenseless body. It was as if he had turned into a complete monster; he continued long after she had stopped moving. I was so hurt I couldn't do anything . . . at least that's what I would love to believe." Kai looked at his own hands as if they were the ones stained with the blood of his mother.

"The truth is that I was too afraid of him. I had escaped death far too many times in one day; I didn't dare risk my life again . . . even if only to call out to the bastard to stop hitting my mother . . . so I witnessed everything . . . including her last breath . . . and beyond . . ."

As tragic as it was, Gary felt elated that he finally had learned about Kai's past, even though the circumstances could have been better. Still, it definitely brought the two of them closer. He now knew that Kai's hatred for the Underdogs was in no way smaller than his own, and the fact that he was Damion's son only made him resent the leader more.

As he held the blade tightly, Kai didn't notice that his palm had slipped above the handle, causing a small cut. But the werewolf in the room immediately noticed the scent of fresh blood.

It was as if Gary was possessed; he got a second wind as he lunged toward his cellmate. The chains pulled till they were taut and his mouth opened wide, dripping saliva, waking Kai up from his reverie.

Gary was only inches away, and Kai saw his sharp teeth that were not human. Nevertheless, he remained standing, fearless, only now noticing the state of his hand.

"You're showing this much of a reaction to blood? I thought only vampires did that," Kai muttered.

It took a few seconds, but Gary managed to control himself, returning to fully human form as he fought his instincts to try his luck once more. Aware that the blood would be a problem, Kai cut off part of his shirt and tied it around the wound.

"I'm sorry, I didn't mean to do that," Kai apologized. "Where was I . . . Oh, right. After he killed my mother, Damion never talked about what happened that day. Instead, he made one thing clear: that I was to become a replacement for Simon.

"He said I would be the successor of the Underdogs. I was expected to train every day, to learn the ins and outs of the business . . . and I hated every second of it. But I decided to commit myself to the training, because I had promised myself that I would get vengeance for my mother.

"As for Marie and Kiki, he seemed to have forgotten about them . . . or perhaps he didn't want them around because they would be a constant reminder of Simon. Either way, they were no longer involved with the Underdogs. But Aunt Kiki felt guilty about everything that happened, and the two of them have been by my side ever since."

Kai fell silent and walked up to the bars, gazing out.

"I'm sorry for what happened," Gary said. "I'm sorry for rushing in here without really thinking about what to do. I understand now . . . I understand why you hate the Underdogs."

He stopped there, lacking the right words to console his friend given his personal situation. They had the same goal, though for different reasons. Gary was fighting to protect his family, while Kai was fighting to avenge his family.

"You mentioned something about Damion waiting for someone to take care of me, so we should probably focus on getting out of here now. Since you came here as soon as you knew I was here, I assume you have a plan, right?"

Kai turned around, and rather than his usual confident smile, he wore a look of uncertainty. "I do, but I have a feeling you might not like it very much. After what I told you, I think you can understand why I want to get revenge on Damion with my own hands . . .

"A small part of me had hoped I would be able to do him in, or at least injure him, but unfortunately he is far stronger than I anticipated. As if that weren't enough, the Underdogs have somehow managed to acquire a shit ton of Anti-Altered weapons, far more than you can handle . . . but if you turn me, we should be able to overwhelm them."

Gary's eyes widened. "T-turn you? I-I can't!"

"Why not?" Kai asked. "You turned Billy and Olivia. What's stopping you from doing the same for me? Don't you trust me?"

"No, you don't understand, it has nothing to do with trust . . . it's not as easy or as simple as you think! You could die!" Gary shouted. "You were there, Billy was pretty much an accident, and Olivia just got lucky! I didn't care whether she lived or died, but I wouldn't be able to live with myself if I caused your death."

Kai took a step toward Gary, but stopped short.

"Yeah, I had a feeling you wouldn't like this plan. You're a nice guy, Gary . . . but in this world, nice guys don't last a long time." Without giving Gary any time to react, Kai removed the wrap around his wound and shoved his hand right into the starving werewolf's mouth.

CHAPTER 36

ALPHA BITE

When Kai lunged toward him, time started to slow down from Gary's perspective. Alas, the werewolf was unable to control his instincts. Since the nice, juicy piece of meat had presented itself to him, he opened his mouth, his teeth extended and sharpened further, cutting through the flesh.

What . . . why is Kai doing this? Has he gone mad? I have to stop . . . but this taste! Gary thought as the blood filled his mouth. Rather than iron, it tasted like the most divine sauce. It was hard to say whether this was because his palate had changed, or because he had never been on the verge of death by hunger. No matter how hard he tried to stop himself, his jaw crushed down harder.

"Arghhh! Shit, how long do I have to endure this? Come on, Gary, turn me! That's the only way we can get out of here!" Kai cursed as he felt the bones in his hand breaking.

Gary tried to unclench his jaw but failed. He stepped back, dragging Kai with him; his friend's weight seemed inconsequential right now.

Not only was he worried that he might turn Kai, but the chains that were holding him had started to loosen. He wrapped them around his arms until he felt the chains tightening again. He tried to reach for Kai's body but fell short.

"G-Gary, you're still there . . . right? You just need to let go. If you let go, I can break us out of here and help you!" Kai tried to reason with the werewolf. Unfortunately, when he tugged his hand away, trying to free it, Gary's mouth opened slightly, only to chomp down harder. Kai knew that his approach would put him at risk, but he was starting to realize just how much of a gamble this situation really was turning out to be.

"Fuck!!!!" Kai screamed at the top of his lungs. "Are you trying to kill me?"

Of course, Gary wasn't trying to kill him. If he wanted to, he could have done that in seconds. In fact, he was doing his darnedest to prevent his instincts from doing anything but take a bite to replenish his depleted Energy.

He was fighting even now, and suddenly he and Kai heard the sound of metal bending. Kai turned to see that the chains were breaking away from their anchor points; even the links looked like they couldn't hold out much longer.

"Gary!" Kai shouted. At such close range, Gary could bite his face off at any second, but if he didn't do anything he would probably be eaten alive.

I . . . I can't fight much longer, and if these chains break free, then nothing can stop me from going after Kai. He will be killed instantly . . . I don't know if just biting him will turn him now that I have a skill . . . but I don't want to kill him . . . but if I don't do anything, he will die either way . . . Please be lucky, Kai!

Forced by the circumstances, Gary decided to risk it.

Skill activated: Alpha Bite

Using the system seemed to be easier than holding back the urge that was growing within him, and he could instantly tell that it had worked. Kai's veins started to bulge in front of him, showing through as a bluish green, and soon the transformation spread to his neck. Kai looked like he wanted to scream, but other than shallow gasps of air, he made no sound.

Still, there was one problem that had yet to be resolved, and that was the fact that Kai's hand was still trapped in Gary's mouth. At the same time, the hungry werewolf's fingernails were starting to grow, and they were inching farther and farther toward Kai's torso.

"Stwb fme!" Gary grunted. He could barely articulate because of the hand in his mouth, but Kai managed to understand the order. Using his last bit of control, he grabbed his mother's pocketknife with his other hand and swung it toward the top of Gary's mouth.

It pierced through his skin, which was tougher than Kai had anticipated. But he continued to push it in, and finally Gary let go. With his wounded hand free, Kai fell to the ground as the pain took over, and he managed to roll away a few times so the werewolf couldn't reach him, until he hit the back of the bars.

With his meal taken away, Gary felt his body weakening again, he fell to the floor, his sight fading.

Was it the wound on his face? With the knife embedded in his flesh, he had no way to heal; he was bleeding out and had no strength. Perhaps this was the end for the two of them.

Slowly, Gary opened his eyes. It didn't take him long to register that he was still in the same cell. However, things had drastically changed from the last time he had woken up. For one, the room was permeated with the smell of blood, his own as well as Kai's.

He touched his face and felt neither the blade nor the wound. That was when he noticed that his Energy was back to normal, and he was no longer chained up.

He turned and saw that the chains had been ripped out of the floor.

Did I do that? No, that can't be possible . . . and how did I heal? Was the blood enough for that?

A bad feeling engulfed Gary as he recalled what had happened. He could see that the bars were bent and Kai was missing, and he could barely make out the sound of fighting in the distance.

CHAPTER 37

ANOTHER TO THE PACK

Trying to determine what had happened, Gary looked around the cell. The chains lay loose on the floor, and the cuffs were no longer around his wrists. They had not been destroyed but merely opened.

It looks like someone went and got the key, and all this blood on the floor . . . there's too much of it to be mine and Kai's alone . . . did I sleepwalk and eat someone?

Even if he had eaten Kai's entire hand, which he was sure he would have remembered, it shouldn't have been enough to heal him, which confused him even more. He decided to open the system screen and assess the Pack tab.

Howlers Pack
Alpha Werewolf: Gary Dem
Grade: Bishop (1/15)
Beta Werewolf: Olivia Pearl
Grade: Knight (0/5)
Beta Werewolf: Kyle Hamper
Grade: Pawn (0/1)

Phew, I'm glad Kai successfully turned into a werewolf . . . But should I be happy or sad that he didn't become a Knight-grade were-wolf? According to the system I received a Pawn point, so I could up-grade him to assign him a class, but according to Olivia's account it takes some time, and assuming he's fighting right now it could be a death sentence. At least I hope he is the one fighting.

Fortunately Gary had seen Kai's name appear in the Pack tab, so he knew he was safe. Still, finding him might prove troublesome. He had already tried picking up Kai's scent to find his location, but it was hard to make out, especially since it had somewhat changed, most likely because he had been turned.

Well, after hearing Kai's story, and judging from where we should be, he must have gone after Damion. I have yet to receive the daily notification about how much I have left until the full moon, so I can't have been out for too long, but I can hear some struggling sounds, so I'd better check up on him.

Stepping out of the cell, Gary abruptly stopped as he discovered a dead person. A gang member who had been brutally slashed across the chest multiple times. On closer inspection, Gary saw that his limbs had been removed and only his torso remained.

Shit! He took a few steps back. *Was it this guy's blood in the cell? . . . It has to be. He smells the same. Did Kai kill him and bring him to me? But how's that possible? The pack rules should have prevented him from taking someone's life unless he was in a life-or-death situation.*

Gary realized that the rule might be a bit more open to interpretation than he had initially believed. He didn't know whether it had been a life-and-death situation for Kai, but Gary's own life as pack leader had certainly been in danger. He made a mental note to experiment in the future whether pack rules could be overridden in cases where his own safety depended on it, or if they were enforceable as long as he made them more specific.

Either way, he would have to thank Kai for replenishing his Energy and Health. He gave the corpse a silent thank-you for becoming his food as he went past it. He was a little worried about what else he might see, and he hesitated to turn the handle of the exit door.

At least I know that Kai is still alive out there . . . wait a second, the pack rules! How much can he actually do against Damion? It's one thing to kill someone to ensure my safety, but how much is he allowed to do once I'm fine again?

He swung the door open into a large room that was splattered with blood. Two guards lay by the door; both had been severely hurt, but Gary heard a faint breath from one of them. He quickly knelt down to check on the gangster.

"Tell me what happened to you . . . was it a blonde-haired boy? Was it Kai? If you tell me, I can save you." Gary bombarded the dying man with questions. His eyes looked weak, and his wounds were still bleeding. Unsure whether he could talk, Gary checked the other person. Unfortunately, he was already dead.

". . . Mon . . . ster . . ." the first man revealed with his last breath. The circumstances spoke for themselves. Although Kai should have been bound by the pack rules, apparently injuring a person so severely that they were close to death wasn't out of the question, and letting them bleed out didn't seem to be a problem either.

Damn it. It looks like the pack rules are not as loophole-free as I had hoped . . . What have I done? As angry as he is . . . What happens if he becomes another Billy? Shit, I don't want to have to kill him . . . Gary ran toward the noise.

He soon realized he was in an abandoned building that used to be a police station, though in hindsight the cell should have been a big hint. There didn't seem to be many guards, which seemed a little strange. He had expected Damion to have brought the remaining members of the Underdogs here, if only to make sure that he wouldn't escape.

Soon, though, Gary heard groaning and a few loud bangs here and there.

Please, let me not be too late . . . he silently prayed.

When he turned the corner, he saw a woman standing in the large reception hall, just by the double-door entrance. She was surrounded by four people, each one armed with Anti-Altered weapons, and two more lay on the ground, seemingly knocked out.

"Screw it, even more of yo— Oh, it's you. That saves me having to look for you." Olivia smiled. "Well, don't just stand there, help me out!"

CHAPTER 38

A TRAINED WOLF

More than a dozen people had appeared in a dimly lit underground parking garage that was filled with black vehicles, all with tinted windows. As if that alone weren't shady enough, each person had a large black sports bag in their hand or strapped on their back, large enough to hold a pair of skis.

Of course, these men weren't just a normal group of enthusiastic skiers, but the inner circle of the Underdogs. The contents of their bags were priceless for any normal salaried worker, which was just another reason to keep them hidden from public eyes. The men were following behind Damion, who angrily paced toward the cars.

Why does it seem that all my problems started after I agreed to smuggle that damn package? Ever since it went missing, I've been haunted by problems. Since Greeny took out Kirk, I couldn't even be happy about doing in Brandon. I just hope that NIRV guy really makes it worth our while for capturing that traitor and takes his sweet time extracting his Altered DNA.

And now we have more problems. Someone has attacked every single one of the Underdog hideouts. Some of them were being used to store Anti-Altered equipment.

Who leaked the information?

Thinking about his prisoner, Damion suddenly stopped, reminded of the other traitor. He had always been wary of a rat appearing in their midst, but learning that it was his own flesh and blood had stung more than he had ever been prepared for. Part of him didn't want to believe it, but in hindsight it made sense, especially how the Pincers had managed to pinpoint every single Underdogs operation after that night.

Well, with this group and our weapons, we should be able to take on any of them that come our way. Then I'll bring back every one of those damn Howlers that he thought were his allies, and force them to fight to the death for their freedom, including that damned brat of mine!

When Damion finally reached his car, he let out a bloodcurdling scream. Only those in his inner circle were privy to the location of this safe house, yet someone had managed to sneak in and slash all of his tires.

This is a private complex, no one should be in he—

Damion's thoughts were interrupted by something crashing down on top of the car. One of his trusted men pushed him to the side, just as he suffered a large impact to the side of his head. It was a strong kick that sent him falling into the car parked next to his.

His head hit the windshield and smashed the glass to pieces before he fell to the ground. He wasn't going to be getting up any time soon, but his shallow breathing was a sign that he had at least survived.

Two more guards pulled him back and out of the way as the third one tried to intercept the enemy. But they were struck by a strange circular device; when it made contact, it opened up and hooked four sharp points into their skin, then sent a strong electric current through their bodies, like a stun gun, and they collapsed onto the ground.

It was worth waiting in the ceiling for the perfect time, Kai thought as he crouched on the hood of the car, using his newfound strength and claws.

Unfortunately, he had been unable to use the element of surprise. Both times, Damion had been surrounded by his men. It was as if there was a force field around him, that protected him from attack.

Kai thought fast and changed his targets to those next to him, taking them out ousing the Anti-Altered equipment he had obtained.

The sound of something swinging through the air caught Kai's attention, and quickly he rolled away from the strike, allowing the batlike weapon to smash a large dent in the hood.

That's not an ordinary weapon. It must give him super strength, or it has some strange technology I don't understand, Kai mused. He climbed back onto the hood of the car using one hand, and leapt into the air with his legs in front of him, kicking his attacker right in the face and sending him flying.

Meanwhile another gangster with a crossbow fired at Kai; he quickly leapt back, allowing three arrows to miss him, and he was now on the roof of the car.

Kai had trained nonstop since the day he lost his mother, and he was thankful for that. He had then put himself in real fighting situations since starting the Howlers with Gary. With his new body, he had reached a potential he had never thought possible.

But now he faced nearly a dozen remaining gang members, all with Anti-Altered weapons. Sure, they couldn't use the weapons properly like the Altered Hunters, but they were strong weapons nonetheless. Strong enough to have captured Gary.

"It appears that there is actually more of me in you than I ever thought," Damion said with a smile as he took out his axes. "You were born to rise to the top and take whatever you want for yourself . . . even if you have to take out your old man!"

"The last part is the only thing you got right!" Kai shouted, his heart rate soaring. He had expected his father to have any number of emotions, whether scared, worried, or angry, yet for him to feel pleased about Kai trying to take revenge just made him boil with anger.

His forearms grew slightly as they bulged, so wide that they ripped his clothing. Now clawed hands covered in gray fur appeared, along with his fierce blue glowing eyes.

CHAPTER 39

CLEVER WOLF

If Kai had known beforehand how much the process of being turned into a werewolf would hurt, he might have been far less eager to go through with it. He was no stranger to pain, but even if he added up every single painful experience throughout his life, it would still pale in comparison to the change that had started after Gary's Alpha Bite.

After what felt like multiple lifetimes, the pain had eventually subsided, only to be replaced by an overwhelming sense of hunger. His stomach was growling in protest, demanding to be filled as it started to emanate an entirely different kind of pain. Fortunately, his nose informed him that a source of food was already nearby.

Without losing a moment to think about it, Kai bent the metal bars of the cell that had held the two teenagers and followed the scent. Behind the door, one lone Underdogs member was busy staring at his phone. The moment he looked up, Kai was already in front of him, using one hand to claw at his chest while holding his mouth shut with the other. The man died without being able to let out more than a whimper.

Then Kai feasted. Before he even realized what he had done, the body providing his meal had lost both its arms. Now satisfied, he felt compelled to make sure that Gary was taken care of, yet he could feel that this was more than just his own thoughts. Nevertheless, he did what he felt was right and fed the werewolf with the corpse's extremities.

Part of him was surprised to see that Gary managed to eat it in his clearly unconscious state. The moment Kai held a leg in front of Gary's mouth, he chomped down on it, and it disappeared as if the alpha werewolf's mouth had been a black hole.

Kai briefly wondered whether this was a normal reaction a conditioned response due to the bloody smell, which he himself found appetizing now. Still, he knew that he should not waste time here. He freed his friend from the chains, not forgetting to pick up his mother's knife.

As Kai made his way out of the abandoned police station, the Underdogs who tried to stop him became his unwilling test subjects, allowing him to get more used to his new body. Things that had taken Gary weeks to learn, Kai had picked up on in around an hour.

Kai had to admit that this kind of body was amazing. Were it not for the gruesome torturelike transformation that had made him wish for death more than once, he might even be mad at Gary for not having turned all the Howlers ages ago. Ever since the day his mother and Simon had died, Kai had trained his body to the best of its capabilities, yet . . . now he could easily surpass his former limits without even trying.

Unfortunately, not everything was great. For one, he found out that something prevented him from using outright lethal attacks against the gang members . . . though it didn't take him long to find a way around it.

Kai also quickly discovered that the more enraged he became, the more his body changed in turn. There was an easy trigger that would always make him angry, and that was remembering the scene that haunted his nightmares . . . the last moments of Eleanor Hamper's life.

"Use your weapons against the Altered!" one of the men shouted as he fired bolts from his crossbow. With his enhanced vision, Kai was able to avoid both bolts as he darted from right to left.

The other crossbows were firing three bolts. That number seems to be their limit, so there should be at least one more before I get a break, Kai thought as he analyzed the situation.

The next second, he saw the third bolt coming toward him as the man started reloading. Seeing this as an opportunity, Kai focused on his legs, and suddenly his shoes ripped apart as long nails appeared.

Spinning his body, the werewolf kicked the shaft of the bolt, knocking it off course and into another person who was approaching him with a strange orb-looking weapon with a rounded end. It looked a bit like a spear, but Kai wasn't willing to find out what would happen if he touched it.

The man was electrified by the bolt that pierced his chest, and he fell to the ground.

Seriously, Gary, it feels unfair that you kept this to yourself all this time, Kai thought, happy to be able to accomplish things with his body he previously would only have been able to dream about.

"Were you just playing with me, so I would throw you in with your buddy?" Damion asked, now holding both axes in his hands, the smile gone. "I don't know how you did it, unless . . . Were you behind this whole thing in the first place? Did you pay off Greeny to bring you the package? Shit, if I had known that there was enough stuff in it to turn more than one person, I would have used it on myself!"

The possibility of one Altered turning others into Altered was unheard of.

"You know, when I gave you one of these axes, I did it because I considered you to have come one step closer to succeeding me as the leader of the Underdogs. I didn't think I would have to use them to take you out. Oh well . . . I bet if I hand two of you over, my reward will be even greater."

While his father was rambling, the other gang members got in formation and surrounded Kai. At the front of the circle, they held out their large Anti-Altered weapons with the sparks on the end.

A couple of the Underdogs now stood on top of cars, pointing their crossbows toward him; between the cars stood more Underdogs with swords, clubs, and spiked weapons.

Nevertheless, the one he was most looking out for was none other than Damion himself.

Am I overconfident after learning of my powers? No, I can still do this, Kai thought as one of his opponents thrust his spear forward.

Kai kicked the head of the spear. The weight and power of the kick caused the weapon to crash into the others, but the second the werewolf's foot touched the end, his whole body experienced an electric shock going through it.

Damn it, these Anti-Altered weapons are proving to be perfect to handle Werewolves as well.

Another weapon prodded him in the back, and the shock traveled throughout his body. In anger, Kai grabbed the spear end behind him and lifted it with all his strength; the Underdog was also lifted into the air before being swung around and crashing into the others.

Now that Kai had one of the Anti-Altered weapons, he was going to use it against the others, until he felt himself being struck in the side by three bolts at once. The shock was larger this time, and the fur on his arms reverted slightly, as he was losing strength.

Damn it, who gave them access to so many of these nasty weapons?

"Stop hiding behind your men! Why don't you fight me on your own, you coward?" Kai shouted toward his father, who had yet to do anything.

"Do you think it's fair for a normal human like me to go up against an Altered like you?" Damion shouted back, shaking his head. In the meantime, a few more bolts were shot toward Kai, but something wrapped around them in midair before retracting back like a toad's tongue.

The bolts fell to the ground with a loud clang. Turning their heads, the Underdogs members saw two figures running toward them. Leaping into the air, they landed right in front of Kai.

"Gary . . . Olivia." Kai uttered their names, unsure what else to say. He was curious to find out how they had found his exact location, since he had only told Olivia the address of the abandoned police station, but that question would have to wait for later.

Gary pulled the bolts out of Kai's body, allowing him to heal a bit. "Looks like I'm not the only one who rushes head-on into things without asking for backup."

Smiling, Gary stood up and looked at Damion, who seemed to be thrumming with anger.

"I don't think this many against one person is fair, either," Gary stated. "You know, Damion, I don't think you're fully aware of what you're dealing with."

Damion scoffed. "Do you really think it matters how many of you losers show up? Even if all three of you were Altered, it wouldn't make a difference."

Now it was Gary's turn to smirk. "You might be right . . . if we were your everyday Altered, that is. There is something you should know about us wolves, we always hunt in packs!"

Skill activated: Full Transformation
-20 Energy
Transformation has begun

CHAPTER 40

HOWLING FORCE

The three of them stood side by side, tall and strong, their presence making all the Underdogs members unconsciously take a step back. After all, what they were staring at wasn't three humans, but three literal beasts.

Now that Kai was no longer being attacked, he was able to focus his anger once again, allowing his arms and legs to be covered in fur once more. Strangely, this time even the side of his face was turning hairy, going down toward his chin.

Then there was Olivia. Only part of her body had changed to show off her black fur, and her forearms were smaller compared to Kai's, yet her fingernails seemed longer and were sticking out more. Gary was unsure whether this difference was because Olivia was a female werewolf, or if it had to do with her being a Hunter-class werewolf.

Meanwhile, he himself was undoubtedly the biggest threat to the gang members. While the other two had only partially transformed, he had used Full Transformation to completely turn into a werewolf.

"Three Altered, all the same type. What is going on?" one of the men cried out in panic.

"Who cares!" Damion shouted. "We have the weapons to fight them! Just think of the rewards we will get once we hand over all three of them!"

The first one to make a move amid all the chaos wasn't Damion or any of his remaining men; it was none other than Gary, who was proving that although he was big, he was faster than any of them.

The alpha werewolf ran straight toward one of the Underdogs who was wielding an Anti-Altered spear. Before the gangster could use his weapon, he felt a stinging pain in his neck, then a warm liquid dripping down, before he fell to the ground dead.

Following his instinct, Gary licked the blood off his claw while looking at the gang members. Ironically, the Underdogs weren't the only ones whose fear this type of action had invoked. Kai had never thought he'd see this side of the teenager . . .

Not too long ago, Gary had chanced upon Olivia in the abandoned police station. With the two of them working together, it had proven relatively easy to defeat the remaining guards. The Lady Boss had then told him what had happened while he had been out.

A team of Pincers, along with the other Howlers members, had raided the few hideouts the Underdogs had left. At each place a token force of members had been left, and the invaders were getting rid of them one by one.

Kai knew this would catch the personal attention of his father, so he had asked Olivia in person to come at the right time and break them out, unless he contacted her. This had been Kai's plan B, in case his plan A of being turned had not been feasible.

"Then we have to go and save Kai! He will definitely be after Damion now!" Gary insisted once Olivia was done speaking. "Kai is one of us now, but he won't be able to take them on his own! We can't let him make the same mistake I did."

"You think I don't know that? Seriously, both of you need to sit down and talk this shit out once all of this is over. I'm aware that each of us is stronger than the average person, but neither one of you was thinking straight when you decided to take on an entire gang by yourselves.

"Look, I'll have to follow whatever you say anyway since you're the boss, but let me give you a word of warning. If you want us to save your buddy, you'll have to fight to the death. Remember when you went into the Pincers gang? Everyone there was ready to kill you, including me; the only problem was we just couldn't.

"It's going to be the same this time, only they seem to have the means we lacked. You were lucky that Kai's suicidal plan actually worked but don't think you'll get a third chance if we lose.

"This fight will be all-or-nothing, so you'll need to fight without holding anything back and allow me to do the same. If you don't, there's a good chance that all three of us will end up dead. Do you understand what I'm saying? You have to be prepared to kill everyone!"

Gary gritted his teeth; he hadn't killed any of the Underdogs members they had run into so far, and neither had Olivia, though in her case it was more than likely due to the pack rules. He wanted to avoid going on a killing spree, but it didn't really seem like he had much of a choice.

Unfortunately, he recognized the truth in her words. The alpha werewolf would have to steel his resolve. He hoped that by the time they reached the end of Damion's Mark, he would be ready to do what needed to be done.

The Underdogs' moment of fear after seeing their fellow member killed soon gave way to the realization that if they did nothing, they would end up as corpses too. So they sprinted into action and thrust their spears toward Gary. Once again, something quickly wrapped itself around each shaft.

The gangsters were yanked onto the ground, and Olivia kicked one of the men right in the face.

"It looks like you made your decision. You're becoming more of a person I can follow," Olivia said with a wicked smile.

Not answering her, Gary picked up the dead body and hurled it toward the gang members before running back to Kai and Olivia, who were repositioning themselves. He easily grabbed his friends and leapt over the remaining gangsters.

Gary had more strength and speed than the two of them combined, because he was a higher-grade werewolf.

"Gary, what are you doing? We can't risk letting him get away! We need to finish him off here and now!" Kai protested.

"I know," Gary growled in response, setting Kai and Olivia down and turning around. Now they were no longer surrounded. They stood on one side of the garage, blocking the exit, while Damion and the others stood next to the vehicles in the center.

"We will finish it here."

The gangsters couldn't understand him, because his speech was full of growls and only the vowel sounds were clear, but both Olivia and Kai understood. Immediately he opened up the system; it was time for him to use everything he had.

First, Gary selected the Pack tab, where Olivia's name was listed. As a Hunter-class Werewolf, she had fifteen Marks available, and as the alpha werewolf he was able to assign them. He used this ability to mark every still-living member of the Underdogs.

The second this was done, Olivia felt her Energy increase. She could see the scents in the air around their targets, and the blue color in her eyes shone stronger than before.

This was an effect of being in the Hunter Class, and on top of that, Gary would gain additional Exp for every target that Olivia successfully hunted.

There was one more thing, Gary needed to change.

The pack rules have been amended.

"Kai, go take care of Damion while Olivia and I take care of the others. If you need help, don't hesitate. After today, there won't be any Underdogs left!"

Opening his maw wide, he let out a large, piercing howl.

Skill activated: Howling Force

CHAPTER 41

THREE BAD WOLVES

The Underdogs immediately got into position, once again using the cars as a higher vantage point and firing toward the three. However, Olivia's presence made their resistance futile. The female werewolf swung her whip with incredible speed, snapping the bolts in two.

"Just take them out, while I make sure none of those things pierce your ass!" Olivia instructed Gary.

The alpha werewolf gladly accepted her support. He charged forward and grabbed the ends of two of the Anti-Altered spears. He pulled the men forward, causing them to fall on the ground and enabling Olivia to run straight past them.

Several bolts shot toward her, but she evaded them by running in a zigzag pattern, using her whip to intercept any that got close.

This is amazing! My body is even faster than it was just moments ago, and there's a new energy inside me. Every time I'm around that brat, he pulls out something that defies common logic. Who would have thought a howl could increase not only my strength but also my speed . . . this power is really addictive!

Throwing out her whip, she wrapped it around one of the Anti-Altered crossbows, stopping it from firing another bolt. The gangster held on tight, aware that the weapon was his only safety net. If he let go, he was sure that it would be the end of him.

The other gangster, perched on the hood of a different car, aimed carefully and attempted to fire toward Olivia, but she used her great strength to pull the first man toward her and quickly stabbed him in his gut with her free hand. As he bled out, she held him in place as her human shield.

Unfortunately for him, the bolts had already been fired, hitting the injured gangster and sending electricity throughout his body. Before it could reach Olivia, she quickly let go of him, making him fall to the ground, spasming.

"That was cute, you trying to hit me with those bolts and all," the Lady Boss said with an evil smile as she lunged toward her next victim.

Meanwhile, on the ground, Gary was causing havoc as well. He was batting the spears away with his claws, unafraid of the Anti-Altered weapons.

Gary's strength was clearly superior against their uplifted swords, and they were unable to do anything about it. Alas, he wasn't able to finish them off, as someone would always be there to cover them, allowing them to come back up and fight again.

I'm being more careful because of what happened last time, and thanks to Olivia I don't need to deal with those annoying deranged losers. Argh, I can't believe I let these guys capture me. They're a far cry from Blake! If only I hadn't gone in alone, Gary thought, ducking under another sword strike and going down on all fours.

He pounced forward with all his strength, hitting the man right in the chest and sending him flying back into another.

"Do your part, Kai!" Gary shouted. He only cared about taking Damion out so that he no longer posed any danger to himself or his family. After Kai shared his story about why he hated the gang leader, Gary didn't think it would be fair to rob him of the opportunity to get revenge.

"Just what went wrong in your upbringing for you to defy your own father to this degree?" Damion said as he watched the situation unfolding behind Kai.

"You mean the upbringing you were never there for? We both know that I've always just been your replacement son. If Simon hadn't died, you would never have even given me the time of the day. Even then, all you've ever taught me is how to take care of the gang business and fight!" Kai shouted as he lunged at his father.

Damion stayed still and swung one of his red axes straight toward Kai's head. The werewolf was barely able to react and leaned back slightly, but he also fell off balance. The second axe was already in the air; he quickly rolled to the side before it hit the ground, creating a huge crack.

His strength and speed with those axes is no joke, even in my werewolf form, Kai thought, taking a few steps back.

"You're a monster, you didn't even hesitate in either of those attacks!" Kai shouted.

"Are you really calling *me* a monster right now? Have you even looked at yourself in the mirror?" Damion sneered. "Did you expect me to just stand still and let you finish me off? When your life's on the line, nothing matters, not even family relationships. The moment you decided to try to take my life, you became just another guy who I will happily skin with my axes!"

With that, Damion threw one of his axes at Kai with all his strength. It spun through the air at a speed he felt unable to dodge. Left with no other choice, he crossed his arms in front of his chest to avoid a fatal injury.

The beta werewolf had a strong hide, but the axe managed to pierce deeply into one of his arms. He looked up and saw that while he had been focused on the flying weapon, his father had closed the distance between them and was right in front of him, ready to chop down with the other axe on the teenager's head.

I can't keep running away . . . that won't work! Kai realized as he twisted his leg and kicked out as hard as he could. His foot hit the handle of the axe, stopping the bladed part from reaching his body.

The foot and axe were seemingly locked in a battle of strength in the air, yet Damion surprised Kai once more by unceremoniously letting go of the axe, then delivering a punch to Kai's guts. Fortunately, his werewolf body had strengthened his overall constitution, allowing him to avoid falling over, but it still hurt greatly.

Although Damion had hoped that his attack would be more effective, he quickly switched strategies once more, pulling out the axe that had been embedded in his son's arm. Kai threw out another kick, but Damion slammed his axe right into the teenager's shin, making him howl in pain; the head of the axe had not just gone through his hide but had struck bone as well.

This time, rather than leaving the axe in, Damion pulled it out and jumped back, picking up his other axe off the ground.

"For a second there, you almost scared me with this new form of yours, but you are still just a brat!" Damion shouted, charging in and swinging his axes at great speed.

Kai was left on the defensive, unable to find an opportunity to retaliate. Worst of all, he could tell that his situation was getting progressively worse. *Are his attacks getting faster with each swing?*

Alas, it wasn't just his imagination. His father was getting a thrill, a boost, out of the fight, which allowed him to draw out more power from the weapons. Soon Kai couldn't avoid the blows from the weapons at all, and the wounds covered his body. Blood was dripping to the ground, and the more Kai was hit, the weaker he felt.

Think . . . there has to be some way for me to turn this around. I trained for years just to get revenge, and I'm even a fricking werewolf right now! How is it possible that I still *can't beat him?! This isn't fair . . . no, I will make sure you die tonight, even if I have to accompany you!* Kai thought in frustration, looking for a chance to use all his remaining power to take his father down with him.

"Is this really the power of an Altered? I could beat you even without my weapons!" Damion taunted, having noticed the change in Kai's eyes. He had been doing his job long enough to recognize the kind of stare he was getting. A cornered rat always tried its hardest to get one final bite in, trying to inflict the greatest amount of damage against its attacker, even if it knew that the attempt would be feeble and pointless.

Since it was clear that his son was about to throw out all caution, he feigned an obvious opening so he could exploit the senseless charge that was sure to follow. Raising both axes in the air, he prepared to deliver a fatal blow.

As his weapons reached the top of their arc and he started to swing downward, he felt them get stuck in place.

Turning his head, he saw a large werewolf holding on to both axes, and behind him, all of the Underdog members had been defeated.

"Let's find out if you really are so great without those."

CHAPTER 42

HOLLOW

I'm glad she's on our side. It's seriously frightening how effective Olivia's Hunter Class is when fighting marked enemies, Gary thought as he watched the female werewolf take care of yet another member of the Underdogs.

He would have liked to take credit for defeating the group, if only to repay them for capturing him earlier, but with the power boost Olivia had received from the marks and his Howling Force, she was making short work of them. Well, he didn't mind, especially since he had discovered that it was smarter to let her do the dirty work, as he received more Exp this way.

What's more, all of them had already given him ample Exp, though he wasn't sure if that was due to the marks or if the Underdogs were considered "elite" enemies, seeing as they had Anti-Altered weapons. Whatever the case, with the last one down, Gary was greeted with another notification.

Congratulations, you have now reached: Level 20
A stat point has been granted

The alpha werewolf would be lying if he claimed not to be at least slightly disappointed by Level 20 being this lackluster. Granted, he already knew that Level 25 had a juicy reward waiting for him, one that was a lot more substantial, but if he ever got the chance to talk to whoever had designed this Werewolf System, he would make sure to complain about these milestones not being epic enough.

After his level-up, he noticed that Kai was visibly struggling against Damion, so he hurried over.

His extra speed boost since defeating and consuming Kirk gave him a great edge, and since then he had thought it best to use his stat points elsewhere, such as on Energy and Health. However, because of the situation, and worried that his Strength might not be enough, Gary placed both stat points into Strength.

2 points have been allocated into Strength
Your base Strength is now at 25

Reaching out, Gary grabbed the axes, and his grip was so strong that no matter how much Damion tried to pull, he couldn't budge.

How . . . how could my men lose against just two of them with all of those Anti-Altered weapons? Damion wondered. *I've heard that Greeny defeated Kirk, but it should have only been by a small margin . . . Just what kind of special Altered DNA was in that package that could have allowed him to become even stronger in such a short amount of time?*

Damion was ready to let go of the two axes, but just as he did in his attempt to turn around, his legs were wrapped by Olivia's whip. Then a heavy foot kicked him in the chest, and now both of the axes were in Gary's hand.

Full Transformation canceled

Slowly Gary started to shrink as he reverted to human form. The clothes he wore had ripped, though by sheer wonder his lower body was covered enough to not show off his manhood.

"Don't transform so much, it takes up too much Energy," Gary advised, looking toward Kai.

Hearing this, Kai decided to cancel the transformation in his arms. He had to focus for a bit, but he was able to keep the transformation at bay. Gary was flabbergasted at how fast Kai was adapting to his new body, which made him feel like an idiot for taking much longer in comparison. With Olivia getting stronger as well, the alpha werewolf knew that he would have to work twice as hard to make sure he could continue being the alpha with pride.

Damion was getting up off the ground, and he immediately threw a kick toward Gary, which the alpha werewolf evaded by moving to the side.

"Your fight is not with me!" Gary shouted.

It was then that Damion saw a leg heading straight for his face; he lifted his forearms and blocked the attack, but he fell and slid across the ground.

"Now, don't you think this is unfair, three against one?" Damion argued.

"Since when is any of this fair?" Gary retorted. "Besides, I don't need to get involved."

Kai was feeling a little drained as his body healed his injuries; he had lost blood as well, but he was determined, gritting his teeth, and with his eyes still like those of a wolf, he was determined to finish his father off.

He dashed forward and went for another kick. Even without his weapons, Damion was still able to lean back and avoid it, However, the first kick was never intended to hit Damion; it was just to help build up momentum.

As it landed, Kai spun his body, throwing out his other leg into a spinning back kick, and the heel of his large foot hit Damion right in the jaw. With a loud crack, the gang leader's face swung to the side.

"I'm not done!" Kai shouted, punching toward his father with his transformed hands. Once again, Damion lifted his hands to protect himself, but Kai's claws ripped through his skin, splattering blood on the floor.

"Why . . . why did you have to do that to Mom?" Kai screamed at the man underneath him as he continued cutting skin and flesh away like a grater.

"What are you on about?" Damion shouted back, dropping his hands in anger and frustration about being unable to fight back. Just as Kai had done earlier, he switched to a more suicidal approach and tried to headbutt his son. "You were the one who called me over in the first place! If she could kill Simon, then that means she could have killed you t—"

Damion didn't get to finish speaking, as Kai had met him head on. A werewolf's skull proved to be far more durable than a human one, and while he was still disoriented, the teenager slit his throat.

"You're a foolish idiot who let Simon do whatever he wanted! If you had only reined him in earlier, none of us would have been there that day! The only reason she killed him was to protect me . . . you could never see what he was. He was betraying the Underdogs right in front of you, and you still never saw it."

Damion collapsed to the ground seconds later, as Kai stepped out of the way. His father had finally died; his ambition, his long-awaited revenge was complete . . . Yet as he looked at the lifeless body, the sense of accomplishment he had been hoping for did not come.

"Why does it still feel so heavy?" Kai asked, touching his chest, looking at the corpse, which could not give him an answer to that question. Unfortunately, neither could Gary; nor could Olivia, who didn't feel like it was her place to meddle in that complicated relationship.

"Don't worry, you have a new family now," Gary said, putting his hand on the other teenager's shoulder . . . but the moment was interrupted by a ping from his system.

CHAPTER 43

FLAWLESS HUNT

In the middle of this chaotic mess, Gary's system still managed to surprise him.

Secret achievement unlocked: Flawless Hunt
Whether through luck or strategy, your pack managed to pull through and successfully finish its first hunt without suffering any casualties!
Reward: 10 Pawn points (use at your own discretion)

The green-haired teenager only knew of a few ways to receive Pawn points, the most reliable ones being to either turn someone into a werewolf or kill them after they had become one. So far, certain quests had also rewarded him with Pawn points, but the most he had ever gotten was the one Knight point he had received for consuming Kirk. With this generous reward, Gary had effectively doubled his total overall count.

"Secret achievement," huh? I got one a while ago for defeating that color gang, but last time the reward was merely Exp, so why is the system being so generous now . . . and what does it mean by "use at your own discretion"?

It's not enough for me to increase my grade once more, so should I convert it to stat or skill points? Or does the system want me to turn and evolve the others?

As he looked through the system screen, Gary saw that Kai was still standing there looking down at Damion, seemingly in a trance.

Now is not the time to be worrying about system things.

"You did it, Kai, you defeated your father! With him gone, Slough will no longer be under the thumb of the Underdogs!" Gary said, trying to cheer up his friend. "Finally I won't have to worry about my family . . . so thank you, Kai."

The words *thank you* managed to snap Kai out of his deep thoughts. He let out a sigh, aware of how he would have fared without the intervention of his fellow werewolves.

"Please, we both know that he was kicking my ass while he was holding on to his axes. This wasn't how I imagined things going down, especially after I forced you to turn me . . . sorry for that. Anyway, you shouldn't thank me; I should be the one thanking you for coming here in time and saving me, not once but twice . . . and also for letting me be the one to end that piece of shit.

"Olivia, I also want to thank you for keeping those guys busy in the meantime."

"Sure, sure, not like I had much of a choice. Speaking of them, what are we going to do? I can sense that a few of them are just pretending to be down, or are unconscious. Do you want me to finish these other guys off?" Olivia asked, since some of them were still breathing, but their legs had been injured so severely that they could no longer move.

"We'll call the police and let them deal with the rest. Without Damion the gang has already fallen apart; there isn't much for us to do in terms of the Underdogs. However, Slough is a different story," Kai replied tonelessly. Usually he might have advocated for a more secure ending for them all, but he felt that too much blood had already been shed today.

"Your family might be safe, Gary, but Slough isn't. The Underdogs were doing someone else's bidding; that's how you became a Werewolf, and that's how someone like Kirk was even with the Underdogs in the first place.

"Right now, we have to focus on getting control of Slough before anyone else swoops in and takes the glory for all of our hard work. Damion was trying to meet someone, probably whoever gave him all those Anti-Altered weapons.

"I think it's best if we don't risk them seeing our faces. We have to force them, give them no choice but to come to the next leader of Slough if they want anything done in our town," Kai said, clenching his fist.

Kai's journey felt far from over. He could only hope that his father's death would bring him the result he wanted, which was why he was using his energy to focus on something else. Whether that was the case or not, he was right about all these things.

"I know it doesn't end here," Gary said. "That's why we promised to go to the top. We're in too deep now."

The two smiled at each other once again, but their touching moment was interrupted by the slamming of a car door, just outside the parking garage.

"That can't be the police. There's no way they got wind of this already, and I only just sent them a tip now, that's too fast," Kai said, worried that it might be the people that the Underdogs were planning to meet up with.

"Damion told me that he would have someone extract the Altered DNA from my body, so it's probably them," Gary guessed.

"Or the gang in charge of the Underdogs. Either way, I've had enough killing and risking my life for you brats today," Olivia complained. The Lady Boss then used her whip to pick up a couple of the Anti-Altered weapons as spoils of war before making a run for it, and the two teenagers quickly followed.

Kai looked at Damion's lifeless body a final time as if he expected his father to rise once more, but naturally nothing happened.

I hope you rot in hell with Simon, Kai thought.

A few moments later, a new group of people entered the parking garage. Three of them wore white lab coats, others wore strange armor and were wielding weapons similar to the Anti-Altered weapons still lying around, and some were dressed in suits and sunglasses.

They were an odd assortment of people; that was because these people were the Recoverers.

"Gather information from those who are alive. Let's try to find out what went on here," one of the men in a white lab coat ordered.

He walked over to Damion, and studied the large wound on his neck.

"It looks like the very reason you called us here was the death of you. I bet you started to think you were invincible. It's a shame, really; I would have loved to see what you could have become." The man spoke seemingly to himself.

A short while later, the rest gave their reports about what the survivors had to say: that they had been attacked by three Altered, all of them displaying wolflike features.

"I see." The leader addressed the man in charge of the Recoverers. "Well, make sure no one else learns of this, and it looks like we might be meeting some new business partners soon. Send someone to link up with this city's gang once they're ready."

"Sir, what if they don't wish to do business with us?" the man asked. "After all, if they have three Altered in their midst, they might already have someone else backing them."

"In that case, you're to follow the protocol. If they don't need us, we don't need them either."

CHAPTER 44

HOWLERS RULE

To most students, today was just a regular day, with only a handful actually looking forward to attending. Among them was Tom Green, though just like the majority of students who weren't cursing whoever came up with the idea of school as an institution, his reasons had nothing to do with the classes being taught. No, he was just happy to finally be back in Slough.

His internship at NIRV had come to an end, and he had learned far more than he had ever thought possible, yet all of it was protected under a very restrictive NDA. Keeping all of those secrets was killing him inside, and so he was looking forward to sharing some of them with the one person he knew would never let anything slip. The fact that they both now had such big secrets made Tom feel as if they would finally be on equal footing again.

After his father drove him back to Slough yesterday, Gary was the first person he contacted, inquiring whether everything was all right in his hometown. However, Gary's reply had been lackluster to say the least, as if Slough hadn't been attacked by crazed Altered—an event that had been reported in more places than just the local news.

Before their first class began, they gave each other a giant grin, but they understood that they couldn't risk being overheard talking, so they agreed to have their lunch on the rooftop.

Gary spoke first. He had decided to come clean and tell Tom everything about the gang business now that the Underdogs were no longer a thing. After what had happened between him and Kai, Gary no longer wanted to keep secrets from his oldest friend.

"You've gotta be kidding me! I've been gone for a week, yet you've basically saved the whole town from those crazed Altered, defeated *the* top gang, created two more Billys, who are both working under you, and one of them is *Kai*? You've pretty much gone from local gang leader to head honcho?" Tom's eyes were basically popping out of his sockets. He had to pinch himself multiple times to make sure this wasn't just a dream.

"Man, with this kind of news, you should've let me go first. What I have to say barely holds up to any of those things." Tom sulked, but he decided to spill his guts anyway, and he told Gary everything he had seen, even the minor things he hadn't planned on revealing initially. Just to be safe, he had intentionally left his phone in his locker, on the off chance NIRV might have planted a bug in it.

"So that's how they are able to make Altered? They seriously have a crystal that can bring beasts back to life? Hang on, with how many Altered there are, and with other organizations, does that mean everyone has access to such technology? How is it possible that people can create monsters, but nobody knows anything about it? You think there would be videos or something," Gary wondered out loud.

This train of thought made him curious if Jayden knew about this as well. The AFC was known to work quite closely with NIRV, who sponsored them after all.

"I know, but if you had been there, you would have seen how serious they are about secrecy," Tom said. "Their NDA alone forbids anyone from talking about anything. The scientists are not supposed to talk with each other about their respective projects, and I only found out about this because my dad called in a few favors. Heck, my entire internship was actually some sort of exception they made because he knew the right people. Honestly, if you weren't you, I would have probably taken all of it to my grave."

It was quite amazing, how they each had their own journey, and the more they thought about what the other was doing, the happier they felt about each other.

"You know, I plan to go and work at NIRV," Tom said. "I bet the things I saw were just the tip of the iceberg, and I want to know more about this world. At the same time, I want to help you, Gary. They should know more about what was inside the package that you had to deliver. Perhaps there's even a way to change you back."

"Change me back . . ." Gary repeated. The thought had popped into his head a couple of times, but nowadays, he was content being what he was. The only downside so far was the full moon, but he had a plan for that, and he believed there was a good chance it would work. Well, he would find out in a couple of days . . .

"Anyway, what is the next step for the Big Bad Wolf of Slough?" Tom asked jokingly.

"Please don't call me that." Gary shook his head vehemently. "Besides, I'm about as useful as a CEO who just signs off on everything; Kai and Olivia are the ones who get stuff done. According to Kai, we took over ninety percent of what the Underdogs used to own.

"However, unlike them, we're not extorting businesses. In fact, both of them keep complaining that we are far too nice, to the point where it majorly eats into our profits. Still, for the shop owners it means that rent is low, and we've even given them back their land deeds.

"Unfortunately, the Underdogs seem to have used up most of their money to purchase those Anti-Altered weapons, so there aren't many funds left to make the changes that I wanted in this town, to really make it a safe place.

"At the same time, we have to try to protect it from outsiders. We're going to have to try to get new businesses to move to this town somehow, at least with a promise that we can protect them or give them something in return. With how much stuff there is to do, I'm really happy I have the two of them to help me out."

Tom couldn't help but pat his friend on the back.

"Gary, I've heard that people can change in the face of responsibility, but your change is a bit too drastic, don't you think? You had average grades, were average at sports, yet now here you are, pretty much doing the mayor's job for him. I was gone for such a short time, yet you're all grown up."

Gary playfully punched Tom's arm, though he made sure to hold back. After such a serious talk, the two of them spent the rest of the break actually eating their lunch before they returned to the classroom.

During one of the afternoon lessons, Gary received a text from Kai. The others hadn't come back to school after the infected Altered incident, and Gary was also considering dropping out. As Tom had put it, with his newfound responsibilities, school did not really fit into his schedule.

Meeting at the Wolf's Pool Club. Everyone will be there, important you come today, Gary.

At the same time, a vehicle was leaving the town of Slough. A bulky student was looking back, aware that he would not return here anytime soon . . . if at all.

"You really think that guy will help us?" Gil asked Raven, who was driving the car.

"He's our best shot. Even if the Gray Elephants had not been dissolved, we would not have stood a chance against Damion's crew, yet the Howlers have defeated them. There's nothing for us to do. My stupid brother had a tendency to piss off the wrong people, but it's just my luck that the last person to have seen him alive happens to be a freaking Altered who even defeated Kirk Summerfield."

"What are you planning to do now?" Gil asked. "I mean in case he won't help us?"

"We'll come back, don't worry about that. That information should be worth something to Sin, but even if he won't interfere, we'll just have to make our name somewhere else . . . and when we return, there will be hell to pay." Raven answered, throwing his cigarette out the window as he drove off to start a new life in a Tier 2 city.

CHAPTER 45

A SECOND CHANCE

It had only been a few days since Gary had last visited the Wolf's Pool Club, but so much had changed since then that it felt surreal. Slough's underground world had already been pretty shaken up with the Gray Elephants gone, but now that the Underdogs had also been taken care of, the Howlers had effectively become the top gang in town.

Truth be told, Gary had expected Kai to contact him far sooner, most likely to send him out on a special assignment to force the small-time gangs to accept the new status quo. However, as it turned out, there had been no need for that. The rumors about Damion's defeat at their hands had proven effective enough for the other gangs to keep to themselves so far.

The only thing left to do had been to take care of legal things, and Gary had been well aware that he would be of no help with that, so he had wisely left all of it to Kai.

As the teenager approached the door, he saw a sign saying that the establishment was closed for today. *Is this because of the meeting? I guess with how much we own now, it doesn't matter if the pool club is closed for a few days*, Gary thought.

It was a strange feeling for him. For most of his life, the Dems had lived close to the poverty line, at least after his father had disappeared. Now he indirectly owned multiple establishments. Even just the bits and pieces Kai had scrounged up from his father's old gang had been more than enough for Gary to pay off all their debts, including the bill for his mother's stay in the hospital.

It made him wonder just how many families were stricken with poverty, unable to get a good night's sleep, while gangs were throwing around the type of cash that could solve all of their problems?

Most importantly, what was that money being used for? Purchasing weapons so they could kill each other, take over the loser's territory, enrich themselves, and start all over again? It didn't make any sense, and it was one of the main things that Gary wanted to change.

I still need to come up with something that I can tell Amy. She already knows something is up, and even if she really doesn't ask about it, Mom will surely start questioning how we can suddenly afford to move into a nicer apartment. Where should we move, though? Burnham Street maybe, or perhaps somewhere more central, so Amy can be protected just in case?

It was unlikely that somebody would try to harm his sister, but he didn't want to take any chances. After all, people like Gil were out there. Unfortunately, it had proven impossible to find his former bully's mark. He had moved far enough away that Gary couldn't see the red scent. However, the fact that he was listed in his marks was proof enough that he was still alive somewhere . . .

Gary shook his head as he entered the club. He was happy to find Miss Degrace and White behind the bar. The younger woman certainly looked a lot happier now that she had settled in. Both appeared to be doing some refurbishments to add more things to the bar.

"The others are waiting for you downstairs," Miss Degrace told Gary with a smile on her face. White also shyly waved at him before resuming her work.

Having learned the tragic past of Marie's mother made Gary want to help them out even more, but he was sure that Kai had everything under control. After all, Kai was in charge of the gang's finances, so Gary knew that he would provide everything they needed to lead a decent life.

As he reached the bottom of the stairs, Gary stopped abruptly, his mouth open wide at the drastic changes that had taken place. The storage room with a desk in the corner had turned into a full-fledged office. There were bookshelves at the very back, with a large wooden desk in front. Two large three-seater sofas, with a table in the middle, added to the picture. What's more, the room was filled with little trinkets, most of them in the shape of wolves.

It looked like the office of some eccentric fellow with a wolf fetish, rather than a gang office. The only clues that this was actually the latter were the Howlers sitting on the sofas. Olivia stood next to Kai, who was sitting behind the wooden desk, looking over some paperwork.

"Holy shit, when did you manage to redecorate this whole place?" Gary couldn't help but ask.

"We told you we dropped out of school, remember? What did you think we've been doing all this time?" Innu replied with a satisfied grin on his face.

"Yes, and all of you did a great job, but that's not why we've called Gary over, now is it? Let's go over the official business first, and then you can go toot your own horn, all right?" Kai interrupted, which rained a bit on Innu's parade; he had obviously been about to list all their accomplishments.

Truth be told, seeing their interaction made Gary feel a bit left out. He hadn't seen the others much because of his school life, and when he had wanted to drop by after that, all of them had been busy with other tasks. Funnily, this just strengthened his resolve to drop out of school and focus on the gang business.

"We Howlers might be a big gang now, but that only holds true within Slough. Once news about Damion's defeat at our hands spreads, it will just be a matter of time until other gangs appear and try their luck at getting a piece of the pie or the whole thing. There are also the small-time gangs we have to worry about. So it's best to keep the main base of operations our little secret . . . and what better place than the one that started it all," Kai explained.

Although the big threat was seemingly over, Kai was already thinking several steps ahead. It brought a smile to Gary's face, as his friend looked better than he had on that day.

"It's good to see everyone again, and I'm glad that no one is hurt," Gary said. "In fact, since you're all here, there's something I wanted to share with you. I've decided to quit school so I can spend more time helping out with the gang."

He didn't know what he was expecting, but a room filled with silence certainly wasn't it. The looks on his friends' faces were a mix of concern and worry.

"What is it? Why does it feel like I said something terrible and wrong?"

Innu and Austin were both looking upward, seemingly wishing they could be somewhere else. Kai let out a deep sigh, while Olivia shook her head. Ultimately, Marie was the one who, after fiddling with her hair, answered his question.

"Well . . . you see, that's actually part of the reason we wanted to talk with you. Please don't be angry about this, and just listen to us before you react, all right? We've been talking the last few days . . . and we all agreed that it might be for the best if you don't stay in the gang."

Gary took a step back out of pure shock. Sure, in the past he would have hated the idea of being in a gang, and he had never planned to be in one forever, but with everything that had happened it didn't seem as if he had much of a choice. What's more, he and Kai had created this gang together and they both had agreed to do their best to make it rise to the top, to improve people's lives.

The Howlers could become a gang that was different from the others, one that could act as a modern-day Robin Hood. In the middle of his daze, Gary saw something flying toward him, and he instinctively caught it.

"Stop freaking out and just read it," Kai said. "Hear us out, so that you don't get the wrong idea this time."

He looked at the card that he had just caught and saw a logo that Gary recognized well: the initials *AFA*.

CHAPTER 46

HIDDEN SYSTEM

The Altered Fighting Academy was a place where the most talented Altered trained in order to join the AFC, the Altered Fighting Championship. The first image that came to mind when he saw that card was Xin. The academy was the reason she had left Westbridge. Shaking his head, though, he had to deal with the matter at hand.

"What do you mean? You want me to quit the gang and join the AFA instead?" Gary asked.

"That pretty much sums it up." Austin nodded.

"We all talked about this, and you've already done so much for the gang. Without you, we wouldn't have made it this far, but we should be fine for now. All of us want you to be happy and do your own thing," Marie added, though Gary sensed a hint of sadness when she said it.

"So we thought of a way you could enjoy your life and still help out the Howlers. Tom told me all about how the two of you have been obsessed with the AFC since you were little. Joining it should be a dream come true for you, right? And it's not like you don't have the skills." Innu gave him a wink and a thumbs-up.

"Think about it, once you become a star in the AFC, you'll have a believable story to tell your family about how you earn your money without dragging them into any kind of gang business. you can also find out a lot of information that might help the Howlers continue to grow, since most of your peers will probably be secretly related to the gangs from the other towns and cities.

"And now that we're the local powerhouse, the Howlers can even act as your sponsor and support you. That way, all of us will benefit. Becoming a successful Altered fighter is the perfect way for you to solve your personal problems while helping the gang," Kai explained.

Gary fell silent as he considered the option his friends had presented to him. He had already composed himself to leave Westbridge, and attending the AFA wasn't a bad thing, especially since there was one person he was dying to see. He would just have to tell Tom, yet he had a feeling his best friend would support the idea.

Still, there were a few problems, and Gary clenched his fists as he considered.

"You know, Kai, I'm not exactly a . . . you know, how can I join the AFA?" Gary asked. He remembered when White Rose had tested his blood and confirmed he wasn't an Altered, at least in the traditional sense.

Kai smiled. "You're worrying about the wrong things. Most Altered your age can't even control their transformations until they're properly trained. Those are the ones who need to get their blood tested to prove their Altered status. You, on the other hand, can just transform. Do you seriously think anybody will bother with any other test once they see it?"

Now Gary was picturing himself. Since he knew that he was actually a werewolf, he had only briefly thought about becoming an Altered fighter. Not that he'd had much of a chance to entertain that idea; until recently he had other problems in his life, yet the most problematic ones had already been taken care of.

"Wait, there are still other things. What are you gonna do about those other small-time gangs, Slough's mayor, my sister, and don't forget that there's that thing I need your and Olivia's help with in a few days," Gary argued, looking toward the beta werewolves because it was nearly time for the full moon.

"Let us worry about that," Innu said. "We aren't completely useless without you, Gary. We can handle ourselves. In fact, Olivia brought over some Anti-Altered weapons, and Kai also has something to show us.

"The mayor will be no problem, and honestly I want to say something. You are and always will be the leader of the Howlers in my eyes. Nothing will change that, and if we really need your help, it's not like we can't send someone over to come pick you up."

"Innu's right," Austin added. "We just want you to enjoy your life. Unlike us, you weren't involved in gang business before. We were already planning to live this life, but the same isn't true for you. But you're the Howlers' leader; if you need help and call on us, no matter how big or small we have gotten, you can be sure that we've got your back."

The atmosphere seemed to be the same throughout the room, even for Marie, who had been close to Kai. Gary had saved her when she was kidnapped, though he had ended up saving all their lives after the twins had transformed into abominations.

"We'll look after your sister. We've done a good job so far, and I'm sure she will understand as well. We can get her a new place, and have her under watch," Kai said. "I have a plan for what to do with her so she won't snoop around on her own, and as for the other stuff, it's not like you'll be gone tomorrow. We still have some time for you to show us the way before you go off."

Gary could tell how much thought they had put into this decision, and his eyes started tearing up. The people in front of him were some of the most selfless people he had ever met. He was aware that they must have all know his secret by now; at least they thought they knew everything, and yet none of them were asking him questions, not even about his past with the Underdogs . . . or how he had become what he was.

No, they were all just planning to move forward, and all of them wanted him to do it in a way that would make him happy first and put the gang second.

"Thank you, everyone. If everyone really thinks this way, then how can I say no? I'll join the AFA and become a champion of the AFC in record time!" Gary pumped his fist. "If you guys don't mind, I'd like to talk with Kai and Olivia separately. We'll join you guys for a couple of pool games in a bit."

The others didn't ask questions and simply left the room, leaving the three werewolves to themselves.

"While I'm away, I guess it will be your job to look after them," Gary said as he approached Kai. "I would hate for something to happen to any of you when I'm gone, so I should do everything in my power to at least give you the strength to help them. Heads up; according to Olivia, this might hurt like hell."

Opening the system, Gary selected the beta werewolf and assigned him the Pawn points he needed to advance.

Congratulations, one of your beta werewolves (Kyle Hamper) has been upgraded to Knight grade
You may now select his class
Hidden conditions have been fulfilled, Special Class available

CHAPTER 47

UNIQUE CLASS

Hunter Class
A Werewolf Hunter is fast, agile, and sneaky. He focuses on killing his prey quickly, out of sight and from the shadows. He is able to track his targets from a great distance and has great focus.
Class perks include: More and better marks, improved tracking.

Protector Class
A Werewolf Protector boasts one of the sturdiest bodies of his race. He uses his own body to shield his pack members from any harm, making sure that they will survive.
Class perks include: 1 extra point in Endurance upon each level-up, faster healing.

Warrior Class
A Werewolf Warrior could be considered the vanguard of his pack. He leads his pack into battle with his strength. He has exceptional fighting ability and courage, but it is because of this trait, and his role, that this class boasts the highest fatality rate.
Class perks include: Wide range of skills to select from, large Energy pool

Shapeshifter Class (Optimal)
This Special Class of werewolf is a master of disguise, capable of transforming into various animals, blessed with an innate understanding of his form. His versatility is unmatched, though limited by his Energy.
Class perks include: Various transformations, big Energy pool

Shapeshifter Class has been deemed optimal
Based on the werewolf's traits and special characteristics, a Unique Class will be assigned

Gary was unable to even read through the choices properly before a new notification popped up that the class was already being automatically assigned. In the same moment, Kai began screaming in pain, falling out of his seat onto the floor.

The veins in his neck began to bulge before he felt his muscles contracting and relaxing over and over again. They were tensing up incredibly hard, worse than any cramp he had ever suffered, and not just in one area but all over his body, yet the worst thing was that this excruciating process was accelerating.

Holy shit, Olivia wasn't kidding when she told me it hurt like hell. Should I have given him more of a warning? No, I don't think anything can prepare you for this type of agony. Perhaps I should've prepared something to bite down on? Gary awkwardly watched Kai suffer, unable to help him. Fortunately, it only took a couple of minutes until he received a new message.

Your beta werewolf (Kyle Hamper) has successfully become a Gray Werewolf Shapeshifter

Gary was quite surprised that the Unique Class was still a Werewolf Shapeshifter, merely with the prefix *Gray*, which coincided with Kai's fur color. This, in turn, raised the question whether it had some other effect he wasn't aware of, and if so, what did it mean for him, who was a brown werewolf, or Olivia, who was a black werewolf.

"What . . . what the hell did you do?" Kai asked, his eyes scornful, yet his voice was too weak to convey his anger properly. He had a hand on the table but lacked the energy to stand up. As the pain started to recede, he noticed a change in his body, almost as if it had gotten lighter somehow.

"Hah, you can consider yourself lucky," Olivia said with a certain amount of schadenfreude in her voice. "At least you got a warning, and besides him and me, nobody saw your sorry state. In my case, I thought I was gonna die in the middle of the street . . . and once I got better, my embarrassment made me wish I had died."

Gray werewolves are a rare breed who gain extra strength while in the company of their kin, even those who are not part of their pack. Because of this, gray werewolves are often feared by their own kind, as they tend to come out on top when fighting their own.

Thanks, system. So that means the color of the fur is not just a coincidence. I guess Kai was always meant to be a werewolf; he learned everything more quickly, and now he even has a Unique Class. Oh well . . . I trust Kai, so it should be okay.

From what he had been able to read from the description, Gary guessed that Kai should be able to change into an actual wolf, and probably even other animals. However, just like with Olivia, although the system gave a lot of information about the class, he couldn't see individual things such as skills and stats.

"I'm sorry, I didn't know it would be this bad. However, I promise you that you didn't suffer for nothing. Like I said, I need the two of you to be at the top of your game when I'm gone. I would hate it if you or the others got hurt in my absence," Gary said. "It's hard to explain what I did, but let's just say as the original werewolf there are some things that I can do that you guys can't."

Kai was obviously curious, but he decided not to press Gary for more. If anything, he was more excited to find out what the changes were in his body and what he could do now.

"Tonight," Gary said, having noticed the eager look in his friend's eyes. Perhaps because of the time they had spent in the cell together, he could tell what Kai was thinking.

"We will meet up in the forest tonight, and we can test out some of the new tricks you'll have up your sleeve, all right? On top of that, we also need to talk about what we're going to do the day after tomorrow, so that there won't be three blood-crazed werewolves running around Slough."

"We need to see if we can get through it, and if we can, we need to make a plan for the future. Hopefully, the two of you will be able to replicate what I've planned, and ideally it will work even if we aren't together."

Remembering what had occurred on the night they had met Billy the werewolf, Kai knew the dangers of what could happen. For now, the three of them headed upstairs. Olivia was going her own way and would meet them in the forest later, while Gary and Kai planned to relax and play a couple of games. After all, Gary wouldn't be seeing them as much anymore.

When they reached the top of the stairs, the others were waiting, playing, joking and having a laugh with each other. In fact, Gary even saw Tyler, the former cashier turned driver who was pretty much a member of the Howlers now.

I guess these are the people who've decided to stay around me. I should be fair to them, right? Gary thought.

"Guys!" Gary exclaimed, and everyone in the room turned to look at him. "There's something important I need to tell you all. I'm aware that all of you already know my secret . . . and I'm thankful that none of you have asked me about it. Before I go, I want to set the record straight. I'm not an Altered . . . I'm actually a werewolf."

CHAPTER 48

A STAR PROMOTION

I can't believe I'm actually here, Blake thought as he took in the sight of the few hundred Altered Hunters who had gathered in this secret base today. Up until now, his father had been the only other Altered Hunter he had ever come in contact with.

It hadn't been easy getting here. His father had taken him across the country into some seemingly random no-name Tier 4 town, where they had been picked up by a guide who had then dropped them off in a parking garage. Before leaving, the woman had pressed a button combination so that the elevator had let them out below the supposed basement that went deep underground.

Unsurprisingly, there was barely any light down there. Fortunately, that wasn't an issue for Blake or the others. Everyone in attendance was dressed in full Altered Hunter gear, including masks capable of night vision.

After a quick verification of their identities, father and son had been separated, then led to their respective rows to be among their peers. In Blake's case, this meant joining the seemingly biggest faction of other unranked Altered Hunters, most of whom were around his age.

"I'm sorry to have kept all of you waiting so long," said a middle-aged man with curly hair as he came onto the stage. He was the only one who wasn't wearing a mask, though his black sunglasses appeared to give him the same night vision as the rest of them.

Nobody addressed the oddity of wearing sunglasses underground, especially given their own attire, but also because nobody dared to disrespect the man. Edvard Heimdallr was in his early forties, yet not only did he hold the title of youngest five-star Hunter in their organization, his Altered kill count was in the triple digits, making him a prime candidate to succeed the current leader.

"Now that we're all here, I won't bore you with a long-winded speech. After all, today is not about me, but all about you! Let us honor those among you who have earned a promotion!" Edvard lifted his hands and was met by loud cheers from the audience.

Blake was surprised to see his usually calm and rational father join in the cheering. This was a first for him, and far more emotion than he had ever witnessed during any of his rugby matches.

"As is tradition, I shall start from the highest promotion. Although we don't have any new five-star Hunters joining us today, there are a healthy number of you who will walk away with your fourth star today. I have high hopes for all of you!" Edvard revealed as he began calling out names, including Ozacas Hunt, Blake's father.

Nearly a dozen Hunters climbed onto the stage. They all removed their clothing above the waist, revealing their shoulders marked with three stars. This was a moment of pure joy for them; each one looked forward to what was to come.

From the side, a large man walked in, holding a glowing black stick with a star at the end. The room became completely quiet; only the man's footsteps resounded until he reached the leftmost Altered Hunter.

Without any warning, he pressed the hot metal to their skin, leaving it there for a few seconds before moving on. The sound of searing flesh filled the room. Each Hunter endured the pain with a stoic face, rather than exhibiting extreme joy at becoming four-star Hunters.

It might have seemed like a mere branding, but every star was testimony to their capabilities and proof of their success. In a way, it was everything to them.

Next came the two-star Hunters who had earned their third star, then the one-star Hunters who had earned their second star . . . until it was finally time for the youngsters who would receive their first star today.

"Ah, it is always a pleasure to see our promising youth receive their first branding. It's a rite of passage that all of us have gone through, one that signifies that you've joined our ranks as fully fledged Altered Hunters. Your generation will be the one to succeed us, and I'm looking forward to your future! First up, Blake Hunt!"

Walking up, Blake proudly took off his robe and mask and placed them on a table to the side; he looked at the glowing stick, then turned to the crowd. From here he saw his father standing with his arms crossed. Although Blake couldn't see his facial expression, he was certain that his father was proud of him.

My first star . . . He wondered whether he truly deserved it. After all, the first Altered he had actually killed was Billy, and he had only managed to do so by teaming up with Gary. Just as planned, the police had found the clues that pointed to the Altered Hunters, allowing Blake to take credit for the kill.

Then the news channel had recorded him killing a few of the infected Altered who had attacked Slough, so upon his return Ozacas Hunt had shared the good news with his son that he had earned his first star. While the Altered Hunters didn't exactly approve of Blake acting in such a public manner, there was undeniable proof that he had taken out those Altered, and taking on Billy had also done its part to convince the leaders that Blake was worthy of promotion.

Blake had little time to overthink the situation. He was forced to grit his teeth, unwilling to be the first one to cry out, even though the smell of his sizzling flesh made him want to throw up.

Once everyone had received their branding, everyone on the stage was told to follow Edvard. The man walked to the side of the stage and pushed in a few bricks, which opened up a secret doorway, and the group entered what appeared to be a giant warehouse. It was so enormous that Blake couldn't see the far end of the walls.

"For those who are new, I shall explain," Edvard said. "Everything the Altered Hunters have gathered over the years has been brought here today. Depending on your star ranking, different sections are available to you. Our best weapons and armor are naturally reserved for our best, so take that as a motivation to improve.

"As much as I'd like to outfit all of us to the teeth, we don't have an unlimited supply, and despite our technological advancement, we're unable to forge weapons that are as effective as those of our predecessors. Not to mention, it wouldn't go well if they got into the hands of the wrong people. Anyway, forgive my ramblings; please choose and enjoy your new weapons."

Blake was excited to look at what he could get. Thanks to his father's influence, he had actually used far more advanced weapons than his peers; he was perfectly aware that that was more of a loan from his father, while these weapons would actually be his.

Just as he started to walk to the one-star section, Blake spotted something at the very back. Even beyond the five-star section, something lay inside a glass case.

"What … is that? … I can feel its energy," Blake wondered out loud.

"That, my young friend, is the most ancient but also the most powerful piece of equipment we own." Edvard put his hand on the teenager's shoulder. "According to records, this Red Dragon armor was a gift from the best friend of our founder."

CHAPTER 49

A DANGER TO ALL

Throughout their long history, which dated back for more than a millennium, the secret society had had a lot of different names; *Altered Hunters* was merely the latest one on that list. One of the downsides of modern technology was that it had become impossible for their activities to remain secret, especially since their targets had the status of modern-day celebrities. Thanks to various news channels, in the eyes of the public they were nothing more than modern-day terrorists.

Despite the public outcry, they nevertheless continued their noble mission for the sake of humanity. While times had changed, the Altered Hunters still used the swords, axes, and shields of their predecessors. According to the history books that the Altered Hunters kept, beasts used to roam the world, and to defeat them they used special weapons made from the beasts themselves. In the past these were called *beast weapons*, but today they were largely referred to as *Anti-Altered weapons*.

Thanks to the recorded techniques of their predecessors, the Altered Hunters were trained in the ways to channel the most power out of those ancient weapons. Being able to focus on one's own energy and passing it through the weapon would bring extra benefits to the wielder, usually granting them extra power, beyond that of a professional athlete, which was what allowed them to have even ground with the Altered in the first place.

The better the weapon, the stronger the buffer its wielder would receive. From what Blake had read, some weapons were even imbued with special features, such as enabling the user to ignite the weapon without a source of fire . . . and he was dying to earn one of those in the future.

The armor at the very back, though . . . Blake could instinctively tell that it was a step above everything else lying here. It was complete and there was a dark deep red color to it, with a dragon-scale pattern on different parts of the armor pieces. Just looking at it made him feel invigorated.

"Why is it locked away?" Blake asked. "How many stars would I have to reach to try it on?" There weren't any visible star requirements, so Blake asked, already expecting that the answer would be humiliating.

Edvard chuckled a little at Blake's eagerness, reminded of the time he himself had first laid eyes on it. Amused, he patted Blake's back. This simple action made a deep sound, but unwilling to yield in front of the five-star Hunter, the teenager stopped himself from stumbling, keeping his feet firmly on the ground.

"That is our trump card," Edvard explained. "Although this place is a well-kept secret, and we do our best to make sure there are no spies, we can't rule out the possibility that one day our enemies might find it.

"If it comes to that, White Rose would send all of its forces over, and should they do that . . . I honestly doubt our ability to deal with them. That's why it is of utmost importance that you choose your targets carefully, pick the right weapons, and plan thoroughly before taking on the Altered of your choice. The less attention you garner, the better it will be for your safety, as well as ours."

"Still, some things are inevitable, and in the worst case that armor will be our saving grace. Believe me, I understand your desire perfectly, it has a very alluring call . . . but the rules are clear: it is only to be used in an emergency when our very existence is at risk. So I can't just give it to you.

"Nevertheless, the rules also state that the strongest fighter should be the one to wear it. If you work hard for the group, gain more stars, then you might one day become an existence worthy of protecting us all."

Blake was a little disappointed by the answer, but he hadn't expected much in the first place. He sighed, then decided to use his limited time to search for decent weapons and armor.

There were many, and black was a predominant color choice for the armor. Blake upgraded his set, picking out a few items that matched him most. His fighting style focused on speed, agility, and dexterity, so he needed armor that was not too heavy.

Luckily, everything had already been neatly organized into sections so they could easily pick what suited them.

After that, Blake headed to the weapon section, where he already knew what he wanted: a pair of short swords. They had served him well, though there was another reason for his choice. A pair of dark red blades had managed to catch his eye.

Usually, he wouldn't have picked red since the color was easier to see in the dark, but these were quite the dark tone, and now that he had seen the dragon armor they fascinated him a little. As he studied the hilt of one of the swords, Blake noticed an emblem on the guard.

I've never seen this marking before.

Usually, blacksmiths in the past put a special marking on all the weapons they created. That way, they could make a name for themselves if a famous warrior used their weapons. Many of the items had one, but a shield with two spears in a cross shape behind it was something he had never seen before.

It's a bit weird on a pair of swords, but I like the weight of them. Blake gave them a couple of swings before putting them away, happy to keep them.

When I was fighting Billy, I saw those white lines mentioned in our books . . . if I can find out how I did it, I should rise quickly, Blake thought.

Roughly thirty minutes after they had been let in, everyone was equipped with new gear. While the one-star and two-star Hunters were free to leave, Edvard instructed the three-star Hunters and above to stay, because he had something important to discuss with them.

Inside the base meeting hall was a large round table, but there were no seats. Edvard stood with his hands on the table, while the others waited patiently.

"I trust in the judgment of each one of you, and while working on your own has worked so far, I'm afraid that we have a very serious situation on our hands. There have been multiple reports of something quite concerning as of late," the Altered Hunter leader explained as he pulled out a syringe and placed it on the table.

"I assume some of you have perhaps seen or heard about this 'black liquid.' It is predominantly being passed around in the lower tier towns. It appears to be either a failed experiment or an early prototype for a new Alterification method. Whoever uses it turns into a type of crazed Altered.

"Its usage so far appears to be limited, but unless we do something about it, incidents like the one in Slough may very well start appearing all over the country. My reason for calling you here is that I need you all to make this our number one priority. We need to find out more about this black liquid, starting with its origin. To do that, we're going to have to be more active in the higher-tier cities, which means your jobs will also become more dangerous."

CHAPTER 50

THE AFA

"Thanks for the ride!" Gary said cheerily as he jumped out of the taxicab, taking in his surroundings. The building in front of him was far larger than anything he had ever seen in his life, and this was just a tiny part of the campus.

"Are you serious? Have you ever heard about tipping? Come on, I drove you for three hours!" his driver complained. The teenager's request had sounded absurd, but since he had paid in advance, the cabbie had agreed to drive the teenager all the way here. Still, part of him had done so in the hopes of a nice tip for this inconvenience, especially given that their destination catered to a special type of people: Altered.

"I'm sorry, I paid you all I had on me. Is it okay if I tip you next time?" The teenager cheekily scratched the back of his head. The cabbie had trouble believing him, but there wasn't much he could do. Muttering a few profanities, he drove off.

This little scene had caught the attention of some passersby, who couldn't help but comment on the absurdity of the situation. "Have you ever heard of someone coming to this academy who couldn't afford to tip? That makes no sense; he must just be really stingy."

"Maybe that's why he dyed his hair green, thinking that it might bring him the green," another commented with a smirk, seemingly proud of his clever pun.

Gary had no problem hearing them, even if they were some distance away, but their comments did little to spoil the mood. Once more, he gazed at the large campus building, a place he had never dreamed of seeing in real life. Truth be told, he still had cash on him, and not a small amount. Kai had given him enough to last a year in Slough, but since he had been warned that his stay here might be expensive, he had lied to his driver.

This is it! This is all me from here on out. I don't have anyone to help me or get me out of any trouble I might cause, Gary thought, as he drew a deep breath and took his first steps onto the soil of the academy.

His heart rate was higher than usual, though fortunately enough to show any signs of transforming, but it couldn't be helped. Unlike everyone else who had come here today, he wasn't exactly an Altered, and if that came out, he shuddered to consider the consequences.

Kai said it would be okay, and he's smarter than me, so he should be right, Gary told himself.

The academy was large, and rather than walking straight ahead through the main building, the students followed the signs pointing elsewhere.

Gary closely observed the group he was now part of. A quick head count put them at close to a hundred.

Man, with their fancy clothes and jewelry, they even make Kai look humble. Did they come here to attend the AFA or go to a nightclub to woo some girls? Gary thought as he internally rolled his eyes.

Speaking of girls, about a third of the groups of students were girls, all of them beauties who could easily be models, and perhaps some of them actually were. Gary wondered how "natural" their appearances actually were. No matter their genetics, money could certainly buy them the best skincare routines, the best nutrition growing up, and if all of that didn't work, then there was always plastic surgery.

Most of them probably are the children of rich and powerful parents, or are so talented that they were sponsored by a big, powerful organization. I might be the sole exception to that.

Gary remembered Kai's advice that if anyone asked about his backing, he should say he was sponsored by the Howlers. Apparently that was on his application form as well.

Eventually, the werewolf's eyes rested on a teenager with black hair parted down the middle. He was about as tall as him, and roughly the same age. He was dressed in a normal blue shirt and an inconspicuous black hoodie, which ironically made him stand out even more in the crowd.

Eventually the signs led the students to a large open field. A few campus buildings were visible in different directions, but they were far away. Still, the students knew they were in the right place because three professors were sat at a long table, apparently having waited for them.

The oldest one had an extremely long beard and wore round glasses, and he was the only one to stand up. "As you all should be perfectly aware, the AFA is a competitive place to get into, and we pride ourselves on accepting only the best of the best . . . Unfortunately for you, we don't consider you as such. You were not invited here by our scouts, nor did any of your families or other backers have a big enough influence for us to trial you separately to let you in."

Gary had to suppress a grin when the faces of his peers dropped. This statement had obviously insulted their egos. For people who must have been pampered since birth, it was not easy to swallow being told that they were simply leftovers instead of truly special.

The werewolf was perfectly fine with being called nothing special; he knew that it was the truth, which was why he had come to the AFA trials. The professor held up his hand, spreading all his fingers out, slowly moving it from left to right, as if to make sure that everyone could get a good look.

"Five. Do you know what that number represents? That's how many open places we have this year. Now, don't be too happy about it. There's no guarantee that all of them will be filled by you. In fact, it wouldn't be surprising if all of you fail and get sent back home today.

"Don't forget, we didn't invite you, so you'll have to prove to us that we were wrong!"

"Of course!" Gary shouted back.

Unsurprisingly, the other teenagers gave him strange looks. The professor wasn't really asking them a question. Still, Gary didn't care because he was just too excited to be here.

Surprisingly, the old professor didn't chide him. No, he actually smiled at his antics. "I like your spirit. Let's see if you'll stay this chipper after the test. The first one starts now. Show us what type of Altered you are! If you can't even do that, then there's no reason for us to waste any more time with you!"

CHAPTER 51

TROUBLED TALENT

Gary watched the participants get called out one by one to show off their Altered forms in front of the three men. He was feeling anxious, though less because of the test and more because he was realizing his lack of knowledge about the academy itself.

Gary had known about the AFA's existence in general, but he had never looked into its inner workings. After all, the base requirement for attending had always been to be an Altered, which would have been impossible for the old him. Alas, even after he had turned into a werewolf, he had been too preoccupied with other things to fill that gap in knowledge.

So the only thing he knew about the three judges were their names because they had name plates in front of them. Unfortunately, none rang any bells for him. Aside from not being Altered fighters, he wasn't sure whether they were merely helpers or perhaps renowned professors who had come today to test them.

Every teenager was told to demonstrate their transformation in front of everybody. They were to show off the extent to which they could transform, and how much control they had. All of it was being recorded, and once they were done, they were told to head farther down, where the man with the large belly and muscular arms asked them questions about what type of Altered they were, if they had any special traits, and what their specialty was.

I'm actually quite surprised that most of the people here kinda suck, Gary thought, scratching his head because so far seven teenagers had come up, and none were able to transform. The eighth one was the first to show some potential, though he was able to transform just one hand.

Still, despite the bespectacled man's earlier claim of making them fail outright, those who had been unable to transform were told to take a blood test before getting a chance to talk about their Altered status.

I guess they must also be looking at potential. Some of them may have a rare and powerful Altered form that will grow in the future. But it's not like they're testing our physical capabilities either, Gary thought, as he noticed that the third judge had yet to say anything, seemingly juggling his attention between his notes and the teenagers eager to prove themselves.

Fortunately, not all of them were duds. Eventually, some were able to turn their hands into deadly claws, change their eyes into those of reptiles, sprout wings from their back, and demonstrate other abilities that were clearly inhuman.

Some of these Altered forms look really fascinating and powerful . . . but if that's really as far as they can change, I understand why they didn't get scouted. Still, they were at least lucky enough to get sponsored by a company. I bet those who are unable to transform are mostly kids of rich families from Tier 2 cities or above.

What about Xin . . . I wonder how far she managed to get? With her skills, she might even be joining the AFC for her debut match soon, Gary thought.

"Numba Cardenez, next!" The man in the middle shouted out the name.

The teenager who came forward was the one Gary had noticed earlier; he had looked so out of place with his lack of brand-name clothes. As he walked up, other students whispered snide comments about his clothing, the way he walked, and his posture.

Gary would have loved to slap all their faces. After all, he didn't have the same upbringing as the people around him. He had relatively nice clothes mostly because Kai had picked out his wardrobe for today, and even then he had turned down quite a few items solely because he felt they wouldn't suit him.

Standing in position, Numba clenched his hands and soon a change appeared on his body. It wasn't on his hands, legs, back, or face like the others, but on top of his head. Two large white horns had sprouted.

"Hahaha, what is he, some type of goat Altered!" One of the students pointed and laughed, and a few others joined him.

"Shut up!" Gary couldn't take it any more. He turned around to face the one who had started it. "You guys have yet to go forward and demonstrate that you're any better than those who couldn't transform even part of their bodies! He's better than all of them, so how can you make fun of him?"

Gary wasn't sure what he'd expected when he came here, but watching a group of rich teenagers make fun of somebody certainly wasn't part of it. After experiencing all kinds of things when he was in the Underdogs, and even more after he and Kai created the Howlers, their behavior just seemed . . . so childish. None of them scared him, so Gary wasn't afraid to speak up when someone annoyed him.

"The boy is right." Professor Humfree, the bespectacled man who had been speaking, chimed in. "None of you have earned the right to look down on your peers. You're here simply thanks to your parents or your sponsors, but at the place you're going next, assuming you're among the lucky few, they won't be able to help you. You should be very careful about how you act before you have earned your place in this academy."

After he spoke, everyone settled down a little, and Numba was told to answer the same questions as his predecessors.

"Well then, young man, let's see whether you have the qualifications!" The professor pointed at him, seemingly skipping over others, though Gary didn't mind. Of course, the teenagers that he had told off just moments ago were scowling and staring at him. Unaware that he could hear them, they were whispering about him.

"I tell you right now, I'm going to laugh my head off if he can't transform after all his grandstanding . . . better yet, I hope he's some type of lame herbivore-looking Altered."

Ignoring those hateful comments, Gary casually pulled his sleeves back, unwilling to ruin his clothes. In an instant, he had transformed both arms. The brown fur was coming through his skin, with little parts of it falling off, almost shedding, as a stronger hide appeared. At the same time, his hands became larger, with his fingernails extending into claws.

Gary looked at the three professors. Noticing that he had their full attention, he transformed his teeth next, revealing four large canines, before his eyes narrowed, though without changing their color. He had made sure to stop just before that point.

"Impressive, very impressive; is that the limit of your transformation, or are you able to do more?" Humfree asked.

Gary looked at the other students, who seemed to be taken aback at what had happened so far, but he told the professor a lie.

"That's my limit," Gary answered, then moved to the next professor to answer his questions.

Humfree locked eyes with his colleague and nodded, which prompted Professor Wood to look up Gary's information and mark him as an interesting specimen.

Figures he isn't one of those fancy pants who come here because Mommy and Daddy sponsor them. So he's sponsored by . . . the Howlers? Don't think I've ever heard—no, wait . . . wasn't there a report a while ago about the Howlers?

Doing a quick search, Professor Wood brought up information about Slough, and he learned a few things. For one, the town was now under the control of the Howlers, a gang that had come out of seemingly nowhere. Nevertheless, that wasn't a problem as far as the

AFA was concerned. As long as the kids were powerful enough, the academy didn't care who was behind them.

A new, rising gang, and one from a Tier 3 town. He has a lot of talent, that's for sure, and his Altered form looks vicious to say the least, but I fear that he might run into a lot of trouble if the others find out about his background. Students like him struggle the most in the AFA, especially if they are truly talented.

But Professor Wood also found an article about an Altered facing the rookie champion of the AFC. The article featured video clips of the fight.

As he watched the clips and looked at Gary, a smile crept over the professor's face.

CHAPTER 52

A SECOND CHANCE

After Gary's little display, the testing proceeded without a hitch. Showing off his transformation had been enough to convince the three men that he was an Altered. He wondered what excuse he would have to make if they asked for a blood test, but in the end he was fine, at least for the next couple of weeks.

25 days until the next full moon

At the moment Gary just had a loose plan of claiming that he was sick on the day of the full moon, which would hopefully be enough to allow him to skip classes. He intended to put some more thought into it, but first he would have to actually get in, though judging by the reactions of the three professors, he was sure that he had passed this test.

Gary wasn't bigheaded but he believed that out of all the students, his transformation was the most impressive.

"All right, we've collected all your data now. I will now read out the names of those who are eligible for the next test!" Professor Humfree began, only to be interrupted by one of the teenagers.

"Hang on a moment! This can't be it, right? All you did was find out whether we could transform and what type of Altered we are! Shouldn't there at least be an assessment of our fighting ability? You can't tell me that just because I'm not that great at transforming, I'm necessarily weaker than those who could!"

The professor raised an eyebrow at the student, and strange energy began radiating off him. Behind Humfree was a black fog of darkness, rising by the second. If one took a deep look, one could almost see a pair of eyes as well. Honestly, Gary didn't know if he was just seeing things, but judging from the looks on the others' faces, they could at least feel it.

Following their instincts, many of the students took a step back; only about a dozen remained where they were, including Gary and Numba, whom the werewolf had been keeping an eye on.

"Do you really think that you're in a position to argue about *our* rules after we already graciously allowed you to even show up today? If you don't like it, then you're free to join one of the other academies." Humfree then cleared his throat and began reading the twelve names on the list.

There were groans, tears, sobbing, and anger from the students who had been rejected, some even going so far as to stomp on the ground in frustration. Meanwhile, those whose names had been called also showed a wide mix of emotions, from smiles covering their whole face to tears of joy. For a second, Gary and Numba made eye contact, smiling at each other.

We all passed because we weren't intimidated by the professor just now . . . they seem to really know what they are doing, Gary realized.

"This makes no sense!" the angry student protested once more. He was better dressed than the majority, though with his black hair gelled back and combed over, Gary felt like he was more suited to take part in a film rather than the assessment for an Altered Academy.

"With all due respect, Professor Humfree, I can understand your decision to pick those who could transform, but what about those who couldn't? How is it fair for you to pick them but deny those among us who were able to transform at least part of our body into our Altered form? You have to at least explain why you picked them over us!"

It was true, three out of the twelve students hadn't been able to transform at all, and their Altered status was only confirmed by the blood test. Gary hated to admit it, but the loudmouth had a point.

"Here I thought that *for once* we would go through this assessment without one of you popping up to cause a scene. So do you believe that you're wiser than us, who have been doing this job for more years than you've been alive?" Professor Hai said as he stood up. Given his mean-looking face and bulky build, many of the teenagers took a step back when he suddenly got involved.

"I'm tired of explaining these things to brats like you, but as the saying goes, 'seeing is believing.' Whoever thinks that they deserve this chance more than the ones we've selected, I'm willing to give you that opportunity. All you need to do is beat one of them in a fight."

The students looked at each other; they had never expected to fight each other this early on, at least not until they had been fully admitted into the academy. What's more, those among them who had passed felt nervous, now that they would have to protect their place, while those who had been denied started to become confident.

"Fine!" The kid with gelled black hair stepped forward, throwing his blazer onto the ground, He kicked off his nicely polished shoes and unbuttoned a few of the buttons on his white shirt.

"I want to fight that guy!" He pointed to a short, calm-looking, brown-haired student, one of the three who hadn't been able to transform. For a second, the student looked toward Professor Hai, who just smiled and nodded.

"You want to keep your place, don't you? There's no need for you to hold back; whatever happens in this fight, the academy will make sure that all of it will be taken care of."

The others made some distance for them. Honestly, the sadness and anger from before had turned into excitement for those who had failed. Some of them thought they might still have a chance to prove themselves.

"Let's do this!" the black-haired student shouted, and immediately his hands started to transform, growing to twice their size and forming into pincers.

If that kid wins, there's a good chance all of us will have to fight for our positions, Gary thought.

CHAPTER 53

A DIFFERENT LEVEL

Running forward, the Crab Altered student swung his arm, but the other student ducked underneath and kicked upward at his opponent, who fell to the ground.

The Crab Altered saw a fist coming toward him and blocked the attack with his larger claw. As his opponent's fist landed on the claw, many of the onlookers winced in sympathy.

Rolling to the side and getting up, the Crab Altered expected his attacker to be in pain, but he wasn't where he had left him. Instead, before the challenger realized that his opponent had jumped up, a kick came down, aimed straight at the side of his head.

"Damn it, that was cheap!" the Crab Altered complained; his head hurt, but thanks to his Altered physique he was at least still conscious. Unfortunately for him, he was immediately forced to defend himself from a flurry of punches thudding against the hard casing of his pincers.

What the hell? How is this possible?! Are this guy's hands made of metal or something? They should be broken by now . . . or at least injured; why am I the one suffering all the damage? the teenager thought in frustration.

Eventually, the Crab Altered's pincer broke with a loud crack. A shooting pain ran through his body, and as he dropped his guard, a fist connected with his face, knocking him out.

Wow . . . I wasn't expecting that at all. Gary was amazed. *Still, this makes one thing clear; we weren't just selected by a fluke. He may not be able to transform, but his body is already stronger than a normal person's. Just how strong will he be when he learns to transform?*

"Well, after seeing this fight, does anyone else wish to challenge those we've passed?" Professor Hai asked with a large grin. Around a dozen students hesitantly raised their hands. "In case any of you wanted to be a smartass, you're not allowed to challenge someone who has just fought."

The hands came down. The majority were now disheartened once again. They tried to put themselves in the Crab Altered's shoes, but they couldn't imagine beating the person who had just fought. They could see clearly how strong he was and how fast his movements were.

Shortly before they dispersed, one person raised his hand and walked forward. He had short spiky hair and Gary recognized him immediately; he was the one Gary had shut up because he had made fun of Numba.

I bet he's going to pick a fight with that Numba guy. Well, out of all those who could transform, those horns looked the least impressive, and after seeing what one person who couldn't transform could do . . . Gary wouldn't blame him if the guy challenged Numba. "If only I could fight in his stead, I would love to shut him up without suffering any consequences," he mumbled to himself.

"I pick the green-haired one." The spiky-haired fellow pointed at Gary.

The onlookers began whispering among themselves, obviously as confused as Gary. Out of everyone who had passed, his transformation had been undoubtedly the most vicious and deadly-looking Altered form they had ever seen. Not to mention Gary had been able to transform at the snap of a finger, something only two others had been able to do, yet his transformation had been far more smooth.

The ones who can't transform seem to have something special about them, which is probably why the professors picked them. They might actually be the strongest among us, and even if that guy was the strongest, there's no need to test out the other two. So if that's the case, then I just need to pick the one who stood out the most, since he should be the weakest! That was the student's train of thought, but he also had another, more personal reason to pick Gary.

Besides, I have a trump card that suits this type of fight very well. Given his image, he won't go back on his word, and as long as I win, it doesn't matter how I beat my opponent. You dared to talk crap to me, so suffer the consequences. The student smirked.

Gary didn't complain as he walked forward and stood in front of his opponent.

"Now, since you are both able to transform, we'll tweak the rules slightly," Professor Hai announced. "Once I shout 'start,' you'll begin your fight, and only then are you allowed to transform. Got it?"

The two nodded, and a notification appeared with a ding before the werewolf.

New Quest received
Honorable Fight 0.5!
Many people are watching, so don't make a fool out of yourself
Win the match!
Condition: Knock out or kill your opponent
Quest reward: 50 Exp
Failure: ???
Optional Quest received
Waste not, want not
Consume the Altered
Quest reward: Additional stat points

Unconsciously, Gary licked his lips as he read the message, but snapped out of it as soon as Professor Hai shouted "start!"

Immediately, the challenger's feet started to transform, turning green and looking like those of an insect. Less than a second later, he pushed off, springing upward.

"Haha, I bet you never expected this, my one-shot-kill. I'll take you out in a single hit and take your place!"

Even the three adults were surprised by this, since previously it had taken him a few seconds to transform his hands and feet. Professor Hai began to worry; even a student in a stronger Altered form might have trouble dealing with such a surprise attack.

It was one of the reasons they didn't host a battle royale. Sure, the challenger might win, but it would be a cheap victory and not one that demonstrated their potential. Nevertheless, since admission to the AFA was on the line, they couldn't blame him for using a cheap trick.

Honorable Fight 0.5 . . . only 50 Exp . . . it means I don't really have to worry about you. Gary sighed as he shifted his front foot, taking a fighting stance. He lifted his heel off the ground slightly and balanced on his toes before getting his fist ready.

You might think you're fast . . . but you're nothing but a snail compared to Kirk!

Bouncing off his toes without transforming, Gary threw out his fist, landing a punch right in his opponent's face, shattering the Insect Altered's jaw and nose with a loud crack. Blood flew backward through the air as he fell to the ground.

Gary stood there looking down at his opponent with a bloody fist, happy to receive a free 50 Exp without even needing to transform.

He's on a different level, Professor Wood thought.

CHAPTER 54

THE FINAL FIVE

The guy might have been an idiot, but that doesn't give me the right to kill him, Gary thought as he looked down on the unconscious body of the Insect Altered. The guy clearly wouldn't be getting up anytime soon. As if taunting him to do it, the optional quest flashed before him, yet the werewolf ignored it, shook the blood off his hand, and stepped back in line.

On some level, Gary understood that the fastest way for him to grow in power through the Werewolf System would be by consuming beasts. However, since those were technically extinct, other than what NIRV was doing, he would have to eat Altered if he wanted the benefit, and that just wasn't socially acceptable, nor was it something Gary really wanted to do.

Fortunately, that wasn't his only way to grow in power. Aside from leveling up, a task that became progressively more annoying because of the increased Exp requirement for each level, he could strengthen himself or his pack through the use of Pawn points.

Gary had evolved Kai into a Knight-grade beta werewolf using a Pawn point. He still had no idea whether Kai had simply been predestined to become a werewolf, or whether his Alpha Bite had been the trigger, but the assigned Unique Class had made even him jealous.

It was a good thing that Kai was on his side, and given his power boost, Gary felt confident in using the ten Pawn points he had earned as a bonus for successfully hunting the Underdogs on himself.

There were three things he could do with them. He could invest them toward reaching the next grade, evolve his pack members into Bishop-grade werewolves like himself, or convert them into either stat or skill points.

The first option seemed wasteful. Gary lacked the necessary Pawn points to go up a grade in one go. He needed to invest fourteen more Pawn points to do that, and no matter how much he racked his brain, he couldn't imagine that it made any difference whether he had 1/15 or 11/15.

The second option, while arguably more useful, also had its problems. Unlike him, neither Olivia nor Kai had any levels or stats. Even if they did, the alpha werewolf had yet to find a way to see them, so he would have no clue how much of an effect evolving them would have.

After the full moon, he knew that they were weaker than him, but Gary preferred not to take a risk in that regard. He didn't need either one challenging him for his position, as unlikely as that might be.

That only left the last option, the one that would strengthen him directly. After nearly dying at the hands of the Underdogs, he had grown aware that a werewolf was far from invincible. He was sure that he could have beaten each gang member individually, but why would his enemies do him that favor when there was strength in numbers?

Of course, the same was true for him, and the Werewolf System had tempted him more than once to increase his pack size, but he wasn't willing to turn his friends, at least not until he found a way to eliminate or at least severely decrease the risk of them dying.

Name: Gary Dem
Class: Warrior
State: Human (Alpha)
Grade: Bishop
Level 20

Exp 478/5302
Health 160 → 200
Energy 278/300
Strength 25 → 27
Dexterity 24 → 26
Endurance 20 → 25

Before coming here today, he had made sure to strengthen himself, maximizing his chances to become a student at the AFA. Alas, ultimately, Gary had ended up with a mere thirteen stat points after the conversion. After half an hour of cursing the system with everything he could think of, the alpha werewolf had assigned his points.

If I had known that my competition was only at this level, I would have saved up those Pawn points. Hopefully, the real students of the AFA have more to offer, though I suppose being able to climb to the AFC in record time should also have its perks.

Honestly, the significant boost Gary had received after consuming Kirk had been enough to put him above his opponent. With his Dexterity even higher, the werewolf was now at a level comparable to the Cheetah Altered. Of course, that was only true for speed alone; skills were a different story.

Without Olivia's interference, the fight would have ended differently, and since it had been televised, Gary intended to refrain from transforming completely while in the AFA, and perhaps even in the AFC, if he could help it. Although he felt in control when transforming, there was something about that form that forced out his wild side.

Once I'm done with the assessments, it appears that I will need to have a word with the scout leader. His men have really failed us this year, Professor Humfree thought, looking at Gary. *Someone of his talent should have been brought before us with the scouted group, especially since he should place highly even among them.*

Not only is he great at controlling his transformation, but he was also able to precisely track a surprise attack, and used his opponent's own force against him. A shame the fight ended so abruptly; I would have loved seeing his abilities more in depth, but the next test will be perfect for that.

After two fights, none of the teenagers who had failed dared to challenge those who had passed, accepting their fate of having to apply to a different academy.

The twelve students who had passed followed the three professors into one of the academy buildings. Strangely, it was an empty hall, which led to a long hallway, which eventually led to an even larger empty white room that had nothing inside.

"This is where the second test will take place," Professor Humfree explained. "While it is remarkable that so many of you have met our standards, the AFA can only admit five of you. In a few minutes, balls will start shooting toward you. It's up to you whether you wish to dodge or catch them; just be aware that the moment one of you comes into contact with a ball, we will enter the next phase.

"A sixty-second timer will appear, and once it reaches zero, you will hear this sound."

BZZZZ

"The last person who came into contact with that ball is eliminated, starting a new round without that person. Any questions? No? Great! You have five minutes to talk among yourselves before the first round starts!"

With that, the three adults left the room. Gary wondered why they would be given five minutes. He was still pumped, eager to get things over with. However, once the timer started to count down, he saw why they had been granted that time.

"Hey, do you want to team up with us? If there are five of us, and we agree not to hit the ball at each other, it means we will have a higher chance of passing on. We can work together to get the others out!" one of the teenagers suggested. It was one of the three who had been unable to transform.

As he contemplated this offer, Gary noticed that once again, one individual was being ignored by the others.

"Thanks for the offer, but I already have a team member, and I think just the two of us will do fine," Gary apologized as he headed toward Numba.

"How about we work together?" Gary smiled as he offered the Altered his hand.

"No" was the abrupt answer, without a hint of hesitation.

"That's great, le— hang on, what did you just say?"

CHAPTER 55

GOING SOLO

"I said that I'm not interested," Numba stated without much emotion, and as if to stress his point, the lone Altered moved away from Gary.

Didn't we have a bro moment earlier? We even smiled at each other . . . was that just me misinterpreting stuff? Gary thought as his cheeks turned red in embarrassment.

"Come on, don't you agree that with everyone else teaming up, we would be better off doing the same?" the werewolf argued, completely aware how pathetic he must sound. Less than a minute ago, he had confidently refused an offer to join someone else's group, and now he was practically begging for cooperation.

"I don't mean to say that I think you need any help necessarily, but working together would increase both our chances of passing the assessment."

Numba let out a sigh before turning back to Gary. "I don't know if you're a good guy or bad guy, but that's kinda my point. All I know about you is that your Altered form looks impressive, and that you punched someone's face in a while ago. While it would be great to have that kind of power on my side, what exactly is stopping you from betraying me during this assessment? This is my only chance to get into the AFA, so I'm not going to take any unnecessary risks.

"One thing I learned growing up is that you can rely on the fact that people will always do things for their own personal benefit. Frankly, I don't see what you could possibly get out of working with me."

Gary wanted to argue, but while his mouth remained open, no words came out. After all, what else could he say to Numba other than that he should trust him? If their positions were reversed, would he be willing to trust the word of a complete stranger?

Left with no other option, the werewolf accepted his defeat and turned around. From the looks of it, he was one step too late. The other two teens who had been unable to transform had been more successful in securing teammates, making them a group of five. Additionally, four Altered capable of transforming had also grouped together.

Screw me, I guess. That's what I get for trying to be nice. I should have just agreed to the guy's offer. Oh well, no other choice but to do this whole thing on my own, he thought.

"Erghh, excuse me, I couldn't help but overhear what you were talking about with that guy, and I totally agree. Since he doesn't want to team up . . . would you mind if I take his place? I really want to get in the AFA, and you were super impressive." A nasal voice interrupted Gary's thoughts.

Before him stood a teenager with straight, flat hair that was cut level with his eyebrows, giving it the appearance of a bowl. Then there were his eyes, which looked like upside-down moons as he smiled.

"You . . . were the guy who could, like, grow his hair out, right? Turning into like a Hair Altered?" Gary asked as he tried to recall the teenager's name. The next moment, he covered his mouth, realizing how incredibly rude his description must sound. Fortunately, the teenager's expression didn't change in the least, but rather he nodded along.

"Yep, that's me. You don't seem to remember my name, but I don't blame you, I'm as surprised as you're that I actually passed. I'm Vik, and it would be my pleasure to work alongside you."

Truth be told, Gary couldn't match his enthusiasm; from what he barely recalled, he couldn't imagine the guy becoming anything but a burden, but after getting rejected he also felt bad for him. "Are you sure you wouldn't rather join up with the group of four? Together, you might have a far better chance."

"What's the point? I'm convinced you'll end up as one of the last five. But even if they change their mind and allow me to join, if it comes down to it, I'll be the one they abandon in the last round. My gut is telling me that my best chance is sticking with you," Vik admitted with a smile as he rubbed the back of his head.

Gary wasn't sure if it was due to pity or appreciating Vik's honesty, but with barely any time left on the timer he agreed. The lights near the ceiling of the room turned on as soon as the buzzer sounded. Behind the glass, they could see the three silhouettes.

"Time's up. We hope you've agreed on your tactics to pass the assessment. Heads up, the first ball will shoot out momentarily."

BZZZZ

In silent agreement, the room had been split up into four parts, each one belonging to one of the groups. A panel on the side of the white room opened up, and what looked like a slick cannon shot a football-sized black ball toward them.

The panel was right behind Gary, and when it opened he had instantly moved away from it. Alas, from the corner of his eye, he saw that his new teammate would be hit unless he moved. A loud bang went off, and the werewolf was barely able to pull Vik aside by his shirt, saving him from the impact.

The ball passed them by at incredible speed, seemingly around a hundred miles per hour. It hit one of the teenagers belonging to the group of five and bounced off his body.

"All right, the countdown will now begin!" a voice announced over the megaphone.

"Hey, I was hit, I was hit, what are we going to do?" Gerald—the teen from earlier who was unable to transform—panicked as he looked for help from his teammates.

"There are no rules about what we can do, so let's grab one of the others and hold them down!" the leader from their group decided.

Immediately, Gerald grabbed another boy from the group of four before they could react, using the body as a human shield.

"Throw the ball! Don't worry about me," the boy demanded.

His teammates didn't need to be asked twice, and the ball hit him right in the stomach.

Under the large timer on the wall, a photo showed the person who had last come into contact with the ball.

Now the timer was at forty seconds.

The group of five split up, keeping their distance from the other group. Seeing that it would be difficult to help out their teammate, their eyes turned to the one player who was on his own.

I see how it is; well, just try it, Numba thought as he started to transform.

CHAPTER 56

EXPLOSIVE POWER

Unlike during the initial assessment, when Numba had been struggling to transform, his horns were now growing at a fast speed, swirling backward just past his entire head before they curved up. The pointed bits stuck out around six inches in front of him. As the ball headed toward him, he dashed forward with incredible speed and perfect timing. The Goat Altered's horns connected and the ball rebounded like a bullet, right past the closest two teenagers from the group of four, then collided with its target.

Surprisingly the ball itself didn't break, indicating that the material wasn't normal rubber. It was far more durable, yet it also kept a solid state on impact, allowing it to maintain optimal speed and force.

Numba, aware that his chances of fighting off four Altered weren't good, had wisely decided to make a fight pointless by forcing the group of five to act. What's more, his target had been caught off guard against this sudden ambush. The ball had hit him right in the stomach, knocking him to his knees. No matter how hard he tried to breathe, he couldn't, to the point that tears were coming out of his eyes.

"Grab the ball, we have to make sure that Tick isn't eliminated in this round! With him gone, we won't have the numbers advantage anymore!" a young girl shouted. Like Tick, she was one of the three Altered who had been unable to transform.

Immediately, the short brown-haired student who had displayed his skills in the fight against the Crab Altered ran toward Numba to knock him out. After all, the only rule was that the last one to come into contact with the ball would be eliminated, and an unconscious person would be unable to do anything after being tagged.

Five minutes had been more than enough time to form teams, so the two groups had used the remaining time to coordinate how they could best complement each other given their respective Altered forms and skills.

If it's just him, I might be able to defend myself until the timer reaches zero," Numba thought, ready to fight since the group of four had already escaped his reach.

"You can do it, Ian!" Izzy, the other non-transforming Altered, shouted from behind. All three of them had attended the same school, and Ian was undoubtedly the strongest among them. Fortunately for the trio, the Crab Altered had challenged Ian rather than Izzy or Tick, which had led to the misconception that all three of the Altered who were unable to transform had to be some sort of powerhouse. Alas, with Numba hitting Tick, their friend was on the verge of losing his chance to attend the AFA, especially with only ten seconds left this round.

Just as Numba was about to push off again, he saw another figure running toward Ian. It looked like a blur, but the figure met Ian's kick in midair.

"What the hell? This fight has nothing to do with you! Fine, if this is how you want to play it, then let's go!" Ian cried out as Gary caught his foot with his right hand.

"Numba might have rejected my offer, but I'm not going to just stand there and watch when all of you are ganging up on him," Gary explained with a confident smile. He grasped Ian's leg harder. Then, seeing that Ian was about to kick him with his free leg, the werewolf prepared to meet the incoming kick with one of his own.

Alas, that kick never came. Instead, a loud crack filled the room, followed by a terrifying scream. The scene was gruesome. Not only was Ian's leg twisted into an unnatural position, but a small part of his leg bone was sticking out of his skin.

"*Shit!* I'm so sorry." Gary apologized the moment he saw the damage he had caused. He had intended to merely use a simple kick, but having seen how Ian had fared against the Crab Altered, he had used a bit more strength and speed to overwhelm Ian's defense. He had succeeded . . . a little too well.

"Hmm, I didn't think that they would go at it with such enthusiasm from the get-go. Should I call in the medics, so that they can collect him?" Professor Hai asked his colleagues.

"There's no need. He's an Altered, and according to his blood test a very powerful one at that. This type of injury is not enough to kill him, so we should let him decide whether he wishes to forfeit or continue," Professor Humfree replied.

None of the teenagers knew what to do at that moment. Their reverie was broken by the buzzer. The image of the last student who had been hit was now flashing under the timer.

"Tick Mybal was the last person to come in contact with the ball and is thereby eliminated from this assessment. Please leave the area," Professor Humfree announced over the speaker.

In the room, another panel opened up, revealing a door. Tick walked toward it, head down. He hadn't fully recovered yet, but he was able to walk on his own. The boy could do nothing but blame himself for not having been more cautious. Still, because his Altered form had been deemed interesting enough to allow him to pass the AFA's first assessment, the silver lining for Tick was that other academies would be happy to take him in.

As soon as he had left the room, another beep sounded. Everyone expected new balls to come flying out, but instead, the sixty-second timer started counting down, showing a picture of Numba underneath.

Immediately, a feeling of relief overcame the others. All they had to do now was make sure not to get hit, and having seen what

Numba was capable of, they were very wary of him. Meanwhile, the Goat Altered ran toward the ball and lifted it off the floor, then threw it slightly up in the air, as if he were serving a tennis ball.

As the ball fell, Numba readied his legs and, once again, explosively charged forward, hitting the ball with his head. It flew across again, this time hitting one of the group of four Altered on the shoulder.

"Crap, let's just go for others, our numbers are the same now, so we should be able to get one of them!" one of them suggested.

For Gary and his teammate, the second round was calm and peaceful. The two teams of four were fighting against each other, the image under the timer changing every other second. The timer continued to count down, and in the end, there were only ten seconds left until the next person would be eliminated.

Izzy was holding the ball. She was bruised and tired, but her face showed conviction as she changed her approach, running toward Gary.

Why me? Do you want to take revenge for your boyfriend or something? Gary wondered as he watched her, ready to dodge. He had contemplated hitting the ball back but decided against it, fearing that she too might turn out to be even more fragile than Ian.

The countdown continued and from a few yards away, Izzy hurled the ball. It was fast, faster than a human could throw, but nowhere near fast enough to hit Gary; he could tell that the trajectory of the ball was off, to the point that he didn't even have to move.

I can see that this is a desperate attempt, but you still have to at least aim properly, Gary thought, a small grin on his face. Just in case it turned out to be a curve ball, he stepped to the side, and the ball missed him completely.

Keeping his eye on the screen, Gary saw something strange. The image had changed, now displaying Vik.

Crap, I completely forgot about him!

Gary turned to try to help his teammate, but the ball bounced off his chest and fell to the floor.

In the distance he saw Vik, his moon-shaped eyes smiling at the werewolf's visible confusion.

CHAPTER 57

THREE SECONDS

Only three seconds remained in this round, and Gary's image was displayed underneath the timer.

Who would have thought that the most talented kid from this batch would lose due to trickery, Professor Humfree thought, scratching his beard. *It's truly a shame, but this should serve as a lesson for him. No matter how strong you might be, you can always lose your life if you put your trust in the wrong person.*

Tests like this one were designed with treachery in mind. Just like in the real world, each trial taker could control only their own actions. So they had to either put their trust in the right person, convince the others to work with them, or try to do everything on their own. After all, life in the AFA would be brutal. If you couldn't make it past this stage, then only a life of hardships would await you.

Gary's eyes turned red as he continued to stare at Vik. The teenager with the bowl cut had seemed so innocent when he had asked the werewolf to help him out. Gary had been willing to help him pass this assessment since Vik had been so up front with his request, but after this betrayal, he understood the situation for what it really was.

"This bastard *came over to me just so he could stab me in the back! I should have realized that something was up when the others didn't let him join their teams. Numba was right . . .*

Unfortunately, Gary's realization came a bit too late. Although he was faster than Vik, he was far away and with just three seconds on the clock, it wasn't enough time to change the situation.

"Wolfboy, kick the ball!" a voice shouted.

Closing the distance between himself and Vik, Numba grabbed him by the arms and held him in place. The traitor had been unable to react, as his attention had been focused on Gary; he was afraid that the werewolf had more tricks up his sleeve.

The ball was right in front of Gary. Two seconds remained, so he did the only thing he could. Not caring about his clothes, he activated Controlled Transformation on his legs. The muscles on his calves grew, and he even left a dent on the floor as he propelled himself upward.

With one step, Gary was next to the ball. Now one second was left on the timer. He had focused his transformation on the foot he would use to kick. His brand-new shoe exploded as long, large toe-nails poked out, revealing the growing fur.

I'm getting into the academy no matter what! Gary thought, disregarding the damage he might cause to Vik.

His foot made contact with the ball, blasting it through the air.

Numba flinched as the impact sent him sliding a few meters back. However, Vik was far worse off. The teenager had been mid-transformation, attempting to use his hair to block or at least partially deflect the incoming projectile, yet he had been unsuccessful.

The Goat Altered, noticing that Vik had gone limp in his arms, let go. The Hair Altered dropped headfirst to the floor, blood pouring from his mouth and nose, with a large imprint of the ball on his face.

Holy shit . . . just how much power did that kick pack? Numba wondered. *It was even faster than my headbutt . . . has Wolfboy been holding back this entire time?*

BZZZZ

The buzzer went off. Gary quickly turned his head to see if his desperate attempt had made it in time. An image appeared on the screen and an announcement was made.

"Vik Scissor was the last person to come in contact with the ball and is thereby eliminated from this assessment. Since he is unable to move on his own, someone will come to collect him in a moment. The assessment will continue after that."

This was music to Gary's ears. He had been confident in his ability to pass this assessment without a struggle. After all, these were just applicants, and they weren't even the ones who were scouted.

Since they were on a bit of a break, he headed over to the Goat Altered. "Thank you . . . thank you very much for helping me out. If it weren't for you, I would have been eliminated. I really, really owe you one."

Numba looked at Gary's face, then down to his feet, which looked human again.

"I told you that you shouldn't trust just anyone, especially those you have just met, but you didn't listen." The teenager sighed. "Don't mention it, I was just repaying you for taking out the other guy. Let's just say we're even."

"No way!" Gary replied straightaway. "I just helped them not gang up on you, but you seriously saved me out there. I would have been eliminated without your intervention, not just beaten up or kicked to the head. And besides, someone with your skills should have been able to at least evade the guy until the timer went down.

"So yeah, I owe you. Unfortunately, I don't really have anything I can give you right now, so how about you get a, ummm . . . let's call it a Gary token. Yeah! Whatever you need, whenever you need it, I'll help you out, no questions asked, all right?"

Numba didn't know what to do. He wasn't used to being around such an upbeat person, though truth be told, Gary wasn't normally this hyped either, but something about the whole atmosphere of the AFA had led to his current mood.

"Fine." Numba shrugged. "I don't know when I would use it. Let's make sure that we both pass first, and maybe after we're both official AFA students, I will get back to you about that favor."

The panel to the door eventually opened up, and a person they hadn't seen before entered. The middle-aged man wore a tight-fitting shirt that showed off his muscles. His piercing gaze moved over each of the teenagers before he saw Vik lying on the floor. He walked straight over and picked up the unconscious Altered with one arm.

"That was a nice kick," the man said on the way back, as he passed Gary. "I look forward to seeing you inside the academy. Make sure to learn from this opportunity." And with that, he left the room.

The feeling he gave off . . . He's better suited for me to go up against than these people. Gary smiled, his blood pumping. He didn't know what position the man held inside the AFA, but he was looking forward to meeting him again.

In the past, Gary's mind had been filled with all kinds of thoughts concerning his family, his school life, and the Underdogs, among other things. Before he turned into a werewolf he had never realized how much he truly enjoyed fighting. Sure, part of him had watched the Altered fights with a dream of becoming as rich as them, but now he wanted to prove that he was better than any of them.

"You look relieved," Professor Hai noted with a chuckle, his belly jiggling.

"Of course. If he had lost, I would have contemplated asking the director to make an exception for the kid," Professor Wood replied honestly. "There is a lot more to him than meets the eye. I believe that we may have the next Kirk Summerfield on our hands, perhaps even better."

Professor Wood's face lit up. He started furiously rubbing the bottom of his chin, which made his colleague wonder if he was all right in the head.

"Really? You rate him that highly?" Professor Humfree asked, now intrigued. "It appears you know something that we don't. I would ask you to elaborate, but it should be more interesting to watch him prove himself. Hopefully, he has learned from his mistake."

BZZZZ

"The next round has begun," the speaker announced, and the picture that appeared was Gary's once more. The ball was right next to his feet, which made everyone else nervous.

"It looks like your plan failed, eh? Were you also the one to come up with this plan?" Gary asked, looking at Izzy.

Turning to her left and right, the teenage girl found herself isolated from the rest.

"Hey . . . hey, what happened to us being a team? Didn't we agree to work together?" Izzy shouted at her former teammates.

"I think you have other things to worry about." Gary smiled, cracking his knuckles. "You see, my plan was actually to remain on the sidelines and let you sort it out among yourselves who deserved a place in the AFA. I thought it would be fairer for everyone that way. However, what you just did *really* pissed me off!"

Pulling up his sleeve, Gary used Controlled Transformation on his arm. His forearms grew larger, his nails gripped tightly around the ball, and his brown fur covered his skin.

"Now, let me personally take you and your whole group out!" Gary said as he sprinted across the floor.

This seems like the perfect opportunity to test out that new skill I got a while ago. Let's see if I can end this whole assessment in this round!

CHAPTER 58

A SPECIAL HOWL

Unlike a few moments ago, Gary kept his legs human and only transformed his hand. Still, even without transforming, Gary was much faster than those taking the assessment, at least before they had transformed into their Altered forms.

Before Izzy could make up her mind about what to do, Gary was in front of her. He raised his furry hand above her, holding the ball.

"Catch." Gary dropped the ball, and Izzy held on to it as she was told. The image on the screen had now changed to hers, but she didn't care about that.

Looking at Ian lying on the ground with his broken leg, she could only imagine what would happen to her. On the other hand, Gary hadn't even transformed back then, nor was he angry.

"For the next few seconds, just hold the ball for me, or you know what, hold it as long as you can."

Then, raising his head, Gary stared at her teammates. He suspected they were all in on the plan together, and there wasn't just one person to blame for all of this.

Noticing his gaze, the teammates started running away, acting as if Gary himself were the ball.

Let's see how this thing works.

You have used Magnetic Howl

It was the first time Gary had used this skill, at least in a fighting situation like this. Before, he had used this skill in his regular practices, but it didn't seem quite as spectacular. However, he believed that things might change for him this time.

In the next moment, Gary suddenly felt like he was choking, and it was as if something was happening to his throat, as if it was changing. Soon his larynx was no longer like that of a normal human. When the transformation was complete, he looked up at the sky and opened his mouth, letting out a loud howl.

"AWHOOO!"

It wasn't short, either. Instead, it bounced off the walls and created echoes, amplifying the sound. It wasn't the strangest thing for the others to see, especially since Gary had revealed himself to be a Wolf Altered.

After hearing this howl, the students running in the opposite direction turned around and headed straight toward Gary. It was as if they couldn't control their bodies.

"What is going on?" Most of the students panicked. Their bodies couldn't stop them from running at Gary.

It looks like it worked. Gary smiled. He had already taken a fighting stance.

As soon as the first student got close, he kicked him right in the side, possibly breaking a rib. Then he threw a fist into the face of the next student, sending him stumbling back.

By now, the other students had realized they had little control over their bodies, and decided to try to attack. However, they had failed to note the claws on Gary's transformed hands.

"This might sting a little, but I'm sure you bastards have experienced a bit of pain before!" Gary shouted.

When they saw the claws, the incoming students froze, and instead they focused on avoiding the incoming attack. However, Gary never planned to hurt them seriously to begin with, so instead he took advantage of their stupor to send them flying with his kicks or punching them in the face, before turning his hands back to normal.

The one-sided beating didn't take long; he had knocked out four more students. As for the others, they no longer felt like they were being pulled toward Gary, but they didn't want to come any closer.

That skill was quite useful for a situation like this, but if I were going up against the Underdogs, I can see how I wouldn't want to use it.

The system had unlocked the Magnetic Howl skill as a reward after defeating Kirk. However, based on the description, he knew he wouldn't be able to use it for most of his battles because this skill was an aggro type.

According to the description, it made the surrounding enemies focus their attack on him. No matter who they were fighting against or what they were doing, they would choose to come toward him and attack him. However, the skill stated that it would work longer on particular types of individuals and less on others.

This skill was also why Gary wanted to continue increasing his Health and Energy; he wanted to become a tank character who could take on all his own gang's enemies, and at the same time, in a desperate situation, this skill combined with Last Stand could work well.

The only drawback here was that the skill had a ten-minute cooldown and took up to 25 Energy points, which was a lot. Of course, Gary would not become a pure tank, but there were other ways for him to improve his stats.

Exp 2788/5302

I got quite a bit of Exp for beating those guys, even though the Underdogs seemed like a harder lot to deal with. Is it because they're Altered? And that damned notification kept telling me to devour them for extra stat points, Gary thought before turning his attention toward Izzy.

"Thank you for holding the ball all this time." Gary smiled at her; her legs were shaking. There was no doubt in her mind that if she threw the ball, she would pay for it dearly, and by then the buzzer had gone off.

Strangely, the timer had stopped with five seconds to spare. It was as if someone had paused the machine to halt it.

"Due to an unexpected turn of events, we have had to pause the assessment. So, can all the able students head toward the exit that will soon open up in the room?"

On the top floor, where the three professors were watching the whole thing, Humfree shook his head.

"Well, this has become quite a headache!"

Soon all the students had gathered in a room that looked like a practice room for fighters. It was quite old, and there were spots on the walls that were used as punching targets.

Meanwhile, the professors were in an adjacent room, along with about ten other teachers; they were here to assess the situation and make a decision on the next step.

Humfree pressed a button and turned off the TV mounted on the wall.

"As you can see, that is how the assessment has gone so far, which is why it has come to this," he explained. "Usually this assessment has worked out for us, and it has done so for years, but if we had let things continue, then those who passed and failed would have been dictated by a single person.

"A few talented students would have failed this assessment before we even went through the next round, which is why I have called all of you to decide who will go through to the next assessment."

Professor Wood handed out papers to all of the teachers, so they could fully assess who would be best. They were also to consider the video they had just seen, so they weren't just basing their judgment on paper.

"I'm sorry I can't really focus," said Miss Hartlett, a teacher who had her hair tied up in a bun and glasses on her face. She focused on teaching theory lessons. "I just keep thinking, how was a student like that not scouted by our academy? "Don't we have scouts in every city to keep an eye out for such talents so a situation like this doesn't happen?"

Several other teachers thought the same thing. Gary was clearly just as good as their scouted students this year.

"I'll answer that," said Gabe, a teacher dressed in a military-style uniform with a large cut over one eye. He was also older than the other teachers but younger than the professors. "The boy hails from a Tier 3 town. Although we kept track of all Altered in each city, this one didn't get on our radar.

"It seems like he is being backed by a group that suddenly rose in his city. This rarely happens, which is why we missed this one."

It was a simple explanation, but a rare one. An uprising in power hardly ever happened. A change in management from a city gang taking over another was common, but not a single person had heard of the Howlers before.

After Gabe cleared that up, the teachers and professors spent the next few minutes deciding who would pass the test.

"Well, there is only one thing left to do before we end this meeting." Professor Humfree sighed. "We need to decide what we should do with Gary Dem."

CHAPTER 59

THE FINAL FIVE?

While the professors were busy discussing what to do, a few helpers brought in a few benches for the waiting teenagers to sit on, while others moved the injured to another room. After receiving treatment, they returned and joined the others.

Gary sat on a bench of his own, since the others had all chosen to distance themselves from him. Ironically, some had taken the initiative to go and talk to Numba, pretending they hadn't treated the Goat Altered like an outcast. Of course, he hadn't forgotten, nor had he forgiven them for the fact that they had tried to gang up on him in the first round, so with his arms folded he was simply ignoring them.

At one point, Gary stood up to stretch, which made everyone else immediately flinch, clearly afraid of him. "I only attacked you because of the assessment. I'm not normally that aggressive," he mumbled as he looked away from them awkwardly.

I didn't exactly come here to make friends, but they could at least try and hide their disdain toward me, Gary thought as he let out a small sigh. *I admit that I might have gone a little too far back there, but I only overreacted because their plan to eliminate me nearly worked.*

This awkward atmosphere continued until the three professors eventually entered the room.

"We won't waste your time any longer, so I shall proceed by reading out the list of students who have successfully passed. Please note that due to the unforeseen circumstances, we've taken into account everything you've shown so far in this assessment and the previous one."

Everyone was nervous and tense, as they had no clue who had passed and failed. Chances were that those who had been knocked out before Gary went on his small rampage were noncontestants, but as for the rest, it was anyone's guess.

"In no particular order, Gary Dem."

The first name came as no surprise, as everyone agreed that the werewolf had proven himself vastly superior to the rest in every way. The real question was who the other four lucky teenagers were.

"Numba Cardenez!"

Numba had also shown great skill during the ball challenge. Many expected this as well, though all but he and Gary had secretly hoped that the professors might not see his potential.

"Ian Noblitt!"

There were gasps from the students as they heard this name. After all, not only was he one of the Altered who had been unable to transform, but his confrontation with Gary had led to him having a large cast on his leg, which would likely take a long while to heal.

Some students looked like they were about to argue, but Professor Hai gave them a stern look, shutting them down instantly. In the end, they had no choice but to accept the fact that his potential had to be high enough to warrant this decision, especially taking into account his display of strength against the Crab Altered.

If it weren't for Gary, then he might have had a great chance to pass this and any future assessment. The other students started to lose hope. They felt like everything would be based on their background, and they all knew that their backgrounds were lacking, or else they would have been invited.

"Izzy Shamone!" Professor Humfree called out.

"Wait . . . me?" Izzy stood up, pointing to herself. The teenage girl was in disbelief; she hadn't done much in the ball challenge, and her background wasn't the best, so why had she been picked? Overjoyed, she didn't even notice that tears were rolling down her face.

"That is the result of our decision. These four students have passed and will be moving on from here. Everyone else, we thank you for your interest in applying to the AFA, and we hope you'll have a bright future elsewhere."

All of the students stood up. They wanted to complain, but the three professors were already leaving the room, telling those who had passed to follow them.

"That's just four! What about the fifth student?" someone shouted.

Without turning around, Professor Humfree reminded him, "I did indeed state that we have five places, but I've also been up front about the fact that I did not believe that five people would pass. It's already quite surprising that four places have been filled, and as for the rest of you, blame yourselves for lacking the necessary talent to impress us."

Gary and the other three felt a little bad, yet this feeling paled in comparison to their joy over getting to be students of the AFA. Out of around one hundred teenagers, only four of them had succeeded.

However, rather than walking to the main building, the professors were leading them off campus. They were quite surprised when they saw a bus, which they boarded, but since they had been told to follow, all of them did so silently.

Fortunately, their destination wasn't too far from the academy buildings. There was an air around the professors that told the group of teenagers that it was best to not question them. Eventually they reached another large building. There was no glass on the outside, so it was impossible to tell what was inside.

One thing was clear, though; it was huge and looked almost like another academy. As they stood outside, the students were told to line up and each one of them was handed a badge.

"Some of you may think that you have already made it, but those two assessments have merely proven that you deserve to have come here," Professor Hai explained. "This is the first step into entering the *real* academy."

At that moment, numbers appeared on each of their badges. Gary's showed the number 120, Numba's 121, Ian's 122, and Izzy's 123.

"Inside that building, the number on your badges will dictate how pleasant your stay will be. It decides many things such as what room you'll sleep in and what meals you will receive, though most importantly, only those who manage to retain their place in the top ten for at least one week may join the AFA."

Although it wasn't quite what Gary was expecting, for the first time he felt like he was actually going to be part of the AFA, and this badge made him realize that he might be one step closer to meeting Xin again.

CHAPTER 60

A SITUATION

Professor Hai went on to explain what their life would be like and how they could rise through the ranks, be it in the form of passing the assessments, completing challenges, or fighting other students. He also explained that there would be teachers inside but no lessons, since the teachers were there to observe and nothing else. Still, they would have the facility to train as they wished, and higher badge numbers meant access to better facilities to train in order to encourage students to improve.

"You will be able to leave whenever you wish, but if you do choose to leave as someone outside the top ten, you will forfeit your only chance to join the AFA. It's in your own interest to do whatever it takes to reach the top positions, and hopefully I will see you all at the real academy again. Once you enter, that will be your next step."

Before the adults left, Professor Humfree looked at Gary and directed a few more words at him.

"Although you've disrupted our assessment, your talent is undeniable. It's hard to say how much you've yet to show us, but from what we've seen, we have a good idea of what you can do.

"Honestly, some teachers even suggested that it might be best if you joined the academy immediately. Ultimately, however, we agreed that this next part is akin to a rite of passage that everyone must go through.

"That building is filled with students who have been scouted. They are just as talented as you, yet for one reason or another they never rose to the top ten. There will be things you have never experienced.

"Gary Dem, stay strong, and I hope you make it through this."

With that said, the professors got on the bus, leaving the four students in front of the stadium-like building.

What did he mean by that? Our actions in here could affect the outside world? Gary didn't know what to expect, but he did have one thought. Xin had only recently become an Altered, and according to Professor Hai, it wasn't uncommon for the ones inside to stay there for months, if not years. So there was a very good chance he would meet her inside.

Looking forward to the possible reunion, Gary was the first to step toward the door. The others, not wanting to be left behind, followed him. Although they were still worried about the harshness of what awaited them, they knew there was no way back now.

There might be groups or factions who have agreed to work together so they can get into the top ten, Izzy realized. *And what the professor said. Are students using their connections on the outside to secure their positions inside? If that's the case, we nonscouted students might have the toughest time in getting higher positions.*

As soon as the four of them entered the building, everyone inside turned to look at them. They had already been informed that the newcomers would arrive today, so now was the time to size up their new competition.

Looking around the large room, Gary was unable to find Xin.

Is she perhaps training right now? I doubt it . . . I'm certain that Xin wouldn't just give up, so she has probably already advanced to the next level. So much for surprising her . . . Oh well, I bet she will be even more surprised once we meet inside the AFA. The werewolf let out a depressed sigh.

As the new students walked in, the others continued to stare at them. None of them looked friendly, and nobody introduced themselves either. Unsure what to do, Gary followed a sign that pointed to the personal rooms, until he arrived in front of his.

"They expect us to stay here?" Izzy couldn't help but complain. "This is supposed to be one of the top academies in the world. They have money coming out of their backside, yet they expect some of the richest, most powerful people to stay in this type of shithole? I've seen closets with more class!"

Ian also was displeased about it, as he covered his nose with his shirt. A certain smell seemed to emanate from the rooms. However, neither Gary nor Numba said a word about it. They simply unpacked the belongings they'd brought, such as some changes of clothes and a few personal items, With no bed or drawers, they could only place them on the floor.

After everyone had settled into their rooms a little, Izzy knocked on the boys' doors, asking them to meet outside. They stood by the handrail, looking down at all the students.

"First, I just want to say that I'm sorry for what happened during the assessment. I'm not as good as any of you three, so I did whatever I had to do to get this spot." Izzy began with an apology, looking straight at Gary since she had done him over the worst.

"I don't expect you to forgive me outright, but I hope you can at least listen to what I have to say. Placing in the top ten is the only way for us to move on to the real AFA, and from what we've been told, it seems nearly impossible to do that on our own. So I propose that we stick together as a group.

"We're the new guys here, so there's a good chance that some people will take advantage of that. Everyone knows that we're the ones who weren't scouted. They most likely see us as easy targets, the bottom of the barrel. So for now, why don't we call a truce and try to help each other out?"

Numba immediately walked away. "That's a great speech and all, but this guy already knows that I don't trust people."

Ian nodded. Unlike the others, he was already friends with Izzy, so he instantly agreed with her.

Gary was still hesitating. Part of him was still pissed at her for what she had done, but another part also understood her reasoning, and now that they were all here together, it might not be the worst idea, but . . .

"I think it might be a better idea if you don't team up with me. There is a good chance that I could cause some trouble here." Gary smiled.

A buzzer went off in the middle of their discussion, and an announcement was made.

"Everyone, please head to the canteen for lunch. Newcomers, make sure to sit down according to the numbered seats!"

Over a hundred teenagers moved in one direction, so the four newcomers followed behind them. Inside the canteen, Gary tried once more to locate Xin, but she was nowhere to be found.

A delicious smell wafted into his nose, and his stomach let out a grumble. One of the tables was far more luxurious than the others. It was reserved for the top students, who were being served first. They had waiters serving them and the students were able to select whatever food they wished, which was cooked and delivered to them, most likely by professional chefs.

"Well, at least the food is good at this place," Gary commented, though he soon realized that he had spoken too soon.

Just like other areas, the canteen had separate sections depending on one's rank. The table for Gary and his group was all the way in the back, pretty much an old picnic table. Sitting down, he picked up a bowl of lukewarm chicken soup and took a sip.

2 points of Energy have been restored
208/300 Energy

This isn't good . . . If I don't get a decent meal, I won't be able to fill up my Energy. The more I fight, the less Energy I will have at my disposal, Gary realized.

CHAPTER 61

YOUR BACKGROUND (PART 1)

With all the food being controlled by the facility, money was practically worthless inside this part of the academy. From what Gary could see, the only way to get access to better things was to increase one's rank.

If this is the level of food we receive for each meal, I'm going to lose Energy throughout my stay! Gary thought, cursing the high metabolism rate of his werewolf body. *Should I fight one of the high-ranking guys right away while my Energy is at its highest?*

Gary's table wasn't the only one with only chicken soup. The same held true all the way to the table with rank 101 sitting on it. Still, the students ranked from 100 down to 76 weren't treated much better. They sat at a normal table, on actual chairs, with their meal consisting of a bigger portion of the soup, with a few simple side dishes added.

Rank 50 was the point when the meal started to look decent, with a big serving of curry with various side dishes, though there was a significant improvement from rank 25 upward. Just looking at the food at those tables, Gary started salivating.

I should probably avoid making a ruckus on the first day. My gut is telling me that the professor didn't warn me just for fun. Unlike me, these guys must have been scouted, and I have no idea how long they've already been here. If I pick the wrong target, I might just waste my Energy, which will just further decrease my chances of improving my current situation.

All right, I guess I should try to get a feel for how strong those ranked higher than me are, and just rank up to the point where the food is more adequate before I try something more crazy.

With the next full moon weeks away, and Gary still having over 200 Energy points, he felt confident that he had at least two to three days of leeway. That should be more than enough time to find a good target to challenge. Of course, if somebody challenged him before that, he would defend himself.

"Bleargh, this tastes horrible." Ian spat the soup out the moment he tasted it. Izzy also had an appalling reaction to its taste. Gary and Numba were the only ones at their table who finished it without complaint.

I nearly forgot, everyone is a rich kid here. I might be sitting next to the poorest rich kids, but those two are spoiled.

Seeing the leftover food, Gary licked his lips; desperate times called for desperate measures.

"Hey, if you guys aren't going to eat that, do you mind if I have it?" he asked.

"Ermm, are you sure you want the food even after I spat it back out?" Ian asked cautiously, thinking it sounded a bit disgusting. However, Gary didn't care, he just casually slurped up Ian's bowl, as well as Izzy's when she shoved her portion over to him.

2 points of Energy have been restored x2
212/300 Energy

"Say, do we get any other food, or is this all we get for breakfast, lunch, and dinner?" Ian asked the table in front of theirs. Since they were ranked at the bottom, he wasn't afraid of them. The student he had asked looked a little bruised up, as if he had just gotten out of a fight.

"This is all we get," the student replied, pointing at the empty bowl of soup. "If you want my advice, you should just get used to it. Trust me, soon enough you will be enjoying every last drop. If you want to get better food, you need to either beat someone higher ranked than you or show off in the weekly challenge. Neither option is really feasible on an empty stomach.

"Alternatively, if you have something substantial to offer, you can always try to strike a deal with someone."

The student pointed to one of the other tables. A teenage boy with the number 86 on his badge walked over to one of the tables in the 26-to-50 range. The others could only see what they were doing, but with a small usage of Controlled Transformation on his ears, Gary was able to eavesdrop on their conversation.

"All right, you win, if you agree, I'll tell the Moro Family to lower the percentage of protection money from your family by ten percent. Deal?"

The other student nodded, and then the two of them swapped food. The others at that table weren't in the least bit surprised, indicating that this wasn't anything unusual.

The Moro Family . . . sounds like they're a gang. Is this what Professor Humfree meant? So much for all of us being equal in this place . . .

Lunch had come to an end, and most of the students returned to the main room, which was apparently where the Altered socialized. Several doors led to where the others slept.

The large room had seats and places for people to read and relax. The center of the room looked like an ordinary circle, but people seemed to stay clear of it for some reason.

That kinda looks like an arena now that I look at it, Gary thought.

Just then, the two students they had seen before entered the center ring.

"I challenge you to a fight!" the lower-ranked student said; the other one nodded. Once the challenge was accepted, their badges lit up, and immediately the lower-ranked student's arm transformed into rock.

He leapt up and swung his fist toward the other's face. His opponent lifted his hands to block the heavy blow. For some reason, he had not transformed, and now lay on the ground. He remained there, and ten seconds later the numbers on their badges changed.

The next moment, the student who had been ranked 47 brushed himself off and walked away.

"I'm a bit confused as to what just happened," Ian confessed.

Something strange was going on in this facility, and it wasn't as straightforward as they had imagined.

CHAPTER 62

YOUR BACKGROUND (PART 2)

Having overheard their conversation in the canteen, Gary was about to explain what he had just seen, but someone else was one step ahead of him.

"It was a trade," Izzy answered. "What we saw earlier must have been them agreeing to the terms, and this was the transaction itself. I thought it was strange what the professor said, but now it's clear. People are definitely using their position and connections on the outside to get certain benefits. It's not just a question of who is the strongest.

"Thinking one step further, this means that if you cross the wrong person or get on their bad side, you may not end up as the only one suffering. Worst-case scenario, it might be your whole family." Izzy gulped.

If that was true, this raised the question of what position those in the top ten held for them to be treated like some type of gods. Others constantly approached them, trying to curry favor. The student who had just traded away his position probably thought it was better to help out his family than himself.

On closer inspection, it didn't seem as bad as Gary had anticipated, since the losing student's badge had gone from 47 to 48. Meanwhile, the winner's badge was now showing 47.

Eventually Izzy asked for another meeting. Ian and Gary agreed immediately, while Numba followed behind and leaned against the wall, not saying anything.

"After that little demonstration, it should be safe to say that this place is more complicated than what we were told by the professors. It's in our best interest to find out more information about who is who, like who is from what city and what their backing is! It might be for the better to avoid fighting those from the same city or town as you, or those in your surrounding.

"As a start, how about we properly introduce ourselves. I'm from Pompano, a Tier 3 town. My family owns a few restaurants, and we've also branched out to the surrounding towns in recent years."

Ian was the next one to introduce himself. "I also come from Pompano. Izzy and I are childhood friends. My family operates an IT servicing company there and is helping out some prominent companies from Tier 2 and Tier 1 cities."

"Both our families are doing quite well financially, but in terms of influence, it's not really worth mentioning. They pretty much invested into us becoming Altered to help with that, but first, we'll need to get into the AFA, of course." Izzy explained. "No doubt there will be someone from Pompano who has a connection to the gangs, or the mayor or something. If we come across them, it would be hard for us to touch them. However, if we work together then someone like you from another town or city can!" Izzy seemed excited about this plan.

Thinking about what Izzy had said, Gary realized that he didn't really need to worry about anyone in here. The Howlers were now the biggest gang in Slough. At the same time, he couldn't think of anyone other than Xin who was an Altered there.

"And what if they're from a Tier 1 city?" Numba asked. "Now I'm not saying that those guys will bother with someone who comes from a lower-tier town or city, but if they do, and they're close with their parents or something, it could be the end of our families."

Gritting her teeth, Izzy felt a little embarrassed, but she did have an answer.

"In that case, the best approach would be to wait. I'm sure there are people who are so big that no one wants to touch them. However, if that's the case, they should easily get a top ten position, and after a week they can leave. There will always be an opportunity at some point.

"There are only so many cities, and so many Altered out there. My guess is that those types have already gone through. This system creates a stalemate in the top ten, as you are allowed to challenge them. Remember, you have to keep your position for a whole week.

"This gets rid of all of those that everyone is afraid to touch, and leaves the ones who are constantly challenging them. We can get through this, we just need to know more about everyone and each other."

Izzy seemed to be a scheming type of person. Always coming up with ideas and ways to push herself to the top. Numba agreed with her rationale, and he even suspected that her being the one who had planned Gary's downfall might have played into her getting the invitation with the rest of them. Although the Goat Altered didn't trust her, he also wasn't sure how far he could get with his own backing.

"I was adopted," Numba eventually revealed. "I was adopted by a Tier 3 electronics company because of my potential. My position is pretty much the same as the two of you; the company is looking to expand, preferably into a Tier 2 city, and they want me to be their public face."

Finally Gary understood why Numba had felt different from the rest, and it was because, like him, he hadn't been born into this position.

"Why are you smiling at me?" Numba asked, taking a step back. "Man, you're seriously weird."

"Sorry, I'm just happy to find someone in a similar position, you know?" Gary admitted, though his sheepish smile remained on his face.

"Does that mean you were picked up by someone as well?" Ian asked.

To be honest, Izzy and Ian were holding out for Gary's answer. With how strong the werewolf had proven to be and with the type of talent that had made the professors consider admitting him straight into the AFA, they were hoping that he was at least from a Tier 2 city. If he was, surely he would belong to some important family with a strong backing.

Most likely, he was just someone that the scouts happened to miss. Which seemed probable.

"Ummm, I mean, I guess you could say I was picked up," Gary replied, scratching the back of his head. "I'm from a Tier 3 town called Slough, not sure if you've heard of it."

There was instant disappointment on all of their faces, because given their backing, none of them had the power to bully themselves into a better position. As for Slough, other than Kirk and a few news reports that had come out from it recently, it was pretty much an unknown place. Even then, Kirk had only been the rookie champion, so only people who really followed the AFC would know of him.

I guess I shouldn't tell them the whole truth. Otherwise, it would be a bit weird, Gary thought.

"In my case, I'm being sponsored by a gang called the Howlers." Immediately, everyone's eyes opened wide when they heard that they were next to a gang member.

CHAPTER 63

CRAZY

Gary had experienced this type of reaction before; he had understood it then, but now he felt like it made no sense.

"What's wrong?" he asked. "Is it really that surprising that I'm being sponsored by my gang? I thought it would be fine to mention that in a place like this. I mean, it's not like I'm the only one, and the Howlers aren't active in any of your towns."

None of them answered his question, so he looked toward Izzy, who had been the most talkative up until now. The awkward silence continued for a few moments, but Gary's gaze continued to put pressure on her until she eventually said something.

"Look, it's nothing against you personally, but . . . well, you should understand that the relationship between gangs and businesses is . . . complicated, to say the least. They pretty much control everything nowadays. What businesses are allowed to operate in their area, how high the protection fee is, and other things that only ever really benefit one side. I'm sure you understand why we feel like we have to be wary of gang members, since one wrong action could spell disaster for us and our families. The sad reality is that all they've built up until now could crumble with one word from a gang member."

Gary stayed silent, since he agreed with what Izzy was saying. In fact, it was a major part of the reason why he disliked gangs so much, and why he had made sure that the Howlers would do things differently from Olivia or Damion.

Admittedly, they weren't completely in the right, either. The property that used to belong to the Underdogs was now in Kai's possession, although following Gary's will, they had leased it back to the original owners as much as possible.

The Howlers also charged protection fees, but their rate was far more reasonable than those of the other gangs, and the contracts even included clauses that allowed business owners to postpone payments if business had been bad in a given month.

The fees were unfortunately a necessary evil to ensure that gang members stayed loyal and could support their own families. Gary could try to explain that the Howlers were better than most, but he doubted Izzy and the others would take his word for it.

"There's more than just that," Izzy continued. "Gang members are just . . . different, usually vicious people who don't give a damn about who they hurt, and I bet that includes the ones in here. If we're lucky, we might meet someone who is prideful and won't ask for help from their family.

"The problem is that just because one gang member might be reasonable, that doesn't mean others in his gang are the same. Let's say I beat a low-ranking gang member; there's a chance that because I wronged one of their own, the whole gang will come after me.

"Even if they're facing another gang that's clearly bigger than theirs, those who are deathly loyal will still risk their lives. Now that we know that you're in a gang, it certainly explains how you were able to do those things before so . . . easily."

Gary understood that she was referring to how he had broken Ian's leg and clawed at the others. There had been next to no hesitation in the werewolf's strikes, because he had already fought with his life on the line multiple times. As for the others, yes, they were Altered, but their fighting experience had been far more limited and curated.

"Should I keep it to myself, then?" Gary asked. "If other people ask me what my background is, I mean. Should I just lie and tell them that some business is behind me?"

He wasn't so sure about that, because the whole point of coming here had been to become a famous Altered, one that the Howlers could actively support.

"No, it's best if you're honest about that." Izzy shook her head. "I'm sure there are people in here who have ways to gather information on us somehow. Besides, your backing is actually advantageous for you. None of those from Tier 3 towns will bother to mess with you unless they're from a gang themselves.

"Heck, even those from Tier 2 cities will probably want to avoid getting into trouble with you, unless they have big connections. Don't rely on my analysis, though. There's so much we don't know; some people still might challenge you, to see what you're like or what type you are.

"After all, you might be a gang's Altered, but that doesn't automatically mean your gang will protect you from anything in here. It's not like you're the leader who can declare a gang war on the Howlers' behalf."

Gary scratched his chin. "Right . . ."

He wasn't the type of person to do something like that in the first place, and besides the gang was busy doing their own thing.

It had been a while since the group had all traveled together, but today was an important day for the Howlers. They had been planning this for a while now, and they couldn't help but be excited in the car on the way to their destination.

"Freaking hell, I never thought I would ever get to step foot in a Tier 1 city, and now we're traveling by limo!" Innu exclaimed.

"Of course, we have to travel in style!" Kai replied. "And with more of us, it was important to upgrade the vehicle. Otherwise, we would be squashed."

While most of them seemed to be excited, one person sat with her hand slumped on her chin, staring out the window.

"What's wrong, Marie?" White asked.

"It's nothing . . . I just wish Gary was here. I know he's busy and all, and he's living his dream, but it would be nice if we could enjoy this together," Marie replied.

"Don't beat yourself up too much. Think about the surprise on his face when he returns. Gary won't have to feel so alone any more," Kai answered as the limo passed the sign stating that they were entering Morfran.

The city was mostly controlled by a group of people, known as the Dark Guild.

CHAPTER 64

THE HIGH RANKERS

The first day passed without any major problems for Gary. Surprisingly, nobody had challenged any of the newcomers. Because of the lack of decent food, Gary had felt hungrier than usual, but since there had been no need for him to act, it had been tolerable.

As intended, Gary had simply spent his time observing those who had been here for a longer period of time, and he continued doing so on the second and third days. His Energy reserve had fallen to 178, but he had at least learned a lot in the meantime.

For one, public fights in the center had been a daily occurrence. However, Gary had discovered that the fights held there were mostly following some secret agreement between both parties.

Far more interesting were the seemingly spontaneous fights that had happened elsewhere.

As it turned out, fights could take place practically anywhere and at any time during their free time, outside of meals and bedtime. Interestingly, even in an awkward space that was relatively small, the teachers would come out to clear the area, making sure the other students wouldn't get hurt. These fights were mostly instigated by those who ranked highly, who didn't seem inclined to show off.

The training facility was one of the places where fighting was prohibited. Gary had visited it, and he had to admit that it was filled with some seriously advanced stuff. At the time, around a dozen low-rank-ing students had been using it, all seemingly striving to get better. Of course, since he had no access to the higher-ranking training facili-ties, Gary couldn't compare the two, though most of the high rankers preferred to chill in the main area as far as he had observed.

At the same time, the werewolf had kept an eye on those who had joined with him. Izzy had taken a far more active approach than he did, and whenever he spotted her, she was with a different set of students. She was obviously gathering information for her next move, but only a few had been willing to actually talk with her.

Listening in, Gary could tell that they looked down on her sim-ply because she hadn't been scouted. Unsurprisingly, this wasn't limited to her. Gary, Numba, and Ian all were being discriminated against since they had entered through the assessment.

Things changed on the second day after Ian challenged a boy ranked at 105. Gary wasn't sure whether Ian's Altered form had great regenerative properties or the AFA had used some means to heal him up so quickly, but he had been able to fight as if he had never been injured. What's more, despite being unable to transform, he had easily won.

After that, people that had gathered and started to talk to Ian a bit more, asking about his background and such. Some even asked if they could do business with him.

I guess it's not all negative, then. If you can prove yourself here, you can even make connections for your gang. You don't just have to be afraid of others, Gary thought.

This morning, Numba had fought a girl ranked 98, and he had won his fight without too much trouble, allowing him to upgrade from the chicken soup that Izzy and Gary were being served once more.

"Don't get your hopes up just because they won," Izzy warned as she sat next to Gary. She had taken an interest in the werewolf, and given his strength, she was surprised he hadn't acted yet.

"What do you mean?" Gary asked after slurping his soup, recovering his Energy to 180.

"Haven't you noticed how those ranked closest to us are on the older side? It's because a lot of them are like us, those who came in here after passing the assessments and have just remained here for a while. They all still seem to be hoping that they can get out of this place at some point.

"From my calculations, we are a long way off in strength compared to the others . . . I'm speaking just about the three of us, of course. You, Gary, are a different story, and honestly, I'm looking forward to what happens once you stir this place up."

The werewolf grinned; their relationship might have started off on the wrong foot, but after getting to know her a bit he had somewhat forgiven Izzy for what she had done. He didn't want to hold a grudge forever; after all, she had just been using whatever she could to get through the test, and in the worst case, he would have lost the opportunity to attend the AFA, not his life.

After their meal, everyone automatically went to the main area, but something was going on. A circle had formed, and a student started to clap. The sound echoed loudly around the halls.

It was a lean student who had four others following him, all of them above rank 50; everyone's attention was on him because of the number 4 on his badge.

"Congratulations on your fight this morning. Now I think you and I should have a little talk," the rank 4 said, pointing at Numba. The Goat Altered looked straight at him and walked off.

Numba wanted to pass the other student and head to his new room, but as he did, the others started to follow, thinking a fight was going to start. But strangely a few others stopped them.

"Everyone, just mind your own business and stay out of it!" their leader told them. They were quick to listen and walked away; they wore badges numbered 5, 6, and 8.

Gary approached Numba to find out what was going on. He owed Numba a favor, so he wanted to help, but after a few steps someone grabbed him by the arm.

"What do you think you're doing? I know I said I was excited to see what you were going to do, but even crazy should have its limits!" Izzy whispered as she pulled Gary in. "You don't understand what's going on, but I do.

"Remember what I said before, about how staying in the top ten for a week would be difficult. From what I've gathered, we came at a strange time. The current top ten have all come to an agreement.

"They announced that they would back each other up if one of them was challenged, and they would not fight each other for a week. Apparently, it's been hard for students to pass because of that rule.

"Once these ten are through, there will be a large free-for-all that goes on for the next top ten positions. That's going to be our best chance, and yours, if you want to get to the real academy."

Holding Gary's sleeve tightly, she could still feel that he was going to pull away, despite her warning.

"As I thought, gang members are crazy!" Izzy yanked on his shirt again, trying to convince him. "Whatever they're planning to do to Numba, it won't be bad. They have nothing to gain from him. He's from a small town, and he's a low rank, so don't worry."

Gary pulled his arm away with just a bit of extra force.

"Worrying is what I do. Maybe it's because I've worried about my mother and sister for so long . . . but I just don't like seeing this stuff. If it's nothing, then you won't have to worry about me either," Gary said as he walked over to the three high-ranking members were.

"Stop!" the rank 8 shouted, and placed his hand out in front of the werewolf.

CHAPTER 65

THE TOP OF THE TOP

A second ago, everyone had been about to leave and do their own thing, worried that staying there might get them in trouble with the top rankers. However, when they heard Gary being shouted at, they couldn't help but turn around to satisfy their own curiosity.

"You think that guy has a death wish?" one of the students murmured to the one standing next to him. "When's the last time someone dared to go up against anyone in the top ten?"

"I dunno about that death wish part, but that fresh blood's stay is destined to be miserable now. The poor idiot probably doesn't even have any idea what kind of mistake he just committed," another replied.

"I feel bad for him. He's going to get killed if someone doesn't pull him out," a third one chimed in.

"You're a Cat Altered, aren't you? If you want to play the Good Samaritan, go sacrifice one of your nine lives to save him. I'll make sure to pray for the both of you after they've sent you to the other side," another one said, ridiculing the notion.

At the same time from the third floor, a trio of students were watching things unravel from above. Because if something did occur, they would probably have to step in.

***

"Hey, Snow, Apollo, did Sty tell any of you that he would be doing this?" a shirtless student asked. He was scratching his short stiff hair at an incredible speed; one would think he was trying to start a fire. His jacket was tied around his waist, and the badge that all the students wore was pinned on it, showing the number 3. This student was called Wu Chen, and many knew his name, as he was the most often seen top ranker. He spent most of his time training in the standard training rooms that anyone could use.

Wu was scowling because he had been in the middle of training when he was called. "Didn't we all agree to sit still for one week? Ha, didn't you guys even bet that I would be the first one to break the pact? Looks like you'll have to treat me once we're in the AFA!"

"No, he didn't warn any of us, Wu. He better have a good explanation. Otherwise, I say we should punish him by reducing his rank," the tallest student among them replied. His hands tightened around the bar, and he was grinding his teeth.

Seeing how Snow Light, the currently second-strongest student, reacted, the person to his left handed him a carrot. Not even looking up, Snow grabbed it and chomped down on it aggressively, his overly long ears whipping up and down while all the tension in his body began to disappear.

Wu couldn't help but pull a face as he continued to blather on.

"I don't think you should be saying anything, Snow! With enough carrots, he could easily bribe you into pretending like you hadn't seen anything." Wu then turned to the largest man in the room.

"I don't mind him taking action," Wu continued. "To be honest, there are already rumors going around that those in the top twenty intended to challenge us all on the last day to stop us from advancing. I'm not sure how reliable those rumors are, but given that their background isn't too far off from ours, we can't just ignore that possibility. Besides, I'm sure our actions have made us some enemies in here." He let out a big sigh, sounding tired of the situation.

"I was the one who proposed the idea of no fighting, so I guess I will also need to be the one that enforces the rules." Apollo Zorian stared at the green-haired student. "I prefer honest people like that guy. At least you know what to expect from his type since they express their feelings openly."

Underneath Apollo's dark clothes was a chest bigger than anyone else's. What also stood out was his incredibly pale skin, which looked like it would be burned just from the lights in the room alone. On top of that, there were visible scars on his knuckles and a few on his chin as well.

Most people would avoid such a person on sight. Not many Altered had scars, because their bodies healed so quickly. This meant that at first glance, it was obvious that he wasn't unfamiliar with the world of fighting, as he had fought before he was an Altered. Yet there was another reason to avoid him. His badge showed the number 1.

I wonder what surprises the rest of this week still holds for us, he thought with a mild grin.

On the first floor, Gary continued walking toward the high-ranking individuals. He showed no fear, and the others had already pegged him as a dead man walking, though they were also looking forward to witnessing a one-sided beating.

The two high rankers looked at each other, wondering what to do, as well as which one of them would fight him, because Gary's number indicated he was one of the weakest people in this place.

That was until Gary stopped about a foot away from the rank 8 student's hand.

"You don't have a problem with me standing here, do you? Don't worry, I won't interrupt," Gary said.

I have no idea what he's thinking. Izzy shook her head in disbelief. *Does he plan to annoy them into attacking him first? Or is he just hoping that if he seems confident, they won't attack him, fearing the kind of backing he might have?*

In the end, the two high rankers simply nodded, unwilling to call the werewolf's bluff. They didn't want to act before they were sure about who this newcomer was, and as long as he behaved they were willing to tolerate his antics.

The reason why Gary had stopped just short of them was simple. From that position, he could hear everything that was happening to Numba. A normal person wouldn't have been able to hear from this distance, but then again, the green-haired teenager was anything but normal.

Inside his newly earned room, Numba sat down while surrounded by a bunch of uninvited guests.

"What do you want? Given her ranking, I doubt the one I defeated was a friend of yours, so you shouldn't be here for revenge." The Goat Altered came right to the point.

"Oh, that? No, you're correct, I don't know her and she's nowhere near my type. I've just come here to talk to you," said Sty, the number 4 student. "You see, I heard that TS Services plans to expand. They're the ones backing you, correct?"

Numba's attitude changed from nonchalance to interest. A smidgen of respect appeared on his face.

"You see, your father, or I guess adoptive father, recently came to my family asking to do business with us. I thought since we are the ones who will represent our companies in the future, it would be in our mutual interest to get to know each other. Besides, I have some influence in here, so I can make sure that your stay will be more comfortable sooner rather than later," Sty said with a smile.

Numba thought about it, because his number one rule was not to trust people, and he didn't understand what exactly Sty would get out of all of this.

"What's in it for you? I have nothing to give you, least of all in this place. My rank is far below yours, not to mention, you'll soon be leaving," Numba replied.

"That's where you're wrong. You have one thing that I desire: yourself. I'm always in need of loyal people. I want to build up my own group, you see, and what better place than the AFA? Agree and I will tell my folks to treat yours nicely. All you need to do is do as I say."

A short while later, the conversation ended. Sty left the room, followed by his goons, and eventually Numba. The Goat Altered looked unhurt, which led the onlookers to speculate as to what they might have been talking about.

Sty headed to the other high-ranking members, and that was when he saw Gary standing there.

"What are you looking at?" he asked.

Gary looked him up and down, before smiling. "Nothing, I just didn't know shit could stack so high."

CHAPTER 66

A PERSONAL PET

Gary turned away, though not before seeing Sty's face turn beet red. Before the top ranker had a chance to say anything, the werewolf had run off. Not because he was scared, but because he knew it would be far more annoying to someone so high and mighty.

He returned to his room to think about what he had just heard.

He had insulted Sty because those had been his real feelings toward the guy. Just listening to him talk, he was convinced that the top ranker was someone who abused his power and position. It reminded him a lot of how the Underdogs and Damion used to act.

In a place like this, there were lots of little Damions all over the place. It took a mental toll on the werewolf to avoid following his gut instinct to punch them in the face.

Still, he understood that he had to bide his time, so he kept his feelings buried. Just from watching how they used their position to abuse others, Gary was learning a lot.

He might not like it, but he knew that what he was seeing was the unfortunate reality of how such people acted. Kai had a lot of experience with this, but Gary, whose social standing had been at the bottom before he obtained his system, knew nothing about it.

Perhaps there would be a day when Gary's suggestions would be better than what Kai could come up with.

"Who was that?" Sty asked, barely holding himself together, his cheeks still a bit red and filled with anger.

"We're not really sure. The guy's rank suggests he's one of the newcomers, so it might be best to just ignore him for now. It's not really worth our time to fight someone like that. Remember, we all agreed to avoid fighting this week," the rank 8 reminded him.

Sty took a deep breath. Before he reached the top ten, he had often stirred up trouble by fighting. He couldn't help it; he found it exhilarating to see how hopeless the other Altered looked once he defeated them.

Still, he had agreed with the other top rankers that he would lay low for one week until they were allowed to advance. Since Apollo had suggested the idea, it was a given that he would be the one to enforce it. Sty knew that he himself was strong, but he also knew that the top three were more powerful than he was.

Even someone of his position could be kicked out of the top ten, replaced with someone else. In the end, he made up his mind to let it go . . . at least in here. If he saw Gary in the AFA, that would be another story . . .

Two more days passed, and Gary had still not challenged anyone. According to the rules, an assessment would take place soon, which was another opportunity for people to change their rank. However, the green-haired teenager didn't care too much about the assessment.

From what Izzy had told him at lunch yesterday, most students shared his sentiment. The main way to rise in the ranks was through fighting.

Ian had participated in two fights just this morning, winning both of them and obtaining rank 77. The Altered had stopped there, claiming it was a lucky number for him. It was quite impressive considering that he was unable to transform into his Altered form.

However, he hadn't been the only one who fought. For the first time, Izzy had shown off her skills. Granted, she had only fought against the student with the next higher ranking, but that fight had looked like carefully prepared choreography.

Without suffering a single injury, she had continued to fight two more times, eventually reaching rank 101. After doing a lot of research into other people's Altered forms and fighting styles, she had set her goal to reach double digits.

Unfortunately, against rank 99, she had also suffered her first loss. Izzy's head had ended up swollen, her ribs bruised, all due to a single mistake. Whether she had overestimated herself after consecutive wins or underestimated her opponent, she didn't know.

However, the loss had been a devastating one; the difference in skill had been obvious.

Fortunately, the medical care in this place was top notch, so Izzy was back on her feet for lunch. Ian had earned the privilege to sit at yet another new table, but he had decided to come over to where Gary was, probably because Izzy had done the same.

Although the newcomers had been told on the first day that they should sit according to the numbers on the table, nobody was actually enforcing that rule.

"Guys, you have got to get out of the hundreds as soon as possible!" Ian said. "They have meat! I admit, it's merely pieces of meat, but it's way better than that soup, I tell you."

By now, Izzy had gotten used to eating the soup, but after her loss she had shown no appetite, playing with her food before handing it over to Gary.

"Don't worry too much, you did well. You had four fights in a row, and we have plenty of time to help you rank up." Ian tried to cheer up his childhood friend.

"My problem is, I don't see how," Izzy mumbled listlessly. "I know my body better than anyone, and I just don't see a way for me to beat rank 99. Not with my current skill set even if I had been at a hundred percent My only chance might be to unlock my Altered form, but who knows how long that will take!"

Gary didn't say anything, focusing on gulping down the soup. Sadly, he couldn't give her any input. After all, he wasn't an Altered in the first place. His system was what allowed him to get stronger, and he wasn't the best when it came to techniques either. One of his good points was his ability to analyze, but Izzy didn't seem to have a problem in that department.

Just then, Numba entered the canteen. The group didn't really have many friends in the place, so they had silently agreed to sit together and talk to each other most of the time.

"I guess he's doing it again," Ian said.

But Numba headed to the table with the top rankers, stopping next to Sty. After a while, the Goat Altered left, then came back with a meal meant for the rank 4 student. Not only that, but while Sty enjoyed his steak and soda, Numba gave him a back massage.

Essentially, the lower-ranked teenager fulfilled all of the top ranker's whims, starting the evening after their talk. The trio of newcomers found it an odd sight to behold, because although they hadn't known Numba for long, his current attitude was a clear contrast to his initial prideful self.

"They might be from the same city, or they're blackmailing him in some other way," Izzy guessed. "There's not much we can do about it. I know it's sad, but it's unfortunate that one of the top rankers has picked Numba to be his lackey. Anyway, without any incidents, he will only have to endure that for a few more days, and then he will be able to do what he wants again, I imagine that's why he's putting up with it for now."

At that moment, a bit of food dropped onto Numba's shirt, and the others began to laugh. Gary stood up from his seat and began to walk over to them.

"Damn it, why does he always move so fast? I didn't even have time to grab that stupid moss head!" Izzy cursed, slapping her forehead.

Gary reached the table and stared at the Goat Altered and his handler. Sty, who had already forgotten their encounter, just looked at him. He thought the green-haired teenager looked familiar, but he just couldn't put a finger on who he was.

Oh, isn't this the same person from the other day? Apollo thought as he recognized who it was.

The rest of the top three, including Snow, who continued to munch on his small pile of prepared carrots, also instantly recognized him, though none of them stopped enjoying their meal.

"Numba, I don't know how you can do this. I don't know if you're scared or what, but I just can't watch you act like this. Is it really worth it? Can't your family make a deal with another company or something? If you're that scared, remember I still owe you a favor, so I will happily beat this person up for you if you want."

CHAPTER 67

PREDATOR (PART 1)

Gary looked straight at Sty during the last part of his sentence, making the rank 4 student experience an odd feeling of déjà vu.

Why am I getting this annoying bubbling feeling about this guy . . . For some reason, his annoying green hair reminds me of something. Am I just annoyed because my mom forced me to eat broccoli? No, that's not it. Sty was left puzzled.

He usually took any small threat seriously, teaching the other person a serious lesson, but the moment his eyes wandered to the number on the green-haired teenager's badge, he chuckled. The scene reminded him of a baby trying to threaten an adult, and he found it amusing.

"Numba, this person is being an eyesore. Make sure he leaves," the top ranker ordered, waving his hand nonchalantly toward Gary as if he were a fly pestering him.

The top rankers sitting next to him at the table laughed, looking forward to what would happen next. They all knew that the teachers would stop a fight in here, but they wouldn't act right away.

Numba moved toward Gary, and the other students smiled.

"Please leave, Gary . . . I understand that you mean well, but if you really want to help me, you should leave right now," Numba urged in a soft, defeated voice.

It was a complete contrast to when the werewolf had first met him. Where was the confident teenager who would never take crap from anyone? The Goat Altered had resonated with Gary, because his gut instinct had told him that the two of them were alike.

Right now, this was also true, but the current Numba resembled the werewolf during his time in the Underdogs, when he had been merely a transporter. Just as Gary had feared Damion, the Goat Altered seemed afraid of Sty; both of them had felt helpless.

Gary remembered the feeling well, and he often wished someone could have helped him. In a way, Kirk had done that, pulling him out of the situation before he drowned, and this time Gary wanted to be the helping hand.

"What do you think you're doing?" the rank 4 student asked in annoyance. "Do I really have to spell it out to you? When I tell you to get rid of him, I don't mean to ask him nicely! Go beat him up! Come on, even someone of your caliber must be able to do something. Or do you really not care about the deal?"

Gary slammed his hand on the table, making their plates jump. He had shut Sty's mouth right there before he said anything else, and his eyes started to glow faintly red. Immediately, the others stood up, ready to jump on Gary at any second if he were to try something. These actions also caught the eyes of the teachers, who started to pay a little more attention.

At the head of the table where the top three sat, they felt the vibration across the table and both Wu and Snow stood up.

"What the hell? That guy made one of my carrots drop on the floor!" Snow complained. "I'm going to kick his ass."

Just as they were about to move, though, someone pushed down on their shoulders, forcing them back into their seats.

"Calm down, you two, things are about to get interesting," Apollo ordered, not moving his eyes away from the low-ranking student who had disturbed their meal.

Apollo himself even sat down, grabbing a large turkey leg, and continued digging into his food as if he were watching a movie.

Hahaha, I can tell from just looking into that guy's eyes. He's a predator, one who has tasted blood! Apollo kept his thoughts to himself, rather than warning the others. It wasn't his business anyway. He only regretted the fact that Gary had come so late, as he would have loved to spar with him. Unfortunately, it would look bad if he broke the agreement he himself had instated.

However, his gut was telling him that the two of them would meet again in the future.

Sty didn't move; a certain chill was going through him. The hair was sticking up all over his body. The eyes of everyone inside the canteen were focused on the scene. If he said nothing, did nothing, then the others might think he was weak.

Realizing the same thing, Numba grabbed Gary by the wrist, though he wasn't particularly strong. The werewolf took his hand off the table and looked at the Altered, who pleaded with his eyes to make him go.

"Fine, I'll leave like you asked; just know that I hate seeing you like this. Remember, I owe you one, no matter what it is."

Gary didn't go back to sit with the others. Instead, he decided to just leave the canteen to calm down. But the other students were surprised that such a low-ranking member was allowed to threaten someone at the top-ranking table without any consequences.

Of course, many assumed that Gary had just lived to see another day, as they were sure he would become a huge target of the person he had crossed soon enough. With him gone, and the top rankers continuing their meal as if nothing had happened, the others did the same.

What nobody noticed was that one of the teachers had been speaking softly into a microphone during the entire commotion.

"This is the first time in a while that I've seen you pay so much attention to a new student, Wood," Hai commented as he took a sip of his coffee. "I understand that it's rare for the scouts to miss someone, but it's not like this is the first time. Don't you think you're wasting your time on him?"

"Perhaps, but perhaps not. You've seen it yourself, he's in an entirely different league," Wood answered as he drank his tea. "He has yet to actually fight anyone, but his actions have already caused ripples."

"From the reports we've received, he's only been observing the others. Sounds to me like he's simply looking for the best opponent to beat; nothing uncommon about that." Hai shrugged.

"Please, we both know that he can easily become one of the high rankers. If that were his goal, he could have achieved it on the first day. I, for one, am looking forward to what happens when he finally decides to act.

"There are already interesting things happening in the AFA, and I predict that he will make it even more interesting, just like that feisty girl who came here before."

CHAPTER 68

A PREDATOR (PART 2)

"Man, I know Gary is strong, but I don't think he can just go around doing whatever he likes," Ian whispered to Izzy. "You've been gathering intel so far. Based on his strength, what rank do you think he could get if he were to fight for real?"

Izzy stared into the distance for a while. They were still in the canteen, and quite a few people were talking about what had happened. She shook her head for a moment before answering Ian's question. "Based on what he showed us during the assessment, he should at least be able to enter the top fifty. As for what rank he would end up with, I'm not too sure. Practically all the high rankers should be able to do what he did.

"Still, the confidence Gary has to just do what he wants . . . I don't know if he is just crazy or he actually has the strength to back it up. If only it were true that this place merely cares about strength . . . With people from Tier 2 and even Tier 1 cities, his actions might actually prove harmful to those Howlers back home . . . yet he doesn't seem to be too worried about it."

"I wish I could be the same." Ian sighed, rubbing his leg. "Every time I get close to him, my leg starts to hurt, even though it has already healed. I have no idea how many people in here might be stronger than him; I just know that he is the last person I would really want to fight."

Later that night, many students struggled to get some sleep. Numba lay in his room thinking about what Gary had said, and to release his frustration, he punched the wall.

A small dent appeared, but since he hadn't transformed, it wasn't too big. However, the wall was quite sturdy, enough that his knuckles were bleeding.

Damn it, Gary, don't you think I want to hit that asshole in his stupid face? I've thought about it . . . but I just can't do it . . . I can't. If I do, someone like him will definitely punish my family. Even if they didn't, they gave me everything.

At the same time, Izzy was having her own difficulties falling asleep. She was restlessly lying in bed, reviewing her match to rank 99. She couldn't help but stare at the ceiling thinking of how to win, but no matter what, she couldn't think of anything but one option.

I have nothing to lose, I have to go for it, Izzy thought. She got up and left her room. Outside it was dark; the lights were turned off after midnight, but there was no rule about students having to stay in their rooms and sleep. It was just that nearly everyone was on that pattern.

Gary's room was not too far from her own. As one of the lowest-ranked rooms, it didn't even have a proper door.

If I want to get better, I have no choice but to train. Who better to ask than the strongest person I know?

Plucking up her courage, she looked inside, but no one was there. *Where could he be?*

Izzy walked around, scratching her head. Places like the canteen were locked at this time of night, and since he had kept to himself, it was unlikely that he was in someone else's room.

Following her hunch, she went past one of the teachers, who stood there like a statue. Theoretically, teachers were supposed to enforce the rules, but just as with the intended curfew, this one appeared to be slacking on his watch.

"It looks like you're lost." The teacher pointed out the obvious.

"Oh, just looking for someone," Izzy replied, surprised that he had said something. "You didn't happen to have seen a certain green-haired boy by any chance, did you?"

The man simply pointed toward the training rooms. He hadn't even needed Gary's description, since the teenage boy was the only other student who had come out this late at night.

I've never seen Gary train since getting here, but I guess everyone has to train at some point.

Thanking the man, she headed to the training room. She opened the door and was surprised to see that the lights were off, but suddenly she saw a pair of red eyes moving across the room, jumping from one side to the other at a great speed. It was difficult for Izzy to keep track of them, but suddenly the pair of eyes started to head right toward her.

Her fight-or-flight response was triggered, but her knees gave out, making her drop to the floor in complete fear.

"What are you doing here?" a familiar voice asked. Izzy could now see Gary; he was shirtless, clearly showing his hard abs, and there was a bit of fur on his chest and arms. It was retracting into his body as he approached her, and the glow in his eyes disappeared.

"I . . . I . . . I just w-wanted to ask you something." Izzy tried to stand up, only to nearly fall over again, but Gary caught her with one hand, making her face go slightly red.

"Thank you," she said. "I wanted to ask you . . . to train me. I want to be a stronger fighter."

Gary studied Izzy for a moment, then wiped his sweat away.

"All right, I'll help you, but not right now," Gary replied as he walked past her, heading toward his room. "I can't let my Energy drop any lower than this . . . so I guess it's time I start doing things. Once I can get a good meal, I'll help you train."

Izzy was left there confused, wondering what he meant by that statement.

CHAPTER 69

WHO'S SCARIER?

The next day, the students were woken up by a loud announcement calling them to the main oval room. One of the teachers stood there with a piece of paper in his hand. The moment everyone was inside, he began reading the contents.

"Due to certain circumstances, the next assessment evaluation has been moved back and will take place in four days rather than today. This also means that the students ranked 1 to 10 will have to keep their position for that additional time period if they wish to advance."

As soon as he was done, he turned around and left the room. Since the ones most affected by this sudden change were the top rankers, the other students just smiled and returned to what they had been doing.

"Has this ever happened before? Am I the only one who feels like they're blatantly targeting us?" Wu asked, visibly annoyed.

"Who knows?" Apollo shrugged. "I'm not surprised that they decided to act. From the start, it was impossible for them to not notice that the ten of us haven't really been fighting since we became the top rankers. If anything, I'm surprised that their approach is this lenient, given that we're circumventing the rules. Still, we should be careful. Who knows what will happen in these next four days?"

The others weren't sure what he meant, but Apollo noticed that there was a different air around the most prominent newcomer.

Izzy and Ian weren't bothered by the announcement and simply performed their morning ritual of watching the fights that were happening before breakfast. Izzy watched mostly to figure out how to counter her potential future opponents, while Ian was hyping himself up before his next fight.

As they watched, Izzy told her childhood friend about what had happened last night.

"Wow, I never thought you would actually go to him to ask for help." Ian gasped at the shocking revelation. "I don't think I could do the same; his presence alone makes me feel off. Still, let me know if there's some secret involved to his strength. Until then, I think I'll just continue fighting until I hit a wall. The more I fight, the more I can feel that I'm getting one step closer to grasping my Altered form! Just you wait, once I can transform like the others, you'll see me rising through the ranks!"

There was a smug smile on Ian's face. He had gained a lot of confidence based on his recent fights. Originally he had believed that he would have a hard time competing with those who had been scouted, but he was doing fairly well despite being unable to transform.

At that moment, two people came up to them on either side. Izzy and Ian wanted to move out of the way, but the two blocked them in with their bodies.

Damn it, what did we do to make the high rankers come to us? Izzy wondered as she stared at the badges of the brothers, rank 44 and rank 42. The former belonged to the long-haired redhead, while the latter belonged to his short-haired brother. They seemed to be fraternal twins rather than identical.

"From what we've been able to gather, the two of you took the assessment along with that Broccoli Head, correct?" rank 44 asked.

They hadn't turned their heads while speaking, acting like they had just joined the duo in watching the fight.

"That's correct, but what's it to you?" Ian replied, not liking where this was going.

"You see, we were told to gather some information on him. So we just wanted to know a few things about him, nothing you shouldn't know. What's his Altered form, his fighting style, and most importantly, his backing?" rank 42 asked.

It didn't take long for Izzy to figure out that these two had to be working for one of the top rankers. It seemed like Gary's confidence had made them hesitate before acting, so they first wanted to verify whether the green-haired teenager was someone they could afford to touch.

"Sorry, but we have no idea. He didn't look impressive, so we didn't pay attention to him during the first test. After that, he kicked all of our asses without transforming, so the only thing we know about him is that he is far stronger than us." Izzy quickly made up a cover story before Ian could accidentally spill the beans.

Just then the fight stopped, and Izzy tried to move away, but one of the brothers grabbed her hand.

"Nice story, but we're not buying it. You've been sitting together during the meals like real chums, so I don't believe that he hasn't told you anything of value about himself. Let me warn you, if you don't tell us exactly what we need to know, then starting today, we'll make your stay here a living hell.

"Every day, the two of us will challenge you two, and during the fight, we will beat you before you can give up, and we'll also make sure nobody else will fight you. We will continue to do that until you eventually leave!"

Izzy pulled her arm away, and Ian moved to stand behind her and the twins.

"Fine, go ahead!" Izzy shouted as she walked away. "Your threats might work on others, but it's not going to work if I'm more scared of the other person!"

"Yeah, if you two want to get involved with that crazy person, then be my guest, but I'm not going to sell him out." Ian shrugged and shivered as he thought back to what Gary had done to him by accident.

The brothers were left dazed, as this was the first time their threats were ineffective. They couldn't believe that these two new-comers were actually more scared of this Gary person. It just didn't make sense, but Izzy's words were true. After seeing him last night, she knew that she should never cross him if she wanted to live.

As Ian and Izzy headed toward the library, another large figure stood in their way. They looked up and gulped at the size of the large person's chest.

"Oh, here I was waiting for just you two. I was wondering if you could tell me a couple of things about your green-haired friend," Apollo said with a toothy smile.

"Umm, Izzy . . . I might be afraid of this person a little more than Gary," Ian whispered.

CHAPTER 70

A NICE MEAL

Gary, just how did you manage to make even the rank 1 of this place interested in you? Izzy thought as she gulped hard. *I asked about what happened at the canteen, but from what I've been told, the only one you antagonized was Sty. Is Apollo asking because of the pact that the top rankers made?*

Was he the one who sent those twins over? No, I doubt it. From the things I've heard, he's the type who acts on his own, just like he is doing now. Unfortunately, Ian has a point; although I haven't seen Apollo act, making an enemy of the strongest person in this place isn't a good idea.

Apollo continued to do nothing but smile at the duo, who looked at him like a pair of frightened bunnies. Ian looked at Izzy for an answer.

"What exactly do you want to know?" Izzy asked cautiously.

After they had answered all of Apollo's questions, the top ranker simply walked away, even thanking them for the talk. The two breathed out a sigh of relief as Apollo headed back to his room. Thankfully for Izzy and Ian, Apollo's actions were more friendly than his looks.

The rank 1's room was large and included everything anyone could ever wish for, rivaling a suite in a five-star hotel.

The king-size mattress, the comfiest sheets, the bathtub, and the rainfall shower were just the tip of the iceberg. In fact, the room was so nice, that his two friends often came over just to hang out, even though their rooms were not far away.

When he came in, he found Wu and Snow already playing a game of cards at the table.

"So, did you find what you wanted?" Wu asked, as he looked over his cards, raising the pot.

"Yeah . . . but it was a bit disappointing," Apollo answered with a sigh. "Turns out he comes from a Tier 3 town, apparently one that hasn't any redeeming qualities. The only interesting part about it was that he is backed by a gang."

"Honestly, what exactly did you expect from someone who wasn't scouted? If he were worth his salt, he wouldn't continue being a low ranker. He's probably just acting tough because he's in a gang," Snow replied, revealing his cards and winning all the snacks that had been in the middle of the table. The first thing he did was munch on a carrot in delight.

"Haha, looks like your killer instinct is getting dull from you not doing anything," Snow said, teasing his friend. "Don't worry, you're not completely to blame for that; given his confidence, he even made a fool out of Sty."

Apollo lay down on his bed, wondering whether there was some truth in what his friend said, but he kept thinking about something he had overheard from Izzy and Ian's earlier conversation.

She said she was more scared of him than the twins. From what I've seen, she's a smart cookie, so she must have realized that those two were sent by Sty or another of the top rankers . . . and there's also the look in his eyes. If he can actually fake that, he deserves an Oscar, Apollo thought.

At that moment, there was a light knock at the door. "Come in."

Sty opened the door and closed it behind him. Immediately, Apollo lay back down on his bed, as he wasn't really interested in what Sty had to say.

"Skip the formalities, all right? That's only for outside this place and when our families meet. Why did you come to me?" Apollo asked without much enthusiasm.

"All right," Sty replied, his voice a little shaky; he was nervous in Apollo's presence. "I'm here to ask for your permission to deal with the annoying guy. You all heard what he said in the canteen. He needs to be taught a lesson before others start thinking they can do the same to us.

"I'm not here asking to break the pact. I agree that it's far more important for us to move on to the next stage and enter the academy, which is why I'm asking if you won't mind me sending my men to act."

Apollo rose up from his bed and looked at Sty. "That's a far more reasonable request from you than I had expected. Sure, feel free to send out some of your guys."

Having been granted permission, Sty immediately left the room, though he found the reaction odd. He had been prepared to convince Apollo somehow, only to be given his full blessing.

Of course, he had no way of knowing that the rank 1 student was already looking forward to how Gary would deal with the twins.

Gary had gone down to breakfast, but as usual, the food really wasn't enough to fill him up. His Energy had finally dropped below 150, which had only strengthened his resolve to act today.

Should I just go and teach that Sty guy a lesson? No, it might affect Numba if I do that. Unfortunately, it looks like he will have to endure this treatment for four more days. Hmmm, what if I go for rank 3 instead? If I win that fight, then maybe I'll have a bit more influence over Sty and can tell him to stop.

Contemplating this possibility, Gary was ready to leave his room, but just then, a pair of redheaded brothers came in. It was already a small space, so they blocked almost all the light coming in.

"Next time, think twice whether you should open your stupid mouth." the student with the rank 42 sneered, as his face started to transform, along with his brother's.

Gary looked around; the small room wasn't the best place to fight, but there was one good point about it. Nobody would be able to see what he was about to do.

"I'm sorry, guys . . . but your red hair and the fact that you're brothers really piss me off. I've been hangry for the last few days and since you came to me, don't blame me for retaliating," Gary replied, his eyes starting to turn red.

Finally, it was time for lunch. The students flocked in, and Ian went to sit with Izzy at Gary's table so they could enjoy their food together. Numba stood next to Sty, who had a large smile on his face for some reason.

"Hey . . . Gary's late," Izzy said. "You don't think someone went after him?"

"I mean, that guy is never late for lunch . . . it can only be that. Do you think that top ranker acted even though he promised he wouldn't do anything?"

Just as they were about to look for their missing friend, they saw him enter through the double doors.

"Phew, he's finally here." Ian let out a sigh. "Hey, Gary, we've been waiting for you. If you don't hurry, your soup will get cold."

Gary just gave him a thumbs-up. "I'll be over in a second."

The werewolf took a moment to locate the seat numbered 42 and grabbed the food from there.

Finally, a worthy meal! he thought, as he stared at the steak, potatoes, and extras.

CHAPTER 71

MATCH UP

BZZZZ

The familiar sound that indicated that it was time for the next meal resounded through the place. Despite practically starving throughout his stay, the werewolf had nevertheless been looking forward to each meal-time. The timing of his two uninvited guests made it clear that their appearance wasn't a coincidence.

Right now, everyone would go to the canteen, and the teachers would be busy making sure no fights broke out. However, one of the brothers was standing slightly behind the other, making it impossible to see inside.

With his head held down, Gary's body started to shake.

"Look at him, Brock!" The twin ranked 42 laughed. "That scaredy-cat is shaking all over from fear. Let's get this over and done with quickly, so we don't miss lunch."

Immediately, Brock rushed toward Gary. His face had transformed into that of a gross-looking insect. He had huge eyes and a giant forceps on top of his head, similar to that of a beetle.

The Insect Altered tilted his head down toward his target. His forceps looked sharp and strong and seemed to be controlled independently. He snapped them menacingly, creating a loud echo.

"Let's see you mouth off after I snap right through your weak bones!" Brock taunted.

"You guys . . ." Gary growled in a low tone. When the Insect Altered was close enough, he transformed both of his hands and grabbed the closing forceps of the intruder.

I . . . I can't close them! Brock realized as he intensified his struggles, but the green-haired teenager's hold on him was absolute.

"What are you doing, Brock? Just cut his hands! It's not like it will be your first time. They'll patch him up anyway," his brother shouted, unaware that the situation was no longer in their control.

"How dare you get in the way of my lunch?" Gary shouted as he used his strength to pull apart the forceps until they snapped. Blood rushed from Brock onto the floor, but Gary didn't stop there, using his leg to kick the Insect Altered in the stomach and sending him tumbling back into his brother, who caught him before he hit the floor.

"Make sure to hold him steady," Gary said as he threw out a fist, hitting Brock right in the stomach with a loud crack, indicating that more than one rib had been broken.

The attack was so strong that both twins flew out of the room and ended up embedded in a wall, both losing consciousness.

A teacher had taken care of the brothers, so Gary had simply headed to the canteen, where he was enjoying the taste of the superbly grilled steak. Of course, the potatoes and sides weren't much worse, but the meat was the real kicker.

10 points of Energy have been restored
158/300 Energy

That really hit the spot . . . but I'm still hungry. I should have asked if I can get seconds. I could still eat a dozen more, maybe even a hundred, after nothing but soup for nearly a week, Gary thought, rubbing his belly as he looked over at the others.

They were baffled at seeing the green-haired teenager sit at their table, but the number on his badge convinced them that he had every right to be there. Looking down at their own badges, they all saw that their numbers had shifted, further proving that a fight must have taken place just before he had appeared. As to whom he had fought, that was also obvious, since two seats were empty.

"Hey, are you guys going to eat that? If you're not, I could do with some extra food," Gary asked, eyeing up their plates full of meat as he licked his lips. "I really just want the meat, you can keep the rest."

The student next to him, who was now the new rank 44, just nodded, handing it over. His rank had been between the twins before, and seeing that the newcomer had been able to beat the stronger twin, he understood that he wasn't his match. Making an enemy out of him over a piece of meat really wasn't worth it.

Over at the top rankers' table, they had known that Sty had received permission to deal with the nuisance, but his appearance made it clear that the plan must have failed. Apollo noticed that Sty was tensing his fists. His head was practically shaking, and everyone at the table could hear him grinding his teeth in frustration.

How is that possible? The twins might not be the strongest in this place, but there were two of them against one of him! Just who is this person? Sty was left speechless.

Given the priceless look on his face, Apollo couldn't help but laugh. He had done his best to hold it in, but Sty's visible confusion was just too hilarious.

"You still think my killer instinct is off?" the rank 1 student gloated, snatching one of Snow's carrots out of the Altered's hands and taking a huge bite.

"Whatever, how far can a Tier 3 bumpkin like him really get in here? All he did was beat up two scrubs who could barely be called high rankers; that doesn't make him special," Snow replied, rolling his eyes before he grabbed another carrot.

Of course, Sty didn't miss that information and shot up in disbelief. "Tier 3 . . . that rubbish dares to spout off when he comes from a shitty Tier 3 town?"

Numba was speechless as well. He didn't know what to think as he looked at the green-haired teenager who was gobbling up meat without a care in the world.

"Gary, how are you not afraid about the consequences of your actions? Your family is from a Tier 3 town like mine. No matter who you are, even if you're a member of a gang, the guys in here can crush the likes of you and me like a bug. Don't you care about your gang members, or your family . . . or is it just . . ."

Having finished his second meal, Gary stood up. He headed toward the top table and made direct eye contact with Sty.

"Your two goons might be incapacitated for a while," Gary revealed. "Once they wake up, please let them know that they only got hurt because you were the one who sent them over to me. I was never planning to fight them myself."

"Damn you!" Sty shouted, ready to go after the Werewolf, but at that moment Apollo pounded his fist on the table, making Sty's plate and cutlery jump.

Getting the message, the rank 4 student glared at Gary but sat back down.

"Oh, I thought you were going to challenge me?" Gary said cockily. "Don't worry, I have no interest in fighting you, not until this guy asks me."

Gary looked over at the table and his gaze stopped at the rank 3 student, Wu Chen.

"I challenge you to a fight."

Wait a second, I didn't say that! Gary was confused. He turned and saw Numba pointing at Sty.

"I challenge you to a fight. Let's get this over and done with. I'm sick of you treating me like your personal butler," the Goat Altered clarified, his eyes burning with fire.

After Numba saw the werewolf act without fearing the consequences, something had been lit up inside him.

"Has everyone suddenly gone crazy? You want a fight, fine, then you've got one!" Sty shouted, standing up. "If you manage to win, I'll follow through with our deal, no questions asked . . . but if I win, you're going to wish you were never born!"

CHAPTER 72

RUMBLE

As they left the canteen, the students were far more excited than any other day. They walked together in a large group, following two specific individuals to their match.

Witnessing one of the top rankers fighting was usually quite a spectacle, because the top rankers only ever fought against others who were close to the top. This allowed the other students to see a high level of skills being displayed and showed everyone how close they were to catching up.

But the students were even more hyped up than usual because ever since the current batch of top rankers had risen to their position, they had made a pact that they wouldn't fight. This meant that no high-level fights had taken place, because nobody had dared to antagonize the top rankers. Ever since Gary had openly mocked Sty, the students had hoped that something would come out of it, and now that it had they were all elated, even though the green-haired newcomer wasn't the one who would fight.

"This isn't good," Izzy said to Ian, concerned for Numba. "Everyone has a right to challenge those in the top ten at any time. It's the whole point of the system, but the others haven't done that because of the pact."

"Ah, you worry too much." Ian shrugged. "Personally, I think this is quite exciting. I mean, let's assume Numba loses. What's the worst that will happen? From what you told me, the primary purpose of that pact was to prevent the other high rankers from challenging the top rankers constantly during the time they have to protect their top rank, not for people like Numba. Do you really think they would waste their time beating him over and over again?"

"You don't understand." Izzy sighed as she stopped walking. "I did some research on Apollo and Sty. They don't just have a relationship inside this place, but outside as well. Sty works for a gang in a Tier 2 city, who works for the leader of a gang in a Tier 1 city . . . which is linked to Apollo. Do you understand why it's so dangerous now, and why Numba has been listening to them this whole time?"

Ian wondered what he would do in that situation, and one thing was sure, he wouldn't touch someone from a gang in a Tier 2 city, much less one linked to a gang in a Tier 1 city. Their whole Tier 3 business could be wiped out in a few seconds by any one of those.

Just then, Gary placed his arms around the two of them.

"Let's just watch the fight and worry about that stuff later. Besides, remember what you said about gang members having pride. Do you really think this Apollo guy would go running off to his gang if he lost a fight . . . or call his gang for help with something like this?"

It was true, but it was always better to be safe than sorry, especially in this world. Everyone had now gathered in the large oval room. The students stood around the outer edge, making room for the fighters, Sty and Numba, in the center.

"It seems like your green-haired friend there has gotten into your head, making you think you can take me on. Let me show you that my background isn't the only reason I'm ranked this highly!" Sty shouted.

The match started and Sty began to transform. Immediately his eyes bulged, turning into compound eyes with a slightly orange color. At the same time, a pair of wings sprouted out of his back. Finally, his mouth elongated a bit, starting to resemble a proboscis, giving him the overall appearance of a fly.

At the same time, Numba was transforming as well. His horns had finished elongating at the same time as his opponent was done with his transformation.

The Goat Altered scraped the floor with his feet a couple of times, like a bull. Suddenly, Numba exploded in speed, closing the gap between the two in an instant. The onlookers gasped, thinking that Sty might go down in a single blow.

But Sty's eyes weren't just for show; He saw the moment that Numba accelerated, and his body was fast enough to react. Using his wings, he avoided the attack at the last second by flying into the air.

Where is he? Numba wondered, as his horns had failed to make impact. He looked up but could not see Sty in front of him. Then his back flared up in pain, and he fell to his knees. Sty had not only avoided the attack perfectly but had positioned himself in Numba's blind spot.

"That was your master plan in going against me?" Sty asked in ridicule. "What else have you got, now that your surprise attack failed?"

Turning around quickly in anger, Numba faced Sty again and pushed off with his feet, aiming for his horns to impale Sty's body, pinning him in place. But this time, instead of moving to the side, Sty flew upward, avoiding the attack once more.

"Haha, I could just stay up here all day, and you wouldn't be able to hit me. You're just a useless goat, and I can't believe you actually thought you could beat me with your level of skills!" Sty laughed, flying in to deliver a kick to Numba's face faster than he could react. Blood dripped from his nose and mouth onto the floor.

Numba swung a fist, but connected with air again. It didn't stop there, as Sty continued his attack pattern, flying in to kick his opponent before dodging back to avoid retaliation. After taking a couple of hits, the Goat Altered had to focus on defending, which left him no room to change the situation.

"Crap!" Gary cursed. "It's my fault Numba is fighting, and he's getting beaten to a pulp."

The werewolf hadn't been sure if Sty was all talk, but this fight proved that his arrogance was grounded in his abilities. Of course, the moment Numba had challenged him, Gary had considered the possibility that his buddy might lose . . . only he hadn't considered that it would be so one-sidedly.

Should I go in and help him? Gary thought, preparing to go in.

"If you intend to interfere in their fight, I'm afraid I'll have to stop you." A deep voice sounded from behind him.

When he turned around, he saw the large figure of Apollo, his arms crossed and a smile across his face, and that was when Gary saw the badge displaying the intimidating number 1.

CHAPTER 73

YOU'RE THE PROBLEM

Apollo was huge, and although most would be intimidated by his size, Gary turned to look at the fight after seeing who this person was.

"Are you looking for a fight? Because you can challenge me any time," Gary said while staring at the arena.

Most of the attention in the room was on the fight, so the spectators were unaware of what was happening, apart from Ian and Izzy, who stayed close to Gary. Besides them, Wu and Snow, who weren't too far off either, listened to everything going on, although they weren't too bothered.

I knew this guy was curious about Gary for some reason, but why? Izzy thought. *We didn't even have time to warn him or tell Gary about his background, but knowing Gary, he wouldn't back down anyway.*

She was nervous, not because she thought Gary would lose the fight, but rather about how it would affect his life.

Apollo chuckled.

"Haha, sorry, I think I misspoke. I have rules that I follow anyway. I agreed to no fighting for a week to move on from this place. There was no one interesting at the time. Anyway, I was talking about the teachers.

"They are overseeing this fight. It's being displayed publicly to everyone. If you try to jump in there, the teachers will stop you, and if you end up hurting any student before they can catch you, there's a good chance you'll be punished, maybe even kicked out.

"And I don't really want that to happen, which is why I decided to warn you."

Gary's clenched fists loosened up a bit. Feeling guilty, he thought he had to do something, but there were rules. It wasn't like the outside. Getting kicked out of the academy this soon wasn't an option; he could only stand there and watch the one-sided fight.

Sty continued to attack while dashing away into the air, making every single one of Numba's strikes fruitless. It wasn't that Sty was too fast; instead, it was hard to predict the angles at which he would come at Numba, and to make matters worse, the Goat Altered's reaction time was too slow.

It was a terrible matchup to pit them against each other, since Numba's strength came from raw power and straight-headed charges. But, unfortunately, he was no match against Sty's swiftness.

What the crowd did find interesting, though, was the fact that Numba was still standing. His face was bloody and had begun to swell. Even his ribs and arms were badly bruised, and almost the whole arena was covered in his blood.

Sty's strikes weren't weak by any means because of the momentum his attacks gained from his speed. It was just that Numba's heart was strong.

"Are you just going to keep running from me? Don't you have any pride?" Numba shouted in frustration with a swollen mouth. Even his teeth had turned red because of the blood.

"This is probably the best strategy," Izzy commented. "Since Numba can't catch him, he's trying to anger Sty to make him act out, but I'm not sure it will work."

Ignoring Numba's words, Sty flew in again. Numba waited patiently, and instead of trying to catch Sty, he remained in place, although it was unknown if this was a strategy or if his legs were on the verge of giving up. However, just as Sty stood in front of him, he threw a fist.

Sty easily dodged, moving his whole body out of the way, and then, zigzagging below Numba's arm, he sent his own punch at his opponent's face. But Sty didn't stop there, as he had finally planted his feet on the ground, readying himself to deliver a few more blows.

"Pride? Who cares about pride? What can pride do?" Sty asked as he punched Numba in the face once again. "Can pride help you win this fight? Can pride get you into the academy?"

Sty punched and punched again, and bearing the pain, Numba threw out another fist, but Sty caught it with his left hand.

"Remember, you brought this on yourself." Sty pulled Numba's arm, drew his face toward him, and threw out a fist with his other arm, hitting him straight in the face again.

Numba's head jerked back, and his body reverted to human form. After a pause, Numba's body fell back-first on the floor, and the match was over.

Sty raised his head and looked at the crowd from one side to the other as silence fell around the arena.

Then, as he lifted both his hands in victory, the crowd instantly erupted in a resounding cheer.

"Boo, boo, you damn bug-eyes!" Ian shouted, cupping his mouth.

Sty turned his head to where the sound was coming from and saw Ian whistling away, staring at the ceiling as if he had just found the most interesting thing in the world.

Everyone had expected the fight to end that way; there were no surprises, but Gary looked down at the arena speechlessly.

Shit, what did I do? I pushed Numba to do this. I should have just dealt with that damned bug myself. No . . . I didn't because Numba said he could get into trouble, but all of this mess is just because I was trying to get friendly with him, Gary thought.

"You want to get revenge for your friend? But in this place, things aren't so simple. You can't just solve everything with your fists like you used to do," Apollo said before walking away.

In the arena, Sty stood above Numba and slowly said to him:

"Tomorrow, you're going to regret everything you did."

After Sty walked away, the crowd of students started to disperse as well, and the teachers moved in to give Numba medical treatment.

Before they got to him, though, they found someone else in the center of the room, kneeling beside Numba.

"Numba, I'm sorry, this is my fault . . . just tell me what to do. How can I fix this? Is there anything you want me to do?" Gary asked, not knowing whether to just beat Sty or challenge someone else for a higher position to fix this.

Opening his eyes and staring at him, Numba had few words for Gary.

"Just . . . stay away from me."

CHAPTER 74

AN ANNOYING FLY

Lying on his bed in his new room, Gary stared at the ceiling with his mind full of thoughts. He was struggling with the current predicament in front of him.

What do I do? This was the question in his mind. The scene at the end of the previous fight flashed over and over in his head.

Numba's bloody and swollen face, so damaged that he could barely see or talk, appeared in Gary's mind, yet Numba had mustered up the strength to tell Gary to get away from him.

Have I done the right thing? Did I believe everything else would be effortless after the Underdogs just because I managed to get rid of them? Either way, I screwed up.

If I take out Sty, then he'll direct his frustration at Numba, and I'm not sure even getting a higher position than him would do anything. The way they treat Numba might even worsen after this.

Right now, Gary was honestly missing the Howlers more than anything. Making decisions on his own was hard. If he could, he would pick up his phone and talk to Kai about the best thing to do in this situation.

He was sure that Kai would have some ideas, and probably would have explained the consequences to him before he acted. But, unfortunately, communication wasn't permitted, at least not via phone, unless Gary wanted to get disqualified.

Once he was in the real academy, it would be no problem.

Wait a second. Doesn't that mean Sty and the others can't really do anything unless they have some way of contacting the outside that I don't know about? Still, as one of the rank ten, he'll be out of here in a couple of days.

Even after he racked his brain for a long time, no solution came to mind. Initially, he planned to take out one of the top ten and wait a week before going through, but now, he didn't want to leave Numba in a situation like this.

The next day Gary went looking for Numba but couldn't find him anywhere. Wherever the teachers had taken him, he had yet to return. Gary did make eye contact with Sty several times, though; he immediately looked the other way.

Tch . . . I thought I could get them to challenge me to a fight, but they seem to be making a big deal out of this pact, Gary thought.

While waiting for lunchtime to begin, Gary had resolved his goal. For now, he would stick to his plan of knocking out anyone in the top ten, but before that, he would eat a nice meal for lunch, so he had enough energy just in case he needed it.

Seeing Sty fight yesterday proved that some of Gary's opponents were close to his level. And he couldn't beat them with a single hit.

Right before lunch, Numba finally returned.

He looked a lot better. In fact, it was hard to tell that he had been in a fight, but Altereds healed at an incredible rate, so it made sense. With the medical treatment at the academy, students were assured that they could take the risk of fighting every day with their full strength.

As he kept an eye on Numba, Gary saw him heading straight toward Sty, ignoring all the stares he was getting from the other students.

Don't get involved, Gary. You'll just make things worse. Gary stopped, wondering for a second if he should get close so he could hear their conversation.

Lunch had finally arrived, and as usual, Gary was one of the first people there. He quickly began stuffing his food down. The meal was decent enough that his energy levels would no longer go down for the day, but neither were they going up.

168/300 Energy

Still, he should be able to beat some of his opponents quickly, and if it was proving a difficult match, he could always go into his complete transformation. After lunch, Gary walked up to Izzy and Ian. They hadn't fought for a few days and were waiting for their next assessment.

While the three were chatting, the top rankers entered, with Numba following closely behind Sty. As before, Numba went to collect food for Sty, but there was something strange about his food.

As Numba placed it down, the others saw something wriggling about in the bowl.

"As you all know, the top ten students can request whatever they wish. They just have to put in the order at the start of the day. This is why I have decided to be nice to my fellow participant and ordered some nice worms for him," Sty said aloud so everyone could hear, even the ones who weren't at their table.

He then pushed the bowl of worms to Numba, who stared down at it. They still had pieces of mud on them as if someone had freshly picked them from the ground.

"This is my treat, and please remember to eat every single one. The staff has worked hard to gather these lovely worms, you know?" Sty smiled.

Some at the table and a few others were put off by this meal, while the rest stopped to see if Numba would actually eat this specially ordered "food."

Numba stared at them for a few seconds and picked up the bowl. He held it a few inches away from his face before opening his mouth with a gulp. He then chucked them in and tried to swallow rather than chew.

However, the thought of what he was doing and feeling them wriggling about in his mouth was too much for him, making him gag. Then, putting the bowl back half-empty, he threw up all across the floor.

In the vomit was whatever he had eaten earlier and the wriggling worms.

"Now that's not very nice, that's not very nice at all," Sty said, standing up. He patted Numba on the back as if he were a good friend.

"Look at all of this. It's such a waste. I think you should eat it. We can't waste food now, can we? I think you should get on the floor and lick up every single bit you just threw up," Sty advised.

Numba's body quivered, but he got on his knees. As he stared at the vomit, his eyes teared up.

I . . . I have to do this . . . I have to . . . otherwise . . . my family. I can't let them down after everything they've done for me. I'm sorry for not being able to do better . . . and Gary, I'm sorry for saying that to you yesterday. I just know that you would get involved, and then you would be in this mess.

Sty put his foot on Numba's back, kicking him toward the floor, but suddenly his attention shifted to something else. Someone was walking across the room.

"Ah . . . look, your hero has come to save you again." Sty laughed. "What's he going to do? Stare at me again?"

Gary continued walking without a word. He didn't slow down his pace and didn't look up either, and when he reached the table, he picked up the bowl of worms with one hand. Before anyone could do anything, and before even Sty could react, he slammed it into Sty's face. It shattered on impact, scratching him up. Then he lost his balance and fell to the ground, and worms covered his face.

"Eat the fucking worms yourself, you damn fly."

CHAPTER 75

A SMALL MEAL

It was as if time had stopped for everyone in the canteen as silence descended throughout the dining hall. Even those at the rank 1 table were stunned and didn't know how to react. As for Gary, he just stood there looking down at Sty.

Sty was hurt, but not so bad that he couldn't get up and wipe the worms off his face.

"You bastard! I'll kill you. I'll kill you and your whole *family*!" he shouted, rubbing away the worms as he stood up.

His body was already transforming, but before he could fully get to his feet, a sudden force enveloped both of them, and a shadow appeared between them, making Gary take a step back.

"Do not act!" a voice said. "Please stay calm until we resolve the problem."

The voice belonged to one of the teachers who constantly kept an eye on all the students. One held Sty before he could take off, and another stood in front of Gary.

"Fighting is not permitted in the canteen. The attacker and the victim must come with us to resolve this case. Please follow us," the teacher instructed.

A few students were shaking their heads at what they had seen, mainly Apollo and Izzy, because they both had the same fear.

Gary . . . Gary, why don't you ever talk to me or think before you act? Doing something like this, attacking him out of the blue without challenging him . . . the teachers could kick you out of this place for this stunt, Izzy thought.

Gary and Sty seemed to have complied and followed after the two teachers, leaving the rest of the students to anticipate what would happen next. The whole dining hall was overwhelmed with commotion as soon as the doors closed.

"Did you see that? He smashed that plate right on Sty's face! Who is that guy? Wasn't he just a recruit, an assessment person?" a student asked.

"Yeah, I think he might have a screw loose or something. If I'm not wrong, this is not the first time he walked to the top table. Honestly, I wouldn't be worried about getting kicked out. Instead, I would worry more about what will happen outside the academy after he gets kicked out," another said.

Numba was still on the floor.

Gary . . . Gary, what are you doing? Are you putting your position in this academy and your whole life at risk just because of one favor? Don't be an idiot!

Outside the dining hall, others were shaking their heads after seeing what had transpired in the hall, in particular, the three professors who had their eye on Gary. They were being updated on everything that happened and had been called to make certain decisions.

"This guy." Hai huffed. "He makes no moves in the facility, and then the first thing he does is cause trouble and break the rules by doing this? You guys know what could happen now, right? That family might even target us for not looking after him."

"Stop being overdramatic," Humfree said, taking a sip of his coffee. "Everyone who enters this place is made aware of the consequences. Just because the person attacking him has a low background makes no difference.

"Besides, there is a simple way to resolve this matter." Humfree smiled, then called a teacher to send some instructions.

For now, the teachers had detained Sty and Gary in separate rooms. They were medical rooms attached to the facility, but the students didn't have access to them unless they were hurt.

Sty was getting treatment with the best available means to heal the wounds and swelling; Gary was under observation while the staff decided what to do next. In Sty's room, the teacher standing beside him had received some instructions.

"There has been a resolution put forward," the teacher said, "to resolve the matter between you two. They wish for you to have a match. This is the professors' suggestion to clear the bad blood between you.

"However, no such scuffle is allowed between you after the match unless it is in an official duel. If you pull off such a stunt once again, we will immediately expel the instigator, if not both of you, without any change of plea. Right now, someone else is explaining the same conditions to the other student."

Sty clenched his fist. It wasn't fair. Gary had started it. But he stood up immediately, because this was what he wanted a long time ago.

"A forced match? That's fine with me. This way, Apollo can't say anything about me starting this crap. Bring it on. I will make that bastard wish he never came before me!"

While the staff was telling Gary and Sty about the decision they had reached, lunchtime was over for the students.

However, almost all of them were still preoccupied with the incident and anticipating the decision made by the teachers.

And they didn't have to wait for long as the double doors were pushed open and two teachers walked in, with the two students following them to the center of the arena.

"An official match between rank 42 and rank 4 will now take place. No one is allowed to interfere with this match until one of them gives up or is knocked out, or if we declare one of them the winner!" the teacher explained.

Sty walked to the other side and turned toward Gary. His blood was boiling with rage after what had happened. He had never been humiliated like that before—and publicly, no less.

"You have made the biggest mistake of your life. I'll rip out all your teeth, break all your bones, and beat the crap out of you until you beg for a swift death! But that won't be the end of it! Because my anger won't calm just with your death.

"I'll find your family, your friends, every single person you care about, and make you watch as I beat them all to a pulp and take everything away from you that you ever owned!" Sty's words resounded throughout the arena, and all the students stopped talking.

Gary didn't reply; he stood there, not acting, not showing how he was feeling.

"Gary, he can win this, right?" Ian whispered, trying not to attract any attention.

"He can, of course he can," Izzy replied, "But it's going to be difficult, and I'm sure Sty will do exactly what he said he would if he wins. He won't let Gary off with a simple beating."

In the arena, the match began. Sty sprouted his wings and eyes and flew toward Gary as if he was about to hit him, but at the last moment, he darted away.

Sty . . . he's flying much faster than when he was fighting me. He must be furious. Numba gulped.

Flying in random directions, Sty was making it hard for Gary to predict where he would come from next.

"I will torture you till your very last breath!" Sty shouted, flying in once again.

"You made a mistake," Gary replied.

He let out a resounding howl, sending a strange feeling through everyone's body.

This is what I wanted . . . this is who I thought you were. Apollo smiled.

Sty was affected the most by the howl. He suddenly had the urge to fly straight toward Gary. There was no other thought in his head other than to attack, and his speed increased once more.

Full Transformation Activated

Before Sty could reach him, Gary's entire body transformed. The hair on his arms and legs grew, and his clothes ripped apart as his body enlarged. His mouth elongated, and his ears became pointy.

Some of the students couldn't believe what kind of monster they were looking at, and at that moment, Gary grabbed Sty's shoulders in midair, stopping him dead.

His sharp claws dug into Sty, causing him to scream in extreme pain, unable to break free unless he could rip his body away.

"Report, report, what do we do!" The teachers shouted for instruction from the higher-ups.

Gary tightened his grip, digging in his nails more, making Sty cry for his life. No matter how much he struggled, Sty couldn't get out.

"You don't threaten my family or friends, no matter who you are," Gary declared as he opened his jaws wide and dug his razor-sharp teeth right into Sty.

CHAPTER 76

LITTLE WOLF

Some Altereds in the facility couldn't believe what they were seeing. The Altered standing in front of them was not typical. With razor-sharp fangs, long claws, saliva dripping from his mouth, and red eyes, he looked like a monster out of their worst nightmares.

Many of them felt a chill just looking at Gary's form. It was a rare sight. Altereds first learned how to transform certain body parts, and as time passed, they would mix it up and change their body to whatever best suited them, but Altereds were rarely able to change into their full beast form.

Some Altereds didn't even know what their actual beast form would look like, since it was hard to imagine what their beast was based on from the few parts they could change. But depending on how they became Altered, companies such as NIRV could allow them to see the beast that had been used for their DNA.

Either way, many people still saw Altereds as human, but it was hard for them to believe that Gary was actually human.

In the arena, Gary stared at Sty. He had grabbed him hard, dug his claws in, and used his large mouth to crunch down on his shoulder. The fang marks reached up to Sty's chest. During the bite, Gary realized what he was doing and restrained himself from chewing off half of his opponent's body.

But the spectators wouldn't have believed that Sty's life was saved just because Gary restrained himself. Blood dripped from the tips of his claws, and Sty had utterly passed out from the shock.

At that moment, Gary let go, dropping Sty on the floor and into a spreading pool of blood.

I didn't mean to transform fully. Gary sighed. *I just got so angry. Why can't I learn to control myself when I'm angry? Although he deserved it, now I've gone and shown everyone what I really am.*

Immediately, Gary started to revert to human form. His clothes were ripped but still covered the essential parts of his body. Once the change was complete, he stared down at Sty again.

Shit, I bit him as well.

When Gary was frustrated and fully transformed, he somewhat lost himself. Especially now, he just had an urge to bite the person in front of him. Maybe his werewolf instincts were kicking in, telling him to eat the prey in front of him to get stronger.

One thing had changed, though: the number on Gary's badge. It had turned to number 4, meaning he had successfully gained the position. The fight was over, but that didn't come as a surprise, considering Sty's state.

Many of the students were concerned about whether Sty was still alive. The teachers quickly rushed in and began checking Sty's condition.

"Damn it, kid! Couldn't you have gone easy on the guy?" one of the teachers said while lifting the unconscious Sty off the ground.

"Don't blame him," another teacher retorted. "No one saw this coming; it was our fault, and he won this whole thing fair and square. So let's just get this student to the infirmary."

Then turning toward Gary, the teacher added, "As for you, don't cause any more trouble. We will be watching you."

The teachers quickly left the arena, taking Sty with them, but there wasn't enough time to clean up the blood on the floor.

"Hey, hey, hey. Was any of this in your calculations?" Ian asked.

"How could it be?" Izzy said, still staring at Gary, but now she knew why she was feeling so afraid of him. She didn't understand before, but now it made sense that her natural instincts told her not to mess with this person.

I didn't know he could fully transform. I don't think anyone did. He was already strong enough, and to think he was still hiding some of his power. Did he lie to us about his background?

It was the only thing Izzy could think of, but Gary didn't seem like that kind of person. Was he just naturally talented? But then what about the Altered DNA he had? If there was something this strong, surely the more prominent gangs would have kept it for themselves, unless this Howlers group was something special.

Other than these two, the most surprised person in the whole arena was none other than Numba, the person who was the epicenter of this mess. As he looked at Gary standing in the pool of blood, his eyes started to well up. He couldn't remember the last time he had he cried and how long he had kept these emotions at bay.

He beat Sty . . . He beat him . . . How was he able to beat him, just like that, and so easily? We have a similar background. So what's the difference between the two of us? Is it strength? Would all my problems disappear if I were that strong and had the power to beat Sty? Would I be able to help my family? A thousand thoughts were running through Numba's mind.

"Gary!" he finally shouted out, seeing how Gary looked lost in his thoughts. "Thank you . . . thank you."

Gary came out of his stupor and turned toward the sound. When they made eye contact, he smiled at Numba but walked away.

Without stopping, Gary went to his room, his mind preoccupied with many thoughts.

I've achieved my goal of reaching the top ten, and I smashed that guy's head in, but why did I have to bite him? Is he going to be okay? He isn't going to change, is he? I remember Billy bit that White Rose agent, but nothing happened to her. A werewolf can't turn Altered, can they? It should be okay. I hope.

Meanwhile, Apollo stared at Gary's disappearing back, his fist shaking. He placed his hand on his chest as he sensed his speeding heartbeat.

I . . . want to fight you so bad . . . little wolf.

CHAPTER 77

AN OFFER IS MADE

Gary put his brand-new room to good use . . . by hiding in it. He even went so far as to skip his next meal to avoid having to face the consequences of his actions. He simply didn't know how to cope with all of this sudden unwanted attention.

Naturally, his absence did nothing to stop the rumor mill that was coming up with crazy ideas about what the strange Wolf Altered would do next. However, the other students were just as curious about how the other top rankers intended to handle him.

Since Gary had won the duel, everyone else's rank was adjusted. Normally, that would be barely worth mentioning, but this time around, one of the former top rankers suddenly found himself disqualified from advancing to the AFA.

Only . . . what exactly could he do about it? By himself, barely anything. Challenging Gary after the teenager had revealed that he could fully transform into his Altered form was akin to suicide.

The only ones who might stand a chance against him were Apollo Zorion, Snow Light, and Wu Chen, and it was questionable whether they would risk their own position with their advancement only a few days away. Not to mention, the duel had been set up by the teachers so that there would be no more bad blood between the two duelists.

"What do you think about the rumor that Gary is going to challenge the top three next?" Ian asked as he and Izzy headed toward Numba's room. "If someone had told me that earlier, I would have called that person crazy . . . but now . . . after what he did to Sty . . ."

"I'm not sure," Izzy replied cautiously. "I asked around, but nobody ever saw any of the three fighting, so it's hard to say."

Ian stopped in his tracks, his expression one of pure confusion. He was unable to figure out how such a thing would be possible.

"Sty was the one actively fighting, until he eventually ended up as rank 1. After that, Wu, Snow, and Apollo challenged him to a duel. Each of them defeated him with a single strike. I don't think I need to tell you that those were all just show matches.

"All of that happened right before we entered the place, and then Apollo suggested that the top rankers agree to a pact so that they could all advance together. Since he had some connection with Sty, who defeated all of them, and all of them stood to benefit from that type of arrangement, they all agreed to it.

"Well, that's when we came in, and now Gary managed to destroy their little utopian dream . . ."

Finally, the two of them stopped before a door and knocked on it. A few moments later, Numba came out, his head held low.

"You ready? All three of us agreed to do this, remember?" Izzy reminded them, and the two boys nodded.

Gary found that staying in his room wasn't all bad. He barely noticed the time passing, with so much to check out in such a luxurious place. Even Jayden's top suite paled in comparison. Gary's favorite boon of the room was definitely the Jacuzzi-style hot tub.

As he was soaking in it, he overheard some students talking outside.

"Hey, it's Sty, he's back," a voice said.

Hearing a knock, Gary put on a luxurious bathrobe before opening the door. Next to Sty were some of the teachers, who were there to help him move his things.

Changing rooms was an annoying process for the students involved, but since this place valued strength above everything else, the top rankers had the most luxurious rooms. So it was always an extra hassle whenever one of them was defeated and had to move.

Sty was in a lot better shape than at the end of the duel. The wounds on the backs of his arms from Gary's claws had healed a lot, but his chest was still banged up, and his wounds were visible where the blood had soaked through the bandages, revealing fang marks.

"Hey." Gary greeted him with a nervous smile. "Are you feeling all right? You don't have a craving for meat, right? And you don't smell things any differently than before?"

Everyone was surprised to see the wildcard newcomer suddenly act so chummy after defeating the top ranker. The strangest thing was that it didn't seem to be an act on Gary's part, but genuine concern. It was genuine; Gary was worried about Sty's condition after he had bitten him.

Although the system had been unable to turn Kirk, Gary didn't have a complete understanding of his mostly silent helper, and after what had happened to Billy, he wanted to avoid any such surprises. The easiest way was simply to ask Sty himself.

Unfortunately, Sty wanted nothing to do with Gary anymore. He headed straight into his former room and started gathering his things. What nobody noticed was that his hands had been shaking the entire time Gary had looked at him.

I can't even look at him without getting like this . . . Sty thought. *He's acting like nothing happened . . . trying to be friendly with me . . . What a joke. Has he finally realized what I might do to his family? . . . If only Apollo would let me. Still, I don't need to tell him that part. Hopefully, he'll suffer nightmares throughout his stay here.*

Eventually, Sty and the adults left. Just as Gary was about to go back to enjoying the hot tub, there was another knock on the door.

"What is it? Did you overlook something?" he asked, only to see three familiar faces.

"Holy shit, your new room is awesome. No wonder you haven't left it at all. You could fit about a dozen of us in here without it getting cramped!" Ian said as he shamelessly entered, passing Gary who just stood at the door.

Hurrying behind him, Izzy slapped him on the back, reminding her childhood friend why they had come here in the first place. As for Numba, he seemed a little more reserved compared to his usual self.

"So, did you just come to enjoy the sight of my new room?" Gary asked, closing the door.

Izzy pulled the other two toward herself and made them stand. Then all three suddenly got down on their knees, heads bent low.

"We've all come here to ask you for a favor, Gary," Izzy answered with her own head bowed as well. "Please train us. With your help, we'll be able to get out of this place and advance to the AFA. In exchange, we're ready to help you with whatever you need.

"If you need backup, we'll fight at your side. If you plan to expand, our families will help your gang with that. Please help us enter the AFA, and we promise that for the rest of our lives, we'll be in your debt!"

CHAPTER 78

TRAIN US

With Izzy suddenly pleading their case with such fervor, Gary was left speechless. He didn't know what to say. He had half processed what they were saying, but at the same time he didn't understand.

"First of all, can you guys please get off the floor? It makes me uncomfortable when you act like that. We're the same age, and I'm just a student like you guys. Heck, technically all of us are still just student candidates for the AFA," Gary said, pinching the bridge of his nose.

Lifting their heads off the floor, all of them had eager faces because Gary had not yet refused their request. He was certain that Izzy was putting on a pair of large puppy eyes, which made things extra hard on him and just made him want to look away.

"Gary, it took a lot for us to ask that of you," Ian confessed. "It's nice of you to say we're the same, but let's be honest, it's obvious we're not. Look at the number on your badge, and then look at the numbers on ours. If we do things our way, it might take us months or years to reach your level.

"Do you think just anyone can challenge someone like Sty? I mean, look at what happened to Numba!"

"Watch it," the Goat Altered retorted, and punched Ian on the shoulder. "I might have lost, but at least I fought against one of the top rankers. I stood my ground."

"Look, that might be noble or whatever you guys tell yourselves, but the whole point of this place is to reach the top and stay there for a week. Right now, we can't do that . . . because we're weaker than them." Izzy sighed. "Gary, we want to form an alliance. Not just between us but between our families as well. It's the only thing families like ours can do in a place like this."

Gary started to pace back and forth . . . It was something he often did when trying to think properly, but the problem was he couldn't really grasp what was being offered.

"Can you explain this to me like I'm five?" Gary asked in slight embarrassment. The idea itself didn't sound bad. Kai did tell him to try to attract more business to Slough, or perhaps even find opportunities to expand, and it might be what he needed. "Is it really all right for you guys to make that type of promise without speaking to your family beforehand?"

"Sorry, I forgot that you're backed by a gang, and that things work differently for you. Our families invested into us becoming Altered, sending us here in the hopes that we would meet other great people and form relationships with them.

"While a gang in a Tier 3 town might not be all that great, all of us are convinced that in the future you will become a great person, and we want to help you achieve that potential. As the future of our respective families, we have the power to help you, even if it might be somewhat limited at first. Once we prove ourselves, though, we'll be able to do more for you!" Izzy placed her hand out, trying to get Gary to shake it, but the werewolf was still looking at it with caution.

I have some open marks, so perhaps I should enter a bond with her. At least that way, I would know in case she tries to betray me in the future, though she seems to be serious about her current offer.

"I'll be honest, Gary," Numba said. "You know I don't trust anyone, and it's the same for my family. I might have to arrange a meeting between our families, but I promise that for what you have done I will have your back, in return for having mine. Just like in that assessment, we can do this together." Numba put his hand out, and Ian and Izzy followed suit.

Scratching the back of his head, Gary eventually put both of his hands out.

"I can't shake all three of your hands at once. Of course, I'll teach you, and this can be the start of our alliance," Gary said with a smile.

The training began that day, more specifically at nighttime. Given Gary's new privileges, he brought the three of them along to a private training room. That way no one could see what they were doing. His Energy was around the halfway mark, but that wasn't much of a concern. He was already looking forward to breakfast since he could now order as much food as he liked, something he planned to put to very good use.

Inside the training room, the first thing Gary did was have the three show what they were capable of. In a way, it reminded him of the days when he watched and analyzed Altered fighters on TV, only now he would actively give them pointers.

The three Altered looked a bit tired after demonstrating their skills. Gary stood in front of them.

"All right, I've seen enough. There are a few things that we should do to make you improve as quickly as possible. Truth be told, I don't plan to stay here longer than I need to, so that gives us around a week.

"The quickest way to improve will be to focus on your respective strengths, since we lack the time to effectively combat your weaknesses. I want you guys to think about what your strengths are. This will be important for your next task."

Gary's arms started to transform, and he got into a fighting stance.

"There is one thing that all of you lack, and that is experience. The experience of fighting with your life on the line. So let's try to kill two birds with one stone! All of you fight me at once!" Gary ran forward as he looked over his status.

Exp 3788/5302

Defeating Sty resulted in a nice Exp boost. Let's see if fighting them might also net me some Exp. If so, I might get something out of our training as well, and get one step closer to Level Up.

The next day was special for more than one reason. Not only was it the day the assessment would take place, but today was the last day the top rankers had to hold on to their rank to be allowed to advance, so many students were expecting things to get quite interesting . . .

CHAPTER 79

STUBBORN

The next day, Ian, Izzy, and Numba woke up groaning in pain. Their bodies felt sore all over after their night of training. It took each one of them half an hour of stretching and twisting until their aches and pains had gone down to tolerable levels, just in time to head to the canteen.

"I knew he was a monster, but if this is his idea of training, I'm worried we might not survive our stay here," Ian complained as they met up in front of the canteen. "It's frightening how much stamina that guy has. Shit, I just realized that he did all of that pretty much on an empty stomach. Doesn't that mean that tonight it's going to get even worse?"

"His stamina isn't the only concerning thing," Numba added. "Even after the three of us finally managed to trap him thanks to Izzy's idea, we were unable to damage him, even though I made sure to not hold back my punches. I might not have been in peak condition . . . but he didn't even flinch. It was as if I was punching an iron wall!"

Unbeknownst to the Goat Altered, Gary had felt it. Fortunately, given his high Endurance and large Health pool, he had remained calm, aware that he could sustain dozens of punches without having to worry about his well-being.

"He's surprisingly good at analyzing fights," Izzy said. "All those points he made about us were spot on. When you showed off, I noticed the same thing as he did. However, his ability to do that during a fight is clearly one notch above mine. It's as if he was practically born to become an AFC champion."

The three of them entered the canteen, bantering casually. The atmosphere inside was unusually heavy. Rather than the normal chitchat, the place was filled with hushed whispers as everyone waited for something to happen between the top rankers and those in the top twenty-five.

"That's right, I nearly forgot that today's the day of the assessment. Apollo and his group just need to keep their positions to advance. Since no one has seen them fight, some people are going to hedge their bets and challenge them. At least that's what most students assume is going to happen," Izzy said as they sat down.

"Well, Gary won't have to worry about anything, then. Truth be told, I hope something will actually go down today. No offense, Numba, but if we ignore the fact that Sty kicked your butt, his fighting was pretty impressive. I wouldn't mind seeing the other top rankers show off their abilities," Ian said.

"Speaking of rumors, I've heard one about our future treatment in the AFA being linked to what rank we end up with before advancing. However, seeing as the top rankers don't exactly seem overeager to challenge those above them, it might only be something the teachers spread to encourage fighting," Izzy said as she ate.

"In that regard, it's actually a smart way to force us to fight each other. It would certainly fit in line with those weekly assessments where the teachers decide what rank each of us should have instead of allowing the rank 11–20 students to become the new top rankers.

"Any one of them who fails to enter the top ten would automatically have an incentive to challenge the new top rankers, thus making it hard for everyone to keep their positions for a week . . ."

"Only Apollo broke that system, so who knows what kind of assessment awaits us today," Numba pointed out.

Numerous dishes were being brought out one after the other. Just the ingredients that were used to make them rivaled the yearly income of the average Tier 3 family. While everyone was staring at this spectacle, Gary had eyes for the food in front of him.

Atop five plates were different types of steaks, but the one thing they had in common was that all of them had been cooked blue. What's more, there were eight to ten per plate, spreading their aroma throughout the canteen.

They weren't kidding about serving whatever my heart desires. This is exactly what I've been dreaming of! Gary didn't care that he was drooling; he started digging in at an incredible pace.

To the onlookers, it appeared that he was barely chewing his food, devouring all of it like a black hole. Even after he had topped up his Energy, the werewolf didn't stop. After all, it was all free! In his eyes, he was earning money for each steak he consumed.

I'm going to eat my fill until my stomach explodes! Gary thought in glee.

"For a small body, you sure eat a lot." Apollo laughed when the rank 4 student asked for seconds.

"Hey, wolf bastard, there are other people at this table. Can't you mind your manners even a little?" a girl whose badge showed the number 8 complained.

"Sorry." Gary apologized while licking the juice off his fingers. He hadn't bothered using a knife or fork to eat. "After having only soup for days, I really needed this. You guys will leave after today, so I hope you can tolerate my behavior for one day."

It wasn't that he didn't have manners; his mom had brought him and his sister up well. It was just that for the first time in his life, he wanted to act as he pleased without having to care about others. Since this place advocated "might makes right" and neither Apollo nor his friends said anything about Gary's behavior, the werewolf enjoyed letting loose for once.

With breakfast over, the students were excited because most challenges and fights occurred between breakfast and lunch, followed by more fights after lunch. As they left the canteen, everyone was looking around for the first challenger.

"Sty!" a voice shouted, and pointed toward the student whose badge now showed the number 5. "I challenge you for your position."

The challenger was rank 11, the student who had left the top ranks because of Gary. Many found it reasonable that the guy would be pissed, and since Sty had been seriously injured in yesterday's fight, he might not be in peak form today.

As for the pact between the top rankers, with this being the last day, it was practically useless. After his fight, rank 11 could use the rules to refuse any challenges today, so he had nothing to fear.

The two of them walked into the fighting arena, and the match began. Immediately, the challenger ran across and punched Sty, who just stood there taking it. He didn't transform and just remained on the floor.

What is he doing? Izzy thought. "If he just wins this match, then he gets through and can join the academy!"

However, the Fly Altered remained on the floor and didn't get up. Only after the match had been deemed resolved and his badge changed to number 6 did he finally get up.

I'll stay here, and I'll make sure that damned goat quits on his own. It's because of him and his green-haired friend that I got so humiliated! Sty thought, as he pointed at the student whose rank was one below his current one, rank 7.

"I challenge you to a fight!"

CHAPTER 80

LAST DAY

Everyone was stunned, as it was hard to tell what Sty's goal was. It was clear that he had lost the last match on purpose, so why was he now challenging his fellow top ranker, especially one he already outranked?

His action was completely legitimate. The rules merely stated that someone who had already fought was allowed to refuse any further challenges that day, yet there was no limit to how often someone could challenge others. As long as a challenger didn't have any severe injuries forcing the teachers to take them away for healing, they were technically free to fight to their heart's content.

Usually, only students in the lower ranks would fight more than once, as the strength disparity between them wasn't overly great. The higher the rank, the bigger the gap became, so fights between high rankers normally resulted in injuries for both sides. However, the situation right now was outside the norm.

Since the rank 7 student had nothing to lose by accepting this challenge, he agreed to it.

"I forfeit the match," Sty announced loudly the moment it started.

He's purposely losing to others. Why would he do that? Izzy wondered, trying to come up with a reason why someone so close to the finish line would act this way. The only thing that came to mind was that he might . . . want to stay. She glanced at Numba, who looked quite tense.

"It looks like we're thinking the same thing. He must want to stay to mess with us . . . and by us, I mean me and Gary," Numba said, although he wasn't sure how Sty would deal with Gary after the werewolf had beaten the Fly Altered in the duel. Nevertheless, he understood that he had to tread carefully in the future.

No, I should see this as an opportunity. If he is staying here, then I can't pass this place until I beat him! Numba thought.

As suspected, Sty continued to challenge those lower ranked than him, until his badge finally displayed the number 11. Turning toward Numba, he smiled before walking out of the arena to his new room.

"Man, that bug guy is seriously weird." Gary said what had been on the mind of every other student.

The rumors had been correct about the top twenty-five planning to challenge the top rankers today. Unfortunately, Sty's bout of challenges had made it impossible for them to enact their plan. Everyone who had beaten the Fly Altered was now protected by the rules and could simply refuse the challenge.

This meant that only the top four could now be challenged. Some of those in the top twenty-five looked at Gary and turned their heads. They knew their own strength well enough to understand that they would be unable to beat Sty, so none of them dared to challenge the one who had beaten him.

"Hey, why don't we just go for it?" one of the students whispered to another. "It's not like we have much to lose. Worst-case scenario, we remain at our current rank. Best-case scenario, they turn out weak and we can boost our reputation so that the others might not want to challenge us during the next week."

In the end, rank 15, a lean student who had been spending most of his time in the training room, walked forward and pointed toward none other than Wu Chen, issuing a challenge.

"Me? Hey, Apollo, you saw it, right? I didn't go looking for a fight, he chose me of his own volition!" Wu exclaimed, jumping up in excitement and over a few of the other students' heads, even kicking off from the bald head of another student to help him get to the main stage faster.

"Come on, let's do this!" Wu shouted, ripping off his shirt and revealing his hard-trained body, already covered in sweat. His body fat was so low that his muscles were visible as he tensed his arms and chest.

The moment the fight began, the challenger started to transform, and an extra pair of arms grew out from the side of his ribs. By the time his transformation finished, Wu was already directly in front of him.

The rank 3 student grabbed one of the freshly grown arms, and, with a kick up, he bent it in the wrong direction. Wu slammed his foot on the ground, or more correctly on his opponent's toes. The blow was so hard that the floor cracked, along with the challenger's entire foot.

Pushing through the pain, rank 15 tried to punch him using his two hands on the other side, but before he could, he suffered a direct punch in his chest. Wu lifted his foot and sent the student hurtling to the other side, where the teachers caught him just before he crashed into the crowd of onlookers.

"A complete defeat," Ian muttered, his mouth hanging open. "It wasn't even a contest and the guy didn't even change into his Altered form either. Looks like they're not just there because of their position. They actually have the strength to back it up."

Izzy agreed with Ian. If rank 3 was already this strong, it was likely that his two friends were even stronger. Seeing how one of their own had been dealt with, none of the other high rankers came forward to challenge Snow or Wu.

Lunch came and passed, turning into evening. During the meal, there had been only a single question on everyone's mind.

What would Gary do?

"Why does everyone expect me to do something?" Gary complained when Ian asked him that very question. The four of them were in his room, getting ready to go to the next training session that Gary had planned for them.

"Because you have nothing to lose!" Ian replied. "You can challenge them without the risk of losing your rank, and it will let you see how you fare against them. If you don't do it now, you might not get a chance to fight them. I heard that in the normal academy, fighting between students isn't allowed without the permission of a teacher. Are you really going to waste your chance?"

"Well, I don't really care." Gary shrugged. "Sure, I like fighting, but if it's meant to be, then I'll end up fighting them sometime down the line. I have no grudge against any of them."

There was another reason Gary wasn't feeling competitive. He knew that he wouldn't hold back, even if just for a simple spar. Having seen Wu in action, he understood that he would have to fight all out if he wanted to win. If that was the case, there was a high chance of something going wrong. After what happened with Sty he didn't want to have yet another Billy scare.

The students here weren't like the Underdogs or the gang members he had been fighting in Slough. Many of them might be arrogant, but none of them had committed any crimes . . . at least not that he was aware of.

"Come on, let's go train. You guys don't want to be stuck here forever, right?" Gary said. Opening the door, he nearly collided with the large frame of Apollo.

CHAPTER 81

HIT RANK 1

Apollo had not expected Gary to come out of his room at the exact moment he had been about to knock. His hand remained in midair for a moment before he took it down and smiled at the werewolf.

The other three behind Gary gulped as they saw why the green-haired teenager had suddenly stopped. Since the day was mostly over, none of them had expected that another fight would break out. However, why else would Apollo appear right at Gary's doorstep if he wasn't looking to challenge the newcomer away from prying eyes?

"Aren't you going to invite me in?" Apollo asked in a humorous tone to break the awkward silence.

"I think that's a bad idea. You see, I have a terrible stomach ache. Must have been all the food I ate earlier," Gary quickly replied, holding in his stomach. Just like everyone else, the werewolf hadn't even entertained the idea that trouble might come looking for him. He had thought that as long as he avoided the others, all would be good.

Alas, the rank 1 student simply entered the room before Gary could close the door in his face. "Your excuse isn't very believable when you have three other visitors waiting inside your room, especially when your outfit clearly shows you were about to head out to train. Don't worry, I haven't come here to challenge you.

"Should the two of us fight, then I want you to be at your very best . . . and I noticed in your fight against Sty that something is holding you back."

Gary wasn't sure how to react to being seen through. Apollo was right; since all their fights were being watched, the green-haired teenager didn't feel safe to fight at his full strength.

"I've simply come to offer you a piece of advice before I leave," Apollo explained. "Maybe you or your friends have already heard rumors that your rank dictates your treatment in the AFA. That is only half of the truth. The time it takes you to advance is also important.

"Given your earlier performance, I don't think I'll have to worry about what rank you end up as. But I have one word of advice; go through at least in the top three if you wish to see me. I'll be waiting for you in the academy then."

Having said his piece, Apollo left, and Gary heard three loud breaths behind him.

"Man, I was only one second away from taking cover behind your bed," Ian blurted out, touching his chest in an attempt to calm down his racing heart.

"Well . . . that wasn't at all what I had expected, but I think this might be the best result in the end," Izzy said as she and the others got ready to leave, but as the door opened, she turned around and saw Gary thinking as he stared at the floor; his fist was shaking.

"I see . . . you're one of those types." Izzy smiled. "Earth to Gary, you promised to train us, remember?"

Inside the personal training room, the three weren't sparring against the werewolf, at least not together. After some intense warm-ups, he asked each of them to use their best skills against him. It was part of the homework he had given them yesterday, when he had told them to figure out what their strengths were and come up with ideas to improve upon them.

This was the way for them to get stronger quickly. The fundamentals were important, but all three already had a good foundation, so rather than try to improve to a master level, he wanted to help them come up with something that would allow them to become top rankers like him.

Izzy and Ian had improved far quicker than Gary could imagine. Ian was focusing on trying to get his Altered form to come out, since it would be hard to do much in terms of improving his strength. As for Izzy, her strength came from her logical thinking and how she used her head to come up with strategies. Honestly, she was seeing a lot of improvement just by being able to fight someone at Gary's level.

"Gary . . . I want to thank you," Numba said when it was his turn. "Your words, the stress I was suffering and the will to push through, I feel like everything that I have learned to do was because of you. Which is why I'm asking you now . . . to be careful and brace yourself!" With that the Goat Altered started to transform and began his attack.

A few moments later, both Ian and Izzy were left speechless, their mouths wide open. Numba lay on the floor, panting and sweating, and above him stood a partially transformed Gary, whose frame had been pushed into the wall, surrounded by cracks.

"Thanks for the warning." Gary coughed, his body a bit tensed up. "I think you've got this."

The next day started with an announcement, informing the students that all those who had been eligible had passed on to the AFA. They were quickly escorted out, as the other students had things they needed to do. They were then told to follow the teachers who would accompany them for today's assessment.

According to what they had learned, the assessments differed from time to time; it could be a game similar to what they had done when joining or just a simple series of tests. As it turned out, today was the latter: a hundred-yard sprint, a strength test, a flexibility test, and a reflex test, among others.

Everything was being done in the open, with no real surprises. Students were allowed to transform during the test, but Gary had chosen to remain as he was. Nevertheless, he gave it his all because Apollo's advice was still ringing in his head.

"Everyone, please pay attention!" one of the teachers called out to the students who had returned to the facility. "The screen will display everyone's ranks. If you're dissatisfied with your rank, do better next time, or claim the rank you feel you deserve!"

The screen flickered as it showed them their results, starting from the bottom, going up.

Izzy's name was the first one to show up. Her new rank was 54, and she was very satisfied with it. While some students were already eyeing her with a challenging look, she felt that after Gary's draconian training, there was no need to fear them. In fact, she might even try to secure a place in the top fifty after a few more days.

The next name to show up was Ian's. His new rank was 23, an impressive feat for someone who was unable to access his Altered form. Like Izzy, he wasn't afraid of having to defend his rank; in fact, he was looking forward to being challenged. Perhaps it would give him the needed push to allow him to transform, even if only partially.

Then there was Numba. He was by far the biggest surprise, ending up as rank 15. Meanwhile, Gary's name showed up as the very last one, right after Sty's.

I could have done even better if I had chosen to transform, yet it was enough to get me to rank 1. Did the teachers take that fact into account? Gary wondered as he looked up at the display. The werewolf had already spent a while in this facility, and this morning the system had reminded him that he didn't have time to idle.

17 days until the next full moon

I have to make sure to pass this week.

CHAPTER 82

THE NEW TOP DOGS

As usual, many were very displeased with their new rankings, especially those whose rank had shifted by a large margin. Many had suspected that those in the former top twenty would become the new top rankers, but other than Gary and Sty, everyone else was a new face. Even the two former top rankers who lost their qualifications had only ended up in the top twenty this time.

It was somewhat like Izzy had predicted, and there were nonstop challenges, even before breakfast had begun. Finally, when they went to eat, Gary finished his food quickly and came over to sit with them.

People always made space for the higher ranks to sit with the lower ranks, but it wasn't the same the other way around.

"Man, do you think you could order me some food?" Ian asked shamelessly. "Don't get me wrong, the menu for the top twenty-five is great and all, but pretty much the entire canteen gets a whiff of your steaks, and my meal just can't compare to that. I would be seriously in your debt if you could sneak over a single one . . . even a bite!"

"Don't you think it would taste a lot better if you actually earned one of those steaks by becoming a top ranker? That way, you can eat as many as you like, and won't have to eat someone's scraps," Numba said. "It doesn't even have to be steak, you could order whatever you want. Aren't you getting sick of eating so many of them, Gary?"

They waited for their friend to answer, but he was clearly distracted by something on his mind.

"Hellooo, meat boy!" Izzy called out after a whole minute had passed, waving his hands in front of Gary's face.

"Hmm? What? No, steak is great. It's super expensive for me outside this place . . . and it's meat, which is all I need," he finally replied, still somewhat absent-mindedly. It was a strange answer, but then again the green-haired teenager was a strange person to begin with, so none of them pried any deeper.

As for what was on Gary's mind, it was the system message he had recently seen.

After leveling up, I've been on a plateau, but that's okay . . . the gang isn't in any trouble or anything, but what I'm more worried about is the next two weeks or so.

I haven't even really figured out what I'm going to do. I mean, with all this food around, can I really starve myself? I don't have help like last time . . . it won't work, and after what happened with Sty I'm worried my hunger might take over . . .

Now at rank 2, Sty hadn't been challenged at all, and he had completely ignored Gary throughout the day. From what he had learned from Izzy, Sty was part of Apollo's group, so she was worried that once Apollo was gone, Sty might have some plans for Gary, but there had been nothing so far.

When breakfast ended and everyone returned to the main hall, Sty turned around and looked toward them, raising his hand.

Damn it . . . here he goes . . . is he going to want another beating? Gary thought.

Sty was certainly getting ready to challenge one of them, but his finger was pointing at the Goat Altered.

"I challenge you to a fight," Sty said, a smile on his face.

Izzy, Ian, and several other students raised their eyebrows. The two of them had fought before, so why was Sty going after Numba, who had a lower rank than him?

Shit, what is this bug doing? Gary thought. *Is he trying to get revenge on me by beating Numba? Does he want to keep beating him up so he won't be able to advance?*

Am I going to have to challenge Sty every day and beat him to the punch, so he can't challenge Numba? Or maybe . . . wait, couldn't I just give Numba my position on the last day? Get Numba to challenge me, and lose the fight on purpose?

However, the moment he came up with the idea, Apollo's advice rang in his head again, telling him that he should try to get through this thing as rank 1. Honestly, Gary thought he wouldn't care about such a thing; it was just a number, and either way he would get into the academy, so would there really be that much of a difference if he entered as rank 1 or rank 2?

As he was worrying about this, Gary felt a hand on his shoulder.

"Don't worry too much about me. You've done enough. I can't even imagine what someone as strong as you has to worry about," Numba said. "To be honest, I want to get into the AFA with you, so I was planning to challenge one of the top rankers later. I just didn't intend to go for Sty . . . at least not right away, but I feel like this is meant to be.

"I've trained with you and I know it hasn't been for very long, but I know how strong you are, Gary. If I can last even a minute against you, then I have the confidence to crush that stupid bug!"

The fight was on, and the two of them moved toward the arena in the center of the room. Since it was a rematch and a grudge match, everyone was excited to witness it. But most of them thought it would have the same outcome as last time. After all, the difference between the two of them was too great, despite the surprisingly high rank of the Goat Altered.

"Look at your smug face," Sty said. "Just because you have a strong friend, you think I can't touch you? He might be strong, but at the end of the day he's just some Tier 3 gangster who can do nothing to help you against my family! But I don't need them. I'm going to make good on my promise to let you experience hell! As long as I'm here, you won't pass!"

The Fly Altered began to transform. "And once I'm out of this place . . . we will see what happens!"

CHAPTER 83

THE GOAT AND THE FLY (PART 1)

If Gary had a disliking for Sty before, he had an even greater one now. All of the students here were working toward the same thing. Gary had seen those them training hard day in and out to reach the top and advance to the actual academy. He had even heard of some that had been stuck here for years.

Sty had the chance to leave but had decided to stay. So he could prove to everyone that he could beat Numba? He had already proven that. He had already won once. Which was why Gary believed that Sty was an incredibly petty person who needed to be taught a bigger lesson than the last one.

However, there was a chance that if Numba could beat Sty in a fight, it would bring an end to everything. Numba would be the one who had humbled his opponent.

"It's going to be hard, we only had a little bit of training, but you were the one who improved the most. If you can get a hit on him like you did me . . . it will be interesting."

The two had transformed, and just like before, they looked no different. Numba had his large ramlike horns that curled past his face. In contrast, Sty had his large bug eyes and the wings on his back.

However, the beginning of the fight was different. Rather than charging in from the get-go, Numba got into a crouch so he could kick off with explosive power when needed.

He looked right at Sty, who flew around to approach Numba from a different angle. Lifting his front foot and swirling around, Numba turned so his body was facing Sty.

Sty kept changing direction, trying to get behind Numba, and each time Numba followed him, not allowing his back or sides to face Sty, constantly spinning around with a bounce in his step.

"Man, just watching Numba is making me feel dizzy," Ian said, holding his stomach. "He just keeps turning and turning. Can't one of them just attack already?"

The spectators were getting restless as well. Although the fight was tense, there had been no action yet, and the bored students hurled insults and began to chant "Fight! Fight! Fight!"

But Numba wasn't going to let anything get to him as he continued to dodge Sty, waiting for the right opportunity.

"You're more annoying than ever. You think you have everything figured out?" Sty said as he flew, no longer trying to find an opening.

Numa waited for Sty to get closer, and closer, and then when he was in range, he pushed off from his feet with a sudden explosive charge. Head down, he prepared to hit Sty with full force.

Regardless, Sty's reaction speed was incredibly fast as he flew upward slightly, spinning in the air before coming back down and kicking Numba right in the back of the head.

It was a strong kick, and Numba saw black spots for a few seconds. He stumbled to the ground slightly with his hands touching the floor.

He's still faster than me . . . he can still avoid my charge . . . but that's not all I have, Numba thought, spinning around on his knees to pivot into position before standing up again.

"Man, I thought he had him there. His timing was perfect, and his speed has improved a lot after doing all those drills," Ian commented.

"I have to admit, Sty is really fast; he might even be faster than me," Gary said nervously. He realized that if he hadn't used his Magnetic Howl skill, maybe even Sty would have been able to avoid the attack.

It was only because of his own skills and raw power that he was able to defend himself. Maybe everyone here, including him, had underestimated Sty.

Faster, faster. I need to move faster . . . maybe if I wait till the last second, or if I swirl and then punch just when he thinks I'm going to change. Instead, Numba came up with another idea.

Once again, Sty was hovering in the air, waiting for his opportunity. He flew from side to side as Numba was spinning as before. At this point, he was testing to see if Numba had slowed down after the last attack, but he was just as fast, so Sty would be cautious once more.

Diving in, he went straight ahead at full speed. Numba waited carefully, again trying to find the right time to push off, and then he saw his opportunity. He blasted off, heading straight for Sty.

As usual, Sty's Altered form allowed him to have super reaction speed, and he flew upward, avoiding the strike again and aiming to come from behind.

At that moment, though, Numba, using every leg muscle he had, stopped his advance suddenly. This caused great pain in his joints, but he kept repeating in his head, *Just one hit . . . I just need to get one hit . . . and then I know I can take him out!*

Using his explosive power, he twisted his body, turning back to face Sty, who was now in front of him.

Sty couldn't believe it. As he attacked, Numba's leg was already in a kicking motion again, only this time, Numba was facing him.

Once again, using all his strength, Numba kicked off with his feet, charging forward.

It was a seamless three-move motion. Charging in, a stop and another spinning burst, and then a final burst straight toward Sty.

Reacting quickly, Sty dodged backward as the horns came toward him, but that wasn't what he needed to worry about, because a punch was heading straight for his face.

Numba couldn't see what he was doing, but he felt the punch land as Sty went sliding across the floor.

"I did it . . . I hit him," Numba said aloud, pleased.

"Well done," Sty said, wiping the blood from his mouth. "So you hit me once, but do you really think that's enough to win?"

At that moment, another part of Sty's body began to transform. There was a lot more that Sty could do, far more that he hadn't shown.

CHAPTER 84

THE GOAT AND THE FLY (PART 2)

Numba could tell that although he had hit Sty, he hadn't made full contact. Sty had still managed to pull back at the last second, allowing most of the energy to dissipate.

Although there was blood, it wasn't a solid hit and Numba knew that Sty wasn't badly hurt, but it did get a reaction out of Sty.

"I see. You think you're someone. You have some sort of strange confidence around you," Sty shouted, but it was getting harder to understand him. Almost as if his voice was getting muffled.

Looking down and avoiding eye contact, Sty had tensed both of his arms.

"You're still nothing!" Sty charged forward.

His wings flapped quickly, and Gary could hear his fast heart rate from here. He was faster than he had been at the start, the fastest he had moved in the fight so far.

It's like I thought. Humfree was right. These scouted students are good. I only got the upper hand because I had the element of surprise. Sty probably never had to go all out against someone before. So he thought he could do the same with me, Gary thought.

Numba, seeing Sty's change in speed, panicked and charged forward again, hoping for good luck.

If he moves faster, I can get to him faster as well, Numba thought, unsure of his timing.

Suddenly he saw something green coming straight toward him. It hit him in the face, and the substance was quite sticky. Immediately Numba threw a punch, but it hit nothing but air as he tried to figure out what was on his face.

"My eyes!" Numba cried; he could feel them slightly burning, and so was his skin. While he endured that pain, a great force hit him in the stomach. It was a strong kick that lifted both his feet off the ground.

Another kick landed him straight on his back. He sensed burning, bruises, and pain all over his body.

Sty flew up in the air, as high as possible, and now that everyone got a good look, they could see the change in his body. His mouth had elongated, looking like a large tube with a few hairs growing around it.

More and more, Sty was looking like a giant fly, something clicked in Izzy's mind.

"That has to be some type of acid that he threw up," she explained. "Before flies eat their food, they have to break it down into liquid form. If he's based on some type of fly beast, that acid must be quite strong."

"You're saying there's like super sick on Numba right now?" Ian asked.

"Yeah . . . and if it got in his eyes, I'm afraid that Numba might not be able to see anything at all."

It was a tense situation, and Gary was getting more nervous by the second. Had he given Numba too much hope in just being able to hit him? Once again, Gary felt helpless. After Numba had helped him get into the facility in the first place, Numba had been met with difficulties, and Gary had just been making his life harder, not easier.

You can do it . . . come on, Gary thought.

Numba had placed his hands in push-up position, trying to get his body off the ground. He had only been hit three times, four if one counted the strange green goo that had already dissolved but was still hurting him.

Yet he was probably in more pain than last time. Still, his body shaking, Numba knew he needed to do something. He pushed off from the ground, lifting his whole body a good three feet into the air.

When he landed he quickly fell to one knee. He opened his eyes, which were stinging badly, and everything was a blur. He couldn't see a thing.

Sty had noticed this along with his slow movements. He thought that now that his prey had been injured, it was time to go in. From this high up, he went into an accelerated dive, faster and faster, getting closer to Numba.

"I can't watch this. How is he meant to do anything if he can't see?" Ian cried out.

"Well, there is one thing . . . but . . ." Izzy had a thought and was wondering if Numba had the same one.

Finally, realizing that nothing would work, Numba stood up and dropped back into a crouch. Gary noticed that his fist was tense as well. There was one thing Numba would never do: give up.

The next second, Sty had crashed into Numba, punching his fist through Numba's horn, which snapped the horn clean off. Blood spilled out and Numba was in extreme pain, but now he knew where Sty was.

The fist continued toward Numba's face, but using all the strength in his legs, Numba jumped up and threw an uppercut. The explosive power from his legs was transmitted to his fist as it smashed into Sty's face. At the same time, Sty's fist landed right on Numba's face, turning his vision black.

Numba and Sty both fell to the ground, breaking the flooring. One thing was clear. Both of the contestants lay still, not moving.

"Is this a . . . draw? What happens now?" Gary asked.

CHAPTER 85

A STRANGE RESULT

The situation became tenser and tenser the longer the two of them remained lying on the floor. It was an unexpected situation, to say the least, but even more so something that hadn't happened before. Even the teacher seemed unsure what he should do about it.

"What happens now?" Ian asked. "Do we have to wait for the first one to regain consciousness? Does Sty keep his position as rank 2, while Numba gets upgraded to rank 3?"

"I'm not sure." Izzy shrugged. "The rules state that a fight is over once someone is knocked out, or when they remain on the floor for more than ten seconds. It's been double that length, yet both badges remain unchanged. Maybe the system just hasn't been programmed for this type of scenario."

Seeing how no one was doing anything, Gary decided to act. Jumping over the guardrail, he rushed down to the main arena. Without any hesitation, he knelt down and put his head on his friend's chest, searching for a heartbeat.

"You guys call yourselves teachers? Don't you know anything about care? Just because they're both Altered doesn't mean they're not human! Come down here and check if the other guy is okay as well!" Gary shouted.

The students were a bit stunned by the green-haired teenager's action, but they knew he was right, and the teacher sprang into action.

He said something into a small microphone on his collar, and a few moments later, both students were being taken away on stretchers.

I hope Numba's all right. That last attack of his was powerful . . . but it was also a double-edged sword. Accelerating toward his opponent made his attack stronger, but the force of his jump added to Sty's attack as well, Gary thought as he watched the two disappear.

For the rest of the day, the students theorized about how the teacher would judge the outcome of this match. Many assumed that the adults might arrange a rematch to clarify who was stronger. Others thought that Numba might be automatically assigned rank 3, or that the current rank 3 would have to defend his position against the Goat Altered.

However, everyone agreed on one thing: the current rank 15 Altered deserved a position in the top ten. He certainly was strong-willed and determined, putting off many who had intended to challenge him before today's performance.

Toward the end of the day, an announcement gathered the students in the main hall. All the teachers appeared in military-like camo uniforms. It was strange to see all of them in one place, and even more surprising was the fact that there appeared to be only ten of them in total.

Standing in the center in front of everyone was a teacher wearing a red beret. He was clearly the leader of the teachers. Whispers that he was in charge of the entire facility quickly spread, though it was impossible to tell since this was the first time he had appeared in front of the students.

On the stage, slightly behind the leader of the teachers, were Sty and Numba. Gary was happy that his friend seemed to be doing okay. His head looked fine, and his cheek was still a bit swollen, but nothing that wouldn't heal quickly. However, one thing that did worry the werewolf was the look on the Goat Altered's face.

"As you're all aware, there was a fight between two contestants earlier today, one that seemingly ended in a draw. I've called you all here today to clarify the matter. After reviewing the match in its entirety, we have decided to declare the outcome of the match as void because of the interference of a certain student!" the leader stated.

"Did someone interfere? I don't remember that happening." Heads started to turn and whispers circulated among the students. The teachers seemed to have expected this reaction, because a clip started to play above the lead teacher, showing Gary running toward an unconscious Numba.

"This student interfered in the ongoing match between his fellow students. As most of you should be aware, only teachers may conclude any match. However, since the responsible student has not been here for long, and his reason for interfering had been deemed a selfless one, we have decided not to punish him. Nevertheless, this match will be regarded as if it had never happened," the man concluded.

Wait a second . . . did he just say that I was the reason the match was voided? Gary thought as his brain processed what had just been said. Looking at Numba, he also understood why he looked so unhappy and frustrated.

"That doesn't make any sense!" Izzy complained loudly. "We all saw the match! We all saw that both of them had been knocked out for over ten seconds! There was absolutely nothing that Gary did that would qualify as interference under any definition! He just came forward because he was concerned for their health!"

The lead teacher listened to her nonchalantly, then simply said, "One voided match won't make much of a difference. If your fellow student deserves that rank, we're not stopping him from earning it by fighting once more."

Izzy understood that there was no use arguing with the man, but she was still miffed that the school would make such a decision and blame Gary, of all people. With the announcement over, the teachers returned to their usual positions.

Numba and Sty also went their separate ways, but not before the Fly Altered made a snide comment. "Didn't I tell you that staying with that friend of yours was a bad idea? You got lucky once, but don't for a moment think that I'll fall for a trick like that again! Good luck, and see you tomorrow."

The Goat Altered didn't even react, still too downtrodden about his loss. He simply walked over to the waiting trio. When he finally reached the others, his arms flopped to his sides in defeat.

"I'm sorry, Gary . . . I really wanted to win. I really wanted to win so the two of us could go through together. If I had won that fight today, I would have been able to pass with you today. We both could have held our ranks for the full week after the assessment. I tried so hard, I tried so hard," Numba said. His legs were getting weak and he started to fall to his knees, but as he was falling his head hit a solid chest.

"It's okay, Numba . . . you got cheated . . . and I have no clue why," Gary replied with gritted teeth. "Since those bastards are blaming me for your loss, let me be the one to fix this situation. We're going to leave here together, and that piece-of-shit fly won't be able to stop us.

"Numba, I challenge you to a fight!" The Goat Altered lifted his head, confused, but Gary's eyes told him to just trust him, so he accepted the challenge.

A few moments later, there was a change on Gary's badge, which was suddenly displaying the number 3.

"What the . . . ?"

CHAPTER 86

BENDING THE RULES

According to protocol, the staff had to send a report of everything that happened within the facility to the main school. Usually, that report was nothing more than a formal listing of the students' changes in rank. Occasionally there would be some notes, for example when an Altered exceeded expectations by improving far faster than anticipated.

Today, the report included the special incident that resulted in an announcement by the lead teacher. Since that note mentioned a certain green-haired teenager whom the professors had been actively keeping their eyes on, it had raised more than a few eyebrows.

"In essence, you've voided a match because of the interference of the student named Gary Dem in that active match, correct?" Professor Wood summed up the note that had made the three of them call forth the lead teacher. "Correct me if I'm wrong, but that doesn't seem to be standard procedure. What's more, effectively the only one who appears to have been disadvantaged by this is the party who had been challenged, even though both parties reportedly fainted."

The teacher sat up straight, seemingly not intimidated by the three professors. "Should that student be deserving of the rank, he is more than welcome to fight once more after he has recovered. With all due respect, Professor Wood, I don't think the nullification of one match is something that should warrant your concern. After all, the assessment had just been completed and the student had already jumped several places."

The teacher took a sip of the tea that had been served to him. However, his polite tone and calm voice belied his heart rate, which was above what could be considered healthy. He was biding his time, waiting for one of them to speak, still unaware why they had taken such an interest in this case.

"If what you claim is true, maybe we should see the video in order to see if the punishment received is appropriate," Professor Hai said suddenly, with his arms folded. "I take it there should be no problem with that?"

The lead teacher nearly spat out his tea. He barely managed to trap the liquid in his mouth, gulping down hard as he let out a few coughs. "I'm afraid that the footage no longer exists. While we reviewed it, my subordinate accidentally overwrote it when I asked him to zoom in at one moment. I intended to punish him internally for that mistake, but I can let you take matters into your own hands if you insist."

"There's no need for that; we don't wish to interfere with your way of handling things in the facility. Since we only have your word to go on, we'll agree with your course of action. You may leave and continue doing your job as always." Professor Humfree waved his hand to send him off.

The lead teacher didn't even finish his tea. He quickly grabbed his beret, and with a short bow, he left the room.

"Well, how shall we proceed? Should we tell the director to swap him out? It's clear he was acting strangely," Professor Wood said.

"Hmm, for now, let's see how things play out, but we should also make sure that no evidence 'disappears.' Since one of his subordinates made a mistake, use that as a reason to get one of our men inside," Professor Humfree declared.

The next day, when everyone had gathered for breakfast, there was a new topic of gossip for the students to talk about. Last night they had already been talking about how unfair the result was . . . only to find Numba sitting at the table with the rest of the top rankers. Not only that, but he was sitting in Gary's place . . . and his badge was displaying the number 1!

"Gary, are you sure this is going to be okay?" Numba asked, burdened by all the stares he was receiving. "Everyone is talking about it, and they might think it's unfair."

"So what?" The werewolf scoffed as he grabbed another steak from his plate. "They were the ones who cheated you first. All we are doing is making use of the existing rules. If anyone has a problem with the current situation, they're free to challenge me."

Before breakfast, Gary had challenged Numba and let him win once more. This way, the Goat Altered was free to reject any challenges for the rest of the day. Gary was still angry with the decision the facility had made, and this was his way of protesting.

Sty was one of the last students to appear, and the first thing he saw was the latest top ranker sitting among them. He had already expected this kind of situation after seeing that he had dropped a rank. Clenching his fists, he turned around and left without uttering a single word.

"Did you see the look on his face? That's the look we want to see!" Gary jeered as he slapped Numba on the back, cheering him on. "Now let's enjoy our meal."

The other students were aware that the two had a strange relationship. Based on the fact that they hadn't heard or seen a fight, they could only guess what had led to the current situation. Honestly, after seeing Numba's performance they weren't too bothered by it, though everyone was baffled that Gary was okay with giving up his rank 1 spot.

Just as they were about to finish breakfast and head over to Izzy and Ian, though, the lead teacher came storming into the canteen unannounced.

"What do you think you're doing?" the man asked Gary.

"I was about to eat a steak. Why? Want some of it? I wouldn't mind, but you don't strike me as someone who would appreciate blue steak, more someone who fancies it well done," the werewolf cheekily answered as he bit into the meat.

"I'm not talking about your meal, but this!" The teacher pointed at Numba, more specifically at his badge. "This place is meant for you students to earn your ranks, not have them *gifted*!" He motioned as if to remove the Goat Altered's badge, but Gary grabbed his wrist.

"That's a pile of bull if I've ever seen one! On the first day I entered this place, there were students 'fighting' each other. Before their match I heard them come to an agreement about exchanging benefits for their rank! Neither you nor any of the other teachers cared about any of it, yet suddenly this facility is supposed to be some righteous place that cares about its rules? Is there something wrong with your head?" Gary went off on a tirade when faced with the audacity of the adult.

"Let go! The rules may not allow me to remove his rank, but if you continue to injure me, as a member of staff, I'm well in my right to kick you out!" the lead teacher threatened, staring into the green-haired teenager's eyes.

Numba pulled at his friend's arm and whispered, "Please stop, it's not worth fighting him over this. Not when you came so far already."

The moment his wrist was freed, the lead teacher turned around and headed out. Like everyone else, Izzy had watched this sudden confrontation and thought there was something strange going on for the lead teacher to personally show himself twice in such a short amount of time.

He only found out about this after Sty had left . . . and he came bursting into the room. This can't just be a simple coincidence . . . Izzy thought. She decided to leave the canteen early, and Ian followed her. After all, his childhood friend was always up to something interesting, and given what had just happened, he was dying to find out what they might uncover.

Izzy waited until no one seemed to be looking her way before opening the door slowly back into the main area. She and Ian exited the room and looked around. The angry adult wasn't hard to follow, given that his frustrated steps were loud enough. They eventually hid behind a large shelf that was used to store books. Hearing voices, they peeked around it, and that was when Izzy saw what she had suspected.

Just as I thought, that guy is definitely on Sty's side. Just what could that fly bastard have on him to make him follow his instructions, she wondered.

"We have to tell someone!" Ian whispered in her ear, realizing the same thing.

They thought it was best to get out of there before they got caught, and perhaps inform Gary, but when they turned around, they collided with someone.

"You're not telling anyone squat!"

CHAPTER 87

WHERE ARE THEY?

As soon as Izzy's eyes fell on the teacher who stood in the way of their escape, her heart sank. There was a sick feeling in her stomach as her fight-or-flight instinct kicked in, rushing her to get out, even though her brain screamed that it was impossible.

Damn it . . . I was such an idiot. I should have realized sooner that if Sty has the lead teacher under his thumb, the other teachers probably also work for him. As her brain raced to find a solution to this insurmountable problem, she noticed a sharp pain before everything around her turned black.

"Izzy!" Ian shouted as he helplessly watched from the side. "You bastard, what do you think you're doing?"

A stinger protruded from Izzy's stomach; it had been injected by the teacher. Almost immediately, she closed her eyes, unaware of everything around her. Ian, knowing the dire situation they were in, delivered a spinning back kick toward the teacher's head.

Unfortunately, the teacher merely had to lift his arm to block the attack. With his other hand he injected another stinger into Ian's body. In less than a second, Ian felt weak and drowsy.

"This is fucking unfair! How are we students supposed to win a fight against the teachers?"

I'm sorry . . . Izzy . . . for being unable . . . to protect you . . . was the last thought running through his mind before he too lost consciousness.

With nobody else disturbing them, Numba and Gary enjoyed their breakfast, even joking around a bit. They used the time to become closer friends. Before they had even noticed, it was already free time, yet surprisingly Izzy and Ian were nowhere to be seen.

At first, Gary just found it odd, but not enough to look for them. After all, he was sure the two of them would join their training. When lunch came, both Numba and Gary noticed that neither of them was present. It was weird but still didn't worry them too much, until they didn't turn up to training.

This was a first, especially since all three had been enjoying the training. The increase in their ranks had been the best evidence to support the use of it, so for the two of them to miss out without prior warning was extremely odd. What's more, with Gary and Numba both being top rankers, the time they would stay here was limited, which should have been all the more reason for Ian and Izzy to not skip out.

"Well, now I'm starting to get worried," Gary admitted, pacing back and forth. "This isn't like them at all. If they weren't feeling well today, they could have at least told us. Do you think somebody challenged them?"

"I don't think that's the case. Before we came here, we passed the guy who was next in rank after Ian, but his badge number is the same. If they fought, the badge numbers should have changed," Numba replied.

"You don't think . . . Sty has got anything to do with this, do you?" The Goat Altered gulped as he considered that possibility. However, how could a single student cause two people to simply disappear? Nevertheless, he had been the first one to leave the canteen earlier . . .

"Maybe . . . he did send over those twins to ambush me last week, so I wouldn't put it past him to do the same thing with them. If they were badly hurt, they could be in the medical bay," Gary answered after thinking it through.

Numba was silent for a while. He had an uneasy feeling in his stomach. "That might be it . . . but maybe he did more than that. I didn't have the chance to tell you this, but before the teachers called all of you out to the meeting, both of us had been informed that the result of our match was inconclusive, and that the teachers would discuss what to do about it.

"To be honest, the more I think about it, the more it seems like he must have bribed some of those teachers. He was all confident and looking at you during the announcement, even though we hadn't been told that they wouldn't count it.

"I know I should have said something earlier, but I thought it might have just been me overthinking things yesterday. I mean, Izzy and Ian aren't even a part of all of this."

Considering Izzy's curious nature, she might have figured this out before them. There had to be a reason why Sty was confident in staying behind even after Gary had beaten him, and it looked like they had just found the answer.

"What should we do?" Numba asked nervously. "We have no idea who among the teachers is on Sty's side. But without asking them for help, how else can we find Ian and Izzy?"

"We'll just ask the one person who seems to be involved in this charade," Gary answered confidently as he left the room. Without caring how it looked, he sniffed the air to filter out his target.

In the main area surrounding the center arena, several large staircases led upward to the students' rooms. Several students were hanging out on the stairs and joking around; one of them sat calmly with his arms casually spread out. It was none other than the rank 3 student.

"Sty!" Gary shouted the name so loudly that it instantly caught the attention of everyone in the vicinity. His voice was aggressive and powerful, making them freeze in place.

"You've got five seconds to tell me where they are before I smash your face in," the green-haired teenager threatened as he approached Sty. Not fazed by this, the Altered stood up and shrugged.

"How am I supposed to know what the hell you're talking about? If you've come here looking for a fight, then I have to disappoint you. I've already been challenged. Try again tomorrow, but you might have to get there *really* early because there's someone who is very keen to challenge me these days." Sty let out a chuckle, visibly enjoying the frustration on Gary's face.

The werewolf continued approaching him, and when he was close enough he stopped for a second before suddenly transforming his legs. Sty had been busy laughing as Gary closed the distance between them. Transforming his hands as well, Gary grabbed the back of Sty's head, clenching it tightly.

"You think I give a shit about whether you've been challenged or not?" Gary shouted, slamming the Fly Altered's face onto the edge of the staircase. Teeth flew through the air and dropped to the floor.

Sty's mouth was now a bloody mess.

"Mwy tweath!" he struggled to say.

"Wrong answer!" Gary interrupted him, slamming his head down once more onto the staircase.

"Where are they?" the werewolf demanded to know, his eyes glowing red with fury and fire.

CHAPTER 88

EXPELLED

There was a reason why most students had avoided interacting with Gary, much less challenge him to a fight, ever since the day they had seen him fight Sty. It was simple . . . they were afraid. The werewolf had not only managed to defeat the Fly Altered, but he had done so seemingly by accident.

After his family had been threatened, an anger had overcome Gary, making him reveal far more than he wanted. Many had hoped to not see such a scene anytime soon. Alas, the students who had just been hanging out with Sty had front-row seats. What's more, the current spectacle was even worse than the match had been.

Sty's mouth was completely red, and the whites of his eyes were fully visible because his eyes had rolled back in his head. And yet . . . the green-haired teenager was not showing an ounce of compassion for his fellow student.

"Answer me!" he demanded, holding the Altered by the head. Of course, being passed out, Sty could not say anything, and his "friends" were too afraid to move.

Gary . . . I understand that you're worried . . . I understand why you're angry at him . . . but when I see you like this, even I'm scared of you, Numba thought as he watched in silence with the rest.

Because there was no answer from Sty, Gary gripped his head again, getting ready to shove him into the staircase for the third time. But suddenly a strong force held both of Gary's arms, and now one of the teachers held the unconscious teenager safely in his arms.

"Student Gary Dem, you're in clear violation of the rules. Stop this immediately and follow me!" the teacher who had followed the noise shouted at the werewolf. "Your punishment will be decided by us. As for the rest of you, get back to your rooms. There will be no duels for the rest of the day until this matter is resolved!"

The students quickly dispersed, while one teacher carried Sty and the other dragged Gary along. Before heading their way, Gary turned around for a brief moment, smiling knowingly at his friend, then leaving with the teachers.

Don't tell me . . . did you do all of this, so they would punish you? Don't you think your actions are a bit excessive? We aren't even 100 percent sure yet that they're the ones behind all of this. Numba worried that his friend's rash actions could lead to something worse.

The werewolf had done a lot of dangerous and unconventional things in the facility during his short stay, but without a doubt this was the worst.

"He's going to get kicked out! He has to! That's what they did to other students who fought anybody who was in their right to refuse a challenge," one of the students commented on the way to his room.

"Sure, but none of those who were expelled had been top rankers. I feel like the teachers are far more lenient on them since those guys have proven that they have the necessary talent to advance to the academy," another student argued.

"Still . . . that meat-loving freak didn't just hit Sty once or twice. This was a full-on assault and battery. I wouldn't even be surprised if he crippled him for life!"

Gary followed the teachers until they reached the medical bay, where he had been told to wait until someone came to pick him up.

he looked around, checking to see if his missing friends were here as well. It was hard to do, as one teacher had remained to watch him, but by sniffing the air he found their scent.

Izzy and Ian . . . they were both taken here. The scent is relatively fresh, so they might still be here somewhere. The AFA is nothing like I thought it was. How can even the teachers be involved with something like this?

Just thinking about it and worrying about his friends was making Gary angrier by the second. Eventually, the teacher received an order to move elsewhere, and they ended up on the outside.

Behind the facility was another building; on the inside it looked like another training room. Already waiting for them was none other than the lead teacher. His arms were folded, and standing next to him were Ian and Izzy.

"Gary!" Izzy shouted out, but the lead teacher held out his hand, stopping her from getting closer. Just then, a teacher entered the room, and the other one left. The door closed and locked behind them.

"I hear you have been looking for these two. Well, here they are, you can have them," the lead teacher said, nodding toward them.

They immediately ran to Gary's side. Izzy even hugged him without warning.

"Gary, why are you in here!" Izzy asked. "Never mind that, this man and the other teachers are all working with Sty! He has them on his payroll or something. We heard him, and then they kidnapped us and brought us to this place!"

She was speaking too fast for Gary to follow, but luckily he had already guessed as much.

"All three of you have broken several rules, which leaves me with no other choice but to punish you by expelling you," the teacher explained calmly.

"You can't do that!" Ian shouted in protest. "Just because you're working with another student. We'll tell the other teachers and report this to the others!"

"Are you really threatening us?" the lead teacher asked, and at that moment the person behind him moved closer. "I am in charge of this facility, and whatever I say goes. None of you will ever set foot in the academy again.

"I was planning to be lenient and allow you to go so you could enjoy your lives at some other academy, but since it looks like you don't understand what's good for you, let me teach you the consequences of ever coming close to the AFA in the future!"

Each teacher had giant hornet stingers emerging from their forearms. Ian and Izzy had seen what they could do and took a fighting stance, getting closer to Gary.

"Kick us out?" The werewolf chuckled. "Don't bother, I was already planning to leave. However, if you thought I was going to leave this place without making you guys pay, then you're dead wrong!"

CHAPTER 89

DOUBLE STINGER (PART 1)

After the two teachers threatened them, the system popped up a message.

Two dangerous Altereds have you surrounded and wish to take you out!
Quest: Defeat the two Altereds
Additional Quest: Complete the quest while surviving with your two allies
Optional: Consume your opponent to gain additional stats

That's not a good sign, not good at all, if the system has decided to come up now. Doesn't that mean this will be quite hard? And judging by the additional quest, it doesn't think I'll be able to survive with Ian and Izzy.

While thinking this, Gary retaliated by using partial transformation in his arms and legs. He had plenty of energy, but the last thing he wanted to do was drain it quickly with a full transformation. Not while he didn't know who his opponents were and what they could do.

"Wait! You're really going to attack us over this! That's crazy!" Izzy said, her whole body trembling. "Surely we can talk this out?"

In her mind, if there was a fight between the three of them and the teachers, even with Gary they would surely lose, and if she knew Gary, he would retaliate quite a bit. Which could cause these eager teachers to accidentally go further than they intended.

However, when Gary looked at the teachers he had one thing going through his mind.

Kirk would have been able to beat both of these guys, and because of me . . . he's dead. I can't lose this fight!

The first one to charge in wasn't the lead teacher, it was the one from behind. At that point, Izzy was frozen. She didn't know what to do. All of this was still so unbelievable.

One of the teachers grinned and lifted his hand. Suddenly the man's stinger rocketed off his arm, flying right toward them.

"Move, you idiot!" Ian shouted as he knocked Izzy to the floor. At the last second, Ian dodged by ducking and rolling, allowing the projectile to fly over their heads. He looked up in time to see a new stinger regrow into place.

"He really tried attacking us," Izzy said, staring at one of the crashed stingers and seeing a drop of liquid fall off the tip and onto the floor. She turned her head to see how Gary was faring. He was using both claws to prevent one of the teachers from jabbing a stinger directly into his stomach.

This guy . . . he's quite strong, I have my controlled transformation to the max, and I'm using two hands! Gary thought.

"You predator types, always think you're the top dog, wherever you go," the lead teacher said. "Strong, fast, and you have this natural instinct inside you to fight, but a bug . . . has more strength than you can imagine."

An explosive force of power gave Gary's fist a quick jerk. It pushed both of his arms away, and he felt a deep pain in his gut. He slid across the floor, away from the powerful attack, and as usual his system was there to remind him of his losses.

–10 HP

190/200 HP

I lost 10 HP, but the attack didn't even hit me, and I have a high resistance as well. I'm starting to second-guess whether Kirk could have really beaten these guys, Gary thought. A single hit said a lot.

But Gary had more to be concerned about. The other teacher had his stinger ready to stick into Gary's back.

"Don't let them touch you with that!" Izzy yelled. "It will make you sleepy!"

Gary was naturally concerned about the stingers; he'd thought they might contain some type of poison, but now that he knew their effects, he was even more concerned.

As he activated his claws, his nails grew longer and he stabbed them into the ground to bring himself to a halt. The teacher charged in from behind, and the head teacher charged in from the front.

Which one should I go for? Taking on two at once at this level . . . is just not possible. One needs my full attention, Gary thought.

Ian slid in from the side and kicked the teacher in the shin. It was quite a powerful attack. Upon landing, he quickly used his hands to flip himself back and assumed a fighting stance.

"Look, I don't like fighting you guys, but you attacked us! It's our right to protect ourselves!" Ian shouted. "Gary, we may not be able to kick his ass, but we will at least hold him back for you until you beat the other guy."

In all honesty, Gary was a bit concerned that his friends weren't dependable after receiving the system message, but after training with them and knowing their skills, he started to feel a bit silly.

"All right, I'll do as you guys say!" Gary said, running toward the lead teacher.

The teacher waited for the right moment to throw a punch from a standing position, as in karate. But Gary blocked by shoving his opponent's arm to the side, deflecting the stinger past his face.

He made a fist and landed a strong counterpunch. It didn't knock the teacher down, as his stance was solid and his body felt like a brick wall, but that didn't matter to Gary.

He followed through, getting behind his opponent, and slashed at the teacher's back with his sharp claws. They ripped through his clothes and a little bit of blood seeped through. Gary's claws hadn't gone in deep; a strange brown undercasing peeked through beneath the teacher's skin.

What is this stuff? Gary thought.

CHAPTER 90

DOUBLE STINGER (PART 2)

The strange second layer of skin didn't slow Gary down; he dodged another attack and kicked the teacher in the stomach. His opponent grunted, and for a second it looked like the teacher was stunned.

I was startled for a bit because of your strength, but so what if you're stronger than me? Gary thought. *What does that even matter? That's not my only trait. I have a lot more things I can do!*

Not all Altereds worked the same, nor were their bodies the same either, even if they had the same type of Altered DNA.

Little by little Gary was racking up offensive damage, but at the same time, the teacher was starting to get the hang of Gary's speed, odd attack angles, and more. Whenever Gary threw a punch, the teacher would block it.

Things escalated in speed until the two of them appeared to be throwing blows out at the same time, bashing against each other simultaneously. This finally carried on until a stinger caught Gary from the side, drilling into him.

–12 HP
178/200 HP

Still, the werewolf continued charging forward.

I have a lot of Health, so I can take these hits, as long as I hurt him more than he hurts me. If I don't run out of energy, I'll win this fight!

He knew putting all his effort into a full transformation would not help; he needed to conserve his energy by taking him down bit-by-bit. He prepared to attack again, but just then a strange pair of thin, light wings sprouted from the lead teacher's back, breaking through his hard skin.

He flew forward, and threw a double punch at the same time. Gary could tell this was going to be a more powerful attack.

If he blocked with all of his weight behind it, the stingers would pierce his hands, so he lined up his claws to stop the stingers before they reached his flesh. Still, Gary was pushed back across the ground much farther than before. Only this time the momentum didn't stop.

Because the stingers stuck in his claws, the lead teacher continued to fly ahead, dragging him along. Gary felt a sharp pain through the center of his body.

What the . . .

−15 HP
You have received a fatal wound
Emergency healing cannot be used until the object has been removed from the body
If the wound is not healed you will continue to lose HP
An unknown substance has entered your body
It is slowly affecting you
Body functionality is now at 98 percent and will continue to decrease

All the messages had popped up at once. Looking down, Gary saw the stinger sticking out of him. It was solid black, and a strange-colored liquid was coming out of the end, along with Gary's own blood.

He knew that the stinger could not have come from his own opponent, which meant only one thing: it was from the other teacher.

Is that really it . . . it has to be . . . but then . . .

Gary looked down and saw his friends lying still on the ground. Neither one was moving, and blood was puddled around them. Just like him, they had large puncture wounds on their bodies from the stingers.

No . . . no . . . Are they dead? . . . What happened?

Body functionality is now at 97 percent

I . . . I created this situation . . . if I had just minded my own business. Who cares about this academy? Their lives are more important, Gary thought.

"How . . . how the heck can you teachers do that to students. What is wrong with you?" Gary's arms were tensing up and his veins were popping through the fur on his arms.

"Why are you listening to some nobody? Are you a machine that just follows orders?" Gary asked, pushing forward bit by bit, moving his opponent back. "Is it just because you two are freaking bugs?"

The lead teacher smiled. "I guess this should teach you. In this world, in this day and age that we live in, you should be careful about who you touch. A nobody like you."

Now Gary was the one who was smiling.

Full transformation has begun
–30 Energy

"You're right, I'm just the leader of a no-name gang from a Tier-3 city," Gary replied. His arms grew larger and his snout grew longer. With all his strength Gary pushed the lead teacher off his body. With both hands, he grabbed the stinger and snapped the end off.

Gary slammed the broken part of the stinger into the teacher's head, driving it into his temple and causing him to fall straight to the floor.

"What . . . have you done . . . you . . . can't get away with this!" the teacher shouted.

"I have already gotten away with it before . . . it's no problem for me!" Gary charged forward in full werewolf form, but he was up against the clock.

Body functionality is now at 90 percent

CHAPTER 91

RUNNING OUT OF TIME (PART 1)

Gary wasn't sure whether the teacher behind him was out cold, badly hurt, or dead. Honestly, he didn't care as long as he was out of the fight, because right now if he stood any chance of making it out of this situation, he would have to defeat the lead teacher in front of him.

Just what the hell is in those stingers? I can already feel that stuff affecting me. Gary noticed that his transformed feet felt strange, as if he had sat on them for too long.

The system had informed him about the decrease in his body's performance, but at first, it hadn't been too bad. However, given the rate at which it was getting worse, he was under a serious time constraint. Gary had intended to conserve his Energy at the start of the fight, to find the best way to deal with the lead teacher, in case he had more surprises in him like Sty's ability to fly.

Now his best chance to win was to go full out . . . for as long as he could.

Gary leapt into the air. The Insect Altered tried to fly away, but he was too late. The werewolf had successfully latched onto his legs.

For a second, the two fell toward the floor, as Gary's sudden weight was added. However, the wings were sent into overdrive as they started to flutter at an extreme rate, lifting the two of them back into the air.

"Get off me, you damn monster!" The teacher lifted his hand that still held a stinger and punched Gary on the shoulder. The stinger pierced his thick hide, and it was the first time a punch had hit him so cleanly.

–28 HP
135/200 HP

The transformed teenager felt a stab of pain from the stinger. The grip and strength in his right arm weakened, forcing him to let go, and now he only held on to the teacher with his healthy hand.

That freaking hurt . . . it was a big blow as well, but I need to hold on.

Gripping his left hand, he used his claws to pierce the lead teacher's leg. Although he was shielded by strong armor on his torso and back, the same wasn't true for his leg. Now that he had a better hold, Gary swung his body up, lifting his weight with a single arm.

Emergency healing in progress

Gary was unable to restore his Health with emergency healing, since only a skill like Claw Drain could do that, but it was very effective to mend his broken bones. Most importantly, it was quick as well.

"Now it's my turn!" Gary shouted as soon as his shoulder was fixed.

Skill activated: Claw Drain
–15 Energy

Gary had wrapped his legs around his opponent's body, allowing him to hold himself up with both hands free. Not wasting time, he swiped at the teacher's chest.

His claws went in deeper this time, ripping off chunks of flesh and flinging them to the ground. With more strength, his fingers were able to go through the heavy, strange armor.

+3 HP

+5 HP

+2 HP

At the same time, Gary was getting his Health back. Fully focused on attacking his opponent, he didn't notice his surroundings. Suddenly he was crushed up against the side of the wall.

The Insect Altered had flown at full speed trying to shake off his furry passenger in any way possible. The second Gary's grip had weakened, the teacher kicked him off, sending him crashing to the floor.

76/200 HP

Gary's chest felt heavy as he got up, but even worse, his legs were weak and wobbly, and his eyes were drowsy.

Body functionality is now at 48 percent and will continue to decrease

"You really are a fool!" the teacher screamed, his hand held over his chest. The attack had been very effective, and a lot of blood was flowing out. The grimace on his face was not hiding the pain he was in. "I admit that you're strong, but you're also an idiot! The more I use these stingers on you, the quicker they will affect your body!

"How does it feel? Are you tired yet?" The Insect Altered laughed at Gary's disheveled state. "All I need to do is avoid you at all costs, and wait for the drug to take proper effect. And let me tell you, once you take that nap, it will be the last thing you do!"

Gary was certain that the teacher was bluffing. After everything that had happened, it was impossible for both of them to make it out alive. Of course, he wouldn't go down without a fight, so he got on all fours and charged forward.

Come on, legs, don't fail me now! Gary screamed internally. *Let's move like you used to, move like you mean it!*

He was fast, even after losing control of over half his body, and against an opponent like this one. It wasn't enough, though, so instead of using his claws Gary threw out a fist.

The teacher didn't even fly away this time; he merely moved to the side, retaliating by punching the werewolf right in the ribs and injecting the stinger into his body yet again.

–16 HP
60/100 HP

This guy is really hard to fight . . . if only his partner hadn't stabbed me in the first place. Maybe I would have had a chance then. I know I would have already been dead if it were the old me . . . but . . .

Gary threw out a fist again; it was still fast and had a lot of power, but just as before the teacher was able to follow his current speed.

Body functionality is now at 40 percent and will continue to decrease

CHAPTER 92

RUNNING OUT OF TIME (PART 2)

Just throwing punches wasn't working, so Gary needed to make a change. He was unsure if it would work, but it was something he'd wanted to test a while ago, and with nothing to lose in this situation he had to try.

"Stop moving!" Gary shouted, and then he released a loud howl.

Skill activated: Magnetic Howl

The strange howl activated something in the lead teacher and he came toward Gary and began to pummel him on the chest.

"You truly are an idiot! So what if you can make me attack you? My punches are stronger than your stupid hide! Fine, if you want to die quicker, be my guest!" the teacher shouted.

"Maybe . . . but at least you're now in range for me to attack you back!" Gary growled.

Skill activated: Claw Drain
–15 Energy

He forfeited his defense to exchange blows with the teacher. After all, thanks to his skill, he was also getting some of his Health back, albeit not enough to make up for the loss he was suffering. Naturally, the lead teacher was not holding back. Blood was pouring from Gary's mouth and dripping from several wounds all over his body.

"How are you still not dead? How are you still standing with that much poison in your body?" The teacher was shocked. He had never seen anyone take as many hits, bleed this much, and still be alive.

He's hurt, I know he's hurt . . . this is it . . . I just have to go on for a little longer, Gary thought as he saw his HP drop below ten points. Fortunately, he had one last trump card he had at his disposal.

Skill activated: Last Stand
–6 HP
1/100 HP
Last Stand has been activated (59 seconds remaining)

Even though Gary's movements were slowing down, and the teacher was managing to hit him twice for every hit he received, there was a large difference between them. With Gary's Health, his Energy, and his skills, he had become an unstoppable force, a frightening being that could take ten hits to give out one. Covered in blood from head to toe, the Insect Altered could only continue to stare into those glowing red eyes. At that moment, another claw went right into his stomach, piercing through him as blood filled his mouth.

"ARGHHH!" Gary screamed as he continued to stab the teacher in the stomach. He stabbed and stabbed, digging into the same place. Blood was now pouring from the teacher's stomach as the hole continued to widen.

"ARGHHH!" Gary continued to scream as he felt a weight on his shoulder, but he stabbed with his claws again and again until finally a message appeared.

Quest completed

Wait . . . what? Gary thought. He could hardly see, not because of his tiredness but because his eyes were swollen and filled with blood. His Energy was extremely low as well.

Still, the system screen was connected to his mind, so he could still see the notification before him clearly. He took a step back, and the seemingly lifeless body of the teacher collapsed and fell to the floor.

He's not moving . . . he's really not moving. Gary fell to his knees next to the body. He reverted to his human form, trying to use as little energy as possible.

Last Stand has come to an end
1/200 HP

Pushing the teacher's body over, Gary flipped him onto his back and saw a lifeless face. There was no heartbeat, and the color from his face and eyes had gone.

Congratulations, you have now reached: Level 21
A stat point has been granted
Congratulations, Additional Quest has been completed
2 Pawn points have been given

Wait, what is this? Pawn Points, does that mean . . .
With the effects of the poison still in his body, Gary could barely make out the two figures on the floor. If the Additional Quest was completed, it meant both Izzy and Ian weren't dead but had just been injected with the same stuff he had inside him now.

Thank you . . . thank you for not making me mess up again . . . thank you. Gary was relieved, but there was another problem. Now that the worry was out of his head, something else was taking over his natural instinct.

My body hurts . . . and I'm so hungry . . . so . . . very hungry, Gary thought as he moved over to the teacher. Gary could feel his mind blacking out, but his body was moving on its own.

Optional Quest (Waste not, want not) is still in progress
Consume the body of the Altered for additional stat points

As if he didn't need to tell his body what to do, he felt himself pick something up and start to chew. He continued to chew . . . Everything was a mist of haze as to what was going on. He only subconsciously heard the sound of dings.

It was the system message, but what the message was Gary had no clue because he was somewhere else right now, asleep but not quite at the same time.

"This is where they took them, Professors," a teacher said, standing outside a separate training room that hadn't been used in years, away from the facility.

"I reported back to you as soon as possible, and I tried getting inside, but the lead teacher ordered me to stay outside. Which is why I decided to call the three of you."

The professors had arrived, but it took them a while, as they had to come from the main academy. One walked up to the metal door broke the lock, and slammed it open.

They all entered the room immediately and stopped when they saw what awaited inside.

"What on earth has happened here?" Professor Wood had to cover his mouth, almost feeling sick, while Professor Humfree was shaking his head, a churning feeling in his stomach.

Standing in the middle of the room, his whole body covered in blood, was Gary. He was unmoving, and his face was pointed toward the corner of the room, where two lone silhouettes lay. It was as if he was sleeping on his feet.

They had never expected to find the injured students, and as for the teachers, there was hardly a body left for them to bury.

CHAPTER 93

EVOLVING

Slowly opening his heavy eyelids, Gary found himself staring into a bright white light. He could see nothing else, and his hearing was still muffled, making everything sound as if he was underwater.

Am I dead? . . . Is this what death feels like? Gary wondered. *What happened to that teacher? I remember him threatening to kill me once his poison worked . . . so I just kept hitting and hitting . . . and hitting . . . I guess in the end . . .*

Soon his blurry white vision became clearer, and he realized that he was staring at the ceiling light. His hearing was also coming back, followed by his sense of touch, allowing him to feel the soft cotton sheets on his arms.

Body functionality is at 100 percent

The system message had confirmed it. Gary really hadn't died. He was still alive.

So that damn poison is finally out of my system. Is that what kept me asleep and made me feel so weak?

Gathering his bearings, he saw that he was in a medical room. What's more, it was a private one with a single bed, and Gary was hooked up to several machines. However, there were no physical wounds on his body. He had been dressed in a light blue robe, but that was it.

Well, I guess whoever put me in here doesn't want me dead . . . at least not yet, he thought. *But in the end, I completed the quest. Ian and Izzy should be all right. Maybe they're somewhere close by?*

Just to make sure he hadn't been dreaming the part about completing the additional quest, Gary decided to open up his system and check over his last notification.

Things looked good so far; he had leveled up after defeating the two teachers, and he now had two unspent Pawn points, which was a relief. If he was in a hospital, then Ian and Izzy would be as well, but when he looked at his stats, Gary's eyes widened in disbelief.

How . . . how could this have happened . . . how could this much have changed, unless . . .

A quick sensation flashed through Gary's mind, of feeling something in his mouth, but he had no clear memories of it. However, the system confirmed what Gary thought had occurred.

Name: Gary Dem
Class: Warrior
State: Human (Alpha)
Grade: Bishop
Level 21
Exp 3788/6789
Health 200 → 250
Energy 78/300
Strength 27 → 35 (+2)
Dexterity 26 (+2)
Endurance 25 → 32 (+2)

First of all, there was a change in his Health value. Eating Kirk had granted Gary extra stats, but Health hadn't been one of them. He had believed that only stat points could increase his Health, but he didn't mind being proven wrong. On top of that, Strength and Endurance had both increased by leaps.

I guess that confirms it. "You are what you eat" isn't just a saying in my case. My body evolves based on what type of Altered I eat.

Scrolling through the list, he noticed another notification he hadn't expected to find.

A passive skill has been gained: Poison Resistance (Low)
Your body now has a base level of resistance against poisons

This body . . . It's amazing! To be able to develop such a thing . . . Hang on, if I have the ability to keep evolving like this based on the enemies I eat and kill . . . doesn't that mean that as long as I eat enough, I'm practically invincible?

Am I really the only one alive? Gary started to wonder. *Were the ones before me hunted to extinction by a group like the Altered Hunters? . . . or maybe it was something else.*

Both possibilities were interesting to think about, and Gary became even more interested in finding out the origins of the Werewolf System. Unfortunately, the only ones who might know were already six feet under.

Now, as his head started to clear, and after he had read all the notifications and further ogled his newly gained passive skill, which would have been heaven sent *before* his fights against the teachers, it was time to face his current situation.

Whoever picked me up and put me here . . . they must have seen the bodies . . . or the lack thereof . . . Shit, what if they came in right when I was eating those two? Am I still in the facility even? If that is the case, and it was one of the other teachers, with two of them dead, then I should expect serious punishment, maybe beyond just getting kicked out of the school. Gary gulped.

With his newfound strength and extra stats, though, if that did happen, he might have a good chance of getting out. Worst-case scenario, he was prepared to hide out in Slough before the teachers could do anything.

That was when he looked at the surrounding equipment.

Wait, I was definitely covered in blood. I had holes in my body. I might have healed from eating, but it wouldn't have been so bad for me to be in this hospital. Have they gotten a hold of my blood? If that's the case, they might have found out what I really am!

Immediately, he started to pull himself out of the bed he was in. He removed all the strange white little electrodes that stuck to his body, and a flatline signal sounded from one of the machines.

Shut up! Gary thought, as he felt a sudden breeze across his backside.

He realized that under the robe, he was wearing nothing else. Just as he discovered that there were no clothes in the room, the handle on the door started to turn.

CHAPTER 94

A WAY IN

Panic started to set in. His heart was beating rapidly as he frantically searched for a way out. Alas, other than a tiny vent and a small window that he would only get stuck in if he tried to use it as a means to escape, there was only that door.

Amid his panicking, the door swung open and three relatively old men walked into the room.

"Oh, this is a nice surprise, you're already up!" Professor Humfree said with a smile and his hands behind his back, so Gary wouldn't feel threatened during this delicate situation. "Mr. Dem, please lie down and rest while we inform you about what happened."

Gary cautiously looked at all three of them, but he couldn't sense any hostility. His rational mind was telling him that if they wanted to hurt him, they would have done it while he was unconscious . . . or at least put him in chains as Damion had done.

Walking backward to avoid showing them his bare tush, the green-haired teenager hopped onto the bed and even pulled the sheets up. At the same time, underneath the sheets, he used Controlled Transformation on his right arm, to make sure he wasn't defenseless in case his earlier judgment turned out to be wrong. After what had occurred, Gary wasn't willing to fully trust anyone connected to the AFA, even the three professors in front of him.

"First of all, we owe you an apology." Professor Humfree began, and he bowed, the other two joining him without any protest. Never in his life had the werewolf expected such a gesture from someone working for the AFA. His shock even made him revert his arm to normal.

"All of our teachers should have been heavily vetted to prevent any student from abusing their status. Unfortunately, it is impossible to stop corruption completely because of how our world works," Professor Humfree explained with a deep sigh.

Gary knew that, and if someone was joining the academy, they wouldn't exactly tell them all the connections they had.

"We deeply regret that one of the students managed to influence the head teacher, of all people, and that you and your friends suffered because of that. We're even more indebted to you because you not only stopped him but managed to save the lives of your two fellow students," Professor Hai added.

For the first time in the conversation, the tension in Gary's body settled a little. He had been worried about Izzy and Ian, so hearing that they were alive and well was certainly great news.

"Gary." Professor Humfree addressed him by his first name with a strong voice. He was no longer smiling, as it sounded like the next subject was more serious. "We have come here to ask for a favor from you. We've already dealt with the student in question, and hope that you can let it rest at that, rather than seek your own revenge against him."

"Are you telling me that you want me to overlook everything he did? You just said it yourself: *All three of us could have gotten killed!* How can you ask me to simply ignore that?" Gary had the right to be upset, after all; because of this one student he had almost died.

"Gary, we understand your fury, but please try to understand our position as well. Unless you have express permission from a high-ranking staff member, fights between official students in the AFA won't be permitted," Professor Wood explained.

"Most students are able to leave behind what happened in the facility, but those who don't and wish to complete their revenge only hurt themselves and other students. There have been several cases where students never came back to the academy again. I'm sure you're smart enough to understand what I mean."

Gary was starting to think that the AFA might be actually one of the most dangerous places in the world.

"In your case, the backing between the two of you is just too far apart. The last thing we want to see is a talented student like yourself no longer be in the AFA, Gary," Professor Humfree said, trying to persuade him.

He let out a sigh of relief, as it looked like he wasn't getting kicked out. At least he had the option to stay, but could he really not hit Sty if he saw him again, if he continued to play his tricks and games?

"We understand that we're asking a lot from you, and we're also not asking you to do it for free. Not only has he been warned that any attack or provocation against you or any of your friends will be regarded on a case-by-case basis and can lead to his expulsion, but as long as you agree to forget about taking revenge, we shall bury any details about the state we found you in."

Gary's heart thumped louder.

"They . . . saw what I did . . . didn't they?"

"There's nothing to be ashamed of. You were in a desperate situation, one where your life was literally on the line, so none of us blame you for what you did. Given your advanced transformation state, your Altered instinct might have simply kicked in. We've not told a soul about it, and we don't plan to, so we hope for your cooperation, Mr. Dem," Professor Hai admitted.

Gary thought about it for a while, but if he was honest with himself, he didn't want to leave the AFA just yet, not when he hadn't even made it into the real academy.

"It's a deal," he agreed. He was about to stand up and shake their hands, but he remembered his lack of clothes just in time.

The three smiled and started to head toward the door, but Professor Humfree turned around.

"We'll send over a teacher with a change of clothes as well as some food. Once you're done, he'll accompany you to the real AFA academy. Let me be the first to congratulate you for passing."

"Huh, I made it?" Gary raised his eyebrows. "So I won't have to wait for the week to be over like the others?"

"A week?" Professor Hai chuckled, as he thought the teenager was joking, before he remembered why they had come to him at his current location. "Mr. Dem, your one-week period has already passed. Compared to your friends, you had a lot more poison in your body, so you slept for a far longer time. Anyway, we will see you soon."

After the door closed, Gary immediately went to check something that he had completely missed.

Your bloodlust grows
2 days until the next full moon

CHAPTER 95

ENTERING THE REAL ACADEMY

Just as the professors had stated, it was not long before a young nurse entered the room with a set of clothes. She placed them on the bed after giving a few instructions. Once he was dressed, Gary was to come out of the room, and she would lead him to a bus that was waiting for him.

When he picked up the clothes, Gary noticed that they weren't the ones he was wearing earlier. Instead, they looked more like a type of uniform. The shirt was tight fitting, similar to a sports shirt. It was mainly yellow with a few white details here and there. Turning the shirt around, he saw a large white circle with a black outline on the back, with yellow letters saying *AFA*.

Is this what I think it is? Gary held it up to make sure. *It's the AFA uniform! The one fighters actually use! That's why the material is stretchy, has cooling ability, and is resistant to certain attacks.*

Gary used his strength to stretch the shirt to test it, and the results came out to his liking. When he let go, it went back to its initial shape. But of course he didn't use his full strength because right now, these were the only clothes he had.

When he put the shirt on, it was a perfect fit, and they had even provided him with shorts to match. The uniform reminded him a little of his rugby days, but this was far more prideful to wear.

All his worries seemed to vanish as soon as he put on the shirt. The fabric was soft against his skin, and when he threw out a couple of punches and kicks, he was even more satisfied with the uniform when he found no restrictions in his movement.

I wonder if I can take one of these back with me and have Kai make the gang uniform from this kind of material? They can analyze this, right?

Finally, Gary stepped out the door to face the music. He had come up with a semi-solution to solve his problem in the next two days, and he was hoping not to encounter anyone who would agitate him.

The nurse was waiting for him when he exited the room, and Gary shyly handed over the robe he had been wearing.

"You could have just left that in the room, you know." She chuckled but took it anyway, then walked him to the bus.

To Gary's surprise, waiting just outside was someone that Gary had seen before but didn't know too well. It was one of the teachers who had been present during the assessment, the well-built man who wore a tight-fitting black shirt.

"It's nice to meet you, Gary. You have been quite the trouble-maker during your time in the facility, I hear. But nevertheless, after our last encounter, I knew we would meet again." The man smiled. "My name is Eddy, and I'm one of the teachers you'll see more frequently."

He seemed friendly enough, which was a good sign, but Gary now had a subconscious desire not to trust anyone he met for the first time. It was somewhat like how Numba was on the first day.

After getting on the bus, Gary noticed that it drove past the facility, which was a good sign. They eventually arrived at the main academy where Gary had taken the original assessment. It was enormous, like a university. Even though the place didn't have many students, it didn't lack facilities for people to use, which was why there were so many buildings.

"First, I'll give you a tour of the place, so you can see everything we have," Eddy stated.

As they walked past each building, Eddy explained that there were different teachers in different facilities who would teach him various things, from fighting to survival. For example, an entire building was dedicated to the fighters' dietary requirements. Every Altered was different, so it was quite the specialist treatment they had.

At the same time, they would teach students about their diet so they could take the information for themselves outside the AFA. There were also massage rooms, infirmaries, and a whole section where AFA students would learn about Altereds.

Then there was a large oval building, randomly plotted. It looked highly secure as if even a missile could not destroy it.

"That is a new facility that we are building. It should be ready soon, but we cannot enter now. Anyway, let's head somewhere else."

Eddy smiled as he said those words. Gary saw where they were heading, and according to Eddy, this was where sparring matches would be held.

There were octagon rings just like in the real AFC matches, and the academy also had many more training facilities in other buildings. They soon stepped into a large room through a pair of double doors, and Gary found his eyes glued to the octagon ring in front of him.

"Wow, it's just like it is on TV, and all the equipment, and . . . and . . ."

Gary paused when he noticed a few familiar people sitting on the bench.

"Gary!" Numba called out as he stood up and rushed over to him. "You're okay? You're really okay? It looks like you finally made it!"

Numba was wearing a yellow uniform just like Gary's, and this made Gary smile. It looked like even without him, Numba had managed to make it through.

"I can see the look on your face, but I wasn't the only one who passed." Sty sat on the bench with his arms folded, Ian and Izzy were there as well.

Although Numba's presence made sense, he was more surprised to see his other two friends here.

"It was a special request," Numba explained. "Because of what happened, they were asked if there was anything they wanted, and they said they wanted to go through to the real academy . . . and now they're here. So we're all here together!"

Gary never thought this would be the case, but it seemed like their set of dire circumstances had worked out.

"What a great reunion, but that's not why you are all here," Eddy interrupted with the same smile as before. It was clear he had something planned.

CHAPTER 96

INTRODUCTIONS ARE IN ORDER

Unfortunately, it didn't look like Eddy had any intentions of sharing his secret. His arms were folded, and he had told the others to enjoy themselves while he met up with Gary. The Altered students had done exactly as they had been told and tried out the equipment after a bit of catch-up.

Now that the green-haired teenager was here, he decided to ask Izzy and Ian about what had happened, but before he had a chance to open his mouth, they bowed their heads in unison.

"Gary, I know you hate when we do these types of things, but we don't know how else to thank you for saving us back there!" Izzy began. "After the poison knocked us both out, we feared we might be goners, but the professors informed us about what you had to do . . ."

A nervous drop of sweat ran down the side of the werewolf's face. He had been worried that they might have seen what he had done, or that the professors might have told them the entire truth, but judging by their actions and words his friends had only been informed about the result, not the aftermath.

"Hey, you don't have to worry about that. I mean, in the first place, I'm the reason you guys got into trouble, right? And besides, we agreed to an alliance, and my part in this was helping you out with my strength. It's the only thing I can offer, after all." Gary smiled, not showing any remorse about taking the lives of two adults.

His friends were more than thankful. Honestly, they had feared for their lives multiple times that day. Never had either of them thought that teachers of the AFA would commit such acts, and if they were willing to go so far, there was always the worry that they could have gone even further.

Ian and Izzy knew how Gary would act, but deep down in their hearts they also knew that they owed him a lot, and they were even more inclined to work with him to repay him for his help.

"Anyway, let's talk about some good things, okay? We managed to skip that whole facility and join you here because of everything that happened." Ian smirked, still staring around the place in amazement.

After giving his thanks, he had wasted no time running over to one of the punching bags that were designed for Altered and gave it a few hits. Naturally, it was a lot heavier than the usual heavy bag used in boxing. A few light hits didn't move it at all.

The others went out to try some of the equipment along with Ian; his enthusiasm was quite magnetic and charming and made them all wish they were as energized as he was. However, one person remained on the bench near the octagon fighting ring.

Sty's and Gary's eyes met for a second, but Gary just smiled and looked away.

You're not even worth my time, and perhaps I should thank you since you have allowed me to get even stronger, so I can protect the ones I care about. However, if you try anything funny in here, I'll make sure that you join those other two.

"Holy shit, you're right. I can't get this bag to budge at all," Numba exclaimed. "Maybe if I transformed, I could do something."

There were several bags in a row and the others were using them to test their strength. So far they had been able to move the bags a bit as they dangled from their heavy chains, apart from the one at the very end.

Ian and Numba had used their full strength when punching it, yet it hadn't moved at all.

"Hey, Gary, why don't you give it a go? Maybe you could make it move," Numba suggested.

Gary touched the outside of the bag, and he could feel that it was sturdy. Perhaps it would even survive a few slashes from his claws, but a lot had changed, and he knew for a fact that his Strength was far greater than before.

I should try to move it without using Controlled Transformation. Gary readied his fist for a big punch. Eddy was watching carefully from the corner of his eye.

Hmm, those three fogies told me that he was special. He's already proven himself to be a fighter, but what about his raw strength? Is he on the same level as the last guy? Eddy wondered.

Storing up his power, Gary controlled his breathing, getting ready to swing at the right time. Just as he was about to throw out his fist, his concentration was broken by the sound of the doors opening.

Turning around, he saw a bright light behind a group of people, allowing them to be seen only in silhouette, but when they stepped forward, everyone could see the shirts that they were wearing, marking them as true AFA students.

"All right, Eddy, please don't berate us like last time. You know that our schedules are busy, okay? If you want us to put on a good show, then we need to be well rested, don't we?" A student with messy, spiky blonde hair scratched his head and yawned a little while giving his speech.

"I understand. Now, if everyone could please gather at the octagon, I wish to introduce you all," Eddy replied nonchalantly.

The others did as instructed, walking over to the teacher. Only Gary continued to look at the bag. It left a sour taste in his mouth to leave it just like that and be the only one who didn't get to test out his strength. He prepared to throw another punch.

"Hey, is he really trying to go for the black bag? If he can do that straight after leaving the facility, without transforming, then I would be quite impressed," the blonde student said.

"Gary, you'll have all the time in the world to do that, so get over here!" Eddy sounded slightly annoyed. Once again, the werewolf paused, but after taking a few steps and turning his head, he stopped completely.

"Did you say *Gary*? . . . It can't be!" a soft voice said.

Gary's heart started to thump.

BPM is rising

"Xin!" he called out.

It had been a long time, and part of him thought that he would never get to see her, yet here they were meeting once again, but with the full moon so close, would it be the reunion he wanted it to be?

ABOUT THE AUTHOR

403

JKSManga is the pen name of UK-based, *New York Times*–bestselling LitRPG author Kawin Jack Sherwin, whose series include My Vampire System, My Dragon System, and My Werewolf System. His works have sold fifteen million copies worldwide, and several have been adapted into comic books.

Podium

DISCOVER MORE

PodiumEntertainment.com